Nude, Not Naked

A love story... sort of

GJ Babb

Matador
9 Priory Business Park,
Wistow Road, Kibworth Beauchamp,
Leicestershire. LE8 0RX
Tel: 0116 279 2299
Email: books@troubador.co.uk
Web: www.troubador.co.uk/matador
Twitter: @matadorbooks

ISBN 978 1838594 053

British Library Cataloguing in Publication Data.
A catalogue record for this book is available from the British Library.

Printed and bound in Great Britain by 4edge Limited
Typeset in 10pt Sabon MT by Troubador Publishing Ltd, Leicester, UK

Matador is an imprint of Troubador Publishing Ltd

GJ BABB

GJ Babb carries with grace the wounds of a long exposure to university education. A great admirer of the unambitious lecturer who teaches with flair and dedication, GJ too is a believer in discourse, birthing pools, oatmeal and wooden toys for the under-sixteens. Being an author who places art at the centre of everything, GJ is naturally disappointed by the state of the world.

One of the big ideas of Britain's Labour government during the Blair/Brown administration was the expansion of university education. Across the country new universities were created by amalgamating regional groups of institutions of further and higher education. Occasionally, one of these new universities found itself in serious financial or reputational difficulties due to poor leadership. On closer examination it was sometimes the case that these difficulties were sufficiently serious to require, overnight, the removal from office of the vice-chancellor. In such circumstances a new appointment was "parachuted in" to put the university back on its feet. The replacements were tough, academic "enforcers" with track records of leadership in the public sector. They were hand-picked by the minister responsible for higher education, in consultation with the Higher Education Funding Council, and were given a great deal of leeway to turn around failing institutions.

This is the story of one such public servant, Professor Clifford Conquest, who was brought in to rescue University London Central where hasty expansion and incompetent management had led to a series of scandals. The change of leadership was swiftly accomplished during the summer months while the students were on holiday and the academic staff on research leave. In September they returned to find a new academic regime in place and change very much in the air.

"The nude alone is well dressed."

— Auguste Rodin

ONE

The administrative hub of University London Central was housed in a building – now named Keynes House – originally built in 1867 for the organisation then charged, by royal charter, with the administration of the wharfs and crossings of the Pool of London. It was one of those Victorian buildings with a frontage facing the main thoroughfare replete with classical flourishes, but providing pinched quarters for many of its inhabitants. Nevertheless, on the first floor, reached by a grand staircase, were a series of offices and meeting rooms that expressed in architectural terms the elevated status of the original organisation's principal officers. Certainly, "pinched" did not describe the quarters now occupied by the new vice-chancellor. Beyond the two outer rooms housing his PA and secretaries, lay a commodious inner office, large enough to have three distinct zones.

Most distant from the outer offices was the vice-chancellor's work area, dominated by a magnificent desk and throne-like chair, hedged in on three sides by bookcases containing his collection of academic tomes, legacy of his background in American studies.

Occupying the centre of the room was an arrangement of easy chairs brought to a focus by two large leather sofas facing one another across the expanse of a low table. The latter featuring an arrangement of expensive books collectively named after the perversely-undrinkable beverage that was served there during the vice-chancellor's informal "chats".

In the third area, nearest the entry point from the outer offices, stood a highly-polished mahogany table, large enough to seat twelve, such as can be found in the offices of old-fashioned City firms. This had been placed there on the instructions of the vice-chancellor for the conduct of more business-like meetings of confidants drawn from the university's senior staff. Needless to say, given the present circumstances, these meetings never numbered twelve participants, nor anything approaching that. Rather, the vice-chancellor utilised the empty seats to suggest a certain imperial distance between him and those called in to account for themselves.

The occupant of these splendid quarters, Professor Clifford Conquest, had nothing about him of the demeanour of an academic. He was a tough, smooth-looking man in his late forties; not tall or imposing, but in some indefinable way formidable. His detractors said he had the look of Hatton Garden about him; the sort who, should you be an acquaintance of good standing, knew a thing or two about blood diamonds. One of the several conditions he had made when accepting the post of vice-chancellor was that Tommy Ballantyne be appointed his director of finance.

'We come as a team, do Tommy and I,' he had explained to the two members of the senior management team who had been at the university to greet him on his first day. 'This university not only has a new leader, it's getting a new broom in finance as well.'

The two of them had worked long hours through August to gain an understanding of the university, its strengths and weaknesses, its human and financial resources. Now it was the Monday of the second week in September, a few minutes before ten o'clock and Conquest was ready for the first of the day's appointments: the inaugural meeting of his senior management team.

The senior management team was the most important internal committee of the university. Its members numbered nine: the vice-chancellor in the chair, the dean of academic affairs (secretary), the deans of the university's five faculties, the director of finance and the academic registrar. Shortly they would be joining him in the council chamber.

Since taking up his post, Conquest had met the members individually, but had until now delayed meeting them as a body. He had read their advice on various aspects of the university's management, he had listened to their views; he had smiled enigmatically and bided his time while he familiarised himself with the terrain he now intended to wage war over. Autumn was here and the students were returning! He felt their expectations impelling him forward. He was their champion and anyone, or anything, obstructing his plans would be swept aside. This was his moment, the moment for plain speaking to those who should be ashamed of their part in allowing the university to fail during the last administration!

Conquest had settled himself at one end of the long oval table, documents laid out before him like ramparts. Behind him on the wall in their gilded frames were the portraits of his predecessors. Soon the members of the senior management team would begin to arrive. When they did he greeted each one with a nod and a pleasant word. He invited them to take refreshments.

If there's a fundamental weakness in the public sector it's when individuals like these get together, slowing everything down, ganging up on the doers, tying decision-making in knots so that this has to be considered, that has to be deliberated on, everything reevaluated endlessly and then put out to consultation. What's the result? Nothing gets done! Process is reduced to a painful crawl. Meanwhile, corruption thrives in the shadows. I've seen it only too often: committee paralysis! I'm not going to be held back by footling, carping, idiotic objections. I expect everyone to be with me; those that aren't I want out of the way.

When everyone was seated with their shortbreads and cups of lukewarm coffee, when the paper shuffling had finally ceased, he looked up with a new sharpness. Seven men, one woman. He surveyed the table, thinking that soon enough he would do something about the gender balance. He smiled, apparently benignly.

'Good morning, everyone. Welcome to a new academic year! As you'll have noticed, there's no agenda for today's meeting. That's because the substance of the meeting is the report I wish to give you on the state of your university as I have come to understand it in the short time I've been your vice-chancellor. I have consulted widely; I've spoken at length to everyone here and I thank those of you who have given me their thoughts on paper.' He made what looked like a heartfelt gesture of inclusion. 'My belief is that our university may have had its difficulties but institutionally, at root, it's sound.'

There was an unctuous, 'Hear, hear,' from somewhere in the room.

'It's no secret that the most pressing problem that confronted me when I arrived was the consequence of a regrettable misunderstanding between registry and the Department of Finance about student numbers. This meant that for a number of years an entirely optimistic assessment of the university's student population was given to the Funding Council as the basis on which our teaching grant was calculated. When this – what shall we call it...? *Fraud?*' At this point he paused and gazed with an air of enquiry, consternation, even accusation, at the members of the meeting. 'When this *fraud* was discovered the Funding Council – naturally enough – instituted proceedings to claw back the overpayment. This threatened the university's financial viability. As a consequence, it was put under review and I am sorry to say that, as a consequence of *that*, a number of other matters came to light. It seems that laxity had taken hold elsewhere. A major misappropriation of funds was uncovered in the finance office, perpetrated by the officer responsible for disbursing petty cash. The Students' Union had been given promises of financial and other support that were, in my experience, unprecedented. Large quantities of books ordered for the library, and paid for, appear never to have arrived, or if they did, the library certainly had no actual books on shelves, or delivery notes. In the circumstances, the Funding Council had no alternative but to receive the resignations of the vice-chancellor, the director of finance and the academic registrar. These and other matters are subject to certain legally binding undertakings and I am afraid I am not at liberty to give further details relating to the period immediately preceding my arrival. Suffice to say that a new team has been drafted in to take matters forward. I agreed to my appointment as vice-chancellor, subject to very detailed negotiations with the Funding Council and the university's senate. And you've all met Tommy Ballantyne –' he gestured benignly towards Ballantyne – 'with whom it's been my pleasure to work before. He has joined the university as director of finance.

'Following the departure of the academic registrar, his hard-working and dedicated second in command, Dr Cornish, has been promoted.' He gave another salute, this time in the direction of Cornish who was smiling sheepishly. 'Subject to these new appointments – we might say "this new broom" – the Funding Council has agreed to write off most of the historic deficit, given certain personal undertakings by me about future accounting. Since he arrived, Tommy has been working hard with Dr Cornish to sort out a budget that reflects actual student numbers on courses – and likely to graduate – rather than the number of students offered places by all and sundry, significant numbers of which, in past years, have been in the habit of not turning up. Dr Cornish and his staff will be working hard to reconcile the student numbers the departments claim to have recruited for this year with those who actually register over the next couple of weeks. So far, so good! This will give us an accurate basis on which to take things forward for the current academic year.

'Unfortunately –' and here Conquest's voice took on a more menacing tone – 'in the midst of the chaos of the past two years the teaching departments have been left to their own devices and several seem to have allowed standards to slip. I am therefore instituting a rolling programme of reviews to assess the quality of our academic provision. I will be asking Murray –' he indicated Professor Murray Woolworth, the dean of academic affairs – 'to draw up a timetable for these reviews based on my assessment of the strengths and weaknesses of the departments' strategic plans for the coming year. Murray, anything to say about this?'

Woolworth looked up from his papers with the glazed look of one whose thoughts were elsewhere. Before he could speak, Conquest had decided that anything he was likely to say would add nothing of significance to what he wanted said, so he pressed on. 'I will be asking senior members of the university to chair the reviews. I will be in the wings, as it were, taking a very close interest indeed in how they go.'

A faint murmuring went around the room. Conquest was curious to identify its source but it seemed to be the result of some form of ventriloquism because wherever he looked no one's lips appeared to be moving. 'If I may return to my theme,' he said loudly, sensing that what he was hearing were the first stirrings of alarm, 'I have to point out that there are more departments in deficit in this university than there are in surplus. This cannot go on! We cannot countenance any department's strategic plan that ignores the need for a sound financial footing. All departments must live within their means. I hope this economic necessity is understood.' Conquest gazed round the room, daring someone to declare otherwise. 'Furthermore, I am announcing that this university is adopting a target of a two per cent surplus for the current academic year. In order to achieve this target there will be an immediate freeze on staff recruitment and a twenty per cent cut in the non-pay budget across all teaching departments.'

The murmuring began again. At this point Professor Blurton, the dean of arts and humanities, was sufficiently ill-advised as to air his disquiet at what was being proposed. 'Vice-chancellor, if I may...? The departments in my faculty already have some twelve unfilled posts waiting the consent of the establishment control committee so that they can be advertised. I cannot run departments without staff to teach and do all the other things that academic departments must do. You yourself have commented on standards not—'

Conquest cut him off with a violent sweep of his outstretched hand. In the silence that followed, while he held the meeting in suspense, he registered for the first time how sloppily turned-out Dr Cornish was: his suit was creased and his tie askew, his face ashen and badly shaved. It struck Conquest that he had the look of a man who had spent the entire weekend carousing. The sight so offended him that he gazed out of the window, thinking what a pleasant summery day it was for so late in the year.

What is the dean of arts and humanities called? Ah, that's it! My memory for names hasn't failed me: Blurton! Blurton, Blurton, Blurton!

'You are so right, Professor Blurton. But then again, let us not deceive ourselves,' announced Conquest without shifting his gaze from the window.

The room waited for the vice-chancellor to reveal why Professor Blurton was deceived. The anticipation was like a palpable thing, big and feisty.

Conquest swung his eyes back into the room and fixed Blurton with a stare. He undressed his stringy frame and saw the soft, pulpy thing beneath the jeans, the knitted tie and the trendy leather jacket.

Oh for a dress code! he thought as he assembled the barbs he was about to deliver.

'From what I see in their strategic plans, the departments in your faculty, on the whole, fail every criterion for continuing good health. Where is the financial planning? Where are the overseas students? Have your staff lifted a finger to apply for research grants?' He pointed to the stack of documents on the table before him. 'Your faculty has produced a set of anodyne strategic plans with no targets, few discernable initiatives of any kind whatsoever! They are a box-ticking enactment! I don't like backwaters, especially stagnant backwaters. We need vigorous leadership and new ways of teaching students with a leaner compliment of staff. I will expect the reviews to pay particular attention to departmental timetables and contact hours for all courses. Departments must be fit for purpose in the new climate we must promote, and the reviews will help us to see that they are. This is a brave new world we are building!'

Such a pitch of rhetoric was entirely unknown to those of the senior management team whose membership predated Conquest's arrival. It left them startled and mute. Only Professor Blurton was not rattled; he had his good-humoured wit to share with the meeting.

'I am sorry if the faculty's plans seem lacklustre, vice-chancellor,' he began in his BBC manner, confident that he could charm with words, 'but my departments have amongst the highest staff/student ratios in the university, their lectures have amongst the largest audiences, and they entertain!'

'Last year,' Conquest interrupted, 'Eighty-five per cent of students in England were satisfied with their universities.'

'As were eighty-five per cent here,' responded Professor Blurton.

'Obviously because they weren't in possession of the facts!' said Conquest triumphantly. 'And "satisfied" is not good enough!'

Flummoxed but unrepentant, Professor Blurton tried to get back on track with his argument. '*We* are the greater entertainers, bringing culture and understanding to places where formerly there was none. *We* charm and dignify the rabble! This is great missionary work and my members of staff are experts. *Experts!*' He smiled winningly at his colleagues looking for support, but all eyes were turned on the vice-chancellor.

'All credit to them.' Conquest touched fingertips in a tiny mime of applause. He reflected that a stooge he had planted there himself could not have done better. He took his time; he was crafting a loosening of his self-control. 'But this is a place of learning and surely we have moved on beyond this attitude to the expansion of the university system? Making higher education opportunities available to all does not mean belittling the very thing that universities were first created for: to carry forth the torch of learning and high endeavour!'

'I did not mean you to infer—'

'In higher education "entertainment value" is not a sound plank in anyone's strategic plan,' he ploughed on relentlessly in full snippy mode, 'let alone in your faculty.' Suddenly he rose up and began to pace round the room as though to vent his rage. 'We need to see more high purpose and political realism from this university!' he stormed. 'Perhaps I should repeat: *every* department in deficit will undergo review during this academic year. We will start with the Department of English in your faculty, Professor Blurton, expressly hoping that you have cleaned up the mess in that department that very nearly landed the university in the courts. They're a bunch of cowboys who need a good slapping.'

A shudder went round the room at Conquest's use of "cowboys" and "a good slapping", terms he had stored away for an occasion such as this, knowing their incongruity in the context of academia would provoke a frisson of disquiet. Even now Professor Blurton was not entirely crushed.

'Vice-chancellor, you will find things much improved, the novels of Disraeli are no longer core curricular reading in year one, but the department does require strong leadership and one of the posts awaiting clearance to be advertised is the head of this department!'

Conquest was now standing by the blackboard, as though about to write on it. To the members of the senior management team it looked very much as though he had decided to turn the meeting into a lesson. He rapped the board with his knuckles. 'Then we must appoint from within. The decision to freeze recruitment is without exception.'

Professor Blurton threw up his arms weakly. 'There are no suitable candidates... really!'

'Have we no cadre of experienced senior staff we can deploy from other departments?' His appeal had been to the meeting as a whole but now he turned to Professor Andrew Czinc, the dean of social sciences, a man he had previously identified as a practised institutional animal and a useful ally. 'Andrew, your faculty could put someone up for a temporary head of department's post, surely?'

'Nothing is impossible,' said the wily sociologist.

'There you have it! We shall discuss it with Andrew and put something to senate. A secondment for this academic year.'

Professor Blurton nodded his acquiescence, his eyes firmly fixed on his diary into which he seemed to be entering a note of their agreement, although in actuality he was writing "bollocks" against the date. Czinc was examining the ceiling moulding. He had ridden to the rescue in a piece of cross-faculty politics – always a source of satisfaction – and he had a troublesome professor of applied linguistics he badly wanted to be rid of, and parking him in the Department of English for a year appealed to his sense of vengeance.

Conquest noted with some satisfaction that there was no further murmuring as he resumed his seat. He had, he reckoned, shown the senior management team that a wilful force for the betterment of the university had entered their lives, disturbing their placid routines, routing selfish mediocrity. They knew now that he had no intention of brooking petty quibbling, parsing and apologies. He could be confident that for the next couple of meetings the senior management team would not question his decisions. What is more, he could rely on its endorsement for any proposal he might wish to present to the university's senate, and that was the only other place where his power could be challenged.

'Fine,' Conquest decided. He gave the meeting a thin smile. 'I know – since teaching is about to begin – that you're all extremely busy. I am sure no one here is slouching towards retirement, and we should not reward those who are. We have excellence in our midst and it will be my duty and pleasure to bring it forth as an example to all. I want you to carry the message back to the shop floor that this university will reward those who excel, and by this means this university will excel. I am sure we will find pleasanter things to discuss at our next meeting. Thank you.'

Ballantyne and Professor Blurton came out of the council chamber together. They proceeded down the grand staircase side-by-side. Eventually Blurton broke the silence. He spoke to the emptiness before him, as though gathering thoughts from the air. 'That man has poor impulse control. I thought he was a charmer. How wrong I was!'

'Yes, we must consider ourselves cautioned,' said Ballantyne in a manner equally opaque, eyes fixed likewise on some distant object on the horizon. He was somewhat nonplussed that Blurton should be so candid, he being so clearly identified with the new regime. He had quietly enjoying the way Conquest had used Blurton to intimidate the meeting. Not that he hadn't seen him do it before; he was familiar enough with the process to have given it a name, borrowed from the lexicon of New Labour: "operation gobble". It was reassuring to see that it worked as well with academics as it had with NHS staff. It was the ease with which Conquest managed to incite some hapless senior manager to sacrifice his self-esteem to help him establish his dominion over whatever committee he was required to work with that so impressed. On the whole, still descending side-by-side with Blurton, Ballantyne reckoned he was in the company of a senior academic whose understanding of institutional politics was astonishingly naive. *What*, he wondered, *were his strengths?*

TWO

It was Friday afternoon, two working weeks after Conquest's first meeting with the senior management team. Much of what he had promised in that meeting had been turned into concrete plans in the intervening days. Now the start of a new academic year was imminent. A celebration was in order. That morning, on Tommy Ballantyne's instructions, a wide-screen TV from the AV store had been delivered to the vice-chancellor's office. Conquest, Ballantyne and Dr Albert Cornish – still ill at ease at his elevation to academic registrar – were doing a spot of gambling on the racing from Cheltenham. They had been drinking for the best part of an hour. Conquest had spent most of that hour prowling the room, sipping occasionally from a glass of vodka. Ballantyne was a recreational drinker and instigated these celebrations. As far as Conquest was concerned, team-building required sacrifice and he indulged Ballantyne's occasional binges out of the superstitious belief that they proofed their partnership against betrayal. Ballantyne's drinking revealed a streak of northern wildness in him, the antithesis of his accountant self, yet never was he anything but sober at work. Conquest, who had known him well for more than fifteen years, regarded it as an act of self-discipline as impressive as his ability to go through a balance sheet. The only discernable effect he had ever noticed his drinking having on him was an occasional abrasiveness with those who worked for him. Abrasiveness was something largely unknown to the staff of University London Central's finance department and since his arrival it had had an entirely positive effect on their collective performance. However, the effect had not gone without comment.

Ballantyne had just come off the phone to the local Ladbrokes office having laid a sum on Winston's Dilemma to win the three o'clock. Conquest stopped his prowling and regarded him speculatively.

'You know what that Marjorie told my PA about you?' he said.

'What, that bloody assistant human resources officer?'

'Yes. She said you're a martinet and a bully, so my PA tells me. Should be dismissed forthwith.'

Ballantyne didn't respond.

'What do you say to that, Tommy?' persisted Conquest.

Ballantyne was sitting on one of the vice-chancellor's sofas. Cornish was sitting opposite him, sprawled behind an assortment of glasses and bottles. Ballantyne cleared his throat.

'Piffle, Cliff. I say "piffle".'

'Very fair,' said Conquest. 'Very fair, indeed!'

'Waste of space,' Ballantyne added.

Conquest said nothing further, but on a Friday afternoon, in a spirit of convivial companionship, he was inclined to indulge Ballantyne's view of the Department of Human Resources.

'I think jumped-up human resources officers should stick to their knitting and not pass judgment on the necessary actions of the senior management,' decided Ballantyne after further consideration. 'Do I mind spending the odd morning in an employment tribunal? *No!* It's worth the odd compensation package to get rid of some trouble-making tosser.' He threw out an arm as though under attack by trouble-making tossers.

Conquest laughed. 'As a union member, I have to take seriously any conduct that may be construed as leading to the constructive dismissal of an employee.'

Ballantyne heaved himself out of the sofa and crossed to the open window to light a cigarette. 'Yes, Cliff, I'm aware you're a union man!' he said, blowing a stream of smoke out of the window. 'But you left behind all that shop-floor-democracy crap years ago. You now take a broad view of matters of efficiency that senior management must.'

Cornish joined in the laughter, thinking this was great stuff. He was younger than the other two and surprised to find himself elevated to the leadership of the university's registry. For him this was all new; never before had he been invited to drink spirits in office hours by his vice-chancellor and was in awe of the scars of previous management triumphs the other two sported. He was fearful of not keeping up. Commuting to work he had read an article on office politics entitled, "How to promote social cohesion". It recommended the telling of jokes. Now was the moment, he decided, to use the tip. 'Want to hear a joke?' he said.

'It better be good,' said Conquest with an air of sufferance as he screwed the top back on a bottle of vodka.

'One night Spencer Tracy took Mark Rothko out to dinner at this fancy club on 5th Avenue. They left their coats with the hatcheck girl. While she was hanging them up the cigarette girl came by the cloakroom to re-fill her tray. "I don't think much of those coats," she said to the hatcheck girl. "Why ever not? They're lovely!' said the hatcheck girl. "They're Mark's and Spencer's."'

Conquest and Ballantyne groaned.

'Here's one,' said Ballantyne, giving Cornish a big wink. 'Two arms salesmen meet at Heathrow. One is returning from Saudi Arabia, the other from Sierra Leone. The first one confesses: "I was bribed in Saudi Arabia." The second one says: "So was I! What did you get?" "Two hundred and fifty-five thousand dollars in a brown envelope," was the reply. "And what did you get?" "Two coconuts and a whittled stick."'

'Too right!' said Cornish with a hoot of laughter.

'The race is about to begin,' said Conquest, his eyes fixed on the TV screen. 'What are we betting on, Tommy?'

'Winston's Dilemma.'

'Winston's Dilemma!' gushed Cornish. 'Lovely name for a gee-gee.'

Winston's Dilemma duly romped home, netting them two hundred and twenty pounds. It was time for a late lunch. They avoided the administrative staff in the vice-chancellor's outer office by taking the fire escape and made their way breathlessly to the main thoroughfare where they flagged down a cab.

'Bloody great,' enthused Ballantyne as they pulled away from the curb. Gleeful, he looked back through the rear widow of the cab as the Keynes Building receded into the distance. 'Bloody hellfire!' he added as he spotted the flag flying bravely from the cupola.

'What?' said Conquest.

'That Palestinian flag's up there again! That's the bloody Students' Onion for you!'

'I don't believe it!' said Conquest. It was the second time that week and he was definitely displeased. 'We can't have the Palestinian flag flying above the administrative hub of the university. We have to be impartial!'

His companions roared with laughter at his discomfort.

'What's the Student Union's president called?' teased Ballantyne. 'Rob Missile?'

'Comrade Rob Mission,' said Cornish. 'Oh, the joys of student politics!'

'He's a pinko *Socialist Worker* ponce, that boy,' responded Ballantyne.

'I'll have to have him in again and tell him to desist.' Conquest was determined that the Keynes Building should be his citadel. How, he wondered, had they managed to get yet another Palestinian flag up to the roof? The security doors were impassable without an entry card, and no student was supposed to have one.

'The Great Escape,' declared Cornish. 'I put my finger up to indicate my completed loyalty to our great enterprise. Fingeeeer... UP!'

'Finger up!' agreed Ballantyne, but without much enthusiasm.

Conquest wanted to say 'finger up' like the other two, but coming from Cornish, the sentiment had struck the wrong note. Cornish wasn't quite part of the team; it wasn't up to him to disparage, even in jest, University London Central like he and Tommy could. They were mercenaries doing God's work, he wasn't. It was, he thought, a decided lapse by the boy.

They travelled in companionable silence as far as a tapas bar near Waterloo station. Here they ate largely and drank white wine.

Ballantyne had reached a plateau of contentment. 'I know,' he decided as the meal came to an end, 'I'll take you two gents to a nice pub where they have pole dancing. My bloody brother-in-law

14

took me there. It's just the place for a pants-down, balls-up-in-the-air wing-ding.'

They went out into the street and hailed a cab. It was overcast and raining.

'I don't know where we're going!' complained Cornish, half-heartedly trying to light a cigarette he had cadged from Ballantyne.

'Oi, no smokin' in the cab, please gents!' said the tinny voice of the driver over the intercom.

Ballantyne, who was travelling with his back to the driver, turned round and explained apologetically: 'Sorry mate, no hard feelings, its medicinal.'

'GET IT OUT!'

In a meek, half-concealed act brought on by the alcohol, Cornish tamped out the cigarette on the plastic seat covering.

'I SAW THAT!'

Cornish, who had been carrying a small holdall all afternoon, started to struggle out of his suit jacket. The other two looked at him, momentarily nonplused. Eventually Ballantyne spoke up: 'What *are* you doing?'

'Changing my jacket. I can't go to a pole dancing club dressed in a suit, can I?'

Ballantyne looked at him in consternation. 'What are we supposed to do? We have to go in looking like businessmen while you go in looking cool, like you're a player? Is that the idea?' Ballantyne made a lunge for the bag and they struggled wildly until he managed to tear the bag from Cornish's grip. Seated in the corner furthest away from the driver, Conquest contemplated the view through the side window and hardly seemed to notice.

'If you lot don't sit quiet and behave, I'm going to stop the cab,' threatened the driver.

Cornish bleated like a goat and the driver's mood grew darker. '*Did you hear what I said?*'

Cornish began to fumble with the handle, attempting to open the door, even though the taxi was moving at speed. 'I don't want to be in your taxi, anyway,' he said.

'Gents, the doors is locked!' yelled the driver. The taxi jolted to a halt, flinging Cornish forward into Ballantyne.

The driver turned round in his seat to address them. 'Give us a break, fellas. My wife's had a miscarriage and I'm trying not to brood. I've got financial worries too, and you're giving me grief. That ain't right.'

'We've all got financial worries,' said Ballantyne with the assurance of a finance professional. 'It's a fact of life. Over-leveraged and all the rest. You can't do without money and there's simply not enough of it. We live in a world where there's more debt than money owed. Did you know that?'

'That's right,' agreed Cornish solicitously. 'More debt than money owed. And we're sorry if we've spoilt your day.'

'Take no notice, cabbie,' said Conquest. 'We'll pay the fare and get out here.'

The taxi driver looked out to check their whereabouts. 'No, gents, I don't think so. This is Vermin Town. Not for the fainthearted or the decently dressed. They'll mistake you for tourists if you get out looking like that, and tourists they skin alive and roll out their arses for prayer mats.'

'There you are, I told you, didn't I?' said Cornish emotionally, apparently imagining he had been vindicated, although about what no one knew. 'You must let us out,' he pleaded, 'we've ruined your day. Your good-natured public service has been abused.'

'Listen, mate,' insisted the driver, 'get out if you must. Don't say you wasn't warned, but if you think I'm opening the doors before you pay, you've got another think coming!'

Conquest leaned forward and flourished his wallet like a small weapon. 'How much?'

'One fifty.'

'One pound fifty?'

'No, one hundred and fifty quid. I saw that dimwit stubbing out his cigarette on my upholstery. Do that sort of thing if you must, but you'll bloody-well pay for the privilege.'

After some haggling, and having brought the fare down to one hundred and twenty pounds, the three men were decanted into the featureless street.

'What sort of place is this?' asked Cornish as the tail lights of the cab disappeared from view.

They looked around. Both sides of the street were lined with high grimy walls, like the perimeter walls of an old-fashioned bonded warehouse.

'Is this Limehouse?' wondered Conquest, equally mystified as to where they were.

'Look!' said Ballantyne, brightening. 'There's a sign says "pole dancing".'

They looked up to where a small neon sign illuminated a dark opening in the run of the wall. The sign read, 'Club Beirut. Pole Dancing a-Go-Go'.

Conquest thought this droll. 'Do you mean to say we've been dropped off exactly where you were planning to take us?' he said, leaning on Ballantyne's shoulder like bosom pals do.

'No, no, I wasn't taking you here, but there's pole dancing, which is what we want... isn't it? I like the sound of it: *Club Beirut.* Paris of the Middle East and all that.'

'But what about "a-Go-Go"?' objected Cornish. 'You can't do anything with an expression like that, can you? It's an anachronism, meaning dolly birds and hot pants.'

'*Cor!* Hot pants!' said Ballantyne. 'What are we waiting for?'

'No, no, it smells rank to me,' insisted Cornish. 'In gentlemen's club terms, it's a bar with flags of St George in the windows.' He broke into song: '"*There may be trouble ahead...*"'

Ballantyne was not to be put off. He headed for the sign. 'Maybe they have fellas with perfect protuberances.'

Cornish still nursed his presentiment of trouble. 'More likely it'll be whippets, ferrets and dogs!'

'Well, I'm pulling rank,' said Conquest, deciding that purposeful direction of any sort was preferable to the dithering nonsense of his companions. 'In we go.'

The entrance was blocked by a burly man in an overcoat: Dirk the Doorman. His mass nearly filled the doorway, and the shadow he cast seemed to be of a special kind of blackness. He leant forward and a placid, pink, round face peered at them from under a bowler hat.

'No cameras or other digital recording devices, no drugs, no side arms or other lethal weapons,' he announced, examining their faces in turn. 'Have you been here before?'

They shook their heads.

Listen carefully, then.' He leant closer. 'You can't touch the girls. Look, but no touching. Correct?'

They nodded in unison.

'Any lewd behaviour in contravention of the rules of the club, and you're out. Any touching and I'll do the throwing myself.' He looked them up and down as if making an inventory of their paltry physiques. 'And don't doubt it will be my pleasure.'

Having delivered his dire warning the outlook turned sunnier.

'Gentlemen, Sister Divine will take your coats.'

The doorway led to a corridor. The walls were brick above and a wooden wainscoting below, much chipped and battered. Here and there posters for obscure theatrical events in the upstairs rooms of pubs and nightclubs, Mondays to Wednesdays, were taped up over brown paint, which had long since lost its original gloss. At the end was a recess with a counter. Standing there, silhouetted against a backdrop of coats and briefcases and watching their arrival with a severe gaze, was Sister Divine. She was a good-looking blonde, aged about thirty, dressed in a pinstripe top with lapels that suggested a business suit but ended above her midriff, which was bare. Below she was wearing harem trousers in black silk. A large white stone adorned the dog collar round her neck. She took a thirty pounds membership fee from each of them, and when they had signed in she addressed them in the following terms:

'Switch off your mobiles and stow them. Our girls are athletes, gymnasts, artistes. They're nude, not naked. We present them for aesthetic pleasure. You show them respect, or I'll know the reason why. Spend thirty pounds per each on drinks and you can invite one of the girls to your table for champagne or cocktails. One, and one only... as a hostess! Remember what Dirk told you: "Look, but no touchee!"' She sent them on their way with a sweep of her hand, watching them attentively as they negotiated the steps down to a gilded door.

'I wanna touchee...' crooned Cornish.

Conquest was on the verge of cautioning his companions against unruly behaviour, but the sight that greeted him as he opened the door was like a blow to his frontal lobes. There, in the

18

centre of the room, in a crosswire of spotlights on a long elevated catwalk was an image that was to haunt him for weeks to come: a young woman of exquisite, ravishing beauty, arms raised above her head, gripping the pole she ever-so-slightly leant against, her body, pale as moonlight, modelled to perfection by the raking light, her auburn hair falling across her cheek, her eyes demurely lowered as though she were absorbed in some private reverie that excluded the perception of all else.

'A miracle!' declared Cornish, craning his neck to see over Conquest's shoulder.

The pole dancer had, it seemed, just taken up her pose for, as they stared, a rumble of percussion filled the room, and that delicate body, stripped bare apart from a loin cloth of metallised fabric, began to gyrate against the pole. Her movements were articulated from the hips and performed in languorous, entrancing self-absorption.

'Yikes!' muttered Ballantyne, pushing Conquest forward as the synthetic drums redoubled their strident beat.

'Boy, can she writhe!' exclaimed Cornish reverently.

All three were shocked into a condition of incapacity; the pumping, thudding disco music reached them as though muffled by felt. The vision drained their expressive ability to its very dregs.

'My...'

'G—!'

'Brrr...'

Then Sister Divine was hustling them from behind. As she drove them forward they became conscious of the room they had entered. It was of indefinable size, broken up by several massive concrete pillars as though a many-storied building stood above their heads,. It was scarcely lit by dim lights hanging down from an invisible ceiling. There were mirrors everywhere and they were vaguely aware that some of the further reaches of the room were reflections. The effect of indefinable space, the throb of music and the girl had all three of them in a state of disorientation. The lights seemed to swing in circles as they stumbled towards the bar across the dark, liquid space of the dance floor, a field of tables with candles and red tablecloths wallowing on either side. Conquest was finding it difficult to make progress as the incline grew steeper. He tried to make his legs work, his eyes swivelling about the room, catching sight of other dancers – one was dancing on a glass platform elevated above the bar, another was undulating within an inch of the face of an unconscious Japanese man in a booth – but it was the hypnotic performance of the pole dancer to which his eyes continually snapped back.

'Get on,' giggled Ballantyne, almost falling as he stepped on Conquest's heels.

'I can't…' gasped Conquest, baffled by the difficulty of the climb.

'Never mind ogling – look where you're going.'

When finally they reached the bar it seemed to Conquest as though they had been on a forced march of interminable duration. 'Tommy, get us some drinks, for God's sake,' he said, suddenly sweating profusely.

At first the barman was disinclined to notice Ballantyne but eventually he paused in his task of recharging a vertical dispenser with bags of salted peanuts. 'Chief?'

Ballantyne fetched out his wallet and put a large denomination note on the counter. 'Give me what it takes,' he said in a brief excerpt of the imitation of Humphrey Bogart he had perfected in his youth. He nodded towards the pole dancer.

The barman leant over towards him, unimpressed. 'You can have the sparkling New Zealand pinot or, for ten more, champagne.'

'Give me whatever.' He took out another note and placed it on the bar.

Cornish laughed, thinking Ballantyne was the very devil. He followed his example, slapping more currency down on the counter. 'One more and we've bought a hostess, mate.'

The barman was unmoved. They all looked at Conquest, who took out his wallet with a show of some reluctance.

'We want company, don't we, Cliff?' said Ballantyne. He slapped another note down on the counter. 'One hostess and champagne for three, please.'

The barman swept up the money and banked it in his pocket.

He pointed in the direction of an empty table close to the dance floor. They followed the gesture attentively but it was a long moment before they understood his meaning. It was a large circular table enclosed on three sides by a horseshoe-shaped banquette. It was only when they had taken possession of it that they realised the music had changed and, to their dismay, the pole dancer had slipped away. Piqued, they grew restless and by the time the barman appeared at the table bearing two bottles of champagne and waxed paper bowls of olives they were complaining bitterly of thirst.

'Ooo! Sophisticated!' said Cornish as the glasses and bottles were being laid out on the table. He took an olive and held it up to show the others the suggestive way it was stuffed with red pimento.

Ballantyne gave the barman a pointed look. 'Where's our hostess?'

The barman's face was veiled, in the manner of one used to drunks. He did not reply until he had unburdened his tray. 'I'll send Miss Divine,' he said with ill-disguised contempt.

Now equipped with essential supplies, the three comrades-in-arms began to enjoy themselves. They started in on the olives and when Cornish tried to squirt Ballantyne with the pimento stuffing, Conquest had to exercise his authority and put a stop to it. Ballantyne poured them champagne, keeping up a running commentary as he measured up one dancer after another, making remarks that, in other circumstances, Conquest would have thought "off-colour", if not cause for "a word", but which in his present condition he indulged. The objects of Ballantyne's comments were, on the whole, blessed with the stocky, utilitarian bodies of housewives and child-bearers rather than those of sirens and nymphs. The consensus was that the pole dancer they had seen when they had first arrived was the only real beauty amongst them. Egged on by Ballantyne, they began to work up a nice little obsession about her.

Sister Divine appeared at the table as the obsession reached fever pitch. 'I hear you three gentlemen want to buy one of the girls a drink.' She looked from one to the other in her challenging way. 'Any preferences?' Her expression said she thought that in their excitable state they were likely to demand something she wouldn't approve of.

Ballantyne spoke up for the three of them. 'We rather favour the young lady who was pole dancing when we first came in.'

'"Young lady" is it? Very gentlemanly. Well, Lady Caroline Lamb is available, if you wish.'

'Lady Caroline Lamb?' Conquest threw himself back on the banquette in surprise. Lord Bryon's mistress! The allusion struck one of his vulnerabilities: historical romanticism.

Notoriety! Scandal! And poetry!

In their present surroundings he found the incongruity delicious. What did it mean that the girl had taken the name of Lord Byron's mistress as her stage name?

'Available for what?' Cornish asked with a foolish grin. 'What's she available for?'

Sister Divine was disinclined to be helpful. 'Pyjama parties and sleep-overs.'

Cornish cackled. 'Does she do anything else?'

Sister Divine put on a satirical pose of thinking. 'No, but Viola is available for dog training.'

'What sort of dog training?' demanded Ballantyne, who was determined he should handle the negotiation.

'Pekinese on Alsatian disciplining.'

'Look,' responded Ballantyne irritably, 'we don't understand the code. Stop shilly-shallying and use words we understand!'

Sister Divine looked him over with her sardonic eye. 'If you don't know the terminology, I can't tell you. Our girls don't want to try doing that sort of stuff with inexperienced clients. It'd be dangerous.'

'Please, tell us!' begged Cornish. 'I'm sure I could do the dog training.'

Sister Divine laughed. 'You'd be the dog, so you'd be the one being trained! Another time, soldier. We'll keep a kennel warm for you.' She had no interest in further talk and leant forward to terminate the negotiation. 'Okay, gentlemen, decision time.'

Conquest fixed Cornish with a threatening look, readying himself to countermand him if he asked for Viola.

'Lady, please give us the pocket Venus,' said Ballantyne, not too far gone to see which way the wind was blowing.

'Good choice, gentlemen. I'll send Lady Caroline Lamb over. I think she'll find you three quite a study.' With that Sister Divine departed.

The three men watched her as she made her stylish way across the room. She stopped to talk at several tables and each time they threw themselves about restlessly, scratching their heads and drum-tight guts in a welter of impatience. After a while Sister Divine disappeared and some minutes later re-emerged at a doorway near the pole dancing stage with Lady Caroline Lamb. Apart from having acquired a tiny Stetson on the back of her head, Lady Caroline Lamb wore no more than when dancing. She looked at them uncritically from across the room – mere objects of financial obligation – as Sister Divine explained her mission. Her instructions delivered, Lady Divine stroked her arm as though in commiseration and motioned for her to go. Lady Caroline Lamb quit the chrome handrail she had been leaning against and became a silhouette crossing the unlit dance floor. On reaching the three revellers' table she stood before them, her chin lowered – almost resting on her chest – causing the long tresses of her hair to fall over her face.

'What might I do for you gentlemen?' she said through the curtain of hair in a voice that Conquest found marvellously chaste. He took a deep intake of breath and pulled himself together. 'Allow us the pleasure of your company, of course. Sit down and have some champagne.'

The barman must have been watching because as Conquest spoke he was there, sliding a Chatreuse-green cocktail onto the table in front of Lady Caroline Lamb.

Close to, Conquest thought her very young, hardly in her twenties, probably younger. There was something gentle, even submissive in her stance, but the way her lower lip protruded added the spice of a dash of petulance. It was his experience – in so far as he was experienced – that beyond a certain point, the more of a woman's body was exposed, as for example on the various beaches he had visited in Spain, the less attractive and desirable it was. He put it down to the loss of the "imagined other", a footloose phrase from his academic baggage. No such effect operated with Lady Caroline Lamb. She managed to retain an effortless grace even when almost nude. No doubt about it, she was a beauty. For a moment, Conquest toyed with the idea of taking off his jacket and covering her nakedness. His throat was constricted by the strange co-existence of desire and protectiveness. Drunkenness swirled through his brain. He couldn't take his eyes of her fingers, they seemed so delicate and elegantly tapered, though her hands looked strong and made for skilled work.

'Would you like me to dance?' she asked, sweeping back her hair. She placed one foot on the seat of the single chair facing the banquette as a steppingstone to the tabletop.

Conquest gazed up at her, vaguely aware that Cornish was tittering into his champagne. He wondered what it would be like to run *his* hands through her hair. 'No,' he said.

Again her hair fell forward over her face, giving her a look of unfathomable concealment, a hidden something that her nakedness couldn't take away.

'Wouldn't you like me to dance?' she asked again... and she looked at him closely, a fresh thought occurring to her. 'We've met somewhere, haven't we, sir?' she said suddenly. 'I know your face.'

The drink, the loaded atmosphere, the sense of intimacy and seclusion that the banquette provided, the sniggering encouragement of his companions – all had lulled Conquest into a sense of security and her question did not disturb it. 'I can't think where,' he said, smiling into her face, all-unsuspecting of what was about to come. 'Where would you and I meet? I can't think!'

'You're not a friend of my mother's, are you?'

The question rather pointed to the disparity in their ages and it displeased him. 'I can't imagine so. What's her name?'

'Hutton. Mary Hutton.'

'No, I don't know her. Anyway, why bother about that? Perhaps you should dance. Now isn't the time for talking, taxing the mind.'

A song started, something by Aretha Franklin. Lady Caroline Lamb laughed as she stepped onto the table amongst the glasses. Conquest had an urge to rise to his feet and kiss her hand in a courtly gesture, an act she seemed to be encouraging since she held eye contact with him as she swung her hips in time to the music. *I can't,* he decided weakly, only too aware that such an action would invoke the 'no touchee' sanction.

Her face was suddenly alive with realisation. 'I know,' she said, 'you're a professor or something.'

He blenched. He did not care to be recognised in his recreation time by a naked woman gyrating on his table in a louche den of a nightclub. He was about to deny any connection with higher education, when he realised that her eyes were growing larger and more lustrous as she recalled where they had met before. 'You're something important, aren't you? I've seen you giving a speech.'

The more she said the more alarmed Conquest was becoming. There was a definite scent of danger in the air, but from where did it come? Then it dawned on him: *he was talking to a student of his university*!

'You spoke at the graduation ceremony last week, didn't you?' Now she turned her attention to his companions. 'They're professors too, aren't they?' She was amused. 'It's a night out, is it?'

Conquest was not so far gone that he could not appreciate the difficulties that might arise if the story got out that three newly-appointed principle officers of University London Central had been caught in the company of an almost naked female student. He could see the *Sun* headline only too clearly: PROFS PREY ON UNI POLE DANCER. It was Tommy's metaphorical pants down and it gave him the horrors. The alcoholic tide receded in an instant. He was sober but not quite sure if his limbs would obey him. He saw that protected by their cocoons of alcohol, the other two were blissfully unaware of what had just happened. He bent close to Ballantyne's ear and whispered, 'Time to go.' The admission brought him out in a prickle of sweat. He leant across him and tried to catch Cornish's attention.

'Isn't she a lovely sight, one of nature's tenderest bud-lettes,' burbled Cornish. He was slumped so far down on the banquette that he was almost lying, looking up at the young woman gyrating hypnotically above his head. 'Shall we ever see her like again? Such rosy nipples, such perfect breasts, not to mention her hips and the way her legs are slim and powerful, both at the same time! She is a miracle!'

In his urge to be gone, Conquest grabbed Ballantyne's arm and tried to drag him upright. 'Tommy, don't you see?' he hissed. 'We're discovered! Caught out! Bert, impropriety a-go-go!'

'Didn't I warn you about the a-go-go? Didn't I?' Cornish struggled to his feet. 'If we're going I'm gonna touchee,' he announced. 'And no half measures!'

'*No!*' cried Conquest. He reached out to stop him, but succeeded only in barging the table. It was enough to unbalance Lady Caroline Lamb and she leapt to safety, landing as agilely as a cat. There was a crash as glasses and bottles hit the floor. Before they could put themselves to rights, Dirk the Doorman was on his way across the room, walking shoulder to shoulder with the barman.

Conquest held out his hands in supplication and surrender. 'It's all right, we're going.'

Dirk had hold of Cornish by his shirtfront and was yanking him this way and that like a ragdoll.

'*An accident! We're going!*' pleaded Conquest, pulling Ballantyne out of the barman's way as he made an unsuccessful grab at the lapels of his jacket.

'I'll pay,' Ballantyne pointed out, attempting to get at his wallet. He began to laugh convulsively.

'You're banned,' said the barman, his fist close to Ballantyne's nose.

'Mind my mobile!' wailed Cornish from the other side of the table. Dirk let him drop to the floor and stood on his hand.

'I think, gentlemen—' Conquest stopped, put his hand to his nose and sneezed convulsively. 'I think we'll say "goodnight".' And with that, to the sound of Aretha Franklin, he shoved and pulled Ballantyne and Cornish away from the wreckage of their drunken spree. As he reached the gilded door he looked back and saw Lady Caroline Lamb across the room. The dark shape of Dirk was standing behind her, turning her into a pale cutout. The contrast was stark: massive/slight, inky/vulnerable, earthy/shining. As the door swung to, in the moment before Lady Caroline Lamb was lost to sight, Conquest saw her sweep back the hair from her face, running her fingers through it as though grooming it free of contamination.

THREE

Eight o'clock on Monday morning revealed a very different Conquest to the one who had stumbled out of the Club Beirut the previous Friday evening. He sat at his desk, alert, impeccably turned out in a dark suit and sober tie, drinking his third cup of espresso. Behind him, standing on a shelf of the bookcase, like a halo framing his head, was the crest of University London Central. University London Central was his. Once he had been a humble professor of American Studies in West Yorkshire, now he was the vice-chancellor, the person responsible for his university's rebirth, its emancipation from the troubles of the past, from the crimes of the previous regime. Now was the first week of a new academic year. Students were flooding back to their departments. Later the Great Hall would be thronged with students registering. As a true professional he, their vice-chancellor, would never be less than pink and well-groomed. His belief in discipline – in order – in the cool evaluation of his options – was absolute.

SWAT analyses I laugh at; I am a master of strategy. No carousing of an evening will ever make sloppy my preparation for the following day. My shaving kit is always laid out with military precision; a freshly laundered shirt always ready to be worn. Concealment is my creed. Let not thy left hand knoweth what thy right hand doeth. Drinking, gambling, young women; never will they be my downfall!

Amongst the returning students, he was convinced, was Lady Caroline Lamb. Over the weekend he had spent a great deal of time reflecting on his stumbling path to rapture at the Club Beirut. Under today's date in his page-a-day personal diary he had written "Lady Caroline Lamb" and beneath it *"nom de guerre"*.

Neither had he forgotten that she had said her mother's name was "Hutton", and of that too he had made a note.

At a few minutes past the hour, Carole, his PA, entered with his appointments diary, primed for a new week.

'Good morning, Carole.'

'Good morning, vice-chancellor.'

'Busy day.'

'Busy week.'

'Just so. I wonder, before we begin, would you ring registry and ask them to check student records for anyone with the name "Hutton"?'

As soon as Carole had left the room he regretted what he had done. He was sufficiently trained in the ways of a vice-chancellor to know that one only took an interest in an individual student in the most exception circumstances. He had already gathered that Carole had robust right-wing views and was married to a detective working out of New Scotland Yard. She was always turned out in the steely way of retired athletes. Clifford regarded her as having something of a policewoman's nose for criminal behaviour. Being head of the vice-chancellor's office, she had been close to the scandals of the previous regime and yet had emerged without a blemish on her character. What she had discovered of the wrongdoing of those around her, and what part she had played in their downfall, was something known only to her and the chair of senate. All in all, Conquest had already concluded, she was rather intimidating. In five minutes she was reporting back with the news that the only student registered at the university with the surname Hutton was a Liam Hutton, a third year student studying marine engineering.

'Ah! Long-lost nephew on my mother's side,' muttered Conquest, relieved to see that Carole did not seem to find anything untoward in his enquiry. He knew it was a misstep though and he vowed he would be more careful in future. Without fully acknowledging it, he was beginning to think about the necessity of covering his tracks.

Carole went through the day's appointments with him and when they had finished he asked her to bring him a copy of the prospectus.

'Oh, and Carole, thank you for clearing up the mess we left on Friday afternoon.'

Carole frowned. 'I don't "clear up",' she said. 'The cleaners must have been in before you arrived.' Then she left to do his bidding, and when she returned she put the prospectus down on his desk without a word.

Hoity-toity! thought Clifford. He let the prospectus lie where she had left it, next to the Club Beirut book of matches he had been carrying around in his pocket all weekend. He waited until the door had closed before taking it up. Tracing Lady Caroline Lamb through her mother's name may have been a dead end but the adoption of the name of Lord Bryon's mistress – assuming that it had not been chosen for her, something he doubted – opened up another line of enquiry. Taking such a name suggested a sensibility for poetry, romance and danger. It was a choice, he reckoned, that would appeal to a student in one of the more literary departments in the Faculty of Arts and Humanities. From the contents page of the prospectus he made a mental note of possible departments: History, English, Drama, Modern European Languages, Fine Art, Philosophy & Gender Studies. As an afterthought he added Sport, Health and Health Sciences on the presumption that a specimen of such physical perfection might well be good at sports, or some other activity requiring a high degree of bodily coordination. The rest of the university he dismissed. He had reduced the odds of finding her from twenty thousand to one to four and a half thousand to one, half of that once one had discounted the male students. Already Conquest was pleased with his morning's work.

FOUR

The remainder of Conquest's very long morning was spent in meetings: first with the university's director of business enterprise, then with the coordinator for equal opportunities and, finally, with the officer for student mobility.

Policy, policy, policy!

At two o'clock Carole brought in a selection of sandwiches. He chose a pack of tuna and sweet corn, and climbed the stairs to the roof of the Keynes Building. The staircase wound upwards from a corridor at the back of his office where the secretaries made tea in an improvised kitchen. It was with some difficulty that he opened the door onto the terrace immediately beneath the cupola. The day was bright and a bracing wind was blowing from the east. He had discovered the stairs and terrace in the days following his arrival and he regularly sought refuge up here when he had time for a break from the press of business. There was an angry flapping above his head and much to his annoyance he saw that once again the Palestinian flag was flying above the cupola.

Another bloody thing I'll have to pursue this afternoon.

The flag had returned despite his request to the head of estates that she ensured it did not. It was rumoured by some – sniggering behind raised hands, he was sure – that the mountaineering club was involved in its repeated appearance. Thinking of taking matters into his own hands, he walked the length of the terrace in the hope of finding where the halyard was belayed. He was disappointed to discover that to reach it required a further climb by a fixed ladder to the lantern, atop the cupola, something he thought unwise to try. For a while he was quite put out, but gradually the sense of equanimity that he came up to the terrace to find overcame his irritation.

My world! he thought, as he looked out across the several blocks of assorted buildings that made up the campus of University London Central. Faintly the clamour of city life reached him on the wind. He turned up the collar of his jacket and cast his eyes down upon the principle walkway that crossed the campus. It was already teeming with students threading their way between the Students' Union building, the refectory, the Richard Dimbleby Lecture Theatre and the George Orwell Library. 'My World!' he said out loud, announcing to the forces of ignorance, superstition and prejudice that all that was stretched out before him was in his care.

Twenty thousand students sailing in this frail barque, with me at the helm! No adversity will prevail against my determination to fill their lives with the light of learning; to keep the flame of knowledge burning bright for the betterment of mankind... and womankind, of course.

Then a figure making its way past the George Orwell Library caught his eye. Was it Lady Caroline Lamb? Even from this height he was almost certain it was.

Can that really be her, he marvelled, *walking the pathways of my world, safe in the groves of academe from the wickedness of men and their recreations? Even wrapped up against the wind in a man's overcoat somewhat too large for her surely there can be no mistaking that singularly graceful figure!*

He followed her progress greedily: the grace of her walk, the springing in her step, the coquettish tilt of her head.

American pioneers wrested civilization from the Great Outdoors for rewards less than this! Log cabins and pale, blonde women! My God, how I love that heroic drama!

He would give her beauty proper tribute he vowed as he broke open the plastic clamshell of his tuna and sweetcorn sandwich.

This university, he swore, *I will make great for you, and your sisters! Amen.*

He ate his sandwich thoughtfully. The note on the clamshell caught his eye. He read it out loud: '"Freshly made by hand by us for you, today! No preservatives. Line-caught tuna and GM-free sweetcorn on wholemeal bread". Amen.'

FIVE

Conquest did not know it, but Lady Caroline Lamb was on her way to the Frank Brangwyn Building for her first appointment of the academic year. The second year of the undergraduate fine art course was about to attend a meeting with Terence Bragg, one of its studio practice course tutors. One could not have a starker contrast in the styles of conducting meetings than between his and his vice-chancellor's. Conquest was a man who knew he was always toying with histrionics; for who every pronouncement was a manoeuvre in a war of rhetoric. Bragg was no orator, and conceived of his job in the most modest of terms. He was a self-effacing person, the maker of a difficult, obscure art of fragments, employed for his standing as a "researcher", by which was meant his record of exhibiting his work. And it was where his next exhibition was coming from that concerned him, not the pursuit of institutional power. The obligation placed on him to produce "research outcomes" meant that somehow the ever-diminishing product of his contemplative reveries in the studio – a rundown fashion warehouse in Bow – had to be put into the public domain, and preferably somewhere prestigious, of "international standing", which he took to mean somewhere the likes of Tate Modern, New York's Museum of Modern Art or the Pompidou. He would occasionally remind himself of this, laughingly. He recognised that he was approaching that mid-term stretch of an artist's life when his work required consolidating into a coherent, consistent style that a dealer could rely upon. He knew this because his hairline was receding and his contemporaries were moving out of town to embrace the rural life. Yet the initial youthful impetus of his work seemed to have marooned him on his own version of Terminal Beach where the fragments of his work grew paler, more elusive, and less and less coherent. It followed that the gulf between actuality and what the university expected of his "research outcomes" simply staggered him, for he was an artist no curator from any branch of the Tate had ever acknowledged, either as "an artist", or as "living". At best he might make the claim that a civic exhibition space somewhere in rural Scandinavia where he hoped – if he were lucky – to secure an exhibition, was a Centre of International Standing for the Promotion of Innovative Contemporary Art. If he did, he planned to face down any colleague who tried to argue otherwise.

It is not to be surprised at, then, that it was with little enthusiasm or sense of mission, but with considerable foreboding, that Bragg faced up to the task of addressing the second year students. He was to introduce them to the first major studio practice module of the academic year. Photocopies of the "descriptor" of the module had already been handed out to his audience. The students were now reading them with something that seemed to him a lot like sullen suspicion. His instructions from the second year course leader, JC McCann – a woman with marketing instincts – were to "sell the students the module" and field any questions they might have. Since JC had dreamt up the "descriptor", Bragg was not pleased to have been left to introduce it by himself. Despite being the department's most prolific author of course documents, JC rarely turned up for occasions like this because her other responsibilities always seemed to preclude attendance. Bragg distrusted her and thought her a danger to his livelihood, but just now what grated most was what any intelligent observer of his art would know: that the module was set in terms at odds with his worldview of open-ended concepts. As an artist, and a man not naturally at home with institutional procedures, or academic trimming, his was not a task to be relished.

Bragg scanned the assembled students. Ominously, he sensed that finding themselves together again after the summer break had induced a mood of militant solidarity. 'Okay,' he began, 'welcome back. Good to see you; hope you had a good summer. This year we're dividing the studio practice course into modules. It's an innovation designed to help you unravel the complexities of art-making. This is module 2.1A.' He paused, giving the students a moment to check the designation at the head of their photocopies, then on he ploughed. 'As you see, the module's called "rhythm and form" and it leads on to module 2.2 in the next semester: "self-initiated studio practice". You can't take module 2.2 until you have successfully negotiated "rhythm through form". If you check with your course handbook you will see that both are core modules and there are no options to this module except module 2.1B: "ceramics: theory and practice". "Ceramics: theory and practice" is obligatory for those on the BA ceramic arts pathway. That includes you, John, with your tailored learning outcomes.'

The distorted young man in the wheelchair signalled his understanding.

'Now, what is the central idea behind this module?' He paused and in preparing to answer his own question he rubbed his lips as if they were tainted. 'It is that rhythm and form are locked in a binary relation; they are a composite from which material things and thing-ness arise. It is the centrality of this idea to the materiality of "stuff" that has led us to entitle this module "rhythm and form".'

Bragg noticed that a bright spark standing near the door had his hand raised above his head.

'Yes, Matthew, you have a question?'

'Is it "rhythm through form" or "rhythm and form", please?'

'I'm sorry?'

'Shouldn't we be clear about the distinction between "through" and "and"?'

Bragg was nettled by the interruption. 'Did I make a distinction? I don't recall saying "through".'

'I think you did. In any case, it says both here.' He waved the photocopy. 'I was wondering whether you thought they were interchangeable? And wouldn't it be best said as "form through rhythm"?'

Bragg regarded Matthew as rather too clever for his own good, and had done so since their first meeting. He recognised his interruption for what it was: an attempt to introduce into proceedings a note of the unruly. He was used to a certain probing of his defences on occasions such as this but it was done, he hoped, in a spirit of playfulness and not motivated by an urge to seriously undermine his authority.

'You're quibbling.'

'Sorry, I was looking for precision in the phraseology, that's all.'

There was restiveness in the room, a collective hope had been born that the disciplining force of the university was about to be challenged.

Bragg felt discomforted, but failed to see how Matthew could engineer any further sallies on this particular topic. 'Let's say "rhythm and form", shall we?' he decided. 'I don't think we want to be straining at gnats, do we Matthew?' He was relieved that Matthew's intervention had not been so daring as to require being trashed with a display of wit, as he had seen done by other members of staff; such was not his forte. He was also mindful of the need to get back on track. None-the-less, this he would remember, he decided, and wait for the moment to repay him for the impertinence of trying to disrupt his introduction.

There was something important he needed to emphasise and he was trying to remember what it was. He glanced down at the course handbook he was holding and saw the word "output". That was it! He cleared his throat. 'You are free to express your ideas in whatever form you wish, but your output must be a minimum of ten pieces of work over the twenty working days allotted to this module.'

A groaned went up from his audience as though he had made a ruinous demand of it.

Bragg's eyes roved over the students; he was doubtful whether the thought he was formulating was at all what he wanted to say, but out it came: 'In the organisation of thing-ness, rhythm, the dynamic motif of compositional relationships, is counterbalanced by the persistence of materiality, as form.' He paused, wishing he could replay his words, to see whether they had made any sense. 'I don't want to be unduly prescriptive about this but...'

Somebody tittered; a woman, one of those smart, privately educated students he admired for their poise.

'...I think it important to emphasise the dichotomy of gravity and grace… so to speak. Sculpture anyone?' He allowed his eye to rove over the group, daring the titterer to reveal herself. *Not enough gumption!* he decided with a sense of triumph. Hopefully he had outpaced them all with words, and could turn to the pragmatics of module 2.1A, a task that he saw as the aberrant necessity of shoehorning the mystery of art into the framework of academic accountability.

'So, turning to the marking of coursework, modules allow you to accrue points…'

'And points mean prizes.'

Another smart Alec!

This one was from Northern Ireland; Bragg recognised the brogue. 'Thank you, Barry. Concentrate! We want you to make an inventory of effects, as well as complete your allotment of outputs.'

There was a notable increase in fidgeting and muttering. Hastily he turned his mind to what he meant by an "inventory of effects", how they should organise it, and how it was to relate to "outputs".

'Your studies can deal with rhythm and form separately, but in your outputs you must try to bring them together as a binary.' He saw Matthew had his hand up and hastily he looked elsewhere. He had a suspicion that Matthew was exactly the discerning observer of his art who would intuit that what he was saying was at odds with his worldview. Unexpectedly, his eyes alighted on Juliette Burton. Her head appeared to be surrounded by a golden halo. That, and the effect of her serious, attentive face was quite enough to endanger his remaining hold on coherence. He scoured the mental sump of his art education jargon for inspiration.

'See rhythm and form as counterpoints to stasis and entropic dissolution and you won't go far wrong. Er… visual metaphors are your stock-in-trade, so do use them… but sparingly: promiscuous visual metaphors look like sub-Heartfield montaging. Are there any questions?'

Avoiding Matthew, he pointed to a raised hand. 'Okay, Frank, what is it?'

'Can I take the ceramics: theory and practice option, please?'

Several hands that had been lowered shot up again and Bragg knew they signalled that others wished to make the same request, which meant he was heading for trouble: there were only three places left on the ceramics option once the students for whom it was obligatory had been assigned places.

'Well you can, but it doesn't make much sense as preparation for module 2.2, self-initiated studio practice.'

'It does if he wants to make pots,' said Matthew in a sardonic drawl.

'Okay, it does if clay is your medium of choice for module 2.2,' Bragg conceded, 'but I only have three extra places on module 2.1B. The ceramics workshop is too small to take any more.'

There was a general groan of rebellion and insurrection.

'There's *no more room*,' Bragg insisted helplessly. 'Okay,' he went on when the muttering showed no sign of abating. I'll pick three by ballot if you all want to do ceramics.' The sounds of discontent barely diminished, making it clear that his attempt to deter the would-be ceramicists had failed.

Juliette Burton had her hand raised. When she caught his eye she smiled sweetly. 'I want to do the rhythm and form module,' she said in a voice, which, as far as Bragg was concerned, was as delicate as an angel's.

'Thank you, Juliette!' he almost yelled.

'Me too.'

'And me.'

It soon became clear that the year was split by gender between the male ceramicists and the female adherents to rhythm and form.

'Okay. We'll do a ballot for the ceramics module. Somebody prepare voting slips. First three out of the hat can do the module.'

Bragg found it amazing that not a single student found it incongruous that the academic progress of a sizable proportion of the year group was about to be determined on the basis of a lucky dip. They proceeded to hold the ballot, and the matter was resolved without further protest, but he could not help but notice that the meeting had promoted an air of mutiny and fractiousness. Was there a self-destructive impulse somewhere in his nature he did not recognise? He wondered. Talking to them individually seemed fine, but was his setting of projects always going to be tinged with farce? He blamed the module system. Who thought making art could be sub-divided into a series of tasks with pompous-sounding names like "rhythm and form"? Only *bloody charlatans*! His complicity left him with a uneasy sense of mortification, as though he had been caught stealing from a charity shop. It would have been nice to have gone to JC's office and told her to stuff the job, but he needed the income. Ending his compromise with teaching was no solution. Reluctantly he resigned himself to expending precious mental energy trying to work out how to manage the group dynamics, otherwise it would always be the same. The only bright spot in the whole farce had been Juliette Burton's smile, and that had been a ravishing ray of sunshine.

SIX

Finally, on Thursday of that first week of the new term, Conquest recognised there was no other way. At five o'clock, as soon as Carole was making her way downstairs, heading for home, he rang Dr Cornish, the academic registrar.

'Bert, are you rushing off tonight? I want to come and have a chat.'

'No, vice-chancellor, I'll be working late. Beginning of the academic year and we're up to our eyeballs – you know how it is.'

'Good. I'll come over to registry about seven.'

The moment that Conquest had been anticipating all day came at last. In the quiet of the evening he strolled out of the Keynes Building and made his way to registry on the ground floor of Kier Hardy House. Dr Cornish slid the bolts and let him into the main office. Conquest noticed a tumbler half full of brown liquid on the table.

'Been non-stop all day,' said Cornish when he saw Conquest looking at the tumbler.

Standing in the centre of the long, high-ceilinged room, surrounded by student records, Conquest found himself suddenly struck by a tremor of excitement. 'I could do with something to lift the spirits myself.'

Cornish nodded. There was a bottle of rum in his office. He bustled about finding a glass from the little kitchen where the registry staff made their tea and coffee. They chinked rims before drinking.

Conquest appraised him silently. His garish tie was askew.

Is Dr Bert Cornish up to the job?

That was the question Conquest was asking himself. He had appointed Cornish to the academic registrar's post on an acting basis only. There had been no time to go through the process of advertising for a new registrar following the sudden departure of the previous incumbent.

Ah, making appointments! Now there's a tricky business! Wish I had a bottle of something vintage for every iffy appointment I've made! Will Bert Cornish stand shoulder to shoulder with me and Tommy through thick and thin?

Conquest had to believe so; nothing else would do. Then there was his dishevelled appearance. He had not yet found time to "have a word", but on several mornings he had witnessed him looking particularly unkempt. Only yesterday he had come to a meeting with an England rugby shirt slung round his neck like a scarf and when it had been drawn to his attention he had professed himself surprised by its presence. Conquest was prepared to indulge the kind of excitable behaviour he had experienced on the evening of their visit to the Club Beirut as long as it remained off-campus, but a shambolic personal appearance was not acceptable.

Here we are on the brink of a new academic year and Cornish does not look the part. All week students registering for the coming year have been passing through the hands of registry, their first encounter with the university's central authority. What kind of example has he been setting? It will not do!'

'Bert, I've seen her!' he announced, unable to suppress the tremor of excitement in his voice.

Cornish took a step back, apparently unnerved. 'Who? Seen who?'

Conquest couldn't help but dab at a small sore in the corner of his mouth. 'The pole dancer.'

'Well, well, the pole dancer!' At the memory of their evening at the Club Beirut Cornish's expression changed to a sly smirk. 'It was bound to happen, I suppose. Did she recognise you?'

'No. No, I caught a glimpse, that's all. The point is to find out what department she's in.'

'Why would you...?' Cornish looked into Conquest's unblinking eyes and saw that he was determined. 'What are you going to do when you find her?' He poured them both a fresh finger of rum.

Conquest's face took on an expression of sanctity. 'Welfare and counselling are an important aspect of university life, are they not? Don't you think a student of ours who has to resort to a job like that – dancing naked for men – is in need of counselling? She's vulnerable; maybe she's in need... In financial difficulties of some kind. I hate to see people exploited, especially vulnerable young women.'

'Agreed, and with all the physical endowments you could ever hope for,' said Cornish, pulling a whimsical face. 'It's enough to provoke strong feelings... I'm not being personal, of course.'

Conquest detected impertinence. He considered that, as someone newly-elevated to a key post in his administration, Cornish should be more circumspect than to express his opinions in such a jocular manner. Cornish was implying that he, the vice-chancellor, might be on the point of succumbing to something little better than a seedy infatuation, and that he resented. He could see Cornish took their visit to the Club Beirut as implying that their relationship had taken on a blokish intimacy and informality.

'Well, she was... *special*,' Conquest suggested, rather mournfully, 'but I do have principles too, you know, Bert, and –' he held up his hand when Cornish tried to interrupt – 'and I didn't get where I am without having an iron control of my emotions. I want to do good works, Bert, whatever the physical endowments – *as you put it* – of the object of my attentions.'

'Ha, ha! Fair enough,' agreed Cornish, taking a swallow of his rum and making an effort at nonchalance. 'Like Charles Dickens, I suppose. Absolutely right to go through students' records in support of pastoral care!' He lowered his voice conspiratorially. 'I suppose you want to see her registration form?'

They went into student records without another word being spoken, Conquest still fuming about the "Charles Dickens" crack. Cornish flipped on the lights as he led the way. The student registration records were kept in rows of grey filing cabinets.

'You do have a name, don't you?' said Cornish.

'No, no name.'

'Ah, tricky!' Cornish hesitated, trying to remember whether what he was about to suggest contravened some privacy law. 'Then the only way to find her is from the photo on her application form. That could take some time.'

Conquest dismissed the difficulty with a flick of his hand. 'I've plenty of time. Show me where to start.'

The student application forms were filed by year of application, subject by subject. Conquest began by going through the forms of the new intake, confining his search to the departments he had already identified as likely homes for Lady Caroline Lamb. Cornish went back to his office to carry on with his own work, leaving Conquest to it. It was a long business. He searched the entire intake but met with no success. With scarcely a pause he turned to the forms of the previous year's intake and there he quickly found her: a little thinner in the face, younger looking, less fully-formed. He held up the form with both hands. 'Here she is!' he said to himself with a gleam of triumph. 'Juliette Grace Burton.'

When Cornish wandered in to see how things were progressing, Conquest was still standing there, holding the form, a pensive look on his face. Cornish went to the filing cabinet where the bottle of rum was standing and filled their glasses. 'So you've found her,' he said, nodding at the application form in Conquest's hand.

'Juliette Grace Burton,' said Conquest thoughtfully. 'She's an art student.'

Cornish offered him the glass of rum.

'No thank you, I've had sufficient.'

Cornish led the way to the filing cabinet where the Department of Fine Art's registration records were kept to see whether Juliette Burton had registered for the current academic year.

'She's already registered: year two, BA Fine Art. What now?'

'Ah! Busy time of year, Bert! You've got your hands full and more! Fine art: that's Professor Pomfret, isn't it? I think the department's senior tutor might be the best person to handle this. I'll speak to Pomfret. Or perhaps I'll pass it over to the student welfare officer...'

'I see,' said Cornish. He lifted his glass to drink, but then had second thoughts and put it down again.

Conquest was done. He saw Cornish perceived he was being

shut out, if only dimly. Of one thing Conquest was certain: Cornish wouldn't find out what he did next. He made his way to the door. At that moment he thought of himself as standing on the crumbling precipice edge, exuding power, able to launch himself into the air and soar away; certainly not dashed to oblivion on the saw-toothed rocks below. He turned to say goodbye to Cornish, and in his vaunting self-confidence he knew that the delictation of identifying Juliette Grace Burton for his own ends was an idea well beyond Bert's imaginings.

He senses, but only in a confused, straitened way, what is on my mind. He is of the kind that has never dared much beyond the filing of application forms. His whole life revolves around sport and drinking, and he has long since lost the desire to escape the dry, fusty line of work that he has drifted into. The sense of ambition that drives me forward is inconceivable to him.

He came to a sudden decision that, all things considered, Cornish was not the man for the post of academic registrar and he would dispense with him when he could.

He lacks gravitas; no academic registrar should be dishevelled, in need of a haircut, a gruesome tie hanging sloppily from his unbutton shirt. How will it look if there are disputes over conduct of examinations and the person responsible is insensible of the fact that he has a rugby jersey draped around his neck?

The wrathful Old Testament prophet in Conquest was let loose; he had his quarry in sight and no petty sense of obligation would stand in his way. He would see an end to Cornish at his university. As he made his way back to the Keynes Building he composed his staff appraisal meeting with Cornish:

'*You have a certificate in municipal administration, don't you, Bert? Well, the bursar's post at the American University in Ankara is for the taking.*'

'*Gosh, really?*'

'*Yes. The money, you know, is rather good. That would suit you, wouldn't it? I mean, that wife of yours is terribly expensive to keep in the essentials, isn't she? Is it true that in Tonbridge they call her Mrs Spondulicks? Ha, ha! Everyone knows that Jaguar of yours is leased, as is her Audi. Right smart they must look on your brick-paved forecourt, even if you are several hundred thousand underwater with that second mortgage of yours. Ankara's a natural career progression. I want you to come back and pick up the thread with a few new skills. I'll make you my Minister for Education when I'm in Number Ten. What we don't want is any disgrace associated with the university, do we? So, it's time to pop along and see those nice headhunters before it's to late. Agreed?'*

SEVEN

Sir Norman Fleet had always been a man of many parts, deeply devoted to the turning over of money to make a profit. And for this he had a genius. In appearance a bulky, over-fed man, he was lightening fast when it came to the pursuit of money. He spoke with a tight-lipped drawl, as though constantly gritting his teeth. The even tan of his face had been expensively acquired but unfortunately the effect was ruined by the sallow colouration of his skin, which made him look as though he was sickening for something. He had a liking for dark suits and narrow silk ties in canary yellow. The canary yellow picked up very nicely on the nicotine stain on the centre of his moustache caused by too many cigarettes taken close to the butt. Sir Norman was restless. Property, property, property! The economy was suffering from what he cursed as "the usual government bungling". Docklands was experiencing one of the financial services industry's periodic retrenchments and the property market had been weak for the past three quarters. Wainwright, Carter & Expandite, the construction company of which he was the CEO, and largest shareholder, was suffering in sympathy. That morning the focus of his particular concern was the property development division that had a troublesome building on its hands: a twelve-storey block of two bedroom flats with oblique views of the Thames Barrier: forty-eight flats for aspiring City workers on a median salary of £70,000. It was eighteen months since the block had been finished and some of the flats were still unsold. And now the plumbing was playing up. For more than two weeks the residents had been reporting an outbreak of leaks: water was seeping down from floor to floor causing staining and dampness in all manner of places. Suspicion had soon focused on the bathroom pods. They had been prefabricated in Belgium with the expectation that they would outlive the life of the building. Four – one for each flat – had been installed at the core of each floor, adjacent to the lift shaft. The pods were not equipped with inspection hatches and the firm of surveyors commissioned to identify the cause of the problem had been forced to do extensive damage to a pod in one of the unsold flats to gain even a partial understand of the layout of the pipes carrying water, both fresh and foul. Jeremy Dashwood, Sir Norman's personal assistant, had been instructed to find out whether the surveyors had completed their inspection and how they were proposing the problem should be rectified, or, put in Sir Norman's more colloquial style, 'Dashwood, get a bleeding grip on the bastards!' And right now Dashwood was standing before Sir Norman's desk, expecting an interrogation.

'What do the so-called experts say about these sodding leaks?'

Sir Norman's demand for the plain, unvarnished truth put Jeremy Dashwood in a situation familiar to all underlings since hierarchical society began: conveying the truth would have the effect of bringing opprobrium down on his head as though he were the responsible party rather than simply the messenger. Unfortunately, much against his own wishes, he had received an ominous briefing from one Hamid Snarf. This suggested that while faulty installation of the pods might be a contributing factor, there was a possibility that some of the leaks were the result of electrolysis occurring between the copper and galvanized steel components of the building's plumbing system. If this were the case it was possible to infer, so Snarf had bluntly put it, "that accelerated corrosion of the galvanized steel components was occurring throughout the building". Then he had gone on to tell him not to expect his formal, written report until further investigation had been undertaken, and Dashwood's watchword was, "Never convey bad news, unless strictly necessary". But here he was "on the mat". It meant adopting the cunning of a fox and the verbal contortions familiar to many a familiar.

'The residents feel—'

'No, no, Dashwood, I don't want to hear about the bloody residents. Tell me how much the bloody surveyors estimate it will cost to fix.'

If he speculated far enough ahead, it looked to Dashwood, who was not without an understanding of such things, that since the pods were craned in as the building was going up, the building might need a serious amount of ripping apart to get at the plumbing, but he was not about to tell Sir Norman that. He also decided to shelve the letter from the leaseholders' solicitor threatening a mass civil action. Instead he began to read from yesterday's email from Snarf, outlining the proposed next step and at the same time waved the surveyors' company prospectus about in what he hoped was an attention-grabbing way.

'"Preliminary findings require that further exploration of the bathroom pods be undertaken." The surveyors propose a day trip to the factory in Belgium, Sir Norman... er... "to correlate the findings observed on site with the details of the plumbing system as observable on the external faces of the pod during manufacture. The integrity of the lining of the pods intended to prevent water penetration would be compromised by cutting further inspection holes." They're anxious to avoid that sort of thing.'

Sir Norman pointed at the prospectus. 'What the hell's that you're waving?'

'Oh, nothing. Just a document—'

'If it's the report let me see the damn thing!'

Dashwood proffered and Sir Norman snatched.

'This is just their bumf, isn't it?' He tossed the prospectus back to Dashwood in disgust. 'Where's the report?'

'As I was saying, they want to go to—'

'I bet they do,' Sir Norman observed peevishly. 'Lunch in Brussels on me isn't going to go amiss, is it? Load of buffoons!' He was trying to maintain a sense of calm and control, but the flats had been marketed with a ten-year warranty and the same nightmarish possibility that had occurred to Dashwood had occurred to him. 'Those pods are an integral part of the building, aren't they?'

Dashwood hesitated. 'I suppose so, although not load bearing.' It was touch and go whether flourishing the surveyors' prospectus had been sufficient to divert attention away from himself – the conveyer of ill tidings – but Sir Norman's ire was ebbing, replaced by gloomy introspection. Dashwood sensed success.

'What if they all develop leaks and they can't be repaired? What happens then? *The building becomes uninhabitable!* How many unsold flats are there?' Sir Norman braced his hands on the desk against the eventuality of bad news. 'How many?'

Dashwood knew perfectly well, of course. Keeping track of Sir Norman's property assets and the flux of monies through the accounts of the property development division of Wainwright, Carter & Expandite were part of his job. Half the flats had been sold "off plan", but sales had been slow since the building had been finished, reflecting the dismal surroundings and the country's financial woes. 'Nine, Sir Norman: the top two floors and a penthouse.'

'Are they being marketed now?' Sir Norman wanted to know. 'We need them flogged off, as soon as possible.'

Dashwood could not believe that anyone would contemplate selling more of the flats before a solution to the leaks had been found, but he appreciated that Sir Norman's mind did not work in the same way as normal people's and some marginal benefit might be had from selling the remaining flats at a discount. 'We closed down the sales office a month ago. One of the estate agents on Canary Wharf is handling sales now.'

'Oh, yes, I remember: cost-saving measure. I want to speak to them right away.'

In a scheme of this size the sale of the last nine flats would normally be all profit, but Dashwood knew that there had already been some discounting to see the scheme off, and the development was still hardly at break-even point.

'Fortesque Curzon.'

'Who do we deal with? Get him on the line.'

'Amanda Fortesque.'

'Woman?'

Jeremy nodded.

Sir Norman looked disgruntled. 'Get the lass on the line, now!'

It took a couple of minutes for Dashwood to contact Amanda Fortesque. When he had, he passed the handset to an impatient Sir Norman.

'Hello! Hello! Damn it, can't hear a thing.' Sir Norman shook the handset and glared at Dashwood as though he had knowingly handed him a defective phone. Just then they both heard Amanda Fortesque's crepuscular voice yelling from the earpiece. 'Sir Norman! Can you hear me!'

'Bloody-well can, lass,' he snapped back, holding off the handset at arm's length. 'Where the fuck are you?'

'I'm... visiting a property.' She sounded put out, as though she was wondering why it mattered where she was.

'Well, dear lady, I would deeply appreciate a report on the sales situation at Titanic Quays.'

'Yes, yes, certainly, Sir Norman. I'm with a client at the moment. Perhaps I could come to your offices and give you an oral, face-to-face.'

Sir Norman pursed his lips, aware that something was not quite right with what she had said, but he didn't have the luxury of time to ponder. 'Tomorrow at nine.' He terminated the call and handed the phone back to Dashwood with a flourish.

'You have a meeting with the Greater Wales Regeneration Authority at nine,' Dashwood reminded him.

'Damnation!' He threw up his hands in despair. 'Rearrange, will you. Get her here as soon as I have a slot. What now?'

'Lunch. You're meeting the vice-chancellor of University London Central at one.'

'Who? What's his name?'

'Er, Clifford Conquest, Professor Clifford Conquest.'

'Ah, vigorous new broom, isn't he? Previously doing something else, wasn't he?'

'Worked for the FA on a bid.'

'That's it: football!'

Very recently Sir Norman had been pressed into joining the university's senate. Speedily following his appointment had come a charmingly solicitous letter from the new vice-chancellor, inviting him to lunch at the Athenaeum to discuss "certain issues I would wish to acquaint you with as a new member of senate. These relate to the university's strategic plan and other governance issues."

Sir Norman was delighted to accept. Surprisingly, because he had taken wine and broken bread in almost every club in London, he had never been in the Athenaeum. The glittering dining room with its angled shafts of sunlight beguiled him. He decided he was going to enjoy himself and order a large glass of white wine, something rather special from Bordeaux.

Between slurps he examined his host. He was a small, neat man, somewhat squeezed into a regulation, off-the-peg business suit, unlike his own more casual, tailored tweeds. He had alert, darting eyes, and sported an academic beard, neatly trimmed and again quite regulation. The man had a confident look about him, although he noticed a rash had installed itself in one corner of his mouth. That might not have meant much had he not noticed how, in the throws of driving a point home, or when working hard on his bonhomie, Conquest succumbed to a scratching tick, rubbing his biceps or massaging the back of his neck. Sir Norman wondered whether the rash might trouble more of his body. He also noticed that when very animated the vice-chancellor's scratching took on a jerky, finger-in-the-collar nervousness as though – so Sir Norman decided – he had an unconscious fear of being apprehended, unmasked or in some way found out. Sir Norman was not a psychologist, but he was a businessman who was acquainted with the fallibilities of the human condition, and his understanding of his fellow humans was acute enough for him to suspect that Conquest was capable of being a bit of a scallywag when in the right company and behind closed doors. Yes, he decided, this was a driven man, probably a clever man, possibly – more speculatively, and interestingly – a bit of a rogue, and definitely he was going to enjoy his lunch!

While Sir Norman's was undertaking his covert inspection, he was happy to let his host talk. He could see Conquest was animated about his topic, although it barely registered that the topic was leadership skills and his arrival at University London Central. He sat back in his chair and admired the room. When he had had enough of soaking up the atmosphere he turned his attention to the diners at the other tables. They were mostly Anglo-Saxon, florid and aged. There was an indefinable tang about the place that he couldn't quite place, perhaps because the Old School prefects' study had never been part of his somewhat foreshortened educational experience.

'You've got an interesting back story, haven't you, Clifford?' he broke in at last, giving him a shrewd glance. 'What is it: national health trust and international football?'

'I worked on the UEFA bid: the one where we lost out to Scandinavia.'

'I remember, honorable runner-up. We didn't want it, did we?'

'I wanted it, Sir Norman. I put together the best bid we've ever made.'

'Oh yes, no doubting your sincerity and endeavour. Top marks. The powers that be, though, didn't.'

Conquest looked discomforted, but Sir Norman dismissed the topic with a casual wave of the hand as if to say, "I know, and you know, what was intended. No need to feel hurt." 'What was your subject, Clifford, before you rose to the top table?'

'American Studies. I did my PhD on "American Literature as a Reflection of the Changing Political Landscape".' He said this with a flourish, as befitted the opening line of his treasured seminar on Emerson and the Great American Outdoors.

'Ah! Useful intelligence for those of us who have to work with the Great Beast,' Sir Norman conceded with a grim smile. 'I'm anti-American root and branch. They've never been a true friend of us Brits. Spent half the last century cutting us down to size. Mongrel culture, mongrel minds. Makes me laugh to see them drowning in Hispanic culture.'

'We study to understand, not necessarily to condone,' said Conquest with a swift, diplomatic smile.

'Oh, I know, I know. Don't mind me if I vent.' He leaned forward as though to share a confidence. 'But don't get me started about the Chinese, eh?' He rocked back in his chair and shook his head with suppressed mirth as though he had just issued a dare.

Conquest responded with a highly theatrical laugh, somewhat incongruous in the circumstances since it was a weapon he had developed to discomfort those he wished to intimidate, so he cut it short. 'I'm writing a book about the Kennedy brothers,' he confessed.

'Ah, the Roman Catholic Micks! Good for you! Surprised nobody's done it before.'

'They have.'

'Oh! Pity! And how did you come to be running a national health trust? Not a medic, are you?'

'No, I was second in command to a medic; he got me on board. Then he fell ill.'

'Did he? Stepped into his shoes, did you? Must have been good at your job!'

Conquest acknowledged the truth of his remark with a shrug.

Sir Norman smiled conspiratorially. He waited in good humour while the waiters fussed about the table with their main courses. 'So –' he began when the waiters had left – 'I had a very interesting chat with your chair of senate, Professor Hingley: human resources expert.'

'Human rights, I think you mean.'

Sir Norman deigned not to hear Conquest's correction. 'He seemed full of enthusiasm for the new leaf. What should I know about this university of yours?'

'I've hardly got my feet under the desk. Of course, given the mess it was in I've been given a great deal of… How should I say…'

'"Discretion", I imagine.' Sir Norman laughed. '"*Latitude*."'

'Yes. "*Room for manoeuvre*".' Clifford laughed too. 'It's weak because its institutions are weak: weak administration, weak oversight. "Perk" Hingley…' He let the name hang in the air waiting to see how Sir Norman would respond. He was not disappointed.

'Yes, obliging and doesn't divide opinion: great virtue in a chair. Not the stuff of an innovator, somehow. Willing enough, but a bit of a milksop.'

'And the academics seem… *demoralised*. One or two bright sparks, but they failed to stick their heads above the parapet when it was obvious that things were going wrong.'

'Best left to their private concerns, I always think. Not the most worldly of people: academics.'

'No, often lacking a spark of realism.'

'So taken all-in-all, you have an opportunity to make an impression, do something memorable. University London Central: unique institution… in its own way.'

Conquest held up a finger and fumbled in his jacket pocket with his other hand. He smiled winningly. 'Yes, I wanted to pick your brains about finances.' He produced a manila envelope and laid it flat on the tabletop. 'I'm beginning to get a feel for the place and it seems to me – and to the director of finance – that if you strip out the unfortunate fraud the last management got itself embroiled in, the finances are in good shape; certainly compared with some of Our Friends in the North!'

Conquest waited for Sir Norman to acknowledge that he understood what he meant by "Our Friends in the North". Sir Norman had no idea what he was talking about, but he gave a wry twist of his lips that might well be taken to indicate he did.

'I've put out feelers to the Funding Council for a capital grant for a new building and it's no go. The university's not considered a case of need; nothing doing until the next quinquennial review.'

Sir Norman was looking at him keenly; talk of property development always stirred his blood. 'What'd you want to build?'

'Well, I'm not quite sure what, but something big.' Conquest leaned forward confidentially. 'Something with a name attached: the Conquest Building. That sort of thing.'

Sir Norman gave a bellow of laughter. 'Ah, I see! You want to leave a lasting memorial to your time as vice-chancellor!'

Conquest couldn't suppress a twitch. He didn't know what part of him had twitched, but he knew something had. Even so, he felt pleased with himself. Even if this particular conversation went no further, the subject was now out in the open and he could come back to it with Sir Norman whenever he wished. 'Well, why not? There's nothing like a successful building project to commemorate one's passing!'

Sir Norman nodded enigmatically and held out his hand for the manila envelope, which he opened with studied care. When he had scrutinised its contents he picked up his knife and fork and began to dispatch his ostrich steak with considerable relish. After a while the speed of his eating began to slow and he eyed Conquest over the rim of his wine glass.

'Tell, me, Conquest, is that lamb living up to expectations?'

'Tender.' He nodded. 'Very tender.'

'And this building of yours?'

'Information technology, cloud computing, digitalisation... that sort of thing. We need to make a transformative investment in IT.'

'Ah! I see, *a hub!*' Sir Norman sat back with an air of satisfaction, as though everything had fallen into place. 'A digital hub would be a lot more than a transformative investment, it would be the future writ large.'

'The future! Yes, I can see that going down well.'

Sir Norman folded the spreadsheet and wagged it at Conquest. 'Good. If you don't mind, I'll show this to my finance guru. He reads financial accounts with more of a penetrating eye than I.'

'Not at all. I'm drawing on the skills of senate, and so on.' He smiled ingratiatingly. 'I think of you as my property person.'

Sir Norman did not care to be thought of as anyone's "person", but for the sake of the moment he was willing to put that to one side. 'Quite, very proper,' he growled, pocketing the envelope. 'I'll get back to you, and we can have a little chat about my chap's suggestions. I'm off to St Andrew's this weekend. Play golf? No, it's probably a bit too much of a boy's thing for a scholarly chap like you. I bet Wimbledon is more to your taste.'

Finally the meal was over, Sir Norman's car had whisked him away and Conquest was free to go. Once out on the street he began to walk towards St James's, too preoccupied to cast around for a taxi. He had found Sir Norman oddly inspiring.

What is my back story? he asked himself, recalling Sir Norman's question. *I think of myself as pretty powerful. Good at my job. Ruthless when I have to be. Sharp when it comes to setting aims and objectives, and achieving them. A motivator. Good at delegating. An excellent grasp of politics in the workplace. Well-connected. My specialty is taking short-term appointments and turning organisations round; putting them back on a sound footing. I expedite change. I clear up the messes others have created. I understand organisations and know how to get things done. I get people fired if I have to. It's never easy being honest with the inadequate. I have credibility and status. Rules, structures, systems and collective endeavours are my building blocks. Anything is possible if you are organised and determined; I prove that every day. I went from being a dean of studies to the chief executive of a national health trust in three years. I've kept up my political connections. I could have run for parliament if I'd wanted to. I'm known to the party machine; consulted on NHS issues. I surprised them when I moved on to the FA. It didn't matter it was football, any more than it mattered when it was hospitals. It was all rules, structures, systems and collective endeavours. I have cultural capital, am recognised as a gifted administrator destined for high office. Then why is it that someone like Sir Norman makes me feel uncertain of myself, ungainly and halting of speech? Is it because he sees me as a mercenary who can be bought and sold? Is that my role in his narrative? I'm bigger than a bit part in his narrative. What about my academic research? That's something I've kept up through thick and thin. When I've finished my book on the Kennedy brothers they'll remember I'm not just an administrator. I'm an academic, a professor of American studies. I offer complexity of character, not a cardboard cut-out or a one-shot academic manager towing the party line. Even so...*

Conquest paused, looking for a way to sum up.

No back story! There's now and the thin red line that leads into the future. I'll make my way along that line and let it lead me where it may.

EIGHT

The Frank Brangwyn Building, home of the Department of Fine Art, had been built in 1897 as the St Agnes College of Needlework and Allied Crafts, "accommodation arranged over five floors". It had bay windows on the elevated ground floor, an Arts and Crafts porters' lodge of exquisite workmanship, corridors paved with black and white marble, and a lift barely large enough for two. In its first flush of youth the building had been requisitioned by the military and formed the backdrop to the heart-rending Great War memoir of Lady Violet Anthrop, later transport minister in the longest-serving Tory government of the twentieth century. During the First World War the youthful, idealistic Lady Violet had served as a nurse in the wards of the hospital that the college had been converted into as casualties from the Western Front began their inexorable rise. Now, some ninety years later, its "characterful but not particularly distinguished façade" (Pevsner) was cloaked in Virginia creeper. Each winter as the creeper lost its leaves a blue plaque emerged bearing the legend "Lady Violet Anthrop, politician and author. Served her country here: 1914–1919". Where once there had been orderlies and nurses, doctors and physiotherapists, there were now the members of the Department of Fine Art: the teachers and the taught. Each day they climbed the curving stone steps that led to the entrance. All memory of the suffering that Lady Violet had witnessed, sought to alleviate, and written so beautifully about, had vanished without trace, to be replaced by the youthful dissipations of the present-day occupants. On its five floors a middle-class, well-mannered bohemia thrived, managed by a changing cast of lecturers who came and went as their careers as artists rose and fell. The occupants of the building consisted of the student body, which, across all of the department's various courses, numbered some three hundred, five technicians, one studio manager, one receptionist, three secretaries (two part-time), and twenty-two academic members of staff, most on two-days-a-week contracts.

Not a few seriously disturbed individuals spent three joyous years in this community of care, which never failed them, never for a heartbeat thought of them as odd or ridiculous. The Frank Brangwyn Building could as well have been a ship of fools drifting from town to town along the lower Rhine. Each year the therapeutic nature of the struggle with the muse of art that graced its studios was attested to by the several students who suffered bouts of depression and shoplifting following graduation.

Besides harbouring the spirit of unworldliness, the department had a proud history of producing artists who, in their maturity, rose to be celebrated well beyond the confines of the art world.

It was to this blessed spot that Juliette Grace Burton came to study each day, along with the other one hundred and eighty or so students who comprised the three years of the BA Fine Art course.

Over the years this charming building, relic of the university's pre-history, had gained a patina, a certain mystic presence. The open space it faced, which occupied the centre point of what had once been one of a number of independent institutions, had always been known as The Green. It had originally been grass, and gated, but some time during the Second World War it had been tarmac-ed and used as parking for an emergency reserve of fire-fighting vehicles. It was more than forty years before it turned back to grass at the behest of the Ecology Society. By 1990 it had been renamed "Tiananmen Square Green" on the fierce insistence of the student activists who then controlled the Students' Union. A generation later and it was rumoured that there was a move afoot to changed the name to "Ramallah Green".

While the Frank Brangwyn Building was very much as it had been before the university was brought into being, the rest of the buildings facing the Green were recent and built on a scale befitting the modern notion of university-education-for-all. To the west was the stern and secretive Biotechnology Building, and to the east the Media and Communications Building, the façade of which was adorned with stainless steel vents, like a factory. Finally, directly across from the Frank Brangwyn Building, stood Emirates House, home of the Department of Oil Extraction Engineering (Marine), an older building than the other two, originally founded as the Lasmo Institute of Oil Extraction in the mid-Seventies as the North Sea became the newest frontier of oil exploration.

Like most art students, Juliette Burton didn't regard art as something to be done in the morning. In her case this was because most nights she was occupied being Lady Caroline Lamb until well into the small hours. For the other students rising late was more a matter of an aesthetic consensus. As a consequence, the studios had about them a strange echoing stillness all morning. And then, after lunch, for a few hours, they resounded to a hundred hammerings. The department's secretaries – innocents who even at close quarters retained a mystical reverence for all art – sometimes declared themselves mystified as to what all this hammering led to. In the majority of cases the answer, observable by those prepared to follow closely the pragmatics of art's manufacture, was either rectangles of battened hardboard or rickety stretchers over which cheap cotton duck canvas was stretched. Both products were finished with a copious application of white emulsion. The images wrought on these grounds were, as a rule, the focus of much despair, if not by their perpetrators, then by their teachers. Their despair found its expression in critical verbiage, a sort of torturing of the soul, that issued like vomit both from the students' mouths, and the mouths of their academic supervisors. Surprising as it may seem, the whole exercise was carried off with a will since the eternal hope was that "practice makes perfect" and everyone concerned, being – despite all – optimists, gave themselves up to the cycle of construction, followed by critical destruction, with good grace.

As has been already noted, Juliette Burton's routine was typical of the student body as a whole. Invariably she arrived in time for lunch, which she took in the students' refectory, finishing a few minutes before two o'clock. This gave her time to chat on the stairs as she joined the queue for the department's shop where she could buy everything she needed for the afternoon's labours.

Her nighttime career meant that she was never short of money to buy materials, unlike many of her peers. For those who were in constant poverty – the vast majority – the shop offered a system of deferred payment, which was enforced at year's end by the simple expediency of denying them their examination results until their debts were cleared. Because of their straitened circumstances many students preferred to source their working materials from the skips, bins and building sites of the city. Nearer to home, the departments occupying the other buildings facing Tiananmen Square Green offered rich pickings. Since they enjoyed a level of funding altogether more lavish than the Department of Fine Art, they junked skip-loads of obsolete equipment and furniture, year in and year out. Substantial quantities of this ended up in the studios of the Frank Brangwyn Building. Most of it assumed the novel guise of art for a few days or weeks, before succumbing to the critical destruction already described above. By this means it was returned to its former status of rubbish, exiting the department by way of the department's own skip kept in the yard at the back of the building. This traffic, in conjunction with the aforementioned critical process, meant that skip rental, as well as being a permanent drain on the department's finances, subsidised the rubbish disposal costs of its neighbours. Despite the expectation that the status of art would only be endowed on these prestidigitations for a short while, a small proportion of them did survive in their exalted state long enough to appear resplendent in the end-of-year exhibitions.

Most days Juliette bought Winton oil paint, something she used a great deal of. She took her purchases up to the second year studio on the top floor of the building and added them to the stock already stored in the locker she kept in her workspace. She shared the space with two other students who found many reasons to defer beginning anything, hence today she found herself in sole possession. She began her preparations to paint by exchanging her outside coat for an old pinstriped shirt of her father's, which looked rather dashing in its post-City afterlife as an artist's smock. The canvas she was currently working on leant against the wall. She turned it round, lifted it up and hung it on two nails driven into her length of wall. The glass top of her locker served as a palette where she mixed her paints. She was a painter of abstracts. Repetition, she was convinced, was a necessity for art, and she never allowed herself to wander far from her chosen *modus operandi*. The commonest criticism she received of the paintings was that "they don't quite work", a criticism she treated lightly since it was generally revealed that what "works" and what "doesn't work" merely reflected her tutors' stylistic allegiances. It flattered them that she pursued them for their views but experience taught her that none could produce a satisfactory rationale for their "it doesn't work" judgment. The consequences were always the same: she deferred to them with a little "Oh!" and was momentarily absent. In this state she looked irredeemably cute.

Not that Juliette was herself analytical about painting: she set great store by "the intuitive leap" in all matters artistic. As far as the other students in her year were concerned she was their pocket abstractionist; the nice, friendly, "*and all that*" student who did the weird, off-colour paintings. They had no inkling that her body was a subversive weapon that men would gladly pay a term's subsistence for to devour with their eyes. Why? Because the paint-encrusted pinstripe shirt – like her over-sized overcoat – concealed her physical attributes utterly.

Her preparation complete, she began. She had been in the thrall of painting for little more than an hour when she received a visitor.

Now, here was Oswald. Oswald: not a fashionable name, but a name with a certain resonance, a name that promised something unconventional – a certain sprightly independence of thought. 'Hi Juliette,' he drawled from the entrance to her workspace. 'Want to go for coffee?'

Oswald is best understood by bearing in mind that in the decade following the turn of the millennium being an art student was one of those archetypal identity positions expressing modernism's indifference to orderly economic production. His art conformed, in the moment of its production, to the expectations he intuited as proper for a full enactment of that identity. Oswald was nearly twenty-one and had, as yet, little experience of productive economic activity. Unlike Juliette, he did not have the economic opportunity of displaying his physical attributes for money. Or if he did, he had not so far come across it. Nevertheless he was not without resource. The previous summer term he had wangled a paid part-time elected post with the Students' Union, performing nebulous duties for the welfare of sporty students. The pay was not great, but it was guaranteed for a year. He had also found employment working nights and weekends for a catering company called The Groaning Board. The Groaning Board was a multi-tiered catering behemoth that could, and did, produce food at every conceivable culinary level, from victuals for prison canteens to magnificent City banquets graced by royalty. Oswald spent several evenings a week in a waiter's uniform serving drinks and canapes at receptions, openings and other catered events. This took him and the rest of his crew – a motley bunch of students, bottom-of-the-pile immigrants, school dropouts and fly-by-night geezers – to all sorts of prestigious and difficult-to-access venues in central London. They spent their evenings mixing with a rich and famous, in proximity to the levers of power, though, of course, they never got their hands on them. As with Juliette, his nighttime life was at odds with his daytime experiences in the studios and corridors of the Frank Brangwyn Building; theirs was a pattern of life that resulted in moments of conceptual dislocation.

'Sorry, Ozzie, I can't go for coffee now, I only just got going,' said Juliette apologetically. 'Later?' Although "later" was an assertion, she gave it a rising interrogative inflection, something of a habit with her, which gave it a charmingly tentative quality. It seemed to him to be all of a part with her delicate comportment. He would have been shocked to know that the only time she put off that comportment was when she was stripped to her sequined loincloth on the pole dancing stage. While economic necessity had suggested the line of work, she found it surprisingly congenial. She knew others would find it strange, but it was at the Club Beirut that she thought of herself as being "in her skin"; it was her emancipation, the only time she felt free from hesitation. Not least it was then, in the guise of Lady Caroline Lamb, that she was liberated from the cares and concerns of painting, something she took very seriously indeed.

'I've got to try and finished this today,' she said apologetically.

Oswald didn't mind that she was busy. He found it a pleasure to watch her work. Everything she did seemed so purposeful: even when she was mixing gloopy masses of paint, her capable hands organised her material with care. He found it strangely calming to watch as she resumed painting, moving with purpose, making tiny corrections to the direction of the colour she was laying onto the canvas with a palette knife. He had no idea what thoughts about painting were directing her actions but he could see that she conducted the entire operation with a sense of precision that other students who chose to paint abstracts singularly lacked. He was impressed, as he was often, by her commitment to her work. He couldn't think of anyone else in their year who came close.

'It looks finished already,' he said, not entirely seriously.

She regarded him gravely as though he had made a profound critical judgment. 'It needs more pink,' she said, 'more pink highlights to lift all this green. Don't you think?'

Oswald nodded. Juliette was a bit of a mystery, he decided. And he warmed to – no, felt positively, *vicariously* engaged in – the problem of lifting her greens. But however much he might admire her absorption in the technique of painting he had another reason for stopping by to talk to her, and now, he felt, was the moment to broach the subject.

'Would you do me a favour?' he asked.

She looked at him cautiously, wondering what was coming.

'Mr Fantastic is in my flat.'

Juliette sensed trouble. She knew Oswald and she knew Oswald's dog. Mr Fantastic was a tramp of a dog that accompanied him nearly everywhere. He was one of those dogs of independent mind that indulge human ownership rather than live in obedience to its lore. The application of health & safety rules by the faculty's academic administrator meant that it had been only a matter of time before Oswald had been banned from bringing him onto the campus. Since he howled loudly if left alone for more than a couple of hours he had become a liability, threatening to prevent Oswald from fulfilling even the modest aims required of him by the course. As a result, Mr Fantastic had become the collective responsibility of his year group.

'Could you fetch him?'

Juliette had found herself in charge of Mr Fantastic before. Walking the brute was a battle of wills, and his pugilistic nature meant that an encounter with another dog was conducted in the spirit of the weigh-in of a world heavyweight championship boxing match. At a deeper level the prominence of his testicles was an affront to her femininity.

'Why? Can't you?'

'I can't...' He waved his hand around in the air. 'I haven't got time. I have to be in Wandsworth by six, and I need to take him with me.'

'Really? Well, I don't like him. He's rapacious of temperament and capricious of temper. Why haven't you got time?'

'I've got a tutorial for my critical studies essay.'

'You haven't! I saw your name on the list. You're tomorrow morning, straight after Helen.'

'Yes, I know, but I had to swop with Cave Mercer,' he explained hastily. 'It was a favour. He's shifting corpses at St Thomas's afternoons all this week. Anyway, how come you've noticed when my tutorial is? Mind, I see you're seeing him tomorrow afternoon, straight after lunch. He'll be in a good mood after all those carbohydrates.'

She was only too aware that a web of favours was an essential part of the student economy; the term was only just underway and already she had bartered her way to a free acupuncture session and the promise of Adobe Photoshop for her Mac: two cash-free exchanges conducted, as she saw it, very much to her advantage. She found herself weakening, partly impelled by the knowledge that Oswald was reputed to have a cousin living in Peckham who was the possessor of a Transit van.

'Okay,' she decided, 'but I still don't like that dog, he's got a rotten personality.'

He was making for the door, heading for his tutorial, when she called him back. 'Don't you need to give me a key, or something?'

For the next twenty minutes Juliette continued her battle to enliven her greens. It was a contest fought out through the thick and thin of the comings and goings of the students whose workspaces were now mostly occupied. While they could not deflect her from her private battle, knowing she had to fetch Mr Fantastic did. Eventually she gave up the struggle. It was already gone four o'clock and she had agreed to be back by five to meet Oswald just outside the perimeter that the defecating wonder was prohibited from entering.

Oswald was one of the most resourceful students Juliette knew; one of the few to find cheap accommodation within walking distance of the campus, not an easy matter in central London. Most students lived deep in the suburbs and made long commutes after the real commuters were already at work. It took her fifteen minutes to walk to his flat, which he shared with two other students, on the upper floor of a house in a mean, terraced street backing onto a railway viaduct. She expected Mr Fantastic to be waiting for her at the door, ready to force his way past her to escape his confinement. Silence. Going from room to room, her search revealed no sign of him. She got on her mobile to Oswald. His should have been turned off, but instead he came on the line immediately, provoking the suspicion that perhaps, after all, he was not in a tutorial.

'Hey, there's no dog here. You sure you got this right?'

'Yeah. You sure he's not hiding?'

She laughed at the idea of a two year old Doberman-cross of doubtful temper hiding somewhere in the flat. 'This place is grossly untidy, but I doubt I'd miss the mutt, were he here.'

At the other end of the line there was silence while Oswald pondered. 'Look, I can't talk now. I'm in my tutorial. I'll call you later.'

Oswald rang off and Juliette tried to imagine the scene – it didn't seem very likely – of him interrupting his tutorial to take her call. She wandered back through the flat to the kitchen at the rear of the house. The mess she regarded dispassionately, as one sees something with no connection to one's own habits of life. Above the sink the kitchen window overlooked the patch of garden to the rear of the house. She wondered if the dog might have been left out there. What she saw made her gasp. In the failing light she could make out the figure of a man digging a hole at the end of the

64

garden, under a wall festooned with Russian vine. He had his back to her. The hole he was digging looked a quite serious undertaking. A large pile of earth lay to one side and she estimated the hole was big enough to bury a fridge. As she watched, the man stopped digging, speared the ground with his spade and reached into his pocket. It was an action she knew only too well: he was reaching for his mobile. And when he put it to his ear he swung slightly towards her, confirming her suspicion that the digger was Henry, one of the two other students who shared the flat with Oswald. The call did not last long. Once he had returned the mobile to his pocket she leant across the sink intending to tap on the window, but before she could she received an incoming call herself. It was Oswald.

'Sorry, I've wasted your time, I'm afraid. Henry's taken Mr Fantastic to Stevie's place in Kennington.'

'I thought you were in a tutorial?' She was now thinking the reason he'd given her for not being able to collect Mr Fantastic was a complete fabrication. 'And *no*, I doubt they're in Kennington with Stevie,' she continued forcefully. 'Henry's here in the garden and he's digging a dog-sized grave.'

There was a nonplussed silence from the other end, then Oswald said: 'Hang on, I'll double check.' He rang off before Juliette could stop him. She gave vent to her irritation by stretching out her hand and rapped on the windowpane with her knuckles.

Henry had resumed his digging and appeared not to hear. She watched, wondering what was passing through his mind. He dug with an unhurried deliberation. He may not have responded to her, but when his mobile rang for a second time he left off digging and clamped it to his ear.

She waited to see what would happen. It was one of those calls consisting of a lot of talk from the other end of the line. Henry hardly spoke and instead listened intently. When his caller had delivered his message Henry made what looked like an attempt to reassure him all was well. Not once did he turn his head in acknowledgement of the fact that she was watching him from the upstairs window. While the call was still winding down, her mobile sounded. She raised it cautiously to her ear.

'Hello. Hello. Is that you, Juliette?'

'Yes Oswald, it's me.'

'Henry's with Stevie. You've got to be mistaken.'

'You talked with him?'

'No, with Stevie.'

She thought Oswald's admission completely unacceptable. Stevie was a notorious "nearly-student" who often hung out with the art students. Juliette hardly knew him but he nurtured a reputation for being something of a wild man and was said to be totally unreliable. 'Have you spoken with Henry *at all*?'

'No, I spoke to Stevie. Stevie says he's there.'

'Both times?'

'Yes, both times.'

'Shit! Stevie's lying.' She was becoming alarmed. 'Henry's here in the garden. He's taking a call on his mobile. It's probably Stevie telling him right now we're on to him. What are they up to?'

'Perhaps you'd better go down and see. You're sure it's him?'

While she had been in the flat the light had been fading imperceptibly. By now it was sufficient to make it difficult to see what was happening in the garden.

'Look, I'm sure.'

'You don't sound sure.'

'I am. I'm going to find out what he's done to your dog. You might be a bit more concerned yourself. What if he's been run over!'

She went out of the flat and down the stairs looking for a way into the garden, but at ground floor level there was only the door of the ground floor flat and, in the other direction, the street door. Then she remembered that to the side of Oswald's kitchen there was a length of passage that ending in a door with frosted glass panels and she went back upstairs. She released the bolts top and bottom, and shoved the door hard. It opened with ease and she almost toppled down the fire escape. She pulled herself up with a jerk and found herself looking into Henry's up-turned face.

'What *have* you done to Mr Fantastic?' she demanded.

Henry didn't reply, but instead he pointed at the grey metal box leaning against the foot of the fire escape. 'I'm burying that.'

'Where the hell is Mr Fantastic? Oswald sent me to fetch him.'

'Never mind that. Help me get this into the hole quick.'

'Why? What did you do?'

He pointed again at the metal box. 'We thieved that, and now I'm trying to get rid of it.'

She put her indignation aside for a moment, descended a couple of steps and took a good look at the metal box. 'What is it?'

'It's a vending machine. We took it from the back of a van.'

'Stevie?'

'Yeah, Stevie. He's split. Left me to it.'

She came down further and looked more closely at the vending machine, her sense of alarm subsiding. She thought she recognised it. 'It's a condom machine, isn't it? Why would you steal that?'

'Not condoms. It's overnight necessities. You put in two pounds and it gives you a kit of overnight necessities.' The ground was strewn with plastic bags the size of a packet of crisps. He picked one up to show her it was a purse-like envelope held shut with a press-stud. 'Toothbrush, toothpaste, comb, shower cap, earplugs, lip balm, needle and thread.'

She laughed. 'What you going to do with them?'

'Bury them.'

'Bloody, stupid kleptomaniac.' She said this without raising her voice or showing the least sign of exasperation. 'Get the cash out before you bury it.'

'I tried already... but there isn't any. It was just being delivered.'

'Great! Somebody's going to be mad. I hope the cops don't catch you; I really do!'

'We left him tied to the railings outside the NatWest.'

'*What?*'

'Mr Fantastic. We came upon this opportunity, you see. We were walking along and saw this vending thing lying in the back of a van. Door was left open while the driver... while he was in the club. Stevie thought it was cigarettes, being a vending machine. He tied the dog up, expecting we'd be just a moment. He walked up to the van and lifted it out. Spontaneous, it was, pure bloody spontaneous brilliance!'

'And the dog?'

He looked embarrassed. 'We had the vending machine and it was suddenly huge... somehow... and we made off with it, quick as we could. Stevie carried first, staggering all over the place. By the time it was my turn we realised we'd made a mistake and we decided to split. So I came round here – this being a garden – to bury the evidence.'

'And that poor dog's still there!' Suddenly she had become the protector of a dog she didn't even like. The irony struck her like a blow.

'We forgot about him. Stevie's been calling me about who's going to fetch him. Oswald's been on to him.'

'Funny, that,' she said, mostly to herself. 'That's what men do for you! You better dig your stupid hole and you can put the stupid swag in it yourself, mate. *I'm* going to fetch that bloody dog before it bites some innocent, dog-loving do-gooder with misguided, benevolent intent.'

She left him staring into the hole he had dug. The doorbell started to chime as she reached the top of the fire escape. She turned round, possessed of the urge to dispense a parting shot. 'That'll be Oswald or Stevie. They'll give you a hand. You know what? You need to air the flat; it's rank with skank.'

She walked straight through the flat, pulled the door to and descended to the ground floor. She turned the front door Yale and was confronted by a large policeman. He looked at her placidly.

'Excuse me, madam, could we have a word?'

Beyond him two police cars and a van were parked in the street.

'Is this your dog?'

And there was Mr Fantastic, wearing a muzzle and looking a trifle put out.

'I don't live here, officer,' she said in a small, meek voice.

'This dog does though, doesn't it?' He indicated the engraved disc on the dog's collar. 'Very thoughtful touch, that. Useful when trying to return a dog to its owner.'

As he finished speaking there was a flurry of activity down the street where a narrow alley led to the backs of the houses. Two policemen came out hauling Henry by his collar. A few moments later a third policeman appeared carrying the overnight necessities vending machine.

The police officer looked her up and down and felt moved to give her some fatherly advice: 'I should keep away from here if I was you, love; they're bad lots.'

NINE

Conquest was living life intensely, vicariously. There were receptions, of course, where important people looked at one another warily over the rims of wine glasses, but mostly it was the business of the university that consumed his waking hours. Each night he went back to his *pied-à-terre* in Bermondsey to sleep for a few hours. He scarcely had time for Marj, his wife. She was a marine biologist he had met at a head of department's training course at Wye College in 1992. He had been beguiled by the intensity with which she had talked of the Burgess Shale, the fossils of which she had studied in Washington the previous summer. He sometimes wondered if the fossils of the Burgess Shale had subsequently come between them. He didn't think so – Marj and he were, after all, mature people with differing academic interests – but his fascination with the development of sea invertebrates had proved a passing thing.

Recently Marj had been diagnosed with an overactive thyroid and was having on-going isotope treatment at Wolverhampton General. While she was radioactive he was forbidden to spend more than one hour in twenty-four in her company. Even accompanying him on the train journey to London from the family home outside Wolverhampton was out of the question. He began to see that Lady Caroline Lamb – or rather the spectral essence of her – had become compensation for a lack of female companionship. When he thought about her – something he resisted if at all possible – he had to admit to himself that he might well be idealising her – after all, she was only a second year undergraduate student, yet she had come to be imbued with an aura, an aura that – so argued his rational self – he had manufactured. Whether manufactured or not, he could not deny its potency. He knew clearly enough that Ballantyne and Cornish had not seen what he saw, but then he considered them to be of coarser fibre. In any case, whether manufactured or not, the aura had attached itself to her; it was – this almost made him laugh out loud with joy – the aura of physical perfection: exquisite, vital, youthful, pure. To him she was an achingly lovely organism. Yes, it was as though he had brought into being – so he had decided – his own private godhead to vitalize the world, although he was not – *of course!* – of a superstitious or religious disposition. No! But he understood the impulse, and there was no denying that it was a rare and precious thing to have discovered in another human being. All around him there were ugly, half-made people, and to have this intense feeling about her physical perfection was a joy.

I am a gregarious man, after all, and yes, the thought of Lady Caroline Lamb more than makes up for the radioactive eclipse of Marj, heartless though that might seem. Some would call it infatuation; to me it is the necessary gilding of this drab day. Harmless, I suppose, as long as it remains an idea and stays in my head.

TEN

Sir Norman Fleet, Sir Michael Rosenthal and Lord N'Garbi were having dinner at the Garrick. The veal pie had just arrived and Lord N'Garbi was in boisterous form, quite a feat considering he had had a gruelling day of it on the cross-benches.

'—bloody ideologues on the right,' he was saying. 'They want spending cuts, but then there's the poor needing nourishment. What is parliament if it is not a source of nourishment for my people!'

Indeed Lord N'Garbi had devoted his life – the part that was not devoted to watching cricket – to getting his stubby, two-tone fingers on the levers of power with the express purpose of ensuring that the taps of cash would flow at his command – and his command only – in the direction of "his people". He did not look a commanding individual, but there lies a misunderstanding of how command works in modernity. He oozed opinion and expertise of an entirely predictable nature, and this was the key to his success: that *never* did he surprise with his views, the issues he raised, or the policies he demanded attention for. He was the reliable minority voice on many committees and worked, in an advisory capacity, for many branches of government. It was a role where originality of thought was not required, which was a good thing because he had none.

Lord N'Garbi was a lawyer by trade and an expert on international law as it pertained to the cruise industry, a subject he devoted a good deal of research to, particularly in January and February. He was rumoured to be assisting the Chinese in the launch of a cruise line in Western waters, although not one word of such an arrangement had ever passed his lips. All in all, he was one of those fat, over-indulged politicos who looked like the smoked salmon *canapés* came a little too easily, and he made the two knights of the realm he was dining with look a little colicky, powdery and dry.

'These Tories want people to stand on their own two feet and square up to the Great Fight, but the world of work is stacked against them; they crucify the worker at every turn! And where's the welfare for the out of work?'

The two knights of the realm indulged him for a while longer, but eventually Sir Norman grew restive.

'Frangi, you don't have constituents anymore. You've been kicked upstairs.'

'But, my dear boy, you don't go to the slums and see the conditions under which my people have to live.'

'Infrastructure,' said Sir Michael. 'That's what we need to be talking about. *We need to build!* Concrete, steel, cladding is the best way to improve the life of the people, to invest in them. Give them the tools...' He lifted his glass dreamily and took a sip of his gin fizz as though contemplating the industry of the people in the crystal arks he was planning to build.

Lord N'Garbi looked incredulously at his companions and gave a bellow of laughter. 'Decent accommodation is not an investment, it's a right! Very well, my friends, let us speak of space, of light... of building.'

'I have a frustrated vice-chancellor who wants to build,' said Sir Norman. 'He wants to put his name to something solid before he moves on. He deserves it: been an exemplary public servant for years.'

'Exemplary!' echoed Sir Michael. '*Most exemplary!*'

His lordship rolled his eyes expressively. 'Exemplary, is he? Has a university, does he? Good for him! And the Funding Council?'

'Doesn't see him as a priority.'

'Shame. Ambition thwarted.' Lord N'Garbi gave a chuckle and tucked into his veal pie. 'Who is it?'

'Conquest at London Central.'

Lord N'Garbi made a scoffing noise. 'What he has there is a middling university doing solid work, needs putting back on an even keel by responsible stewardship. He got up that UEFA bid that nobody wanted us to win, didn't he? He's what Stalin called a "little cog". Am I right?'

'Medium, I'd say,' said Sir Norman carefully, 'but set aside the university's recent unfortunate—'

'Scandalous.'

'Quite, *scandalous* mismanagement... But set aside the recent scandal and one finds that the university's been run on a conservative basis.'

'Conservative!' Lord N'Garbi spat out the word as though something in his veal pie had displeased him.

'Yes, my financial chaps think that despite the deficit in last year's accounts, there are assets,' said Sir Norman smoothly. 'We were thinking of a digital hub.'

'*Are you!* Is he, though? Has he the gumption for a digital hub?'

'I think he has the gumption, if he gets a little steadying. This conservative... "*propensity*", shall we say? Came from the former director of finance. Long-serving but recently... *retired*. Conservative, but not really on the ball, it seems.'

'Ah!' exclaimed Lord N'Garbi. 'Now I understand! The old fashion sort: good at balancing the books, but *didn't leverage his assets*!'

'Seems so.'

Lord N'Garbi dismissed the thought of such a director of finance with a brutal chop to the back of his imaginary neck. 'Have you any push or shove with the university's governing body?'

'Just joined,' confided Sir Norman.

'Then shove and push is what you must do!'

'If the Funding Council will go for it, he can be steadied, definitely steadied,' Sir Norman had the feeling he should give N'Garbi a fuller account of how things stood. 'I've seen the university's accounts. Their accommodation is not entered as a cost on the expenditure side of the budget. The estate is a fat mortgageable asset lying idle... and the university's in dire need of investment.'

'*Investment!*' Sir Michael, who had been slumbering into his gin fizz for the last few minutes, suddenly woke up. 'In business that would be a sin. Shareholders would be all over him, telling him to gear up the balance sheet.'

'Yes,' agreed Lord N'Garbi, 'tell him to gear up and do something to catch the Funding Council's eye.'

'Wainwright, Carter & Expandite have digital hubs off-the-peg for twenty million,' Sir Norman reminded them. 'Cafeteria, lecture theatre and administrative staff sauna all part of the package.'

'Ah-ha! *Vested interest!*' said N'Garbi with a knowing harrumph.

Sir Norman held up his palms as if to show their shining whiteness. He might be the beneficiary of a contract awarded to Wainwright, Carter & Expandite but that didn't mean he didn't know his business ethics. The air of jocularity had disappeared and instead they had grown conspiratorial.

N'Garbi was the first to speak. 'You've just put one up at Severn Estuary University, haven't you?'

'Excellent addition to facilities, rated top attraction in the student survey! *Oh, good garden stuff,* how I love those student satisfaction surveys! Ministers actually take them seriously!'

'Student opinion is greatly valued from where I stand.'

Sir Norman pulled a wry face. It was his belief that most students were too bone-idle ever to fill out a student survey form, and it was well known that a few students, appropriately "prepped", could sway an outcome hugely. Suddenly they were all roaring with laughter.

'So what's the thinking here?' said Lord N'Garbi as he mopped his eyes with a red silk handkerchief. 'That this splendid educational establishment can borrow money on its buildings?'

'...And all we need is the sanction of the Funding Council for a capital project. The university puts put up a very nice digital hub and the vice-chancellor gets his name on a building.'

Lord N'Garbi seemed to find the whole thing a delightful prospect. Suddenly, for the sake of Sir Norman, he was prepared to indulge the vice-chancellor of University London Central. 'Sounds a bit of a thruster, your man, eh, Sir Norman?' he teased with a twinkle in his eye. 'We want to see universities showing initiative with their development plans; they can be eligible for top-up funding for new lecture theatres with an audience capacity of more than four hundred. Building class size, you see. The Funding Council can encourage efficiencies of that nature.'

'Wainwright, Carter & Expandite's digital hubs have lecture theatres at basement level with seating for five hundred, fitted out with full AV capability for performance, complete with stage lighting and mini revolving stage.'

'Very good: student recreational activities!' Lord N'Garbi slapped the table energetically. 'By Jove, there are ring-fenced funds for the provision of those kinds of dual-purpose facilities! If you can get him into bed with the Students' Union he could be on to a winner.'

ELEVEN

The next day Conquest received a phone call from Sir Norman.

'A brief meeting about your planning strategy. I'll be at the House of Lords for a wine and cheese do this evening. Come along and have a word, a brief word. Lord N'Garbi will arrange things.'

Conquest took a taxi at six and sure enough, when finally he found the right entrance, his name was on reception.

'Ah, there you are, Clifford!' Sir Norman greeted him. 'Glad you could drop by. Thought we should have a word about your building. Here comes a laddie with a tray. Get yourself a glass. My finance chap has been through your figures – pretty positive response. Thought you ought to be able to arrange a perfectly manageable mortgage with RBS for fourteen million. There's leeway in your current budget for the interest payments if you defer the reappointment of a few academic posts for a few months. Nothing a bit of temporary job-sharing couldn't take care of, I'm sure.'

Conquest looked duly appreciative. 'Fourteen million!'

'Should be able to get that up to twenty if you put the right sort of project together. Digital hubs are very sexy at the moment. Put some interdisciplinary initiatives together – you know the sort of thing: the creative melting pot. Lord N'Garbi's had a word and he thinks the Funding Council might look kindly on something of that sort. Yes, he thinks they'd warm to the idea.'

Conquest rubbed his hands together thoughtfully. 'Media and communications would go down on their knees for a digital hub; marvellous anchor tenant.' He had second thoughts. 'Sociology would have to have a look in too, of course, not to mention visual anthropology.'

'I'll leave the division of the spoils to you,' Sir Norman

laughed. 'Don't think I'm beating my own drum but Wainwright, Carter & Expandite have an interest in that type of building, as you probably know. Being in the business, I'd have to recuse myself from any meeting of senate that discussed the awarding of the contract. Small conflict of interest. In fact – ha, ha! – I'd probably find myself on a cruise when the contract was awarded. Now, what we need is a good site with a high profile frontage.'

'Ah, yes: site! I was thinking we could buy a site.'

'*Buy a site!* You're in central London, Clifford! What do you think a site would cost for the size of building we're talking about? Any idea how much land costs where you are?'

'No, sorry, I haven't. Well, the campus is pretty much all built on!'

'Deary, deary, Clifford, buy land around there and you'll be putting up a Nissan hut for that twenty million! What you need is an estate development plan. You'll have to rationalise your stock of accommodation.' Sir Norman almost prodded him. 'What you need is some advice from consultants; the Funding Council will expect you to take impartial advice on a development of this scale.'

'Ah, yes, consultants!'

'I know just the company – it's called Urban Tomorrows; I'll get my secretary to email you their contact details.'

'Goodness, we're moving rather fast, aren't we?'

'Clifford, word in ear. If there's a window with the Funding Council it might easily shut to. Top-up funding: need to have the cooperation of the Students' Union.'

'*Students' Union!*' Conquest groaned inwardly at the thought of having to negotiate with the union's president, Rob Mission.

'That's the spirit; seize the initiative! And by the way, I want you to get Sir Michael appointed to senate. He's a good man to have about when you're planning a big project. He'll help keep the quibblers in line.'

As the taxi took him back to his flat behind Butler's Wharf, Conquest found himself musing on Sir Norman's style.

I've always thought of myself as a forceful character, but I can see that Sir Norman pursues a policy of brutal... no... brute self-assurance... far more successfully than I do. He sees himself as always in the superior position and with right on his side. Sublime self-confidence! That's something I can work on, he being a no better man than I. And maybe he lacks my ability to proceed by stealth, disturbing the equilibrium of those I'm required to exercise power over. I can't think that I've met quite such a forceful personality before, and I can learn from his methods; with practice I might even out-do him.

TWELVE

As soon as Conquest arrived in his office the following morning he asked Carole to call Norma Hupplethorpe, the head of the Department of Estates and Services. The layout of the university was not as familiar to him as he would have liked, having made only a few hasty walkabouts since his appointment, and none since the start of the new academic year.

'What I'm going to need, Norma, are some up-to-date plans of our buildings and plant. And I would like a tour of the campus today, so could I avail myself of your services?'

Hupplethorpe's department occupied a warren of rooms in the basement of the Keynes Building. She was taken aback: previous vice-chancellors had tended to show little interest in the university as anything other than an abstract idea. It took her half an hour to sort out a set of campus plans – some so old they pre-dated the granting of full university status – before she took herself up to the vice-chancellor's office.

'I think I'm prepared,' she said as, greatly flustered, she tried to control the armful of plans.

'Leave them, Norma. We need to walk the bounds.' Conquest went to fetch his coat and the plans were abandoned on Carole's desk.

'I would like to build something, Norma,' Conquest confided as they descended the stairs. 'What would *your* priorities be?'

Hupplethorpe's eyes were fixed on her shoes as she tripped down the steps and for a moment Conquest thought she was too timid to give him an answer. 'The caterers would like the kitchens extended,' she said at last. 'Some of the boundary railings need replacing and the concourse of the Dimbleby Lecture Theatre is not really ideal.'

'I see. All very sound, I'm sure. But what about something a little more innovative, something that would transform the student experience?'

'Well, I couldn't say about the students,' she simpered, emboldened by his interest in her views, 'but perhaps we might think about a new building for the Department of Estates and Services. We are rather cramped in the basement and the porters' rest room has no windows.'

'Yes, I think the students would be gratified by some improvement there.' Conquest laughed, not unkindly, though he had begun to suspect that anything that would directly enhance the student experience was, for her, a low priority. As they reached the pavement outside the Keynes Building he paused dramatically. Already he could not recall a single one of Hupplethorpe's suggestions. 'Perhaps I want to think strategically about the academic life of the university, something memorable and frankly rather magnificent.'

'Oh yes, I know,' she exclaimed in a sudden rush of recollection, 'doesn't the Department of Psychology want a new sensory deprivation tank?'

'I think we should put on our thinking caps and come up with a list of priorities,' he decided, deftly putting an end to the conversation.

Ten minutes later they reached Tiananmen Square Green, and while Hupplethorpe discussed the Media and Communications Building, the newest building that edged the green, Conquest found himself gazing at one he could not remember having noticed on his previous expeditions. Architecturally, he realised, it complied so perfectly with his idea of what a university building should look like it had escaped his notice. Now he regarded it with a growing sense of intensity. A monstrous thought had begun to form: somehow he knew that within it he would find Lady Caroline Lamb.

'Isn't that fine art?' he said to Hupplethorpe, already certain of the answer.

'That's the Frank Brangwyn Building, vice-chancellor.'

'Yes, Professor Pomfret's lot, isn't it?' Conquest may not

have visited the Department of Fine Art but he had made it his business to garner impressions of Archie Pomfret, the head of the department, from senior members of the university.

Hupplethorpe closed her eyes with a look of the sanctimonious for she saw herself as the custodian of buildings, and rarely approved of the usage her buildings were put to by the student body and attendant academics. 'That's an academic matter, vice-chancellor, of which I know nothing.'

'Quite. Forgive me for asking. I think I should like to take a closer look at that building sometime.' He raised up his forefingers and thumbs to the Frank Brangwyn Building as though framing it as a target. 'But not when the students are about. Might start rumours flying about an accommodation audit... re-allocation of space, that sort of thing.'

Hupplethorpe intuited some intent in her vice-chancellor's jest, which chimed with her own vindictive thoughts. 'Quite right, vice-chancellor; we wouldn't want the little rabbits alarmed, would we?' she agreed with a repellent smile, thinking with relish of the consternation and disruption that a reshuffle of accommodation always caused.

THIRTEEN

Conquest knew there was a key person he had to persuade in order to mortgage the university's estate. Since it involved what Tommy Ballantyne would regard as "financial jiggery-pokery", he was certain that he would be resistant to the idea. Now Conquest had seen the Frank Brangwyn Building, he had begun to think of the digital hub not as an abstract idea but as an actual building, situated on Tiananmen Square Green, flanked by the Biotechnology Building to the west and the Media and Communications Building to the east. The more enthusiastic he became about the idea, the more he pictured his director of finance as the stern naysayer. For several days he kept his own counsel, imagining Ballantyne's disapproval, until finally he decided to confront his apprehension and had Carole request he come over from the finance office. When Ballantyne arrived Carole had a cup of coffee ready for him. She smiled sweetly in a way that warned him something was up.

'Tommy,' Conquest began briskly when finally they were seated across from one another on his sofas, 'I've had an advisor go through some of the spreadsheets you gave me a while ago now.'

'They're okay, aren't they?' said Ballantyne, going red in the face.

'Well. There are a few pointers I'd like to "have at you", if you follow my meaning.'

Ballantyne's alarm was deepening. In all their working relationship, throughout their work for the National Health Service Trust and the UEFA bid, Conquest had never once queried his bookkeeping and in return he had ensured that Conquest could present a well-ordered set of books to whosoever their paymasters were. 'What's going on, Cliff? We got auditors on our backs for something?'

'No, Tommy, it's opportunities. Opportunities come knocking and we've got to grab them, right?'

Ballantyne was still apprehensive about where the conversation was going. 'Is that right, Cliff? And what is it you want doing?'

'Tommy I want you to cut me some slack.'

'I live and die by the auditors, Cliff, you know that.'

'I know that, Tommy, but we need to be a bit more expansive in our thinking. I want the university's senate to sanction a mortgage on some of our properties.'

'Mortgage? All our property was bought outright years and years ago. We don't want to be servicing debt, do we?'

'If we raised some money we can attract funding – top-up funding – and invest in our infrastructure. If we don't do something big we're just going to look like caretakers, Tommy. I want you to work up the figures for me. I expect there'll be a few doubting Thomases on senate I'll need to blind with figures. Go and see the banking people. RBS'll swing for fourteen million, I'm told. Then we can put our names to something important for this university.'

'Like…?'

'Like a digital hub.'

'What in the name of bally hell is a digital hub, Cliff? It sounds Trekkie as hell.'

'State-of-the-art digital facilities. A – big – shiny – piece – of – infrastructure! A fitting memorial to our passing.'

Ballantyne went quiet. Conquest could see he was wrestling with his doubts.

He's wondering if I'm going too far, taking one too many risks. No, you don't have my imaginative leap, do you?

Then Conquest saw it quite plainly in his face, whatever his doubts, Ballantyne had decided to put them aside. It was all over in a moment.

'If that's what you want, Cliff. You're the one with the vision thing.'

Yes, unquenchable certitude wins the day!

Conquest had every reason to be pleased; if he could win over Ballantyne without a fight all the rest would be easy. The senior management team was already cowed. The only committee with the power to stop him was senate, and with Sir Norman by his side there should be no problem there. The only cause for caution was the chair, Professor "Perk" Hingley, and he would see to him personally.

'We're going to get this university motoring, Tommy. Enough of being stuck in first gear!'

FOURTEEN

The excesses of Freshers' Week were just a memory. The student clubs' stalls had gone from the assembly hall, as had the free copies of *The Guardian* from the students' refectory. Book lists had been issued and departmental photocopies had run hot with the surreptitious copying of copyright material for coursework notes. Lecturers young and old had dusted down their set pieces and checked them through to ensure they were still current. In the senior common room there was talk of politics and pensions. The great machine that was University Education had begun to gather traction. The George Orwell Library filled up and its books began to circulate; in the lecture theatres audiences changed hourly on the hour. The autumnal air was crisp with discourse and debate. Conquest called a second meeting of the senior management team. It considered a presentation on external relations given by the director of external affairs. Dry stuff. The same dullard gave a presentation on the design of the university's new stationary. Clifford was satisfied with the muted responses to both topics. The balmy days of late September had given way to more bracing times. Conquest still climbed the stairs to the roof above his office to be sure – so he said – that the members of the mountaineering club were not flying the Palestinian flag from the cupola atop the building. More to the point was his hope of catching sight of Lady Caroline Lamb crossing the campus on her way to the Frank Brangwyn Building. It seemed so right to him, this vantage point high above the campus: in physical terms it duplicated his psychic relationship with her. She was both one of the student body that he regarded as general, multiple – a homogeneous class – and conversely, in all her splendid specificity, she was the singular object of his tender, sensuous, romantic regard. It was now four weeks since the momentous night he had come across her at the Club Beirut when nudity and the nude had taken on a new meaning for him. The intervening period had not dulled his desire. Even so, the biting winds of autumn were discouraging and it satisfied him less and less to watch out for her from his eyrie. The time was approaching for him to come down from on high, and that, he knew, could only happen at great personal risk.

FIFTEEN

Conquest had made a point of meeting individually all the heads of academic departments. He was consulting them, so he told them, "concerning the university, its strengths and future". He knew there was little enough to be expected of the exercise but it had flattered them and collectively he thought of them as a potential counterweight to the power of the deans if ever the senior management team began to agitate for something he didn't wish to sanction. The head of department who had somehow slipped to the end of Conquest's list was Professor Archie Pomfret of the Department of Fine Art. There was a sense in which Conquest had come to conceive of him as the custodian of Lady Caroline Lamb and as a consequence he had developed an unconscious aversion to meeting him. But Carole held his diary and it was inevitable, however much he tried to put it off, that she would ensure the meeting occurred. Finally they met at half past eleven on an unusually bright morning with sunlight pouring through his office windows.

'Archie,' Conquest said, moving up a gear after a few pleasantries, 'I'm sorry we haven't had much of a chance to get to know one another before now. I've been doing my best to get round all the heads of departments to find out what they think about things. Get a steer, as it were. Such a busy time of year! I know you're busy too. I'm a great admirer of some of our former students who've made quite a name for themselves in the art world. Always nurtured my interest in the arts. I remember splashing out with my first salary cheque on a rather good Picasso print one of the Sundays commissioned.'

Archie Pomfret looked at his vice-chancellor guardedly. As a one-time member, when a student, of a Conceptual cooperative that had terrorised the art school staff for their adherence to the

Ecole de Paris, he still had ambivalent views about Picasso, or anyone who admired him.

'Your department...' Conquest paused, exercising his skills of dramatic effect. He let the pause drag out; he had the man sitting on the other end of his sofa summed up: *intellectually limited with a plain wife and ducks in the garden*. In these respects he was close to the truth, but in thinking Pomfret was a follower of artistic fashion, resting on his laurels, his best years behind him, he was somewhat askew. Little did he know that during the week, on account of the austere calm of his 'Islamic' pattern paintings, Pomfret lived in a grace-and-favour Kensington mews studio at the behest of a Saudi Arabian prince. Conquest's attention was much taken with the flowery tie Pomfret was wearing, which ran counter to the muted browns of the rest of his clothes. And by his white plimsolls. He should have heeded the warning they sounded. These incongruous touches were the very thing that should have told him he was not dealing with a known type. At least, not one he had yet come across in his many years of managing people.

'We've been... I've been looking at your department's strategic plan for this academic year.' Conquest indicated the slim sheaf of papers on the coffee table. He then picked up a substantial wad of paper lying next to it and waved it at Pomfret. 'This is sociology's.'

Pomfret took his time assessing the relative weights of the two documents before offering a response. At last, 'Brevity is a virtue,' he pointed out.

'Of course, true!' Conquest smiled winningly. 'The reason why sociology excels at this sort of thing is because they see it simply as another exercise in social relations. This –' he waved sociology's strategic plan – 'is a defence mechanism.' He gave a bark of laughter of such ferocity that it surprised even him. 'We all know sociology would take over the entire higher education system if it could. But...' Again he employed the dramatic pause. 'But there's a feeling abroad that your department is not setting itself very challenging aims and objectives. This wouldn't matter quite so much if you weren't in deficit.'

'Aims and objectives,' snuffled Pomfret. 'Never can work out which is which.'

'Your sole objective for the year is – and I quote – "to persuade the university to stop charging the department one hundred and thirty thousand pounds for cleaning it doesn't want or need".'

'Yes.'

'Doesn't want?'

'That's right. The cleaners are the single greatest threat to the students' work. Sometimes they even *throw it out!*' Pomfret clapped his hands together gleefully. 'Mind you, they're not to blame, it's hard enough to distinguish student art from rubbish at the best of times.' He pulled a face, momentarily awed by the absurdity of things. 'I blame Schwitters.'

Conquest had no idea who Schwitters was but he joined in, laughing uneasily.

'It would be so much better,' urged Pomfret, pressing on, 'if the studios remain dusty and we save the money. The students clean them up very nicely at the end of the year for their final exhibitions. And removing the charge for cleaning from the expenditure side of our budget would take the department from deficit to surplus in one fell swoop.'

The logic left Conquest cold. 'That's all very well, but I've looked into this and the university signed a new five-year contract for cleaning last winter. It was negotiated by the facilities manager.'

'I see!' Pomfret looked bewildered. 'Well, I'm sure he didn't asked me if we wanted a new cleaning contract. Perhaps you could enquire?'

'Well, he was dismissed in the summer, apparently.' Conquest was flustered to have to confess to this. He felt forced to offer further explanation. 'He turned out to be not what he said he was... but that's hardly the point.'

'Really? So! Was that Mr Fisher?' Pomfret's face had taken on a look of intense introspection as he tried to remember if he had ever come across the facilities manager. It was a task he was unlikely to succeed in since he tended to the belief that anyone working for the university who didn't teach was of little consequence. 'I think I saw him skulking about the building once,' he decided after long moments during which Conquest wondered whether what he was witnessing was genuine bumbling or some kind of act. 'He had ginger hair and was asking after tissue paper.'

'Quite. Perhaps we—'

'The point is, we can't afford unnecessary cleaning. We wouldn't wish this deficit thing to result in a cut to the teaching, would we?'

Conquest had heard quite enough about the management of the university's central services. 'Cleaning is not a matter of election. Finance has confirmed the validity of the cleaning contract and your department's share of the cost reflects the amount of accommodation it has.' Conquest's aversion to meeting Pomfret was becoming a palpable dislike. He decided the time had come to counterattack and he again took up the department's strategic plan.

'Of course, if your accommodation was less extensive your proportion of the university's cleaning bill wouldn't be so high. Your square meters of space per student is extraordinary – highest in the university, apart from science and engineering. Have you considered hot desking?'

Pomfret looked baffled. 'Hot desking? What's that?'

'Well, let me put it this way: are your students always in their studios? No, because they have to attend lectures and seminars... and then there's your workshops! It's perfectly possible to have two students share the same space and never meet if you organise the timetable properly.'

Pomfret had no idea how to respond, the proposal was utterly alien to everything he believed in. An artist's studio was his studio, plain and simple; it was a temple, a sacred place of individual endeavour, looking out on the abyss of creation. Hot desking sounded like the concentrated essence of everything he detested about the Department of Media and Communications. He sat there dumbfounded.

'I hear,' continued Conquest, not one to stick in a knife without twisting it, 'there have been some problems with your joint degree with the Department of European Languages, have there not? Professor Misha finds your department less than wholehearted about the course.'

Pomfret was not dented by this sally. In fact, here was a topic he was eager to discuss. 'Well, that joint degree is another sore point. We provide those students with studio accommodation, handle admissions and student selection, course administration, all pastoral care *and* teach them three days a week, and yet Professor Misha's department gets fifty per cent of the teaching grant. *And* of the overseas fees, which are high-cost to reflect the fact that our half of the course is a studio practice course. What we provide is high cost, what they do is not. Seems all wrong.'

'It is, after all, a joint degree.'

'Even so...' Pomfret made a "hey presto!" gesture that expressed his belief that what he had just said utterly justified his department's lack of enthusiasm for the course.

Conquest did not approve of administrative nitpicking from heads of departments and he reached for his favorite mantra. 'In matters such as this we have to be collegiate.'

'*Quite!*' agreed Pomfret.

Conquest saw that Pomfret had taken his comment to mean that Professor Misha – not he – needed to be more collegiate. 'I think we're at cross-purposes,' he said hotly. He was beginning to see in Pomfret's attitude a kind of bland anarchism, which, by a strange twist of the unconscious, brought to mind the book he was writing about the Kennedy brothers; a book that was proving extraordinarily difficult to finish. The longer he struggled with the seemingly irresolvable puzzle of what made Bobby Kennedy tick, the more he felt his claim to academic credibility was diminished. Was it to be, he wondered, that whenever he felt himself to be opposed he would feel intensely self-conscious about his failure to find a convincingly original narrative of the post-war American dream? He was suddenly alarmed by the thought that Pomfret had somehow discovered that he could not solve the puzzle of Bobby Kennedy. He was beginning to perceive cunning behind Pomfret's bland exterior. As the conviction took hold, it became impossible for Conquest to see that Pomfret was so wrapped up in his own shortsighted sense of reasonableness that he was blind to Conquest's hints that he should tow the line and bend to the will of his superior.

'Doubtless we could clear this up in two minutes if Professor Misha were here,' said Pomfret.

Conquest sensed that this was an appeal for him to referee a meeting with Professor Misha, and frostily he ignored it; he was sufficiently aware of his status to know that negotiating the relationship between two departments, especially ones in the same faculty, was beneath him and should be left to their dean, even if the dean was the hapless Professor Blurton. Even more to the point, his priority at that particular moment was to rid their conversation of its negative psychic undercurrents. He felt an urgent need to assert his authority. And now was the moment, he decided, to stake out his claim to Lady Caroline Lamb. It was a testament to his habits of mind that these impulses took an administrative turn.

'I'm beginning to think that we need an outside view,' he murmured, as though talking to himself. 'Someone without an axe to grind; someone impartial and qualified to offer us advice. Don't you think so?'

It gave him a rosy glow of warmth to think of the inevitable moment when Lady Caroline Lamb would look up and he would be standing over her, shaping the world around her, disposing of her department like *this*, and her academic future like *that*. He would smile, and she would understand that he was in control and her future was in his hands.

'We –' Conquest corrected himself – '*I* am not inclined to believe that a department with only one objective, namely to rid itself of its share of the university's cleaning bill, is quite firing on all cylinders.'

'Well, of course, we do teach,' Pomfret observed reasonably. 'And our students do seem very content.'

Conquest felt a strong urge to silence him, to crush him, if not physically, then psychologically. He experienced a sudden pulse of rage. Had he been more circumspect he would have realised that it was an illusion that he was engaged in a battle of wills with Pomfret, and that to believe that he *was* was a sign that he had lost touch with what was right and proper to his status. Instead of shelving their conversation and sending Pomfret on his way he was on the verge of taking a bludgeon to the situation.

For his part, Pomfret appeared to have no inkling of the effect he was having. 'There doesn't seem to be any room in a strategic plan,' he said with a slightly aggrieved air, 'to say that we're going to keep on doing what we're already doing rather well.'

'*Quite so!*' Conquest flung back at him. 'Strategic plans are about development! Only a dynamic, forward-looking department can improve its standing, don't you think? An organism that stops moving dies, does it not? I am a disciple of dynamism!'

Pomfret gave a polite laugh that seemed to suggest that Conquest had said something absurd, although in actuality he was struggling to think of an appropriate rejoinder to what struck him as an admirable sentiment.

Conquest concluded that now was the time for the *coupe de grace*. 'The senior management team would like to help you with your financial difficulties and with the problems of the joint degree, and I think the best context in which to do that would be a departmental review, don't you? We could address your aims and objectives at the same time. It would help you to develop a SWOT analysis for the department.'

'Sounds ghastly. But I'd be happy to follow your advice, of course.'

'Fine, I'll put the dean of academic affairs on to it. The sooner the better, I would say. In the meantime I would rather like to be shown round. I trust you still have a life drawing studio; I'm rather a fan of all those old traditions.'

Pomfret gave a disconcerted guffaw. 'Well, there aren't any new ones, I suppose.' Although he gave the appearance of being at ease with Conquest's enquiry, in truth, he was not certain how much life drawing went on in his department. 'Life drawing is something we do attempt to provide, though it is a minority interest, on the whole,' he said, hoping he was playing it safe.

'I see, not a discipline for all, then!' said Conquest, incensed afresh at Pomfret's apparent levity. 'This has been a most illuminating discussion, wouldn't you say?' For the moment his sense of dignity was satisfied; their conversation was at an end. He had placed a ligature round Pomfret's neck and would draw it tight at his leisure. With great suddenness he rose to his feet; then the moment turned awkward since Pomfret remained seated, seemingly unaware that this was the signal for him to leave.

'Is there something else you wish to discuss?' asked Conquest.

'One thing, vice-chancellor. The last vice-chancellor: have we commissioned a portrait to hang in the council chamber yet?'

At the mention of his disgraced predecessor Conquest's face took on a decidedly disagreeable look. 'I'm not sure the university will be commissioning a painting of—'

'I have a suggestion: David Quant. He paints like an angel and I know he'd be willing to consider it. Can't have another dreadful mistake, can we?'

This last was a reference to the painting by Arthur Godbold, the ex-Kitchen Sink artist who had been, in his own words, "let loose" on Sir Finbar Russell, the most famous of former vice-chancellors.

Conquest's belief was that the best thing that could happen to his predecessor was for his memory to be consigned to oblivion. It might have been admissible to shock the senior management team with such an opinion, but Professor Pomfret was a mere head of department, and in the presence of someone so close to the business of teaching students, Conquest was not about to undermine the convention that vice-chancellors, however appalling, were never wrong, never mind booted out in disgrace. Such an admission would have been a breach of the code of solidarity that he knew Top People were initiated into for the protection of other Top People, although he could not recall when or where his initiation had occurred. 'Yes, we should ensure that something sober and appropriate gets commissioned, shouldn't we? I'll have a word with the chair of senate about it, and get back to you.'

'Thank you, vice-chancellor.'

'Do call me Clifford… or Cliff, if you like. It's more my style. "Breezy": that's the note I want to strike. Titles can be rather pompous, don't you think?'

'Oh, I rather like them,' said Pomfret, as he rose to his feet. 'They're like awards and uniforms: full of stuffed shirts and rather fun.'

SIXTEEN

When Pomfret had gone Clifford sat for a while reliving their conversation. The meeting had left his nerves jangling. In his judgment, Pomfret lacked the slightest sense of the *realpolitik* that he expected of a senior academic, and yet there was something alarming subversive about the character notes that dominated his recall of their conversation. How could it be that he felt he had, in some way, been shown up by a man whose sense of what it was to be a senior academic was so awry? It made no sense. Determined to throw off the feeling of having been probed and found wanting, he left his office and made his way to the office of Professor Woolworth, the dean of academic affairs. Suddenly he was in an impetuous rush to launch his campaign to bring Pomfret and his department to book.

Dean Woolworth was a blandly affable medieval scholar who had jumped ship from the Department of Religious Studies just before it had been closed down, many years since. He had scarcely any talent for teaching, but carried about him the air of one who was an accomplished pedagogue. What he had become was a pen-pusher and an able maker of rules and meaningful acronyms full of hot air. Over time his office had become one of the best listening posts for the affairs of the university. He had served as dean of academic affairs during the tenure of the last three vice-chancellors, partially because he had a talent for the thankless task, partially because no one else had ever shown the slightest inclination to rotate into the post. In the course of his tenure Woolworth had developed an unparalleled grasp of the administration of examinations. He knew the university's courses by their units of examination, its examinations by their regulations. He knew the reliability of the subject sub-boards, and of their chairs, and – one of his greatest sources of entertainment – the quirks of their external examiners, which he could read in the boards' propensity to mark laughably high, or miserably low, as the externals came and went. Famously, his office used more photocopying paper in a month than any other office in the university in a year.

Woolworth's office occupied a kind of half-floor undercroft behind the grand staircase that led to the first floor. It was low and there were many recesses, nooks and storage spaces off the chief area. Little daylight filtered in through windows that were small and for some reason fitted with frosted glass, the myriad indentations of which had gathered much grime. Papers were stacked on every side in a system of cataloguing known only to Woolwich and his secretary, Di, an elderly bluestocking who dwelt in an adjacent cubbyhole.

When Conquest entered he rose up from behind stacks of papers relating to the management of the academic board, of which he was the secretary, another of the means by which he exerted a subtle but pervasive influence over the academic life of the university.

'Ah, Murray!' Conquest exclaimed warmly.

'Vice-chancellor, do come in!'

Conquest sat down opposite him and they eyed one another with crooked smiles while Di brought in cups of tea. Since his arrival, Conquest had spent two rather dull evenings at dinner with Professor Woolworth. He knew he was an entirely different sort to Professor Pomfret. Woolworth could dowse any minor academic insurrection or administrative flight of fancy with rules and regulations, but whether he was worth cultivating as an ally Conquest found it difficult to decide. He suspected him of being somewhat spineless, so idly he began to wonder about staring him down.

'My programme of departmental academic reviews...' Conquest began when Di had left the room. He took a sip of his tea, looking steadily at Woolworth over the rim of his cup. 'I've decided we need to change things round a bit. I want to move the Department of Fine Art to the head of the queue.'

Woolworth recoiled noticeably. 'Professor Pomfret's motley bunch! What for?'

'Their strategic plan is thin, very thin. They're in deficit, over-provided with accommodation and they have inter-departmental problems. Professor Misha's been complaining about their attitude, and without their joint course her department would be shit creek *up*.'

'I see.' As a high Anglican, Woolworth was somewhat startled by Clifford's use of the term "shit creek". It didn't seem quite right coming from the mouth of a vice-chancellor. 'And what about English? If I remember aright, you had harsh words to say about them. There's a third year student claiming a member of staff has been selling exam grades for sex, not to mention the Students' Union being up in arms about the absence of a joint monitoring committee.'

Conquest acknowledged his objections with an airy wave of his hand. 'All true, Murray, but fine art is another of Professor Blurton's little charges, isn't it? It seems he needs every assistance in getting his faculty back on track. Don't doubt we won't bear down on all miscreants, but priorities change, I'm afraid. I want fine art first, then English, and I want them both reviewed this term.'

Woolworth blenched and shook his head. 'Impossible, vice-chancellor. Think of the logistics of doing two reviews in the next ten weeks! We have to find chairs, and external advisors, then give the departments time to work up their paperwork.'

'"*Work up*"!' Conquest was outraged. 'Whatever the timetable, their paperwork is not going to be "worked up", as you put it. We're going to use existing documentation, and if they haven't got it I'll want to know the reason why! No featherbedding on my watch!'

Conquest saw that Woolworth looked rattled. He knew that Woolworth believed in running collaborative processes and allowing departments under review to get their paperwork in order before they were subjected to scrutiny. It was to be expected that course handbooks, examination protocols, minutes of meetings, student records and so on would all need refreshing before they were presentable for a review of any stringency. It was Woolworth's belief that it did no good for a department to fail a review. One might point out things requiring reconsideration; one might even end up with a few criticisms, expressed as recommendations, but what one did not want was a loss of confidence in the university.

Conquest was aware of these views; he waited for him to express them.

'Vice-chancellor, I feel this may be unwise. We must ensure our competency for course delivery remains unquestioned even when we choose to test our academic colleagues. There is a trade-off which we would do well—'

'Enough, Murray! This may be my first university in charge, but I know a thing or two about quality assurance. I have run several organisations of note! Accountability and transparency, Murray; they are what we're about! I am painfully aware of how lax this university has grown and I am of the opinion that a bit of cold steel would not go amiss in the early days of my time here. Undoubtedly I'm expected – and want – to make my mark here before I move on to bigger and better things. Men – and women – of my experience are of short supply in the public sector.'

This was, metaphorically speaking, a blast from an improvised explosive device and it left Woolworth peppered with shrapnel. 'Fine, vice-chancel—'

'Call me "Cliff". I think it helps to set a breezy tone.'

'Fine – er – Cliff, we'll get these reviews up and running. I'll speak to the dean and Professor Pomfret today about fine art and get a date sorted out. I'll ask Archie to recommend an external expert and we'll get the invitation sent off.'

'Splendid! Now, that's what I call decision-making, Murray, the sort that when successfully implemented justifies a bonus, or what, in vulgar circles, might be termed a "performance bung". The government believes in meritocracy and that means performance-related bonuses for senior administrators in higher education. I intend to ensure such a scheme is implemented here.' He gave Murray a reassuring smile, not at all the martinet. 'After all, this –' he gestured to the cluttered surroundings – 'is the engine room of the university!'

As Conquest mounted the stairs on his way back to his office, he was smitten by a sudden glimpse of what he was doing and for a moment he wondered whether prioritising Professor Pomfret's department was a good idea. How great a part did his desire to get closer to Lady Caroline Lamb play in his prosecution of Pomfret?

Not much; the man deserves it!

A first step – so he reasoned –was just that and in any case, in his experience, visibility rarely extended more than a step or two ahead. It could not concern him that he had no clear idea of what future he was planning for his shimmering beloved of the Club Beirut. Nothing would happen for several weeks and that gave the prospect a delightful sense of abstraction. The anticipation was *thrilling* and not at all something he had expected!

SEVENTEEN

Although Conquest had been in the job barely three months it was already an established ritual that he met once a month with Professor "Perk" Hingley, the chair of the university's senate. Perk had been elected by acclamation when the previous chair had indicated his intention to go and live in Cyprus. He may have been a well-thought-of professor of international law, but the chief reason for his appointment was his public profile as advisor on human rights legislation to the London Assembly. A man more circumspect in his opinions it would be hard to find; it was fitting that his faith manifested itself in his membership of the silent wing of the Quaker church. The scandals brought on by the previous administration, which Perk had found himself plunged into almost as soon as he was elected, had been resolved largely by the foolhardy impetuousness of the transgressors rather than by his determination to set things to rights. But Conquest was very much his appointment and he wanted him to be a success. He saw their meetings as an opportunity for Conquest to unburden himself of his problems and anxieties. Above all he wanted to be useful. Conquest had become aware of these sentiments, and if anything saw them as weapons to use against him. He knew that convincing Perk of the desirability of building the digital hub would clear away the last meaningful source of opposition to his plan and it was very much on his mind that particular morning to honour by imitation Sir Norman's technique of conversational mastery.

As far as Perk was concerned the important business of their meeting was to discuss the agenda items for Conquest's first meeting of senate, due in early November. Conquest had already sent him a list of topics he would like to discuss at the meeting and he allowed Perk to lead him through it until they came to "capital projects".

'Ah yes!' declared Conquest, suddenly all spiky animation. 'Look, Perk –' he led with his chin – 'what we're going to do is mortgage the estate to raise some money, attract some top-up funding and invest in our infrastructure. Only then can we put our names to something important.'

For a second, Perk was thunderstruck. 'Like...?'

'Like a digital hub.'

'What is... Help me out here, Cliff. Digital hub being?'

'It's what it says it is, Perk, it's a hub for the university, and it's a hub for digital media: university and digital media brought together in a purpose-built environment. It's the ultimate learning resource!'

'Sounds a bit speculative for us, don't you think? I thought the future of computing was for them to be all-pervasive, not put in some "hub". And mortgaging the buildings is not our sort of thing either. I mean, Cliff, we'd be mortgaging the inheritance that the thrift of previous generations of academics and administrators have bequeathed us!'

'Perk, we'll be making our own contribution and investing our resources more efficiently. If we don't invest we stand still.' He was gazing at some golden goal on the horizon, over Perk's head. 'We must do this; it will be a glorious achievement.' He noticed that Perk seemed to have shrunk by quite a few inches and it crossed his mind that if he continued long enough he could shrink him down to nothing at all and be rid of the bloody, damned impediment.

And then I'll have my way with that crowd of cowed twerps and arselickers on senate who come for the sherry and will probably never give me a damned word of encouragement, curse them.

'Is it an investment, Cliff? Or is it a divestment of reserves? You know, just consumption?'

'Ha, ha! Nice distinction, Perk. I look at it like this: my biggest investment is my pension pot. It's guaranteed, no risk. I could sit down and in five minutes tell you what I'd receive if I retired now, but here's the truth: it's a bloody, huge Ponzi scheme!'

He noticed Perk flinched at the expression, "bloody, huge Ponzi scheme".

'You know this, don't you?'

'Well, I – I would quite put it—'

'Every five or so years the fund managers have to go back to the universities and ask them to top it up: insufficient investments to cover future entitlements because vice-chancellors and senior administrators are driving up their salaries and when they retire expect more than is reasonable, right or proper. It's a Ponzi scheme for all those eager little lecturers that come after them! Now, take this digital hub. We build it; the students come. They keep on coming. They have access to proper digital media, same kind of kit they work on out there in the IT industries. That's proper investment, Perk: investment in students. And just as we invest in them, so our investment will bring us a return from the increased value of their labour. That *is* investment – proper community investment – and we will be the beneficiaries of that investment!'

Perk was massaging his brow and gazing thoughtfully at the floor. 'I don't know, Cliff, but when you put it like that…'

'I have been in contact with the Funding Council – off the radar, of course – and there's a window, definitely a window, but we need to put ourselves forward.'

'Ballantyne on side?'

'Of course. One hundred per cent.'

Perk looked up. 'I suppose you have to lead, Cliff. The Promised Land beckons, I see.'

Capitulation! The last hurdle has been leapt! As simple as that! Now is the time to change the subject.

'Fine, I'll prepare a position paper for the meeting. You'll see, this will be a great modernising project. Now, Perk, my predecessor.'

'Ah, yes,' said Perk rather gloomily, 'that unfortunate business.' He knew the sudden departure of the previous vice-chancellor was a stain on his reputation.

'It's been suggested to me that David Quant might dignify his time here.'

'Ah, yes, a portrait. It's the usual form for a vice-chancellor, isn't it?'

'Something modest: half-length, seated perhaps. It'll have to be done from a photograph I suppose, since he's gone to Malaysia.'

'I see. You've taken advice?'

'Quant has rather a line in politicians. We wouldn't want to be thought vindictive, would we?'

'No, no, naturally not. Perish the thought. Something small would be most appropriate.'

'Then I take it you'll propose Quant to senate?'

Perk nodded mechanically, the other matter already beyond retrieving.

Conquest could now be confident that there would be no meaningful opposition to the digital hub. He would see to it that his colleagues on the senior management team endorsed it as a priority capital project and Perk would do the same at senate. It would be known as the 'Conquest Digital Hub', about that he was determined. He felt a surge of power, of certitude.

Now was the time to come down from on high.

EIGHTEEN

He was an earnest, slightly shambling figure in rimless glasses and a tweed jacket, a general appearance that somehow conveyed the careless self-assurance of an Oxbridge background. It was Mr Rubin Felt of Urban Tomorrows.

'Mr Felt,' said Conquest, recognising that this was a type he loved to discomfort, 'this is the university's finance officer, Mr Tommy Ballantyne.'

They shook hands. Ballantyne, who was still reluctant to see the university being dragged into debt for the sake of the Conquest Digital Hub, allowed him a dour nod.

'The university, Mr Felt, is looking for a firm of consultants to advise on the way forward with a major building project we have in mind.'

Rubin Felt frowned meaningfully. 'I see, interesting... You want us to short-list architects for you?'

'No, we thought we might go for a design and build package, if you thought it suitable.'

'Well yes, there are some very reputable... What kind of project are we talking about, if that's not confidential information.'

'No, no, of course it's not confidential. Why would it be?' Conquest let out a queasy laugh, unable to escape the feeling that the fact that Sir Norman had brought them together lent their meeting an air of subterfuge. 'We're thinking of upgrading the university's IT provision with a digital hub.'

Felt sat back with his mouth open. 'I see,' he said at last. '*A digital hub!*'

'Yes, a digital hub. Are you familiar with the concept?

Felt roused himself. 'Of course, it's what any self-respecting institution must have.'

'Can you come up with a process for the selection of a firm to build such a thing?'

'Yes, I think we can... Of course! We would need to take advice, naturally, but we could certainly come up with an excellent shortlist and offer you advice about the tendering process. You would want a tendering process?' For a moment he looked comically uncertain, as though he had said the wrong thing.

Conquest rescued him. 'Good! Yes! And a fee for work such as this?'

'Well, we normally expect to work closely with the architect, and we'd charge a percentage of his fee.'

Conquest gave him a knowing smile. 'And the architect's fee is normally a percentage of the building's cost. A very statesmanlike answer, I'm sure!'

Conquest noticed that Ballantyne was still regarding Felt dourly. 'Tommy, any questions for Mr Felt?'

Ballantyne declined the invitation.

'We'd want to move ahead with this without delay,' Conquest continued brightly. 'How soon could you let us have your initial proposals?'

'A month, five weeks...'

'How about ten days?' said Ballantyne.

'I see. Well, very preliminary. Yes, we can do that.'

'Good. Any questions?'

'No, I think we need to get on with it. I'm sure I'll have some for you in the fullness...'

'There's another thing,' Conquest confided as he rose to usher Felt out of the room. 'In order to build we have to find a site. There's no money for land purchase, so we'll need to find a site within our current perimeter.'

'I see, do you have any unused land?'

'Well, that's also what we need to take outside advice about. It may be we need to rationalise our current stock of buildings. Always a contentious issue, as I'm sure you know. We'll need someone to take the flak. That'll be you.'

Felt looked flummoxed. Conquest felt moved to be merciful and shook him heartily by the hand. 'I jest, of course, but we would be grateful for an indication. Now, our wonderful Norma Hupplethorpe, head of estates and services, is expecting you. She's been briefed by me. She'll give you all the information you need and a tour.' He then handed him a visiting card. His voice took on its confidential tone. 'A little tip, Mr Felt: Wainwright, Carter & Expandite have built a digital hub at Severn Estuary University. A model of its kind, I'm told.'

'I have seen photographs…' mumbled Felt.

'Good. I'd like you to go to Bristol and take a look at it. Contact Mr Goodwin, head of facilities; you'll find his number on the back of my card. He'll show you round.' He gave the biceps of Felt's left arm a chummy squeeze. 'I'll expect your report on my desk in ten days.' He gave him a carnivorous grin and sent him on his way.

NINETEEN

Module 2.1A, rhythm and form, was already into its third week and the moment Juliette Burton had been dreading for several days had finally arrived. She was at a loss quite how to put it, but she'd had an intuition for some time that Terry Bragg was developing some sort of... well, *thing* for her. She had tried pretending it wasn't happening but it was difficult to ignore: he was always so considerate, and on occasions she found him looking at her with an unexpected and peculiar intensity. She was not sure what depths of feeling she sensed from these glances and moments of attentiveness, but *how could she be expected to*? She knew him so little, apart from what she saw in the studios. Seeing him, as she did, at a distance, she saw a man she could respect for his sincerity and his idealism. What he was like close to she had no idea, although she was a great admirer of his hesitant, self-effacing installations made of tissue paper, balsa wood and not much else. When the list posted on the second-year notice board told her that her first tutorial for the rhythm and form module was with him her immediate thought was to ask for Oswald's help in devising some way of getting out of it, but the more she thought about it the more she came to think that that would be a cowardly way of dealing with him. In any case, she was touched by his earnest commitment to teaching and genuinely wanted to hear what he had to say about *Blue Gash*, her first major response to the rhythm and form module.

Only very recently had she finished working on *Blue Gash* and the thickly painted surface was still wet. She had hung the painting in her space and spent some time before he arrived gazing at it. The overall effect was of the big elliptical green shape set at an angle in the centre of a field of dabs of vivid colour. The central elliptical motif suggested a centripetal stellar phenomenon throwing off gobs of yellow and cadmium orange from its outer rim. Her latest addition had been made only that morning when she had decided that the ellipse should be cleaved by a jagged line of cerulean blue: the gash. The one word that came to Bragg as he sat down beside Juliette and looked at it was close to gash: garish.

'Very colourful,' he said. The symbolism was clear enough, it was the female pudendum, but that he chose to ignore. 'Tell me,' he continued, going straight to the nub of their reason for meeting, 'how do you see this demonstrating the relationship between rhythm and form?'

She took her time answering. She had been expecting to be asked how her painting fulfilled the module brief and had prepared an answer. None-the-less she spoke so diffidently she secured the impression of spontaneity. 'I've been thinking form is visual but rhythm is mainly an acoustic phenomenon.'

So neatly did her answer side-step the project's central premise that Bragg took a moment to digest what he had heard. 'Really? I see, so only form is visual! But what does that mean, claiming rhythm is acoustic?'

'Well, I'm saying sound is always secondary to the visual; the soundtrack is always secondary to the movie: there's an implicit hierarchy. And so it is with rhythm and form.'

Bragg had suffered some cockeyed verbiage during previous tutorials. In comparison this seemed sublime. 'I don't understand. You're not meaning this literally, are you? The project is intended to be purely visual. Are you saying it fails to take account of the nature of it's concepts... or what?' He was thrilled to think she had subverted the conceit of JC's module.

She looked at him full in the face for the first time, a little colour in her cheeks. 'I don't know. I was wondering whether I did think that, but maybe it's just an analogy. However much I read the brief I can't grasp the words in the way you explained them at the meeting.' She gave a modest laugh. 'I try to adopt an intuitive approach when I'm working, and I suppose rhythm and form are both in there somewhere.'

He was touched she should back away so charmingly from being

109

doctrinaire. He felt moved to say something graceful in return, so he turned his attention back to the painting, wanting to be effusive, but something held him back. He was dismayed to think he was struggling in a tar pit, the words he was fated to utter just one more application of the fashionable phrasebook they were stuck with.

'No good worrying about the acoustic when what we have is gesture,' he said at last.

'I'm sure I don't mean it literally... *perhaps*. After all, it is only a oval with a jagged blue line drawn through it.'

'Well, that's a materialist way of seeing it,' said Bragg hastily, still wanting to override her modesty with a burst of compliments. 'There are other things at work in your painting. It has a kind of dynamic presence.' He faltered. The image of dynamism was in danger of again bringing him face to face with sexual symbolism. The association was most likely only his, yet he felt on the verge of sexual frisson, it was in the air, unbidden. An unwelcome hotness – but also something invigorating – had taken him over, as though a unaccustomed vitality was flowing through him; he had never experienced anything quite like it. She was gazing at the paint-splattered floor and seemed to be lost in thought. For him the pleasure of their exchange was to be near her, but what made it so giddying was that, being focused on extracting meaning from the tutorial, she lacked the least suspicion that that might be the case. This spoke to him of her lack of vanity, which doubled his pleasure since the idea that she was modest, unassuming, amplified her physical grace.

'I think it's marvellous the way you've combined the elements. The kinetic energy... it's impressive, if a little faulted.' Immediately he cursed himself; he had slipped into the "having said that" way of talking, the "on one hand this" and "on the other hand that" manner – all equivocation and reasonableness. In the circumstances it seemed mealy-mouthed.

'Oh! Faulted? How?' She looked crestfallen.

'The colour... I don't mean faulted in a bad way.' He was determined to recover the situation. 'I mean it in a way that gives the viewer access to the artist's vivacity, their... her... your nature...'

She looked round from the painting sharply. The frown on her lowered brow told him she suspected he was joking, but when she saw he was serious a definite tenderness of expression stole over her. It was, he thought, as though his remark had pierced a certain barrier that protected her vulnerabilities. He dared to think – a little sentimentally perhaps – that he had rediscovered the child in her. She glanced at him, her expression full of innocent enthusiasm.

'I suppose I must accept my faults, then.'

'Yes, but I mean to say the palette is highly individual. Nothing is perfect, but you might improve too. That, after all, is what we are here to do!'

The idea that he and she were somehow in it together flattered and delighted her. 'I'm not sure I should improve; it might be better to stay imperfect!'

They both laughed at such a droll idea. He was suddenly aware of how warm their laughter was, how much it signified their accord, their sense of being together in a state of affairs they both loved and cherished. All awkwardness over his role as her tutor seemed to have slipped away; they were confidants sharing a enterprise of great importance.

'Art is a hard taskmaster,' he said, 'but it brings its rewards.'

She agreed wholeheartedly, although, even in her present mood, it was difficult to say anything in response to such an inanity. But what they were talking about, she knew, was *not* inane. They might be moved by different creative impulses, but the imperatives of art were a guild mystery they shared; they could not be trotted out like the catchphrases that attested to a common political outlook: so much to the Left, thus far to the Right. She sensed the exaltation that lay behind the commonplaces of "taskmaster" and "rewards".

Unconscious of what he was doing, he reached out, thinking – so he supposed – to examine one of her brushes – simply an idle gesture – but in so doing he inadvertently brushed the back of her hand and she recoiled as though in shock. The moment was gone, he knew, gone absolutely! He froze in horror, realising he had overstepped the mark and that their sense of being compatriots was broken. Nothing, now, would bring it back in their present exchange. Even if he had the guile, he doubted words of any kind could resurrect the moment.

'I think,' he said, 'you need to do more of the same.' He was sliding towards the precipice of an ending. 'Practice *does* make perfect.' He was ashamed to have arrived at such a conclusion – he wondered: was it possible to be more trite than this? He despaired; however he might try, it seemed he was fated to be impaled on utter banalities. If all he could dispense was cornball he should stop immediately, hang the steady income and make of himself an honest man! Still, she did seem to be enjoying their encounter; he felt he had touched her with his concern; he would now show her it was truly altruistic by walking away, so he dug deep to find one more homily and would then leave her to sort through the pieces.

'Forget about the project. Well, perhaps you have already. Let's not be too literal; you have accomplished something. You should do more. Be bold, paint from the shoulder, not the wrist. But if you don't think it's working use smaller brushes and try and work more with the detail.' Detail: that, it seemed, was what it had come down to.

The tutorial, which Juliette had expected to be something of an ordeal, was over. Despite the touch of his hand on hers it had been an elevating experience; it was as though she had for the first time glimpsed one of the inner circles of art's professional life. He had – she was convinced – been genuinely interested in what she was doing; had found something of value in her painting. She felt she had moved on, that with *Blue Gash* she had come one step closer to her goal of real artistic expression.

While she was turning over all this in her mind, Bragg had taken himself off to the corridor. He dawdled there, his heart beating a little faster than usual. He felt energised and ready for the challenge of the rest of the day; for the task of imparting wisdom to the next four students he was timetabled to meet, most of whom, he suspected, would present little or nothing of substance for his attention. He checked his list and saw that his next appointment was with Matthew, the boy who had given him grief at his introduction to the rhythm and form module. He grinned to himself and went down the stairs to the seminar room, which Matthew had booked for their meeting.

Matthew greeted him with a silent nod. Bragg returned the nod. A video installation was set up in the blacked-out room and Matthew was dressed in black to match. He was standing in front of a wall-sized projection, each quarter of which showed continuous footage of the view out of a window of a train. The trains were travelling at high speed through different types of countryside so that objects close to the track flashed past in a blur, while those in the middle and far distance crossed the frame at a slower pace, allowing for the recognition of fields, houses, warehouses and parked cars.

Bragg watched in silence for five minutes, his mind almost entirely occupied in reliving his meeting with Juliette. 'This is one piece, right?' he said finally.

Matthew nodded.

Bragg had decided that the work was a monumental conceit, a challenge thrown down by Matthew, and he was not about to duck it. 'What's this about, then, Matthew?' he asked.

'You tell me,' said Matthew. 'I'm interested in what you – representing the interests of the audience – make of it.'

'Oh, are you? I see, an open-ended puzzle! Well, obviously it's about relativity. We take the camera's position, so we're in motion, yet we appear to be static and everything in motion around us.'

Matthew gazed through him, picking at his nose absently. 'Ha, ha! That's rather a modernist interpretation, isn't it? I don't want to see that. I'm much more interested in the journey. That's Osaka!' He pointed to the bottom left hand projection where low grey buildings we're passing by, and then to the top right. 'And that's somewhere between Berlin and Stuttgart. Life's a journey; the train carries us thorough the landscape. It's a parable!'

'Well, a modernist parable attracts modernist criticism, I suppose,' responded Bragg.

Matthew was piqued. 'Come off it, you're doing a totally perverse reading! I'm simply not the modernist subject!'

Bragg laughed with relish. He sat down on one of the two chairs drawn up behind the projectors. Matthew took the other one. It was as if they were squaring up for a fight.

'So is this about rhythm and form, or what?'

'No, not really.'

"No, not really", thought Bragg. *Oh yes, you're far too cocksure and smart to follow a brief!* He had made up his mind to show Matthew that the videos were a reflection of the banality of his imagination. He sensed that Matthew had an equally strong desire to negate, if at all possible, anything he might say.

'What kind of subject are *you,* then?' Bragg cajoled. 'Look, Matthew, when are you going to do something that doesn't shout "me too"? The problem is we know your agenda inside out. It's to impress us, by whatever means, that you're ultra-hip. You've spent the summer with the juggling nomads of Mongolia. That sort of thing. There's *everything* here –' he gestured at the piece – 'they're fragments, they're rich in narrativity, the indefinability of existence, they're autobiography as the only available art form, linear narrative without content yet overflowing with detail. It's all there… in a way, but not there too, not there in any way that really makes a point or sticks its neck out. It's timid and well-mannered art for the civic space. It's like you: opinionated without having anything original to say.'

'Well, you're remarkably frank today,' said Matthew with a sullen grin, 'but I don't think you've got it… *at all.* All your criticisms are based on a wrong premise. It's the premise of the unified, purposeful, creative subject. I'm not that subject. None of us are: it's an ideological construct, and it's the one you're speaking from. It's rubbish, actually.'

'Look, the train is just a lazy person's cameraman. You set it up, certain consequences flow… La dee dah! It's literally and metaphorically set on rails, fuelled up and allowed to run. It's got nowhere to go, nothing to do, except comment on the condition of its being. It's the modernist turn without even a hint of irony. If it's not journeyman conceptualism – as I suspect it is – where's the transformative act?'

At the back of his mind Bragg was already plotting his exit. He didn't have his usual urge to bolt, in fact he was enjoying himself, but he knew that even a knock-down, drag-out fight should only go on just so long, and this one, he sensed, had reached stalemate. For the moment Matthew had a sulky, battered look, but it would not last. Bravado would demand that he found some way to wriggle out of his present discomfort, but Bragg knew that this particular video piece would never be seen again.

'I tell you what, Matthew,' he resumed in a conciliatory voice, 'forget all the incidents you've captured on video, which you believe are so telling, and think of it as a storyboard. Then you'll see what I mean. At root this is real-time video and real-time video has an ideological stamp you can't escape... and multiple projections just makes matters worse. It ends up as a collection of tired tropes. Think about it, and let's talk again next time I'm in.'

There was nothing Matthew could do but submit. 'They only let me book this seminar room for three days.'

'Well, I'm not in again this week and I have a lot of people to get through, so we can't argue the toss till lunch. In any case, I don't need to see it again. Recalling its content won't be a problem. You read the biography of John Cage?'

Matthew shook his head.

'I'd recommend it if you want to get to the heart of your dilemma here. I'll leave the details in your pigeonhole.' And with that Bragg eased himself out of his chair, giving a deflated Matthew a wave as he left the room.

Bragg was elated at having crushed Matthew's cocky piece of nonsense. He went upstairs at a dash and found Juliette still in her space, still gazing at Blue Gash.

'Juliette, would you like to go for a drink later, when you've finished?'

'Oh,' she said. For a moment her face was full of eagerness, but her eyes slid away as though, on reflection, she thought it seemly to conceal her willingness.

It was a reaction he took as a hopeful sign.

'I would... I would like that,' she said, 'but I can't...' She stole a look at her wristwatch; she was on early shift at the Club Beirut. 'I can't today. This week and next I'm busy. Maybe after that? Yes, I'd like that, if that suits you. When you're here, I mean.'

'Okay, Monday week maybe?' he offered. 'I'll be here then. We can go to the Students' Union bar... *perhaps*?'

Ritual hesitations aside, he decided, their date was as firmly fixed as it could be. He was exultant at the thought of it, and was proud of himself for having had the courage to ask. It was only when he was once more alone in the corridor, looking back on what he had done, that he began to feel less comfortable with his actions. It was not his invitation to Juliette that was the cause of his disquiet. Now that his mood had cooled, a creeping sense of remorse possessed him at the way he had steeled himself to do it off the back of trashing Matthew's videos. Something primitive had been stirred up by his tutorial with Juliette that had made him determined to out-man Matthew. Matthew might have made a typical piece of self-absorbed art school rubbish; that was not the point. What was obvious now was that once he had crushed Matthew's self-esteem he had been able to go back upstairs and ask Juliette to go out with him, something he had been too timid to do before. He could now see that his treatment of Matthew was contemptible; he had used him as though he were a rival to be dominated. It could only be, he decided, that to do such a thing meant he was becoming someone without scruple; it was a complete charade to suppose he had had a coherent critical position, he had merely bludgeoned Matthew into submission from a position of authority. He went down the stairs at a rush and did not stop until he was out in the open, standing on Tiananmen Square Green. It was a relief to find himself in the open air, breathing the cool autumnal air. Not for the first time he thought he should give up teaching to save his integrity, his respect for art… *His soul*. Was that too much? No, he didn't think so.

TWENTY

Conquest was putting away the papers that through the day had gathered on his desk, and as he did so sought to clear his mind of the matters he had been dealing with for…

Let me see, what exactly is the time? After seven o'clock. Yes, for ten hours!

It had been a miserable day, he decided. He was not one for self-pity but his mind had been running away with him mercilessly. The image of himself as an educational mercenary, doing God's work, required to command strangers far from home, had haunted him all day. No wonder his thoughts kept returning to Lady Caroline Lamb!

But I am the vice-chancellor, and she a second year BA student. Never has so wide a gulf separated a man from his desired object!

In his steely way he yearned to see her. And here was Mr Rubin Felt of Urban Tomorrows come to trouble him with more details. It was only with great reluctance that he had granted him an interview. He sat Felt down on one of his sofas, but did not join him; he remained at his desk, bastion of the administrative turn.

'I appreciate you want *us* to give *you* advice,' Felt was saying, 'but we are experiencing some problems identifying a site for your… Ahem! *Hub.*'

Conquest noted that the word "hub" was still giving him difficulty, as if skirting an embarrassment. He wondered how long the invisible presence of Sir Norman would trouble their association.

'We thought I should come and consult; pick your brain, as it were. We thought you might be able to give us some idea of the institutional thinking on sites for the digital… hub.' All this Felt said with a gratifyingly humble and apologetic air.

'Didn't our wonderful head of estates and services, Norma Hupplethorpe, brief you?'

'Yes, she did, but—'

'You're the expert,' Conquest pointed out testily. 'I expect she's quite happy to defer to you.' The truth was that in his present mood he didn't see why he should be helpful to somebody the university was paying a consultancy fee to to make a recommendation that would comply with his wishes.

'If we were to consider demolition, well... It seems it might be a rather political decision.'

'That is a ridiculous thing to say,' said Conquest, supporting his head in his hands and resting his elbows on the desktop. 'I am trying to renew this university,' he reminded Felt, as though he had been caught in the act of stopping him.

Felt took fright at his tone. 'Believe you me, we've been over the campus with a magnifying glass and we cannot see where a digital hub could be built.'

'Haven't we a subject in this university in dire need of modernising: fine art? Their building is old and unserviceable. Surely we can see a brighter future for them housed somewhere else?'

'I see.' Felt's brain was spinning.

'Look,' said Conquest, suddenly all reasonableness, 'it's not up to me or anyone else here to tell you the best way forward on this issue, but some activities require less specialised accommodation than others. We wouldn't want to be pulling down any of our science buildings, would we?' He laughed good-naturedly at the idea. '*No, we would not!*'

'But you think the Frank Brangwyn Building might be a suitable candidate?' Felt was warming to the idea. 'It is a bit of a warren. And it has a large yard at the rear.'

'Mr Felt, I ask you for your professional opinion, clearly stated with reasons for having arrived at it. If that's political I'll be damned. Now, how about digital hubs? What have you got to tell me on that score?'

When Felt had finished describing the Wainwright, Carter & Expandite digital hub he had seen at the Severn Estuary University,

Conquest was stirred, uplifted. The digital hub was the future, a paragon of progressive thinking; fine art was a minor subject that could be housed practically anywhere, provided the roof didn't leak. He knew every step he took increased his influence over that department but what he was able to conceal from himself – fleeting moments aside – was that his every act circumscribing the authority of Professor Pomfret was designed to advance his own influence over Lady Caroline Lamb's future.

'Goodbye, Mr Felt. I expect your report on this vexed issue in due course.'

Rubin Felt shambled out. Still Conquest was not satisfied. An idea occurred to him. He reached for the phone and put a call in to Professor Woolworth, dean of academic affairs.

'Murray, it's Cliff. I wonder, might I ask you to get Professor Pomfret to put together a panel of students for the fine art review?'

'What d'you have in mind, Cliff?'

'I rather think we need a sort of "brains trust" to help us get under the skin of the department. Students need an opportunity to express their true feelings. I'll chair the meeting.'

'I see.' Murray was startled that the vice-chancellor wished to be so hands-on. 'Don't you feel——

'I *feel* – as a newly arrived VC – that it would be an excellent opportunity for me to acquaint myself with the grassroots. I don't want that department misdiagnosed as in excellent trim when the students are restless but in chains.'

Despite his personal scepticism concerning their efficacy, Woolworth was not about to argue with Conquest about student panels: he had heard tales of Conquest's devastating employment of patient panels against middle managers in the NHS. 'Quite so. We'll call it "student feedback", shall we?' Nor was he the person to tell his vice-chancellor that he considered it inappropriate for him to be so closely involved in the mechanics of a departmental review. Nevertheless, Conquest detected his lack of enthusiasm for what he was proposing.

'Call it what you like,' he said brusquely. 'And I want to see the list of students. Make sure Pomfret does it this week.'

'Will do,' agreed Woolworth hastily. 'I'll see to it directly.'

Conquest banged down the phone and paced his office with his outdoor coat on, unwilling to take himself home. Suddenly he decided that it was not, after all, so difficult to see Lady Caroline Lamb; all he had to do was take a taxi to the Club Beirut and buy a bottle of champagne. In the absence of any evening appointments he resolved to do just that. His mind made up, he was relieved of a great pressure somewhere behind his temples. He no longer felt the sense of doom and despair that had been hanging over everything he did or said; all the bad feelings had quite cleared away and he felt some small but important part of him was renewed. He did a second check of his desk. The blotting paper pad he liked to press against when he was writing was parallel to the edge of the desk and his pens were in a line just beyond it. All his current documents were stowed away in their wire trays and his computer was switched off. Nothing called for his attention. The university would manage without him for the rest of the day, and tomorrow could wait. The lights in the library would burn into the night as the university's cadre of doctoral students followed the research trails of their theses, but now *he* was free to follow his private destiny, and that led straight to Lady Caroline Lamb.

He went out into the street and hailed a taxi. He took a seat behind the driver. In his hand was the Club Beirut book of matches. He turned it over restlessly, thinking that once he arrived he would need to get into role. What was his role? Did he have a role? How could he bridge the gap between himself and Lady Caroline Lamb AKA Juliette Grace Burton? Thinking about that was something he wanted to avoid. He began to feel his courage seeping away, as though, like so much bagged sand, he was running out of his worsted suit. He was overcome with nerves and his heart was in palpitations.

This is excitement, this thrills me!

He leant forward and read out the address to the cabbie, holding the match folder up in his line of sight.

The cabbie laughed. 'You going there solo, mate? A filthy reputation, that place has! I hear they have live sex shows on the billiard table.'

Conquest was affronted. He spoke sharply. 'Nonsense, they don't have a billiard table!'

'Well,' replied the driver, not in the least put out, 'it's owned by a well-known Russian white slave trader. Be careful you don't get fleeced. Very good cocktails for insomniacs, they say.'

'Actually,' Conquest decided, suddenly repelled by the thought of the taxi driver taking him there, imagined him watching him enter, laughing at his folly, 'I've changed my mind. I have other plans. Would you take me to Butler's Wharf instead?'

TWENTY-ONE

The prospect of the review greatly distressed Archie Pomfret. His first impulse was to ask his secretary to arrange an appointment for him with the dean of academic affairs. Professor Woolworth's diary was full and at short notice he was only able to manage what he called "the breakfast slot", at eight thirty on Monday morning. It was a stretch for Archie who normally arrived after ten, and it said something about the depths of his anxiety that he agreed to it at all.

'Listen, Murray,' he began once the croissant and the cup of instant coffee had been placed before him, 'as you know only too well, we're up for review. Aware we can't duck it, but I need some advice about being properly prepared.'

Murray expelled his breath in a long sigh. 'Can't help you much, Archie. I'm on a terribly short leash. The VC wants no stacked decks. He wants the unvarnished truth.'

Archie was appalled. '*The unvarnished...!* I've never heard of a review not being prepped by the bods in the know.'

'And he's set the review for the beginning of November.'

'November!' Archie groaned and slumped in his seat. 'That's practically tomorrow! What's our vice-chancellor up to, Murray?'

'Don't ask me; makes me feel uncomfortable too. But Cliff's adamant. Strictest instructions. New broom and all that.'

'I see.' Archie was overcome by foreboding. 'I'm feeling a bit in the firing line here, Murray.'

'Sorry, Archie. You'll manage.' He didn't sound particularly hopeful. 'He's asked Andrew Czinc to chair the review panel.'

'What, the bloody dean of social sciences! *That Hampstead hypocrite!*'

Woolworth spread his hands in disavowal of responsibility

for the choice. 'We need an external member for the panel. Any suggestions?'

'External, eh?' said Pomfret wearily. 'You'll have to let me think about it. Someone rigorous but sympathetic?'

'That sort of thing.' Woolworth hesitated before he continued. 'Have you heard word about rehousing your department?'

'No.' Promfret looked shocked. 'Should I have?'

'Well, what with a new kid on the block…'

He gave a wry laugh. 'That's not your kind of language, Murray. What's got into you?'

'You know what I mean.' He looked embarrassed. 'Change is in the air.'

'But rehousing fine art? Where does that idea come from? We've been in that building since forever.' Pomfret's worries were multiplying. Rehousing on top of the review and the threat of hot desking: it was beginning to seem like persecution. 'This is about downsizing and all the other drivel, isn't it? I can't believe it's come round again. The last vice-chancellor had a go before he lost the plot!'

'This may be just gossip, Archie, but Cliff – the VC – wants a digital hub. I hear he's been talking to the chair of senate.'

'How did you hear that?'

'I have a neighbour who works for a thruster in the Labour party. There's a policy on Inclusion And The Digital Economy coming down from on high, and it seems we're being lined up for a digital hub. There's something in the wind: Cliff's being smiled upon.'

'God bless him! They all want to make their mark, I appreciate that, but so what?'

'Well, space, Archie, space. There's nowhere to build.'

'What, knock down the Frank Brangwyn building! Ridiculous! *Digital hub!* – sounds like millenarian stuff, doesn't it? Trample all else to make the future!' Pomfret grew pensive, but if he had further thoughts he was guarded about sharing them with Woolworth. Woolworth was, after all, the dean of academic affairs, and his office a well-known gossip exchange.

'Somebody rigorous,' said Woolworth, bringing Pomfret back to the organisation of the review, 'but sympathetic.'

Pomfret made an effort to throw off his sense of nightmare. 'I'll get back to you on that, Murray. I suppose I'd better be gathering my paperwork.'

'All I'm saying is, watch your back,' said Woolworth. He offered Pomfret a sheet of typescript, suddenly formal. 'Here's a checklist of the documentation we'll need. Can you let me have five sets for the panel, one for me and however many you think are necessary for your team? You have to follow the colour-coding guide so we can search them easily. I'll need them before the end of the week to get it off to the panel members, so you better let me know who you want as the external member sharpish.'

Pomfret came away from Woolworth's office thoroughly alarmed. He could not think why, of all the departments in the university, it was his that had become the focus of the vice-chancellor's attention. Even Pomfret, who could be blithely indifferent to the workings of the minds of others, had the distinct feeling that beyond his comprehension there was some dimension of personality at work.

Why my department? he said to himself. *We're small and not particularly expensive. Why is he gunning for us? Are we to be made an example of?*

The thought horrified him, but in his apprenticeship years as an itinerant lecturer he had heard of such things, and worse. He knew art smacked of middle-class privilege and bohemian indolence to many on the progressive wing of the Labour party, and he thought that he had the vice-chancellor's political sympathies pretty well identified.

After a fretful morning spent in the company of Jennifer Cross, the department's senior secretary, Pomfret called a minicab and went out into the street to wait for it. The cab headed west towards the Arts Club in Dover Street where he met an old friend, and together they travelled on to the rough-and-tumble of the Chelsea Arts Club. They had a corner table in the dining room, very suitable for conspirators.

'I'm afraid I have to touch on matters academic,' apologised Pomfret once the Chilean red had arrived. 'The nabob bureaucrats at my place are threatening to run my department through the cheese parer.'

His companion, Perry McBride, a dark, saturnine man with a stooped carriage, stopped picking at his walnut wholemeal bread. 'Are they now?' he said, his interest piqued. 'On the rack, are we?'

'I should bloody-well say so! We're very small fry in the scheme of things and shower that place with newsworthy tidbits. Now, suddenly, I've got a serpent at my throat: a new vice-chancellor imported from some quango or other. Lots of energy, you know: sprauncy in a New Labour sort of way. A bit short, executive suits and Pierre Cardin ties.'

McBride was a sculptor and Camberwell Marxist whose usual attire was a denim jacket and desert boots. He had risen to prominence a couple of decades previously as a result of the Percentage For Art Scheme for public buildings, or what he called "the public sculpture lark", and was now the principal of the Alma-Tadem Academy of Fine Arts, Berkeley Square, a well-endowed private art school.

'It's always The Time Of The New Man, Archie, and they're always repellent.'

Pomfret nodded, acknowledging the truth of McBride's remark. 'I suppose he must have his points,' he said reasonably. 'Just needs to mellow, I suppose. There's a rumour going round that fine art's in the way of a digital hub, whatever ungodly type of thing that is. You'd think he'd have his hands full at my crock-of-shit university, but for some reason he's taken exception to my strategic plan – not enough high flown aims... or is it objectives? He's instituted a departmental review.'

'So... what are you going to do?'

'Well, Perry, to tell you the truth, they've asked me to propose an external member for the review panel and I was wondering whether I might put your name forward. I thought you could be the man for the job.'

McBride looked wistfully at the broken pieces of his bread. 'I don't suppose there's a fee, is there?'

'I didn't ask. I'd not be very hopeful, if I were you. You know how it is: only the apparatchik get fees for their flummery.'

'I suppose I could agreed to do it and them wrangle over a fee when all the arrangements have been made. Threatening to pull out usually does the trick. What do you want me to do?'

'Oh, observe sternly and then at the final meeting be genial and forthright, I suppose.'

'General, all-round clean bill of health.'

'Exactly. I'd need to brief you, of course.'

McBride quaffed his wine and looked shrewdly at his old friend. 'How serious is this, Archie? Times is hard in the university sector and the government carries on as if the culture industries are synonymous with art, but we know what they really mean, don't we? Tossers working for Sky TV channels.'

'He's only just arrived, Perry. I can't believe he's grinding axes already. Asked me if we have a life room. I think I'd better make sure we're running one. Haven't seen a life drawing in an art school for donkey's years.'

'We still run one, Archie. Got a very fine blackamoor model for the debs. Enormous success; covers the foundry's running costs for most of the year.'

'We made a big political thing out of the life class when I was a student,' reminisced Pomfret wistfully. 'Had a notable success with the feminist exploitation angle... until it was hi-jacked by actual feminists. There was an ideological falling-out when we tried to claim the male model as one of our own. We were oppressing them, apparently, by claiming him as gendered. I was branded ideologically suspect; hadn't read enough to follow their arguments, according to them. Didn't have the heart to fight them on their own ground so mostly I made art as a big "fuck you"!' He smiled ruefully. 'Those were the days, eh?'

'Quite right. Show them the edge of your palette knife. I've got an unveiling in a couple of weeks. On the Fifth Plinth.'

'Fifth Plinth? I've heard of the Fourth Plinth. Is there a fifth?'

'Oh yes. Actually, it's not too far from your campus: Liversage Square. There's been a spare plinth there since the Henry Moore was stolen in '94. The Royal Sculpture League's asked me to put my Laocoön there.'

'Really? That I'd like to see. Won't it cause a bit of a furore?'

TWENTY-TWO

As soon as Pomfret arrived at his office the following morning he began, in an entirely scatty way, to scan the review documentation Jennifer Cross, the department's senior secretary, had managed to assemble.

'Coloured tabs,' he kept saying to himself. 'We need coloured tabs.'

At ten thirty there was a knock on his door. It was JC McCann. JC was very pink, like a rose, and very blond. She was also rounded and soft-looking, pneumatic. Short of stature, she had the walk of a duck. In a department of gaunt men she made an altogether cosy picture. Considering her appearance, it might seem strange to report that she had a vindictive streak, something that only Pomfret was unaware of. She lived by what she thought of as the prevailing academic creed: 'do as you are done to, and dish anyone of lower status than you if they stand in your light'. The other lecturers cordially detested her; a detestation tinged by a certain begrudging admiration. She had started work in the department as a part-time ceramics lecturer and swiftly worked her way up to becoming the second year tutor on the undergraduate fine art course as well as being the course director of the several recreational and part-time courses the department ran. The reason for her swift rise was that Pomfret needed a fixer in a department prone to rickety academic procedures; she was the one person in the department he could rely on to understand things like course regulations and examination protocols. Without her he would have floundered; the department sunk into anarchy. To his face she was pally, apparently rather taken with his casual way of running things. Behind his back she referred to him as "one of the boys", patronising him as unduly privileged, incorrigibly laddish and "part of yesterday's problem".

Pomfret threw aside the document he was reading with an air of despair. 'JC,' he said, 'come and have a seat. I need to discuss this departmental review. Have you heard about it?'

'Week after next, Archie. I've cleared my diary and made a list of the members of staff we're going to have to hide.'

'Hide? Is that necessary?'

'Some of them are positively unpresentable, and you know it. They'll put their foot in it if they're questioned by the panel; incapable of projecting the right ethos for a university department. They're chauvinistic, prejudiced and prone to... *French practices*.' She raised an eyebrow and looked meaningfully at him.

'I see.' Pomfret looked crushed. 'How are we going to manage this review, then? I feel as though we are in danger, JC. I don't like the look of our new vice-chancellor. He's one of those Labour party technocrats. There's a rumour going round he wants to knock this building down.'

'Can't be true.'

'Unimpeachable source... Well, reasonably reliable.'

'Can't believe he's thinking something like that.' Her eyes blazed.

'New building. Something to do with the digital economy.'

'We can't have that! Do you know yet who's chairing this review?'

'Professor Czinc.'

'Really?'

'Our new vice-chancellor has a definite leaning towards the social sciences.'

'I know Andrew Czinc; his specialism is diasporas.'

'There you are! It's not reasonable to bring a sociologist whose specialism is diasporas in here! Can we do business with someone of that ilk? It's chalk and cheese!'

'We've got to move with the times, Archie; there's a sea change going on. I've got some contacts at the London Institute – they have experience of handling these sorts of affairs. I'll get their advice.'

'I've asked Perry McBride to be the external on the panel.'

'Hmmm. Bad move.'

Pomfret was increasingly nettled by her discouraging tone. 'Bad move? Why?'

'You need a woman. You need to show the panel you're not trying to protect your boys. If they suspect your external's a friendly they'll turn against you.'

'Oh dear, I was hoping for a stitch-up.'

'Wrong move. He's too much of an old lag... like you! Show them you don't feel vulnerable. They'll respect you for that.'

'Any ideas? All the women artists I know are mad.'

'Marta Cramp. She's on the ball with her research: feminist discourse, photographic practice. Footballers' wives, etcetera. All the rage.'

JC had lost Pomfret, but feeling beleaguered he was inclined to follow any advice she offered. 'All right,' he decided glumly, 'I'll put her name to Professor Woolworth. You'd better give me her contact details. I don't think Perry'll be too disappointed: he wanted a fee.' He rubbed his brow. 'You'd better spend today putting coloured tabs on our documentation.' He gestured to the documents lying on his desk. 'This is all Jennifer's managed to find. I want you to chase up what's missing. What about this new modular system you're introducing?'

JC laughed. 'We've hardly begun; most haven't been written up yet! We'll have to use last year's course handbooks. Nobody wanted to spend the summer writing modules!'

'Oh dear! What about our external examiners' reports? I can't recall reading any. Have we considered them formally?'

She shrugged. 'I think so, but I doubt all the minutes have been written up.'

'You'd better get on to it.'

'I am supposed to be teaching the Chinese students today. You know: the Study in London Certificate course.'

'Chinese? I thought they were Taiwanese!' Archie looked alarmed.

'Same difference.'

'That's your foundation group, isn't it?'

'Not foundation, Archie. We can't call it that, we don't teach at that level; that's further education stuff.'

'Yes, yes, I know.' He made a frantic gesture of dismissal as if he wished the Chinese students would disappear. 'Give them some sort of project and leave them to it. Our documentation needs sorting.'

She nodded and made for the door.

'Oh, another thing JC, the vice-chancellor wants a "brains trust" as part of the review. Can you put together a list of ten or so willing boys and girls who won't let us down? Find some normal students if that's not too tall an order.'

JC had been feeling gleefully combative about the review, but this last bit of news positively alarmed her. She gripped the door handle. 'A "brains trust"! What, in the name of bally hell's that? A chance for them to tell tales behind our backs?'

'Seems so. Can't be helped.' Pomfret shrugged helplessly.

'Bloody hell, it's total war! We'll have to find some way to spike that! In the meantime get Marta Cramp on board.'

JC pulled the door to with a little more energy than strictly necessary, leaving Pomfret alone with his thoughts. In a while he sighed wearily and picked up the phone. In a matter of moments he was through to Professor Woolworth, the dean of academic affairs.

'Hello, Murray. Change of plan on the external member of the review board. Inject a note of radicality, gender balance and all that. Suggest an artist called Marta Cramp. Apparently she's all over the place, exhibition-wise. I'll get my secretary to fax her details over.'

'Fair enough, if that's what you want.' Woolworth had not yet sent out a letter of invitation to Perry McBride and he had no objection to Pomfret changing his mind. 'But Archie, you still faxing? The thing now is email. You do email, don't you?'

'Yes, right, email. I'll get Jennifer on to it right away.'

TWENTY-THREE

It was several days before the list of students that Conquest had requested for his "brains trust" came through from the office of the dean of academic affairs. After a hasty perusal of the list he was on the phone to Professor Woolworth.

'I don't like the look of this list, Murray. I'm not for accepting any old list of students the department proposes; I suspect these students will just give the review panel the department's line. Anyway, the gender balance isn't right: too many male students. Send it back, will you, and ask Professor Pomfret to try again? Tell him I don't want any first year students on the list either, one month into the year they won't have any worthwhile perception of what they've let themselves in for, will they?'

Conquest suffered another long wait before a second list came up from the dean of academic affair's office, during which he went about his business in a furious state of impatience. When Carole placed it on his desk it was with what looked to him like the crooked smile of someone in on his secret. He ushered her out of his office, aware of a faint, diabolical urge to shove her hard, squarely in the back. Only when the door was closed did he dare scan the names.

He was quite resolved: *If her name's not here I'll send the bloody thing back again.*

But there it was, fourth on the list: "Juliette Burton". It was not in his nature to blush but, for a moment, vapour rose from his brow. Now he knew she was within his grasp. He rejoiced at his cunning.

The virtue of patience!

He congratulated himself that he was not one to be stymied by the problems of protocol; at last he had found a way to be in the same room as her, even talk to her. She had come to him – on this point he was quite clear.

Without me asking, without me admitting to any desire to be close to her she is on her way. No one can say I have sought her out; she has come to me by pure chance, but she has come to me!

However great his need, he would never implore.

Things needed to be moved on. Movement is my friend. Only by keeping moving will I confound those who are comfortable with things as they are.

He picked up the phone; put it down again. He had a headache. His pressed his fingertips to his temples, trying to limit the way the pain crowded out all other mental activity.

It is no use, you cannot escape.

He knew the spectacle of an older man made to look a fool by beauty was not uncommon in his line of work. At one time or another he had witnessed colleagues enduring the torments of regret that followed hard drinking, the pursuit of young flesh and the spoils of the chase. It led where it led and the guardians of moral rectitude would catch you out and drag you down if they could. Those were the pleasures, the rules and the costs.

He paced his office for several minutes before calling in Carole and asking her to have Professor Woolworth come up to discuss the review. He was too excited to leave it alone.

'Second try and I have my brains trust, Murray,' he said with triumph as soon as Woolworth arrived. 'This time Pomfret has come up with a proper cross-section of the student population. How go the rest of the arrangements? We need to make sure the review panel speaks with a single, strong voice. When the report comes in I don't want anyone saying it was a weak panel that misconstrued what it was reviewing.'

'Aren't we rather jumping the gun there, vice-chancellor?'

'Let's have no misunderstandings, Murray, I'll be delighted if the department comes out with a glowing report, but just in case I don't want any doubts about the credibility of the panel.'

'I'm sure that's right. Would you like me to go through the panel's members?' He fished out a piece of paper from the folder he had brought with him and held it out for Conquest to inspect.

Conquest had no need to consult the sheet of paper; he was already fully aware of the composition of Professor Czinc's panel. 'Who is Ms Cramp, for instance?' he said.

'She's the department's nomination: external subject specialist.'

Conquest fixed him with a stare, eyes glittering darkly.

'It is usual,' Woolworth assured him.

'Oh, I know it's *usual*, Murray. I was wondering if I we ought to bring in our own subject specialist; find some hungry young art and design dean from one of the newer universities with a thing about privileged London art schools; he'd see through any elitist nonsense, if that's the way they want to spin it.'

Woolworth was on the verge of protesting, but thought better of it. 'I don't think Archie is capable of "spinning" something like this,' he said mildly. 'It's late in the day to be appointing another subject specialist, and wouldn't the panel be getting a little large: four internal members, two externals? The catering!'

Conquest waved his objections away impatiently. 'Cut the chocolate biscuits!'

'I still think—'

'Yes, yes!' Conquest could see his intervention was becoming too pointed and he decided to pull back; perhaps the "brains trust" was enough. 'Maybe you're right, but let's make sure we do this thing right.'

TWENTY-FOUR

Not so very long after Woolworth arrived back in his office he received a visit from Professor Andrew Czinc, dean of the faculty of social sciences and chair of the fine art review panel. Czinc favoured light grey suits, rimless glasses and bow ties. He looked every inch the well-travelled intellectual. Lately he had been having a creeping feeling that he was not the person for the task he was there to consult about. In some ways his feeling was patently unreasonable; he enjoyed committee work, especially when he was in the chair. He was good at policy, an organisation man, a networker who was careful to cultivated academic relations with senior academics at the LSE. He was a cautious innovator, a spotter of ideology disguised as pragmatism; a believer in systems, in post-structuralist thought, in birthing pools, oatmeal and wooden toys for children. Son of the renowned Marxist sociologist, Adolphus Czinc, sociology and academia were in his blood. His caution and clear thinking had kept his faculty aloof from the mess that the rest of the university had got itself into during the last administration. If the university had someone who represented continuity, good practice and prudence – so he thought – it was he. Although some found him preening, in an academic sort of way, all the above were estimable qualities in a dean of social sciences, but *none* were necessary prerequisites for passing judgment on the activities of an art department, even more so if one's appreciation of the visual arts was nugatory, as was his.

Woolworth was quick to note that he was in a state of some agitation. Czinc heaved himself into the chair across the desk from Woolworth and played moodily with a pencil. Woolworth waited, content to allow him his moment of drama.

'Murray,' Czinc said at last, having arranged his thoughts to his satisfaction, 'I have no sympathy for the subject here. It strikes me that fine art is not really – in the university sense – a subject at all. It's a vocation or something, but not a subject in the way we understand such a thing.'

Woolworth was somewhat taken aback. 'How do you mean, Andrew?'

'It doesn't have a discourse, does it? We might as well be training chefs.'

'I think that's rather—'

'Have I received all the documentation there is for the review? I mean, is there no more?'

'No, it's all there. I brought it over to your office myself.'

'I'm surprised.'

Woolworth knew the review documentation was thin and he shifted uncomfortably in his chair. 'You have concerns?'

Czinc took a photocopied booklet with a brown cover out of his briefcase and wagged it at Murray. 'This is their undergraduate course document. I can't find any course content. All their course documents are the same; they've absolutely no content.'

'Ah, that'll be their commitment to open-ended, student-centred learning.'

Czinc looked pained. 'Is that a joke?'

Woolworth laughed a little nervously. 'Not at all.'

'"Open-ended, student-centred learning"! I don't know what that means, Murray. It's is not a concept I understand. Where's the structure of learning, *the syllabus*, if you will?'

Woolworth was not inclined to expend effort proselytising for open-ended, student-centred learning. 'Can't you take this up during the review? I'm sure they have their pedagogic reasons.'

'If there is no syllabus their criteria for assessing student success – or failure – can only be subjective. I'm not a great one for dabbling in the arts but I never realised...' He pulled a face of distaste.

Woolworth could see this was an ideological mismatch that was not going to be overcome easily. 'It's hardly to be compared with a sociology degree, Andrew.'

Wearily: 'I should hope *not*! Am I witnessing a magnificent fraud? That is what I find myself asking! I'm concerned I'm being maneuvered into approving an educational Pushmi-pullyu, Murray.'

'Look, you have a subject specialist on your panel. Leave it to her.'

Andrew looked at him sharply. 'Oh yes! And who *exactly* is Marta Cramp?'

'Well...' Woolworth reached for his notes. 'She's highly recommended, so I'm told. Impressive CV.' He began to search through the review documentation on his desk. 'She's supposed to be very on the ball.'

'Supposed to be? Who recommended her?'

'The department... well, Archie.'

'Hah!' Czinc wiggled a finger at Woolworth. 'In addition to my reservations I'm not being landed with a Trojan horse, am I Murray?'

'No, of course not!' He gave an awkward laugh. 'It's all above board.'

'If I was going into a review with course documentation like this,' declared Czinc, gesturing in the general direction of his briefcase, 'I'd certainly be thinking about some form of sabotage.'

'Andrew, I know Cliff values your high standards; that's why he's asked you to chair this review. You're going to have to allow a little leeway for subject differences. Fine art is not sociology, and I admit it can seem to lack the makings of a straightforward university subject.'

Czinc shook his head sorrowfully. 'Thank you, Murray. I find it reassuring that you share my view, but I had hoped for better from us. Perhaps you'd better tell me about this Marta Cramp. Can I rely on her?'

Murray had found Marta Cramp's CV and he pushed it across the table. 'For some reason Archie changed his mind.'

'Changed his mind, did he?' Suspiciously, Czinc leafed through the pages of Marta Cramp's CV, wondering what Pomfret was up to. 'This woman was educated in Yale and Cologne. That's good: international outlook. She's had exhibitions all over the place – a great deal in Israel, I note.' Something caught his eye

136

and he stopped scanning the pages abruptly. 'Murray, "Freelance installation artist" is not the job description of someone with an academic post! I can't see any academic background here at all. There's a list of conferences she's been to as long as my arm, but she's not worked at any university for more than a day!'

'She's an art expert, Andrew, not an academic assessor. That's the job we're expecting from the rest of you.'

'Does the vice-chancellor know about this?'

Woolworth looked uneasy. 'He'd rather have had an academic, like yourself. But it is usual for the department to nominate the subject specialist.'

'This is another bloody anomaly, even before we get into the substance of their submission.'

'Oh come on, Andrew, you know how it is with fine art. They're an ornament. It's good for our student profiles and all that.'

Czinc – who, after all, had a humorous side to his character – made a pantomime of going limp. 'Yes, I know well enough, I suppose. I can see I must take my concerns away and bury them in a box. However, forewarned is forearmed, and I shall prepare myself accordingly.'

'Look, you're the man to tidy them up, give them a thorough spring clean... and all that. But you know Archie's reputation. Let's not strain to make them something they're not.'

'You always were so understanding, Murray. I wish I had your generosity of spirit.' He sighed and returned the course document to his briefcase. 'I have a feeling I'm going to end up doing the university's dirty work for it.'

When Czinc had gone Woolworth spent some minutes turning over in his mind whether he should warn Pomfret what was coming. He knew it was quite contrary to the vice-chancellor's wishes, but he did wonder whether he might drop a hint or two; something coded that he couldn't be reproved for later.

Little did he know that while he fretted about the review, a related scene was taking place on the stairs outside his office. Professor Czinc, descending, lost in thought, had met the vice-chancellor ascending.

'Ah, Andrew!' Conquest was on his way back to his office

following a brief visit to the basement to see some hall of residence refurbishment plans being drawn up by the Department of Estates and Services. 'Good morning to you.'

'Good morning, vice-chancellor.'

Both men halted on the same tread.

'The review?' said Conquest, nodding in the general direction of Professor Woolworth's office. 'You've been consulting Murray?'

'As a matter of fact, I have.' Czinc grappled in silence with his apprehensions. 'The fact is, Cliff,' he said at last, 'I'm rather concerned about some of the documentation I've received for this review. I was checking with Murray that I'm not missing something.'

'I see. Did you get what you were looking for?'

'What I was looking for doesn't exist, apparently.' He shook his head gravely. 'I suppose it could be regarded as good news. It means I don't have to read anymore of the ghastliness they've concocted.'

Conquest stepped closer, thinking they should lower their voices. 'It's that bad, is it? Their strategic plan was grossly lacking, you know.'

'They don't appear to know how to use the spell check!'

'Don't they have secretaries?'

'I believe they have three.'

They exchanged scandalised expressions.

'I can't say I'm very happy about their choice of subject specialist either. Her academic experience on our side of the counter is absolutely nil.'

'Ah, yes, Ms Cramp!' Conquest relished the name. 'I did notice that. I did think her a high risk choice but I didn't want to meddle.'

'She's not an academic, nor was she Archie's first choice. Seems odd!'

'Why don't you have a word with him: see why he changed his mind? I'm sure he'd see reason if you were to advise him that she isn't suitable.'

'Short notice to change.'

'Well, you'll get to the bottom of things, I'm certain. That's what departmental review is for!'

Good, the bit's between his teeth! No need to risk revealing my hand by giving him specific instructions. All I have to do is cheer him on. Thank God he's unmoved by their liberal, syndico-anarchist educational clap-trap.

'Don't expect a whitewash.'

'Heaven forbid. You must tell it as you see it.' Conquest touched the sleeve of Czinc's jacket, the lightest of touches. 'I'll be right behind you. You can expect a shake-up of this university that'll put lots of interesting things your way. Let's not hold back, eh?'

At that they parted. Conquest rose towards the shaft of sunlight that entered through a south-facing window of the cupola and fell across the upper landing in a golden path that led to his office door. Andrew Czinc proceeded downwards, towards the ground floor lavatories.

TWENTY-FIVE

Later that day, still beset by apprehensions about the coming review but decidedly unenthusiastic about breaking protocol by discussing them with Professor Pomfret, Czinc had the good fortune to run into him reading *The Guardian* in the senior common room.

'Hello Archie.'

'Ah, Andrew, I've been hoping we might meet. You're chairing the review next week, aren't you?'

'That's right. As a matter of f—'

'I was thinking you might like to see – as part of the review – some student work: an exhibition of some of the things the students have produced so far this term: a little offering, as it were.'

'Well, I'm not a very good judge of visual work, more at home with the written word, but I'm sure our subject specialist would appreciate seeing something like that.'

'Yes, of course. I'd forgotten about her.' Archie struggled for a moment to find her name. 'Ms Cramp, isn't it?'

'You should know; you nominated her. As a matter of fact, I've been wondering why you changed your mind about who to have as your subject specialist.'

'Not my idea,' explained Pomfret with a touch of helplessness. 'I was told I needed to get with it. I don't know much about this kind of thing, the niceties, you know.'

Presented with unexpected news, Czinc was quietly startled. 'I see. Well, how was she chosen then?'

Pomfret scented awkwardness. He imagined he'd been caught out doing something questionable, but he was not one to dissemble. 'I was advised... strong representations by my staff. It seems she will bring something fresh to your deliberations, but don't ask me what, because I only saw her CV very recently and

I've no idea what I read. I won't say it was gobbledygook, but I didn't get all the references. I think she's one of those get-naked performance artists, rage against rape and all that sort of thing. I didn't think we'd see their like again, but there we are, one never knows. Nothing wrong, is there?'

'No, no. At least she's a truly independent voice,' said Czinc, rather pleased by what he was being told. Pomfret's guileless confession that he was as much in the dark about Marta Cramp's likely contribution as he was, helped set his mind at rest. Now he knew she was not the Trojan horse he had feared. No need to change the external adviser after all.

TWENTY-SIX

'Good morning, people!' said the vice-chancellor as he swept into his outer office. Carole, his PA, and his two secretaries were already hard at work: typing, typing, typing.

What are they typing?

He often found himself wondering, although not with much curiosity since his affairs always seemed to be in excellent order. He supposed they were writing polite replies to invitations he didn't want to accept from people he didn't want to meet.

How nice to think of them making up delicate phrases of refusal on my behalf. How ponderous must be the deliberations that go into those letters!

In the early days of his career, before his academic post warranted a secretary, he had managed his own administration efficiently and with a minimum of fuss. Here was the reward for all that attention to detail: staff who performed an ever-expanding version of himself! As his career continued to blossom, and he moved closer and closer to his goal, he saw himself with more and more staff. He imagined a future in which they would develop evermore-exquisite protocols to deal with every eventuality, spared of which he would – so he imagined – devote his time to Byzantine machinations. Where would it end? In his secret counsels he harboured the dream that the very pinnacle of his career would be the leadership of the Labour party – *why not?* – a Labour party wrought in his own image: centralist, meritocratic, closely tied to enlightened forces of organised labour. "Administrative oversight", coherent policies of "community", "culture" and "advancement"; terms like "equality of opportunity" and "inclusion" no longer empty slogans. From there it would be but a small step to the office of prime minister. Maybe he would never reach that lofty goal, but he would strive. It was perpetual war, a war fought with words, by combatants armed with secret alliances, maneuvering to secure strategic appointments that took them one step closer to the ultimate goal. And, by all that was serious, measured and proper in his character, how he did aspire!

But today these musings did not lighten his spirit. He was still recovering from a head cold and for some days had been oppressed by the feeling that none of his plans would ever come to fruition. His university had taken on the aspect of a desert island and he that of a hapless Robinson Crusoe.

Carole had followed him into his office. 'Good morning,' she said, regarding him with a quizzical expression.

Another Friday, another dismal weekend ahead. The day will come when my commitments will be unceasing, shielding me from the interruptions of weekends, public holidays, rest days and their like; then I will be on call in the small hours, followed around by code books and secure telephone lines.

The vision barely warmed Conquest. He gazed out of the window, apparently oblivious to Carole's greeting. 'The day is blustery and carries portents of winter,' he intoned without turning round. 'The dead leaves scurry along the paths, collect in the drains and mass on the edges of lawns.'

That morning, on her way to work, Carole had calculated that she had been working for Conquest for the best part of four months and she could no longer disguise from herself the fact that she found him really, *really* annoying.

'You have a delegation of Japanese academics at ten, a working party on research funding at eleven and the Director of Finance has phoned to say can he come and see you before lunch,' she said.

Conquest acknowledged the message with a slight inclination of his head, and she flounced off to the outer office.

At twelve thirty he was again standing at the window, again staring into the distance, when Ballantyne arrived with the news that the bank had agreed to grant the university an overdraft facility of fourteen million pounds secured at a very favorable rate, fixed for five years, against certain properties fronting the main thoroughfare. Now it was *glad day*!

'I've been wanting to prove to the bloody incumbents that there's something innovative and startling this university can do even when times are hard,' Conquest exulted over a fresh pot of coffee that Carole had been commanded to provide. 'It calls for a small celebration!' He went to the drinks cupboard and poured two generous brandies. They drank them with the excellent coffee.

'I tell you what I feel like doing,' confessed Conquest when the coffee and brandy had begun to do their work. 'It's Friday and I feel like cancelling the rest of today's engagements and buying you a damn good lunch. You made a bloody fine case to those bankers and they bought it. A day like this makes me feel like sitting down and knocking off a thousand words of my Kennedy book. I'll buy you lunch and then you can drag me back here and I'll go to it. No train to Wolverhampton for me tonight! I'll sit here till nine or ten and knock them out. I've wrapped up Jack and Ted. It's Robert I can't get an angle on, somehow. It's all been said about Robert and I still can't work it out why he did some of the things he did, what made him tick. I think there was something Irish in his character I don't quite get.' He ruminated on that for a while until eventually Ballantyne spoke.

'I'm half Irish,' he said.

'Are you now? I didn't know that! *Well, good luck to yer, sir!*' Conquest laughed a self-satisfied laugh and ignored the opportunity to ask Ballantyne what he thought about the Kennedys or their Irish background. He rose to his feet, relishing the idea of mounting a sudden literary attack on Robert Kennedy. He reached for the phone, thinking that after all it was a fine, productive day, and asked Carole to come in. Almost as soon as he replaced the receiver there was a perfunctory knock at the door and she entered.

'Can you book us into Franco's for one thirty and cancel my appointments for the rest of the day? Something's come up and Tommy and I need to confer.'

Carole consulted his appointments diary with a slightly insolent air. 'You have a meeting with the president of the Students' Union about outstanding issues at three and the planning officer from the borough is booked in at four to discuss the introduction of parking restrictions on our roads.'

'Put them both off. They're not that important. Send apologies; tell them it's a Friday thing and offer them other dates. I'll pick up the pieces next week.' He gave Carole a wink. She pulled a face of disapproval and was gone.

'Handsome woman, that,' said Ballantyne.

Conquest pursed his lips and his face took on a satirical twinkle. 'Don't get ideas,' he warned, 'her husband's a policeman.'

Outside the Keynes Building they hailed a passing cab. At the restaurant Franco greeted them personally, and put them in a discreet alcove in the restaurant's inner room. They were well into their lunch and the service was beginning to wind down when they overheard Franco greeting a new arrival towards the front of the restaurant and out of their line of vision.

'…I have very lovely beef for you today. And we have Whitstable oysters too. So lovely, they taste of the surf, the cool depths of the sea. We adore them, don't we? Incredible risotto with truffle. Yummy! Everything so fresh, fresh as my naughty niece who we christened Eglantine.'

'Love to meet her,' said a booming voice.

Conquest recognised it instantly. He dragged a protesting Ballantyne to his feet and led him in the direction of the voice.

'Sir Norman!'

Sir Norman looked up from the place setting, which he was still arranging to his liking. 'Clifford! Having a spot of lunch, eh?'

'Delighted to see you, Sir Norman. Can I introduce our Director of Finance, Tommy Ballantyne? Tommy, Sir Norman.'

Sir Norman shook the proffered hand. 'Pleased, I'm sure. Keeping him solvent, I hope? Finance is a marvellous thing, backbone of everything, Wouldn't know how to make a move without my finance people giving me the say-so. I expect you fancied a treat, didn't you?' he added with a jovial air of condescension. 'Well, well! It's progress when chaps like you – men of affairs – can find time to luncheon here. Sit down a moment, my guests haven't arrived yet.' He gestured to the other two chairs at his table.

'It's fortuitous, finding you here,' said Conquest, leaning forward confidentially, 'because we've had great news from the bankers: they've agreed the financing for the digital hub. Made us a very reasonable arrangement.'

Sir Norman was delighted; he rubbed his hand vigorously on his napkin before clapping them on the shoulders with a great show of bonhomie. 'That's bloody marvellous! We must have a drink on it in the fullness of time, but look-ee here, my guests have just arrived.' He had his eye on the entrance where Sir Michael and Lord N'Garbi were divesting themselves of their coats.

There followed a moment of confusion as the arrivals were introduced. With many pleasantries Conquest and Ballantyne were eased away from Sir Norman's table and back to their own. At last calm and order was restored, and at Sir Norman's table the business of enjoying a good lunch was set in motion with many a guffaw and droll aside.

Conquest was delighted by their chance encounter and slightly piqued that Ballantyne seemed to habour the impression that they had been dismissed like a couple of functionaries. 'I knew this was going to be a better idea than meeting the president of the Students' Union, that mendacious fellow with his Palestinian flag,' said Conquest as their desserts were ushered smoothly onto the table. 'What good fortune we should meet Sir Norman; one of those little touches that helps put us in the inside lane. I expect they're politicking. Lord N'Garbi is a great one for the dispossessed.'

'Aren't they a bit right wing company for us to be keeping, Cliff?' said Ballantyne as he gave his glass of wine a speculative glare.

'Right wing! You've got your political compass one eighty degrees off, Tommy. They're Labour, through and through.'

'Ballantyne looked dubious, even scornful. 'They may have been on the donkey since Blair got his hands on the reins, but they're not proper left in the sense my dad would understand. Listen to them roaring away. That's self-interest letting off steam and public money being squandered.'

'Left and right is just name-calling these days. You tell me who belongs to which and I'll tell you differently.'

'Ah, that's the academic talking. I forgot about that distinction between you and me.' Ballantyne cocked his head in the direction of Sir Norman's table. 'You sure you want this digital hub, Cliff? It's risky borrowing a squillion quid on a whim.'

'Whim! Tommy, *please*, moderate the language! A digital hub is not a whim! You'll see, it'll be a triumph and a lasting tribute to your stewardship.'

'Mine? You're the one who'll have his name on it!'

'That's as maybe, but we'll all know who did the spadework, won't we, Tommy?'

'That man's company is going to get the contract, isn't it?' He nodded in the direction of the noise coming from Sir Norman's table. 'How are you going to handle that?'

'Look, Tommy, "that man" as you call him is an ornament to the Labour party. He's gifted hundreds of thousands. He doesn't expect – or need – favours. Wainwright, Carter & Expandite will come in with the keenest price, you watch. And Sir Norman has already promised to recuse himself from any decision of senate on the awarding of the contract. What more could you want?' He saw Ballantyne was not convinced. 'Look, stop worrying, this digital hub is going to be the monument to our time here. Then we move on! How old d'you think those three are?' With a twitch of his eyebrows he directed Ballantyne's attention to the sound of Lord N'Garbi's rich bass. 'They're all in their sixties, living off the fat of the land. Where are they going to be in ten years time? Gone! A coronary here, a stroke there. They'll be gone. Then it'll be our turn, Tommy. Our turn! Believe me?'

'Yeah, all right,' said Ballantyne, relaxing into a reluctant smile. He glanced around and a sly look came over his face. 'I tell you what, when we've finished here I'm going to give you a treat and take you back to that pole dancing place. How about that?'

Warmed by the food and the wine, Conquest was overcome by a wave of gratitude towards his companion. He emptied the last of the wine into his glass and called for dessert wine. In all their time working together, when his need was greatest, Ballantyne was somehow always there with the right suggestion. Now, because of him, he was cruising towards an escapade he had only very recently dismissed as mad, sordid, repellent. 'If you want, I'm game,' he said in his most dissembling voice. Again, without him trying,

Lady Caroline Lamb was being drawn into his orbit. He may have been thrilled at the prospect but he didn't abandon all thought of the Kennedys without a pang.

I will write that piece on Bobby, even if I have to forego altogether my weekend in Wolverhampton. What was his relation with Jack? That's got to be the secret! The younger brother syndrome! How about hero worship? No, even though I keep coming back to it, it's too obvious... but I mustn't forget it.

He reached for some compliment, some way of expressing his gratitude, but Ballantyne was oblivious and being carried along by a theme of his own.

'I think women...' Ballantyne paused as though on the brink of formulating an idea of some importance to him. Nothing came and he shook his head in a befuddled sort of way. 'To tell you the truth, I've no idea what I think about women.'

Conquest regarded him with amusement. 'Come on Tommy, you've got a damn fine, loyal wife in Janis!'

Ballantyne brushed aside Conquest's praise. '"Nubile"! I like that word. Never seen a nubile. Fact is, we don't live in primitive enough times for my tastes. Modern courtship is all computer compatibility tests. Where's raging passion? I work with numbers. Numbers, numbers, *numbers!* That's not likely to generate much passion, is it?'

'No, Tommy, it isn't, but don't get philosophical on me. The wife's happily at home in Dorking and fun in the playpen of the primitive is yours for the asking. You remember Lady Caroline Lamb, don't you?'

'Yeah.' Tommy let his tongue hang out in a jokey sort of way. 'You're right, she was nubile all right. Nubile as...' His store of adjectives failed him and he made a vague wiggling gesture with his hands.

'Loveliness so close to sin,' said Conquest with a far away look in his eyes.

'*Get on!*' said Ballantyne, sipping his wine.

They finished their meal in high spirits, topping it with large brandies.

'Club Beirut awaits your pleasure,' announced Ballantyne when the goblets were empty.

They set about a humorous wrangle with Franco over the bill, which resulted in them having two more brandies. On the way out they stopped for a few words with Sir Norman and his guests who were sitting behind their desserts with affable expressions on their faces. Feelings around the table were well expressed by Lord N'Garbi when he said, 'We all love a good time, don't we? But what unites us is we serve the public good. "The public good" may be an amorphous term, but we all know what it means, I truly believe.' He embraced Conquest and Ballantyne with his politician's smile.

They all nodded; it was a moment of perfect communion.

'Indeed,' said Conquest, realising they should go but wanting to leave Sir Norman and his guests with a final thought, 'and another day we hope to find you having desserts just as good as those look!'

The three diners looked at their desserts, then up at Conquest, trying to divine his meaning. Finally they laughed uproariously. Sir Norman rose with a grunt and, throwing his arms round Conquest and Ballantyne, propelled them towards the door. 'Digital hub!' he cried as they were engulfed by the portière.

'Smooth!' said Ballantyne, once the two of them were in their cab. 'I liked that line about their desserts.'

'Can the sarcasm, Tommy. I can't get you out of a tight social spot every time.'

'What you need is a good lap dancing traffic warden experience. Money comes and money goes, but women go on forever.'

'What I'm saying is that you have to learn to chat your own way out of the paper bag.'

'What the hell? You're drunkener than me.'

'No. I'm not, I'm exercising my unconscious. I always let it out to stretch its legs when I'm thinking about writing. Don't let me forget I'm committed to Bobby Kennedy. I'm depending on my unconscious to come up with the goods. You'll see, it has an attitude to him, even if I don't. All I've got to do is get it limbered up and let it loose.'

'That's why you're an academic and I'm not.'

'Too true. I've got an active unconscious, yours is as dead as a dodo.'

They both laughed.

Their taxi crossed town, moving from one traffic snarl-up to another. They were largely oblivious to what was happening beyond the confines of the cab, the little they did note being not the result of direct observation, but conveyed by the commentary of their sorely-tried driver, whose curses greatly amused them. Eventually they drew up at the doorway in the featureless brick wall. Unlike last time, they had arrived at the Club Beirut in broad daylight and they could see the full extent of its dismal surroundings. The club, they now realised, was not at the base of a large building, but was shoehorned into a space beneath the arches of a vast, brick railway viaduct. Overhead, two railway lines going in different directions crossed, one above the other, leaving visible only a small wedge of sky. They piled out and Conquest paid the cab driver handsomely under the watchful gaze of Dirk the Doorman.

'Good afternoon,' said Conquest, his breezy manner tempered by the fear that Dirk might recognise them from their previous encounter.

'Good afternoon,' replied the giant placidly as the cab drove away. 'I'm afraid we're closed for a private function.'

Conquest could not believe what he was hearing. 'We've come right across town to get here,' he said in a plaintive voice. 'Surely there's some way?'

''Fraid not, gents.'

During the journey the idea of seeing Lady Caroline Lamb had blossom into a thing of spiritual intensity and now it was crushed. Conquest could have sat down and wept with frustration.

Ballantyne was of a different mettle. It was the general trajectory of his fun that was under threat. It was late on Friday afternoon and he had committed himself to a cathartic dissolution of his working self in the vale of alcoholic pleasures. Dorking could wait. To prevent the parabolic curve of his intention being thwarted he flourished a twenty pound note. 'No harm in us asking, is there?' he said, pressing the note flat on the double-breasted front of the colossus, who flexed noticeably before its force.

'It's a private catered event for executives in the swaps market,' said Dirk in a manner that suggested it was a form of words he had been required to commit to memory. 'You can ask, I suppose. The event organiser is at the desk, but she'll expect you to have a lapel badge.' With that warning the twenty-pound note vanished and he ushered them into the corridor, content to put the responsibility for a final refusal in someone else's hands.

At the end of the corridor, where they had encountered Lady Divine on their previous visit, they found themselves confronted by two young women in the PR mould: well-dressed and of the type willing to submit to gross inconveniences of the flesh in pursuit of elegance. Their physical attributes, thus buttressed, would undoubtedly ensure they married well – providing some serious flaw of character did not intervene – but not yet awhile, not while the stuff of business fascinated them, and they still had youth and vigour. They guarded the entrance like Furies; hair extensions wreathed their heads like serpents.

'Hello, gentlemen, this is a private function. Are you guests?'

'We have invites,' said Ballantyne brazenly. 'But lapel badges we have not – yea, nay, yea, nay.'

'Oh!' The women looked them up and down, waiting.

'Can I see your invitations?' asked the taller of the two when Ballantyne showed no sign of producing them.

'Bah,' replied Ballantyne, blithely patting his pockets. 'We appear to have left them at home.'

The two women exchanged sceptical looks. 'We can't let you in without your invitations or lapel badges. I'm sorry.'

'Wait, what if we're on your guest list?'

'If you are and can prove you are who you say you are we will most certainly let you in.'

At that point Ballantyne lost his nerve and placed a fifty-pound note on the counter. 'We have to see somebody in there,' he pleaded with obvious insincerity. 'They are bleeding; we are bleeding!'

'I'm sorry—'

'No, you don't understand: *bleeding*!'

The two women were becoming extremely uncomfortable. Conquest felt the hair rise on the back of his neck and turned to find Dirk the Doorman standing behind them.

'Are you two dafties bullying these ladies?' asked Dirk in meditative tones. 'Bullying is one of those things I can't abide.'

'*Us?*' said Conquest indignantly.

'No, I suppose I am,' decided Ballantyne, suddenly contrite. 'I hadn't thought of it that way until you put the idea into words, but I can see that "bullying" is what it is.'

'These ladies are susceptible to bullying, same as anybody else. They have feelings. I suggest you exit this establishment before things turn unpleasant.'

'We will, if…' Conquest stopped, deciding that attaching conditionality to their departure was a waste of time. He groaned in frustration.

'Wait a minute!' said Ballantyne. 'Where did my fifty quid go?'

Everybody was taken aback. There was no sign of the note on the counter or the floor.

'Now you have to let us in!' said Ballantyne accusingly, pointing at the two women.

'Now wait a minute…' Dirk placed himself between Ballantyne and them. Ballantyne's response was to raise his fists in the manner of a nineteenth century sporting plate.

Conquest's antennae for trouble were signalling danger. Matters were getting out of hand, and their chances of getting into Club Beirut were disappearingly small. Before he could take control of Ballantyne, Dirk had enacted his own form of discipline. He had Ballantyne laid out on the ground with much of the front of his shirt and jacket trapped in his fist.

'Don't I recognise you, sir?'

Conquest was quick to respond. He put out his hands and stooped into Dirk's eye line. 'Let him go and we'll be off. We don't want a bit of silly cheekiness to end in trouble.'

One of the women had come round from behind the counter and made a flailing attempt to grind her heel in Ballantyne's groin.

Conquest stepped back hastily and collided with the counter. 'Let him go and we'll push off!'

Dirk hauled Ballantyne to his feet and began to propel him backwards, along the corridor.

'We only wanted to have a look. Disappointment got the

better of him,' pleaded Conquest with as much dignity as he could muster.

Dirk reached the entrance and sent Ballantyne staggering across the pavement. He almost saved himself from falling but at the last moment he fell on his back with a heavy thud. He lay there, looking up at the sky, laughing silently.

'Excuse me,' said Conquest as he sidled past Dirk. He took hold of Ballantyne's wrists and hauled him to his feet.

Dirk watched impassively from the doorway.

Conquest turned to address him. 'Thank you,' he said, grateful for his restraint in ejecting Tommy. 'Come on Tommy, we need another drink.'

'There's another club on Lower Siding Street,' Dirk said and he pointed to his left.

'Yes, thank you. We'll try there. Thank you very much.' He took Ballantyne by the arm and began to lead him away.

The women who had tried to castrate Ballantyne had come to the door and was standing beside the doorman. 'Don't you rats come back here!' she screamed 'You'll get more of this!' She raised a finger in an obscene gesture.

'Thank you, and the same to you,' muttered Conquest.

Ballantyne was still laughing. He reached in his trouser pocket and fished out the fifty-pound note.' Let's go and blow it,' he said. 'Jesus, that bastard's crippled my back!'

'Yeah, well, thanks a lot, Tommy. Thanks to you we're on the loose in Vermin Town. Around here if they're going to mug you they first soften you up by rolling over you in a car, so look sharp!'

TWENTY-SEVEN

At 8.30am on Monday, the third of November, Professor Andrew Czinc convened the opening meeting of the panel for the review of the Department of Fine Art. He had had a relaxing weekend and felt well prepared for the task ahead. The other members of his panel were Professor Dodds, Department of Music, Cyril Tang, reader, the Department of Psychology, Dr Dafna Goldstein, senior lecturer, the Department of Visual Anthropology, and the external subject specialist, Marta Cramp, artist.

Czinc had met Marta Cramp outside the Keynes Building when he had first arrived. She was leaning against the balustrade at the foot of the steps, a tall – much taller than he – muscular woman, smoking a roll-up with mannish nonchalance. He had introduced himself and enquired whether she were Marta Cramp. She had looked him up and down and tapped the ash from the cigarette. Instead of responding to his enquiry she had studied the ash lying on the ground. 'There's something dead about universities, isn't there?' she had announced with a pronounced mid-European accent. 'Pity to incarcerate the young in them.'

As the university employed the other three members of his panel, Professor Czinc knew, more or less, what he could expect of them. He had previously worked with Dodds and Tang on committees, and knew that in most circumstances they could be relied upon to follow his lead. He was not familiar with Goldstein, who was new to university committee work. She came highly recommended by her head of department, although in Czinc's opinion the state of the Department of Visual Anthropology did not entirely inspire confidence in his judgment. Apparently, Goldstein was an expert on "the Anthropology of the Self". He looked round the table, reflecting that undoubtedly he would find out more about them all over the next two days.

He tapped on his pile of documentation with his pen to get the panel's attention. 'Good morning, everyone. I think you all know who I am. I'm Professor Czinc, dean of social sciences. Please call me "Andrew". Before I ask you to introduce yourselves, I'd like to make a few general remarks.' He paused and straightened an errant paper. He looked around, his mouth gaping slightly. The manual of the Quality Assurance Agency appeared in his right hand. 'You all have one of these in your packs. This is our guide in assessing the quality of the education the department offers. We are looking for thoroughness and consistency. Does it aspire? Does it have ambitious targets?'

Czinc turned his attention to an array of binders running down the centre of the table. 'They contain the statutes, ordinances and regulations, the framework for achievement that the university underwrites. We need to check that practices in the department tally with them. Finally, we have the documentation provided by the department. Did everyone received their copies of the department's course handbooks?'

There was a murmur of assent round the table.

'Good. We need to confirm that these are coherent, comprehensive and consistent. The department must demonstrate that the students understand what its expectations of them are, particularly what it expects of them when it comes to examination. In addition to these, we have supplementary documentation of departmental meetings and other decision-making processes.' He gestured to a table behind him, which was stacked with additional folders.

'The primary aim of review is to determine whether all this documentation gives a full and accurate account of the department's academic procedures. Further, we will consider whether or not the documentation demonstrates that the academic provision is of a high quality. Are there any questions?'

There were none.

'Since you have already had time to study the department's course handbooks,' Czinc continued, 'you will doubtless have already identified issues and questions you wish to pursue. If you have already formed judgments you will need to verify them. Now –' he looked at his watch – 'we have fifteen minutes before we have our first meeting with the senior staff of the department, so I would like us to do our introductions and go round the table to give you the opportunity to share any impressions you've already gained from the documentation.'

TWENTY-EIGHT

Conquest's weekend in Wolverhampton had been drab. The weather hadn't helped, and a series of small domestic chores – changing dud light bulbs, fixing the drying rack in the airing cupboard, sorting out a blockage of leaves in the kitchen drain – had proved reason enough to forego tackling Bobby Kennedy. The fact was every weekend was Bobby Kennedy time, something he'd grown to hate. Nevertheless, it was now Monday morning and he felt grand. It helped that for once he had had a good night's sleep and he felt buoyant as he made for the main staircase of the Keynes Building. This was the week of the first of his departmental reviews; this was the day he would seriously begin the task of knocking his university into shape; this was the day on which, finally, he and Lady Caroline Lamb would be together in the same room.

I will speak to her, I will invade her consciousness, and she will look at me and consider how to respond to my questions.

As he began to climb the staircase he saw below him a group standing outside one of the committee rooms. He realised they were the senior staff of the Department of Fine Art waiting for the review to start. It braced him to see them; a little forlorn group, they looked. Probably, he thought, they had been inconvenienced by having to arrive earlier than normal. Their travails put an extra spring in his step as he rose towards the heavens.

I'm going to modernise this university and do something about the gender balance in the senior posts. If you stand in my way, Professor Pomfret, you're going to find yourself back on the studio floor doing whatever it is you do with first year students.

Below, the team from the Department of Fine Art was, indeed, forlorn. It had been waiting for some time. Victor Montour, third year tutor of the undergraduate course and the senior technician,

Will Forsyth, both gaunt men of the smoker type, had arrived first. The department's senior secretary, Jennifer Cross, arrived next, her arms full of extra copies of the department's documentation. Then came Andrew Deepwell, head of sculpture and gauntness itself, in the company of Sid Bartrum, head of painting, and petit, ambiguous Sarat Patel, head of print media.

There was not much conversation as they gathered. They glanced at one another with a faint air of trepidation since none of them apart from JC – missing, as usual – had ever previously submitted to review. An unasked question hung heavy in the air: where was their leader, Archie Pomfret? Most ill at ease was Sarat Patel. He paced the corridor, muttering: 'Foolish bureaucratic fellows make fools of everyone who tangles with them! I know, I just *know!*'

'Don't upset yourself, Sarat,' said Jennifer complacently, shifting the weight of her burden from one arm to the other. 'It'll all be over by teatime.'

'No it won't,' he retorted bitterly, 'there's more tomorrow!'

Just then two things happened: Professor Czinc appeared at the entrance of the committee room, holding the door open in an invitation for them to enter and, from the front entrance, at speed, came Professor Pomfret, the tails of his old gabardine mac flapping. Czinc took in the flying figure, saw the beige safari jacket and the plimsolls and thought, gloomily, that the man had no idea how to dress for a review.

TWENTY-NINE

It was customary for the first meeting of a review to be confined to introductions and an opportunity for the chair of the review panel and the head of department to make their opening statements. It was the occasion when the head of department could "lay out his stall", as recommended by the dean of academic affairs. The senior staff of the department trooped in and spread themselves out around the committee table, which was more than capable of accommodating the twelve people now present.

Professor Czinc opened the meeting by repeating almost verbatim what he had already said to the members of the panel, and then he asked Professor Pomfret if he would like to speak for the department. He sat back expectantly.

'Yes, thank you,' began Pomfret, casting a humorous eye over the members of the panel. 'Welcome. I don't want this to be a lost opportunity, when all's said and done. Art is a marvellous thing, and teaching towards that possibility – the possibility of art, I mean, which is elusive, as we all know – is an endlessly fascinating task.' He looked round at his staff. 'We enjoy it anyway.' He gave the panel a beatific smile and they nodded encouragingly, thinking his words thus far were the preamble to a detailed exposition of the department's strengths.

'Yes, we have excellent students, and that helps. You can't teach someone without talent. A lot of our competitors don't spend enough time on the selection process. Select the wrong applicants and you'll have dimwits to teach. Get your selection processes right and good students teach themselves. Marvellous facilities. And tradition, of course. Ah, can't say enough about tradition! I like to think that Vincent – never a happy man, a thorn in the side of his family, but a marvellously sinuous line – would have enjoyed being a student here. Not to say that Mondrian wouldn't also. We are at your disposal for the next thirty-six hours, night and day.'

And that was it. Since there was no other business, the meeting came to an end. As the department's staff were filing out, Pomfret was heard to say, 'What was that all about?' as though the panel had disappointed him.

This did not go down well with Czinc. 'I'm afraid we've hardly had a declaration of their educational policy, have we?' he announced to the panel, once they were alone. 'I was expecting detailed claims for excellence, but no matter…'

Across the table Marta Cramp muttered something beneath her breath.

'Now…' Czinc held up a sheaf of papers. 'I'm passing round copies of the timetable for the review. Although our process places great emphasis on the documentation, we have an opportunity over the next two days to see the facilities and meet with staff and students. We have a lot of ground to cover and you will see that for some events we will divide. The vice-chancellor is taking an interest in this review and he's ask me to tell you that he will be chairing a brains trust of students later today to give them the opportunity to speak about their experiences of the department. He wants two of us to join him as observers. Finally, we are expected to deliver a preliminary account of our findings, and our recommendations, to the department at three o'clock tomorrow afternoon.

'Can I draw your attention to the six criteria on which to base our judgment. If you'll please turn to page fifty-nine of the Quality Assurance Agency's manual?'

By now the members of the panel had spread out their individual piles of documents to the point where the table, despite its size, was a sea of papers. In response to his instruction there was a gust of rustling and fumbling as everyone searched for the manual. Czinc hardly paused.

'For each criterion we can score from zero to four, depending on our assessment of the quality of the provision. Any ones or an overall total of less than fifteen will require a further inspection by the panel in three months time, a period during which we will expect improvements to have occurred.'

He turned to Professor Dodds. 'Paul, I'd like you to tackle examinations and external examiners' reports. I want you to do a paper trail on the issues externals raise and see how the department acknowledges and responds to them. I want someone else to look at the relation between the curriculum and examination. I've got a real concern here because I can't find any clear statements about what the students are studying.' He stopped and threw up his hands in a little pantomime of despair. 'I can't see that the department makes any attempt to define the field of practices supposedly taught on the courses it offers.'

'Ceramics,' said Marta Cramp.

'Yes, all right,' agreed Czinc, nettled that the flow of his remarks had been interrupted, 'I'll give you ceramics, but *in general* I have no idea how the students know what they are being examined on.' He looked up from his notes, hopeful that someone would endorse his concern.

'I don't know what you mean,' said Marta Cramp, 'but I'll focus on that for you.'

Czinc contemplated her, doubtfully about her suitability for the task. He knew that although members of a panel were expected to read the documentation from start to finish, some didn't bother. It had already occurred to him that she was quite likely to be the latter. 'Very well,' he said finally, enable to see a way of avoiding her offer. He consoled himself that since she was not a professional academic, he would be able to out-argue her on his own ground. He was very clear about the insights he had gained from reading the department's submission and felt the criticisms he could bring to bear on it were irrefutable.

The other tasks Czinc had identified were quickly allotted; evidence gathering and preparation for further meetings with the department's staff being the first priorities.

As the day proceeded he began to think that the members of the panel were working together rather well, the exception being Marta Cramp. It was not only her lack of academic experience, even more worryingly, he had began to suspect that socially speaking she was seriously dysfunctional. As part of evidence gathering he had sent her and Professor Dodd on a guided tour of the workshops. She had made it her business to talk at length to everyone they met, putting his timetable in complete disarray.

When they reconvened after a delayed lunch, he asked her to report on her progress on the curriculum issue.

She rolled her eyes to the heavens, as though looking there for help. 'Oh, yeah, I suppose!' she said in tones that suggested she would share her views, but only under sufferance. 'I've checked... the staff list... particularly the visiting staff... over the past three years...' She shuffled halfheartedly through the papers she had amassed, but failed to produce any list. 'I *did* have a comprehensive list.'

Czinc waited and when it became obvious she had nothing further to add he could contain his exasperation no longer. 'The members of staff are not the curriculum, are they?'

She sat up with sudden severity. 'I think we can say they are. And that the students are being taught well.'

To Czinc this statement was confirmation of her blindness to her lack of academic experience, a social dysfunction if ever he had come across one. 'How do the students know what is expected of them? Where are their topics? I can't find the syllabus!'

'They're studying art. It's not a matter of topics; there's only art.' She said this with several diminishing shakes of her head, in a manner that suggested she were uttering a self-evident truth that was denied him for the simple reason that he had no idea about art. 'Look through the staff list and what do you see? A lot of eminent artists teaching here. So, what's the problem? As far as I'm concerned you're trying to make a salad with sea cucumber.'

The latter remark left Czinc baffled. He wanted to object but had no idea what she meant. His only recourse was to stick to his point. 'For the sake of wholeness – and for the sake of the students' sanity – the department must tell them what it is that they are studying. There is no differentiation in here –' he waved the fine art course handbook at her – 'between year one and year two. *Or year three!*'

Marta Cramp seemed to find this very droll. 'Oh, I see! You're stickling.'

'I'm sorry?'

'You stickle. You understand "stickler", I think? It is also a verb, no? Well, I say you *cannot* make vegetarian food using slices of animal, can you?'

Czinc goggled as he finally understood what she was driving at, although he was quite unable to comprehend the justification for her analogy. 'I regard your comparison as somewhat strained,' he said with dignity.

'Oh, do you?' Marta Cramp laughed scornfully. Well, you're the chair. Let's see where that gets us!'

Czinc inferred from this that she had already decided that, unless she stopped him, he would wield his institutional power without recourse to her opinion. 'Thank you,' he said, through gritted teeth.

Marta Cramp climbed to her feet. 'I enjoy such exchanges, but now it is time for the delights of your brains trust. If you will excuse me, I must *observe*.'

Dafna Goldstein, the second observer, rose to her feet and, clutching her documentation, hurried after Cramp, fighting her way noisily through a pack of spare chairs to reach the door. During the day she had occupied the far end of the table, largely invisible. What *was* noticed, now she had gone – and Professor Dodds was particularly struck by this – was that during the day she had removed from her documentation the coloured tabs designed to assist the reader in finding specific sections. They were now arrayed, fringe-like, along the edge of the table in imitation of the spectrum.

THIRTY

Conquest could not trust himself to study the students as they trooped into the room. Nonchalantly he browsed through some documents he had brought with him for the express purpose of giving him something to do while they were taking their seats. Then he caught a glimpse of Lady Caroline Lamb swaddled in her outsized men's overcoat and his heart leapt.

It is time! I have come down from on high. Now is the beginning, the true coming!

'Thank you for taking part everyone,' he began, once they had all found a seat in the circle of chairs. 'I'm Professor Conquest and, as you probably know, I'm the vice-chancellor. That means… well, it's not very important what it means. The real point is for you to know I'm an enthusiast for our university. So, you can say: I'm an enthusiast for higher education and for art. Now, if I may, I'd like to begin by asking you to identify yourselves.'

In subdued voices the students dutifully told him their names. Across the room the sixth name rang out like a clarion call to arms: 'And I'm *Juliette Burton.*'

'Thank you everyone,' said Conquest with an avuncular smile when they had finished. 'And sitting over there –' he pointed to where, in a corner of the room, the two members of the review team were seated – 'are Dr Dafna Goldstein and Marta Clamp, observers from the review panel. Welcome!' He cleared his throat and turned his attention back to the students. 'As someone interested in everything that that goes on here, I wanted to use the opportunity of this review to give you a chance to speak about your educational experience. Perhaps I should start by asking you to mark the university from one to ten, where ten is excellent, and zero is, well, not very good!'

There was a moment of strained mirth. 'TEN,' said the students in a ragged chorus as though on some narcoleptic drug.

'Well, that *is* a good start! And what about your experiences of your course? Is it made clear what is expected of you... as students?'

After a little prodding the students began to speak. For fully ten minutes they rambled on, giving Conquest answers as anodyne as his question.

'So,' decided Conquest, bringing things to a halt, 'on the whole, you'd say you're experience of the course has been positive?'

There was a muttered response in the affirmative.

'That's good.' Conquest had lost his focus; his eyes were fixed on Lady Caroline Lamb. He knew his thoughts were invading her consciousness. Her head was lowered in a way that sent her hair tumbling forward; it brought back the image of her standing across from him at his table in the Club Beirut, her limbs deliciously composed. He knew she recognised him from that evening. He knew that she knew he had seen her in that disarming state of near-nudity. She also confirmed to him, by the manner of her sitting there, what he had always believed: that it was their secret; she had told no one of their meeting at the Club Beirut.

'Now, perhaps I can ask you a question? You're Juliette, aren't you?'

If Juliette was startled to have been singled out, she didn't show it. Her delicate features were untroubled as she waited expectantly for what was to come.

'Are the department's technical resources appropriate to the kind of work you want to make; the workshops and so on?'

'Yes, I think they are, very.'

'There's a thought going round that the Frank Brangwyn Building is perhaps no longer fit for purpose.'

'In what way?' she asked, leaning forward, seemingly eager to understand what he was driving at.

'Well, I don't know... not modern. Perhaps a building that allows for more efficient use of space, flexible, not so difficult to clean, would be more appropriate.'

There was a murmur of protest from the students. It went

round the room like a contagion and Conquest realised that the atmosphere would become frigid if he didn't turn the implied threat into a vague-sounding generalisation.

'Well, sometimes new accommodation is an opportunity; an opportunity for something new.'

'We don't want it all spruced up, like the other departments,' said one of the boys.

There was a murmur of assent from the meeting.

'Yes, I quite understand.' Conquest knew better than to allow the perception take hold that he had been rebuffed and he swung his attention back to Lady Caroline Lamb. 'And do you do life drawing from the nude?'

There was a faint stir in the room, as though an indiscretion had been committed. The students' interest had been quickened by Conquest's previous line of questioning, and they sensed the voyeuristic potential of his new topic. Juliette continued to look composed, despite the weight of attention that was now directed at her. Marta Cramp, who had been sitting in the corner with half an eye on her mobile, flicking through texts, failed to hear the question but sensed the subtle change of mood in the room. She looked quizzically at Dafna Goldstein.

'I don't mean to embarrass you, my dear,' said Conquest, still addressing Juliette, a foolish smile on his face, 'but I was wondering if there are some in the department who think the life room is dead, and drawing from the nude not the discipline it once was?'

'"Dear"?' whispered Marta Cramp to Goldstein. 'Did I hear him call her "my dear"?'

Conquest felt it necessary to offer an explanation for his question. 'The nude being such a motif in classical art... I'm curious to know what you think.'

'Well, the practice of observational drawing is rather marginal to my work,' said Juliette with a self-possession that was entirely charming, pitched perfectly between opinion and modest deference, 'but when I have the opportunity I prefer charcoal to pencil.'

Conquest felt himself giving way to the enchantment of the moment. He was engulfed by twin sensations: one, the intoxication of the memory of his night at the Club Beirut and, two, the vivid presence of the same young woman across the room, whom he saw as incomparably beautiful, modest and witty. He would have liked in some way to have succumbed – *it is truly all I wish* – but duty told him that he had to have an answer to his question so that he could move on to matters that would shine a spotlight on Professor Pomfret and his management of the department.

'I think there is vivid beauty to the human form that demands our special attention, don't you? I mean –' he could hear himself prattling on in a churchy voice, but was quite unable to stop himself – 'we're all susceptible to the admiration of the female human form, are we not?'

Across the room Marta Cramp bristled.

'I'm not sure I quite see...' said Juliette falteringly.

'You've seen Goya's marvellous paintings of the clothed and nude Maja? Some say she's a type, not a specific woman, but her flesh makes her so palpable!'

Marta Cramp was beginning to find Conquest's line of questioning sinister. 'Isn't he hounding that student?' she hissed to the frightened rabbit – Dafna Goldstein – sitting next to her. 'That's practically sexual intimidation!'

'It's fascinating,' Conquest continued, unable to escape his train of thought, 'that the nude... that when nude we're still cultural beings, aren't we? I've always rather liked Kenneth Clarke's distinction between "naked" and "nude". "Nude" can suggest the opposite of "prude". Yes, I find "nude" is rather an unfashionable word.'

Marta Cramp had heard enough. 'If I may,' she broke in, her voice a little shrill, 'I would like to ask Juliette, not whether the technical resources of the department are appropriate to the kind of work she wants to make, but if they are *comprehensive*?'

Conquest went rigid. He had been looking expectantly at Lady Caroline Lamb and she had been returning his gaze, apparently with great concentration, but now he had lost her attention to Marta Cramp. It took him but a moment to realise he had been sidelined.

That bloody woman has taken over!

'Oh,' said Juliette, gladly, 'they are, yes.'

Conquest sat there in a daze while the other students talked at length about the cost of oil paint and the bottleneck in the photographic studio. The sense that something had gone awry, that somehow the interrogation of the students had slipped from his hands, enveloped him like a grey fog.

Was it a mistake to address my question to Lady Caroline Lamb? Do they suspect that the great engine of this review was set in motion to create the opportunity for me to speak to her? Look at her now, taking such a lively interest in what that Cramp woman is saying! Such generosity of spirit! Will that dreadful woman ever stop enquiring into these irrelevant, fatuous details?

Time was getting on. Marta Cramp was talking about ideology and the teaching ethos. Conquest felt the touch of despair at the tenor of the students' responses. He had begun to realise that criticisms of the kind he had been hoping for were not going to surface.

I must wrest control of the meeting from that idiotic woman.

Yet, he couldn't help but notice that she had a way of talking to the students he did not. Now she was asking them about access hours to the studios.

I'll tell you what, Marta bloody Cramp, they'll all say they want "twenty-four-seven" and if we paid security to keep them open all the time they'd be empty twenty-three-seven!

Some of the students were becoming restive and he could tell that the meeting was close to having run its course. 'Last but not least,' he announced loudly, 'I think you should be asked if the food in the students' refectory is to your liking?'

Somebody said "pasta sandwiches" and there was a round of muted laughter. Conquest supposed it was some sort of joke, but if it was, he didn't understand it. A few minutes later and it was all over; the students were stretching in nervous release and shuffling out of the room. He caught a glimpse of Lady Caroline Lamb as she made for the door. *She must look back* – so he said to himself, but she didn't.

At least she isn't leaving on the arm of one of those boorish male students whose half-witted observations I've had to endure for the past forty-five minutes.

Suddenly he was alone with his thoughts, and from inside, unbidden, came a cringing sense of embarrassment.

It seems to me, said his Cautious Self, *that you have made an utter fool of yourself in front of members of the panel.*

No, no! disagreed his Bold Self, *that's a ridiculous thing to say. I am not the kind of man who sabotages himself. Don't be deflected from your mission! You have to look deeper to find the rot in this department, that's all. The students are loyal, but theirs is a misguided loyalty. Like Lady Caroline Lamb, they are tolerant and easygoing. Professor Czinc has no such liberality, and the views he gives me before he goes home tonight will be a much better indicator of what is going on in this department than anything I have heard here. He is not the sort of man to have the wool pulled over his eyes. Then we shall see! And I will find a way to get closer yet, and closer still. She is spoken for… by me! And I will pull the department down around their ears if I must.*

THIRTY-ONE

The first day of the panel's deliberations was drawing to a close and Professor Czinc was experiencing a growing sense of unease. True, Professor Dodds of music, who was the kind of academic stalwart one could always rely on, had provided him with several pages of notes that would be useful in drafting sections of the report, but the dark cloud in his sky was Marta Cramp whose appetite for being the panel's dissenting voice seemed unquenchable. So far her relationship with the other members of the panel had been cordial if distant, but from the very start she had picked him out as an adversary. During the course of their discussions she was inclined to dispute every principle he cherished for the proper running of a university department. He found it impossible to predict when next she would strike with her contrarian's views because he could discern no consistent ideological stamp to her attempts to undermine him. His final disenchantment with her came when, as they were taking tea, he asked her to report on her findings at the vice-chancellor's brains trust.

She digested his question for a few moments before leaning forwards as if she wished to attack him across the table. Her brow was creased with disapproval. 'Leaving aside the lovely contributions of the students, *sexual intimidation* is the word that springs to mind!'

'That's two words,' said Czinc weakly.

'A *disgraceful* display of sexual bullying by *that man*!'

Before she could elaborate, Czinc stirred himself to defend Conquest. 'I'm sure the vice-chancellor would not—'

He got no further. Marta Cramp wagged an accusatory finger in his direction. 'Oh, yes! I am shocked that this man is your vice-chancellor.'

Her dudgeon, he reflected, was high and possibly still rising.

'This vice-chancellor of yours… He has little conception of what art is, and he's a bully! He needs to be told that art is not pictures; it is induction, process and election.'

She said this in such guttural fury that Czinc had difficulty making out what she was saying, although there was quite enough in her tone to deepen his alarm.

'He took salacious delight in putting one of the female students on the spot over the distinction between "nude" and "naked". It was nothing short of predatory sexual innuendoes.'

Czinc appealed to Dafna Goldstein. 'I'm sure you found everything… less suggestive?' His slack jaw allowed his mouth to squint at her, hopeful that even if the vice-chancellor had had some kind of… *lapse,* her collegiate sense of loyalty would be enough to ensure that she disassociated herself from Marta Cramp's claim. Little did he know that Goldstein's faculties were engulfed by a fog of anxiety. Being an expert on "The Anthropology of the Self" she was acutely aware of the "Self-in-Others". This term, self-theorised, was what she found most daunting about all social transactions, especially her own. The "Self-in-Others" led – via several chapters of her PhD thesis – to the "Self-under-Review", and here she was in a review in which the self was being… *taken apart, piece by piece!* At the present moment, with Czinc staring at her with half-opened mouth, she had the reoccurrence of the uncanny and unnerving feeling she had had every time he spoke: that a great third eye was scrutinising her. Nearly everything she had experienced during the day had intensified the atmosphere of intrusive surveillance that hung – so she felt – over the proceedings. What threat this implied, or from what quarter it came, she could not say: it was an insidious, indescribable thing. She felt there was a bully in the room, but who it was she could not tell; she feared she was being bullied, but how she did not know. What was clear to her was that Marta Cramp, sitting next to her, provided a sense of refuge – a rock in a sea of maleness.

'Irregularities,' she croaked.

Czinc leant towards her with a quizzical expression. 'I'm sorry?'

'She's saying there were irregularities in the conduct of the meeting,' said Marta Cramp with murderous calm.

'With the greatest respect – and I don't wish to quibble – *you* said that.' He switched his attention back to Goldstein, fixing her with his double stare. 'Please?'

'Now *you* are definitely quibbling,' Marta Cramp insisted, placing herself defensively between him and the quaking Goldstein. 'I heard what she said and "irregularities" is exactly right. The fact is that this brains trust idea – whoever's it was – was squandered in typical male foreplay. Women of our generation do not appreciate this form of social intimidation. It's Freud all over again! You understand, I hope, that I have no objection to sexual relations of whatever kind, but where the economy of power is in play sexual mutuality is quite impossible, and this is *precisely* where abuse and exploitation begin! *Objectification... Scopophilia... Fetishisation...* the man was plainly out of control! Am I making myself clear?'

At this point Czinc, who had a sophisticated grasp of the manners and customs of university liberal arts discourse, understood with the greatest clarity that nothing good could come from continuing with this particular exchange. Further, what was in jeopardy was his hope that she would be willing to follow his lead on major issues relating to the judgment of the panel. 'This all seems to me somewhat beside the point,' he said with infinite weariness. 'It's the Department of Fine Art that we are here to pass judgment on, nothing else.'

'Very well,' said Marta Cramp with fine contempt, 'let's get to the real issues, then. The students seemed hugely supportive of the department and the courses they're on. There, is that what you wanted to hear?'

'And Dr Goldstein, do you concur with that view?'

'I...'

'Can *I* say something?' This question came unexpectedly from another quarter: a member of the panel who had been conspicuously quiet for most of the day. Cyril Tang, senior lecturer in the Department of Psychology, the panel's expert on staff development and the dissemination of good practice in teaching, had finally broken cover. 'Where there is brilliance clearly we can applaud, and here there is some first rate stuff going on... *Right?* But there is very little system to their pedagogy. Their staff development programme is hardly worth the name. I have come to the view that this department is – *right?* – a fly-by-the-seat-of-the-pants organisation. I wish to challenge them with this observation.'

There was a moment's reflective silence before Marta Cramp leapt in. 'This is just another version of the "structure" argument, isn't it`?' she said dismissively. 'They're passionate, you're not!'

'I *beg* your pardon?' Tang looked hurt and clearly had more to say in his deep, seductive baritone.

'All we hear about is "structure",' steamed Marta Cramp, before he could speak. 'The academy is the structure that murders invention, radicality, creativity! How can they even *begin* to achieve if the university doesn't understand that it is the imposition of structure here, there and everywhere that turns everything to mortuary dust? This is the phallic principle in modernity!'

These remarks Czinc did understand, every word. Here, he decided, was more stuff he'd have to put in a box and bury. 'Fair enough, we have disagreement,' he said in his most emollient tones. 'I ask: what collective judgment is possible here?'

Marta Cramp turned to Tang, 'I say: go ahead and ask your question, but don't expect to understand the answer!'

Tang threw up his hands, exasperated and taken aback in equal measure.

'Very well, Cyril,' decided Czinc, speaking with infinite caution, 'tomorrow morning, during the "identification and dissemination of best practice" session with the department, you shall put your observation to them.'

THIRTY-TWO

Professor Czinc felt sapped of energy as he climbed the stairs of the Keynes Building. It had been a long day and he felt the weight of his responsibilities. He noted that Conquest greeted him heartily, and he had no particular wish to spoil his mood.

'So tell me, Andrew, how goes the review?'

Czinc closed his eyes for a moment as though gathering his thoughts. 'I can't say I'm moved by the evidence myself, but to my surprise the department has some support on the panel.'

Conquest's brow darkened. 'How's that?'

'It's their enthusiasm; it's infectious, apparently.'

'Enthusiasm? Enthusiasm for what?'

'Oh…' Czinc made a circular motion with his right hand. 'Their enthusiasm for art, for teaching, for… for students, actually.'

'But Andrew, *the strategic plan is a complaint about cleaning!* They're not in the least bit strategic! Pomfret isn't a strategist. You've seen how flimsy it is; how can that be a basis for success? Without a proper strategic plan how can they know where they're going?'

'I know, I know; I don't get it either. There it is. What can I say? They don't seem to think about going anywhere. It's all *ad hoc*-ery.'

'Are you saying—?'

'I'm not saying anything, but there is a peculiar *esprit* at work that I'm having some difficulty—'

'Andrew, I'm relying on you to keep your panel on the straight and narrow. I don't want any sentimentality.'

Czinc digested that for a moment while he examined his shoes. 'Then there's Marta Cramp,' he said, the name emerging from some dark place in the recesses of his mind.

'Ah, Professor Pomfret's fireship!'

'Apparently not.' Czinc shook his head. 'Somebody suggested her to Pomfret. He'd never heard of her; never met her. I'm inclined to think she's joined the wrong event.'

'Do you mean…? I must say, she was quite the disruptive presence at my brains trust. What are you going to do about her? Can she be managed?'

'She's not the least bit coherent; never had any academic responsibility. One wishes one could discount her views.'

'Ah! Some sort of minority report we can give attention to in due course?'

Czinc looked doubtful. 'She's a persuasive presence, Cliff. I'm not sure she sees herself as a minority. To be frank, she can be quite intimidating.'

'Bullying?'

'Vehemence.'

'Well, we can't have that. The anti-bullying code's on your side.'

'I said "vehemence". That's the difficulty.'

Conquest examined him carefully. *My God,* he thought, *this man's losing it! What has that woman done to him to reduce him to such a state?*

'What *is* her position, do you think?'

'Her idea of a university is, basically, what I would call a retreat, a retreat from the world of sensible propositions.'

'That sounds like Pomfret. You sure he doesn't know her?'

'Yes.' This came out of Czinc's mouth like a bleat.

Conquest frowned. *Czinc is definitely not living up to expectations. I can't believe that one woman, unattached to the university, can be having such an impact on what is, except for her, an internal panel of my senior staff, led by my most respected dean.*

Conquest groped for an explanation. 'Is there something here I'm not getting?' He waited for an answer; Czinc's mouth, he noted, was working fretfully.

'Well Cliff, there is the brains trust.'

The turmoil of emotions that had engulfed Conquest at

the scene of his double failure flooded back. 'Well, yes, bit of a damp squib, and not a particularly instructive intervention by that Cramp woman, not that we could hold *that* against her.'

'No, she thought *you* were being rather… *tough*… on one of the students.'

It was all Conquest could do not to scratch himself vigorously. 'Probing, Andrew, *probing*.'

'Too probing?'

'*Me?* Goodness, cotton wool-itis, Andrew!' He was beginning to feel a crawling sense of discomfort at the amount of attention his little flirtation with Lady Caroline Lamb had attracted. 'I'm not a newcomer to questioning students, am I? Did the Cramp woman claim I was too probing? Is that what she said?'

'Heated words, Cliff, that's all it was, but there were two of them there, you know.'

'*What*: colluding to monster me in some way? That's outrageous!' Conquest was now in extreme discomfort. An image of Lady Caroline Lamb swaying above him on the table at the Club Beirut extruded itself into the forefront of his consciousness. 'An interrogation is an interrogation, and that's all there is to it.'

Czinc did not know what Conquest had in mind by "an interrogation" but he thought it politic to agree with him. 'I understand entirely… *entirely*.'

'Good.' Conquest was determined they should consider the matter closed and he batted it away with a vigorous motion of his arms. 'Work Cramp into a corner, Andrew. You must stiffen the resolve of the other members of the panel; we cannot allow ourselves to wilt before a disruptive outsider.'

Strange to report, Czinc was relieved. He had raised Cramp's reaction to Conquest's conduct at the brains trust and got away with it without it becoming the cause of major unpleasantness. He had, he felt, done his duty, and now he could go home. He hoped that by tomorrow Marta Cramp would have lost interest in the issue and he would do his best to rein in her obstreperous behaviour. On a visit to Taiwan he had experienced a typhoon and, for a reason he could not fathom, he kept thinking that a typhoon was a hurricane by another name.

THIRTY-THREE

Since the review required all the attention of the senior staff of the department (barring those who, at JC McCann's urging, had been given leave for the duration of the review to ensure they did not express inappropriate educational ideas in the hearing of the panel), it was left to a rump of junior, part-time staff to maintain a semblance of teaching-as-normal. As it happened it meant – a rather telling administrative oversight, this – that only one tutor was actually teaching in the studios of the undergraduate course that Monday: Terence Bragg. And the consequence of this was that his tutorial schedule was even more jam-packed than usual, and ran late; it was gone five-thirty before he was finished. For the past couple of weeks he had been eagerly anticipating his date with Juliette. Today was the day and he was dismayed to discover how late he was. He went up to the third floor studio and found her workspace empty. When he enquired he was told that she had left some time ago. Now flustered, he raced back down the stairs and out of the building, hoping to catch her. He thought that perhaps she had decided he had forgotten about their arrangement, but then it occurred to him that perhaps they had agreed to meet at the Students' Union building, not in her workspace. He was almost sure he caught a glimpse of her leaving Tiananmen Square Green, heading in that direction. Yes, he decided, that almost certainly had been the arrangement. As he approached the Students' Union building he saw her standing outside the entrance, talking to Barry Duffy, one of the third year students. He was overcome by a sudden doubt about what he was doing; his courage almost left him. Bolstering his nerve with the thought of the intimacy of their tutorial in front of *Blue Gash*, he went on. Miraculously – so it seemed to him – Barry Duffy walked off before he reached her, leaving her standing alone at the foot of the steps. She saw him coming and broke into a delighted smile; all the confirmation he needed that she had been waiting for him.

'I'm sorry I'm so late. I went up to your space. I thought I was meeting you there.'

Her face clouded. 'No, I'm certain it was here.'

'Yes, no, my mistake. For a second I thought I'd missed you.' He laughed at his own foolishness.

She looked around as though to get her bearings. 'Shall we go in?'

He nodded and followed her up the steps. As they reached the door he reached forward to push it open, suddenly close to her. In the moment of intimacy he caught her scent.

'That perfume is very nice. Is it—'

She laughed. '*Head and Shoulders*: anti-dandruff shampoo.'

'Oh!' He was embarrassed, caught out trying to be gushing; something he knew was not his style.

Through the foyer she led him down a short flight of stairs to the bar, which occupied a large, lower ground floor space at the rear of the building. It was dark and noisy. There was a music system mounted on a dais, manned by several shadowy figures. They were served rapidly and sought a refuge from the music in a distant corner where a few tall slit windows gave a view of the service yard to the rear of the building.

'How are you getting on with your painting?' he asked, once they had found seats.

She looked at him and smiled to herself while she added Coke to her rum. 'The first thing I noticed about you,' she said, 'was your overcoat. Do you remember?'

'No.' He was taken aback that she had not gone along with his opening gambit. 'I mean, I remember my coat, of course, but... When was that?'

'Oh last year, when I first started. I was pretty scared, starting at uni. I thought you looked very sophisticated, like a proper artist, in that coat. Mysterious, I suppose.' She sat back, well contented with her evocation of her first memory of him.

He didn't know what to say. 'When I first saw you...' he began, unsure where his sentence was going. 'Talking of coats, the first time I saw you, you were so well wrapped up you looked like an Oxfam shop.'

She pulled a face of mock indignation. 'Me? Oxfam shop?'

'Yes, it was before Christmas, when the cold weather really got going. It was in the shop. You were buying canvas and paper. I remember you had mittens.'

She looked doubtful. 'I don't remember that. I've never had any mittens.'

'And a manky fur hat pulled down over your ears.'

'I do remember seeing you in the shop. You said, "You've pushed the boat out, haven't you?" And before I could think of a reply you'd gone.' She pulled a face as though the memory irked her.

'I could have been more inane,' he pointed out.

'I'm not so sure. I wasn't pushing; there was no boat.'

'I suppose it was the stuff you were buying.'

'Don't you remember?'

'No,' he lied.

'I wondered if you were talking about my coat,' she said, but immediately waved the subject away, as if she had tired of it. 'So why did you decide…?' She smiled, provoking him with an unfinished question that hinted at her pleasure at having been asked to go for a drink with him.

'When I saw your painting, it turned me on.'

'Oh, yeah?' She looked sceptical. 'How did it do that?'

'It was so ferocious. I was impressed. You being so quiet and well mannered… compared to the rest.' He had foregone the dramatic impulse and said the latter with real feeling. In truth, he had undergone a change of heart since their tutorial. Her use of colour, which he had thought of as garish he now considered her painting's most distinctive feature. 'Some of your year are pretty… well, wankers. I mean, this ceramics business… Thank you for saving me from that.'

'Saving you?' She laughed, delighted by the notion she had saved him. 'How did *I* do that?'

He thought for a moment, wondering how candid he should be. 'I was being ganged-up on, wasn't I?'

She shook her head incredulously. 'I thought you were in total control! You explained it so beautifully. You made me do the painting.'

'No, your response to the project has been *really* considered! I was spoiling for a fight with Matthew, and I behaved badly towards him.'

'Really?'

'I was unkind, when there was no need.' He looked glum.

'I don't think you should reproach yourself. Matthew's a bit of a...'

'I'm not sure I should be in this line of work, you know: teaching. It rots the soul; there need to be more rules when it comes to criticism, don't you think? It's easy to be unfeeling.'

'But you brought my ideas to life.'

'No, no, that was you.'

'I owe it to you... that I did that painting.' She said this very deliberately, as though the full import of what she had said had only just come to her and it startled her.

Her insistence was a great reward and, to a degree, it eased Bragg's feeling of remorse over Matthew. Such was perfection: flattery from a pocket beauty, a gamin sylph, an *ingénue* of the first water. Were the memory of his behaviour to Matthew easier to forgive, he decided, *I would be in seventh heaven.*

'I was in the vice-chancellor's brains trust this afternoon.'

'Oh yeah!' Bragg threw off his introspection. 'Did he try and get you to dish the dirt on us?'

'He got onto me about life drawing. Is that traditional or not? I think he's a bit of a weirdo.' She wasn't going to tell Bragg – or anyone else for that matter – that she had entertained the vice-chancellor as a client. Bragg had no idea she was a professional pole dancer and she honoured absolutely the rules of client confidentiality. The vice-chancellor could count on her discretion about everything and anything that happened at the Club Beirut, but that didn't stop her from expressing an opinion about his behaviour at the brains trust, unaware that in his mind the two were commingled in a way she would have found shocking. 'He talked about Goya! He was going on about the nude. I mean, I think he has a thing about young women.'

'How's that?' said Bragg.

'It was like he was talking about flesh, *naked flesh!* From what I see, men like that are a bit obsessed… in a sexual way. They talk about the nude but they're imagining having some woman stripped naked. There's a big difference.'

Bragg smiled a crooked smile, doubting that Juliette had a very developed understanding of men's sexual proclivities. 'Do you mean a thing about you?'

She thought for a moment before replying. 'I'd be flattering myself to say "Yes", but he does like me, I can tell you that. I don't say he doesn't have cause, in a general sense. I mean: he looks the frustrated type. You know, buttoned up in a suit all his life.' The thought of solitary men in suits brought her back to the circumstances of her employment and suddenly she realised that she had work to go to and already they were running out of time.

He saw her look at her wristwatch. *God,* he thought, *she's hurrying her drink. She's going to leave!*

'I'm sorry, Terry, it's later than I was expecting. I have to go.' She saw how he shifted in discomfort as she pushed aside her empty glass. 'I'm really sorry, but I've got to be somewhere very soon. I'll be late if I don't watch out.' His look of disappointment was all too apparent but she had promised to be at the Club Beirut by seven: Cindy, the other pole dancer, was off and the boss had said, "The other girls *will not do*". She was about to offer Bragg some encouragement when he spoke.

'I know some paintings you should see. Will you come and look at them with me?'

She leaned forward eagerly. 'What d'you think I should see?'

'I'm not saying. You'll have to come with me.'

'All right, I will.' She felt released by her promise and stood up, ready to go.

'I'll see you tomorrow to arrange when.'

She nodded as she pulled her overcoat about her.

'It was nice to see you, Ms Burton,' he said, saluting her. 'I raise a glass to you. May you have a pleasant evening.'

She dipped her chin demurely and gave him a flashing smile.

Bragg watched her cross the bar, thought temporarily blocked.

His drink had become redundant and he swirled the dregs around once, twice, before abandoning them. Suddenly he got to his feet, overcome by a desire for one last glimpse of her. He reckoned she would have a wait at the bus stop and he might catch up with her there. He took the stairs to the entrance of the building two at a time. In the doorway he came to a halt, hoping she might still be in sight. Unable to see her, he backed his hunch and headed for the main road and the bus stops. He walked swiftly and felt sure he must soon overtake her. Sure enough, as he approached the edge of the campus he saw her beyond the railings, but she wasn't at a bus stop: she had her arm raised and was hailing a taxi. He stopped and watched as it drew up and she climbed in.

Never in my life, he thought, *have I ever seen a student hail a cab! Students don't take cabs. I never think of taking one; they're too expensive.*

It reinforced his growing conviction that there was something unusual and mysterious about Juliette. Was she rich? She didn't act, or dress, like one of those rich overseas students who lived in Nell Gwynn House.

Maybe, she has a rich lover. That would explain the self-contained confidence. That's it, she's the beloved of someone powerful, rich and far removed from the narrow confines of a university campus.

He felt crushed by the thought, but intrigued, as if he was discovering in her a secret being more exotic than ever he had imagined.

THIRTY-FOUR

It was 8:30am on the second day of the review and Professor Pomfret was brooding in his office. He looked at the timetable of the day's events on the top sheet of his review documents and for a moment felt an unpleasant sense of vertigo. He pulled himself together, gave the desktop a sharp rap and resolved to navigate through the day as best he could. At that moment there was a knock at the door and, without being invited to enter, JC McCann poked her head in.

''Morning, Archie.'

'Ah, JC! Not a glorious new dawn.'

'I know, this review does grind on somewhat, doesn't it? Never mind, right now Marta Cramp is at work on your behalf. Rest assured that she will not allow them to do a hatchet job on this department.'

'I tremble to think of it! I really would have preferred Perry McBride, you know. He's an old chum and understands these things. He would have done everything with discretion.'

'Believe me, it's warfare and Marta is the nuclear option.'

'That,' said Archie miserably, 'is precisely what I'm worried about.'

'Don't be, she's doing Czinc's head in this very minute. Here's an odd one, Archie: she's been waxing miffed about the behaviour of your boss.'

'My boss?'

'Yes, the vice-chancellor. Seems he hit on one of the students at his stool pigeon exercise.'

'JC, slow down! His what?'

'That brains trust trap he set for our students. You remember, I sent up their names.'

'Yes, I do remember that, JC. It's happened, has it?

'Yesterday afternoon.'

Archie looked crestfallen. 'What's the damage?'

'No damage; own goal. He wouldn't leave her alone; talked dirty in front of everyone.'

'And this Marta Cramp told you this?'

'Yes, she's been telling everyone.'

Pomfret could not approve of a member of the panel leaking, whatever the reason: it was bad form. 'How come she's talking to you in the middle of the review, JC? Most improper!'

'She had a row with Professor Czinc about it, so she says.'

'Did she! Anyway, she must be exaggerating.'

'Oh, I expect so.'

'Picking a fight with the vice-chancellor is not the way to go. I expect Czinc'll sit on it; he's an expert at that sort of thing. Any idea who it might have been? I'm thinking it might be Megan: she's a pert little madam if ever I saw one. Or Lindsey. Now she's really something to set the heart racing.'

'Archie, you're getting carried away. Lindsey wasn't even on the brains trust.'

'Oh, really? Well she should have been.'

JC had a list of all the students on the brains trust. She read out the girls' names: 'Clair, Suzie, Juliette, Megan or Mikko. Marta thinks he's got "a thing".'

'"A thing"? What's that?'

'Yeah, I don't know, it's just what she said. She thinks all men are disgusting, predatory fuck-ups, so watch out!'

For a long minute Pomfret sat with a thoughtful expression. 'Things are not as they were, JC, not at all. I remember the days when members of the professorial class were like gods. *Gods,* JC, *gods!*' He shook his head in despair. 'Now look, I've got to give a performance to the review panel over in the Keynes Building on –' he checked the review timetable – '"identification and dissemination of best practice". *Grief!* And the vice-chancellor's coming over here to tour the building at eleven. I want you to meet him and start the tour if I'm not back. Will you do that for me?'

'Yes, sure. Don't you want to know who caught his eye?'

Pomfret looked at her blankly. 'Whatever for? No JC, but if you find out, make sure she's kept out of sight while he's about. Much the best thing.'

JC looked at her watch. 'You've got twenty minutes before I&D. Any idea what you're going to say?'

'What's I&D?'

'Identification and dissemination.'

'Oh, ha, ha! Very clever. Well, don't worry about me, I've had a few thoughts. Just make sure you meet the vice-chancellor here at eleven. And do we have a life class up and running for him to see on his way round?'

'I think that's all arranged. Derek's booked a model.'

Pomfret rose to his feet with sudden urgency and ushered her towards the door. 'Right, I must prep my identification and thing, so leave me to it.'

On her way upstairs to the second year studios, JC ran into Terry Bragg.

'Listen Terry, you were in the studios yesterday, weren't you? Know anything about the vice-chancellor hitting on one of our students at his brains trust?'

'You mean Juliette?'

'Do I, Terry? Juliette Burton? Oh, happy day! How come she's been talking to you?' Her voice had become stern. 'She's one of my girls.'

Bragg was annoyed by the implication that Juliette had no business sharing confidences with him; once more JC was playing on his sense of guilt. It was something she had a trick of doing. 'I don't know, JC. We had a chat. No harm done, I suppose.'

'Let's hope so. What's her story?'

'Oh, he went on about the nude. She felt he was more than a little persistent.'

'Relentless?'

'She thinks he's got a crush on her, salacious turn of mind as well. Dirty old man stuff, by the sound of it.'

'That's interesting, Terry. "Relentless, salacious, dirty old man." Sort of thing someone in a position of authority ought to know about, don't you think? Duty of care and all that?'

Bragg was beginning to find JC's presumption that the only basis on which they could converse was one of jocular menace exasperating. 'I don't know, JC. We're all in love with Juliette, aren't we? You're her year tutor, I'll leave it to you.'

'Oh, *catty!* Always better to pass on these sorts of things, Terry. Line manager knows best. Lovely sprat to catch a mackerel!' She gave a raucous laugh and continued on her way up the stairs. 'Thank you, Terence, and good day.'

THIRTY-FIVE

Professor Czinc had left Professor Pomfret's presentation on "the identification and dissemination of best practice" early. He had done so in order to join the vice-chancellor for his tour of the Frank Brangwyn Building. As he crossed the campus he found himself reflecting on how much he regretted seconding Cyril Tang – the review panel's expert on staff development and quality assurance – to the task of chairing the meeting. He had every reason for believing that his colleague had the expertise to guide the discussion, but what he had witnessed had greatly disappointed him. He suspected Tang of a failure of nerve, and to know the reason why one had to look no further than Marta Cramp's verbal trouncings. The day had started with her throwing her weight about in the panel's early morning progress meeting where she had continued to insist that everything he considered anomalous about the Department of Fine Art's educational philosophy were in some way a critique of the evils of universities. If anything, her virulence seemed to have intensified overnight.

'This is what happens when politicians start taking an interest in art,' she cried at one point, as though in torment. 'They must tame it, regulate it and turn it into entertainment: that is the impulse of politicians. It's cruelty to wild beasts!'

'Might I suggest,' remonstrated Tang, 'that that's a trifle extreme?'

Czinc had a nose for such things; what he suspected was actually the case: Marta Cramp had come to see Tang as one of her pet hates: the lecture theatre performer, the Lothario of the Lectern. She stared through him as she replied, as though she had turned him to vapour. 'You're all happy enough to live with capitalism; mistakenly, it seems, you believe you can tame the whirlwind. We artists know we have to fight for our cause, or we will be found wanting!'

Tang gazed at her with the silent reproach of a wounded animal. Dafna Goldstein was still possessed by the spirit of a frightened rabbit and could scarcely be expected to utter a word. Professor Dodds was so busy writing his notes he might as well have been absent.

In contrast, when it came to "identification and dissemination of best practice", Professor Pomfret was a sprightly barque clefting through this sea of troubles. He introduced his presentation by saying, "Well, everybody does their best, so best practice is everywhere, and other than that we don't differentiate". This simply would not do in the circles where identification and dissemination of best practice were taken seriously. Even so, Tang had only half-heartedly taken control of proceedings, and inexplicably failed to challenge Pomfret about his department being "a fly-by-the-seat-of-the-pants organisation". Instead he had allowed him to waffle on to no great effect with barely an interjection. Watching from the sidelines, Czinc had little doubt that Pomfret would continue in the same vein until his allotted time ran out.

Pomfret's notion of pedagogic discourse was one thing but Marta Cramp's depredations on the panel were altogether another. Since its members were now, at every turn, caving in to her, Czinc was beginning to despair of curbing her ideological impositions. Never had he come upon such an extreme example of the polemical madwoman. It induced a pang of melancholy in him to think that he had been landed with her at a moment full of potential for professional gratification, if not advancement. Although he was not entirely aware of it, his confidence in himself as the supreme institutional animal had temporarily taken a beating. What he *did* realise was that the review had reached some sort of crux and he had no doubt that the cause was Marta Cramp. At least, he reflected, she was no longer castigating the vice-chancellor for his performance at the brains trust.

As he approached the Frank Brangwyn Building he was turning over in his mind the degree to which he would have to bite his tongue when Pomfret came over to join them. Pomfret, he reflected, had something of the fifteen-year-old autistic boy about him. He was too much of a logical animal to believe in shamanism, but somehow he suspected Pomfret of it. Why else would staff and students follow him? It was a puzzle!

The sight of the vice-chancellor striding across Tiananmen Square Green interrupted his reverie. Conquest's evident self-confidence made him feel wan and shabby. *Now that,* he said to himself, *is the supreme institutional animal, a man without doubt!*

'Good morning Andrew,' called Conquest as soon as he was within hailing distance. 'Sorry to take you out of your review meeting, I know you're very busy.'

Czinc tried his best to pull a cheerful face. 'Not at all, Cliff. Only too glad to find you taking an interest.'

They were now close enough to lower their voices.

'So, tell me,' said Conquest, 'since you've already had a good look round fine art's accommodation –' he indicated at the Virginia creeper-clad façade of the Frank Brangwyn Building – 'is it fit for purpose, or should we be looking for something better?'

'I think the way it's presently used would probably be condemned out of hand by any self-respecting health & safety officer,' said Czinc, trying to match Conquest's mood with a touch of forced levity. 'Last week, I'm told, a student completely blocked the fire escape between the first and second floors, doing some kind of performance with an upright piano.'

Conquest gave him a confidential look. 'There's a redundant Church of England ladies' teaching academy in Potters Bar the DOE wants us to take under our wing. Rationalisation, you know. It might be an idea to move them out there. Plenty of space, all at ground floor level. They could spread out as much as they liked; bring a little sophistication to Potters Bar, where things have gone a little... stale. I think fine art might be a good ambassador for our way of doing things... in the arts, you know, in the arts.' Conquest paused as though to make sure Czinc had understood the limits he placed on fine art's ability to represent the qualities of their university.

Despite the ill-feelings towards the department that the review had engendered, and forgetting for a moment the several monologues his wife had suffered on what he had disparaged as "that man Pomfret's asinine conceits", Czinc still had sense enough to recognise that this would be widely interpreted as an unjust act. 'Whatever else, they do see themselves as part of the metropolis, Cliff.'

'Oh, I know, I know. Nothing enforced you know, Andrew. Consultations with stakeholders before we commit to anything. Probably take a year or so before we're ready to demolish, what with planning permission and the like.' Conquest took a vigorous intake of breath and – so it seemed to Czinc – took aim at the Frank Brangwyn Building.

'Demolish it?' said Czinc, thoroughly startled, for it was the first he had heard of such a thing.

'Fewer faculties, bigger departments, Andrew; that's the way to go. Digital hub! I see you doing good work in reshaping this university.' He nodded sagely.

'Well, I appreciate you confidence in me, vice-chancellor. But first things first.' In his mind's eye Marta Cramp had taken on the form of the jaws of the killer whale he'd taken his children to see at the National History Museum. He was, as he saw it, about to do battle with a behemoth. He smiled wanly. 'Let's get through this review. Professor Pomfret's been leading a very enlightening session on identification and dissemination of best practice.'

Conquest understood they were trafficking in irony. 'That good, eh?'

'Not his forte.'

'Not really head of department material, is he? I mean, not in a modern sense. Might have sufficed once upon a time, but not now, not with the imperatives of today. Takes a man of the world... or woman.'

'What do any of us academics know of the world?' said Czinc, with the pathos of a wounded sheep. 'We, of necessity, must plough a lonely furrow.' He wasn't quite sure why he'd succumbed to poetic melancholia. His grandfather had known Freud and, contrary to what he had just said, he considered himself a man of broad accomplishments and worldly understandings.

Conquest seemed to feel the need to comfort him. 'I think you can exempt yourself from such judgments, Andrew,' he chided.

Czinc shook his head, still overcome by the tragedy of his situation. 'The problem with art is that it's not a proper subject, in the university sense. I still think that's what we're all struggling with.'

'Quite right. I hope your panel will reflect on that. A university must be led by worldly folk. It's true that some of those we lead take advantage of our endeavours, but there must be men – and women – of experience in command. It's the public sector where innovation and endeavour are most at home, I always think. Pomfret is unworldly, no doubt. I cannot abide those that place personal interest above the interest of the collective, whatever we may mean by that. It was the same with the FA. Some of those footballers… It's news flow, you see; it's too much for some.'

Czinc had a feeling he had been trumped and took it upon himself to steer Conquest back to their immediate concerns. 'Pomfret'll be here soon; the meeting was about to wrap up. I'll take you to his office. He said one of his staff would meet us there.'

'No need for you to come. You've important things to do, a panel to muster.'

'Oh! Of course, if you think not. Let me show you where to go.'

'Thank you, Andrew, *tell me* where to go; I'll find my own way.'

By that point they were standing before the steps of the Frank Brangwyn Building. Czinc saw the vice-chancellor was determined to return him to the fray and he pointed out the window of Pomfret's office to the left of the main entrance.

For some reason Conquest grasped his hand and shook it. 'Thank you, Andrew,' he said gravely.

Czinc watched him climb the steps, reluctant to make his way back to the Keynes Building, knowing that Marta Cramp awaited him.

THIRTY-SIX

As soon as Conquest entered the Frank Brangwyn Building he was struck by the atmosphere: the faint knockings of history seemed to come at him from the walls. Here was the Arts and Crafts porters' lodge of exquisite workmanship and there the lift – barely large enough for two – with its retractable diamond grill doors. The corridors leading left and right were paved with marble and there were plaster cornices and big paneled doors. Altogether too fussy for Conquest's taste; he preferred swept-clean, Mies van der Rohe simplicity, which he thought of as the house style of The Modern University As Teaching And Learning Machine. He turned left and almost immediately found himself at Pomfret's office door. He gave it a cursory tap and walked in, thinking how good it felt to be on Pomfret's own turf.

How understanding I'll be as he shows me around. How carefully, how judiciously I shall listen to his explanations as we walk through the studios! How I shall smile at his droll, inconsequential asides! How carefully I shall inspect—

Standing in the middle of the room, studying him uneasily was Lady Caroline Lamb. For a moment Conquest was at a loss. 'Am I in the wrong room?'

'I was asked to wait here for someone,' said Juliette, looking at him steadily, 'to show him round the department.'

'Well, I am expecting to be shown round. I didn't expect…'

What in God's name! That man Pomfret knows! How did this happen?

For a moment he felt overwhelmed.

No, no, straighten up, this is an opportunity. You have this department totally within your grip. If Pomfret wants to act the procurer, let him! Stay cool; see where this goes.

'Well, Juliette, what a surprise.' He took her in with a vivacious smile. 'Quite unexpected.'

'I was asked if I'd guide a VIP… I had no idea…'

'Well,' responded Conquest warmly, 'as I'm very much an admirer, I'm delighted by Professor Pomfret's choice. If I…' He hesitated, for once uncertain about the wisdom of what he was about to say. 'If I was over-pressing yesterday afternoon, I apologise. I didn't mean to put you on the spot. I feel I over-did my enthusiasm for life drawing. I know you said you don't, but perhaps I could see what you *are* doing in your studio?'

She seemed doubtful as to whether that would be appropriate. 'I suppose…'

'I suspect, Juliette, that there's a plot afoot to bring us together. I think, in the circumstances, we should allow it to unfold and prove the conspirators misguided.'

Conquest saw her expression had clouded over and he assumed that *he* was the cause. 'I'm sorry if you find this upsetting—'

'No, no, it's all right. You're the only one who knows… about the club. And I don't want the others to find out. It's private.'

'I see. Well, your secret's safe with me, of course,' he said gallantly. 'I hope you don't think it's something to be ashamed of, I thought you were glorious.'

This made her laugh and for a moment she hid her face behind her hand.

'Come on, let's get out and about before we give them cause to think badly of us!'

They left Professor Pomfret's office and began their tour, Juliette in the lead. She took him upstairs to the first floor where the studio accommodation started. They walked through every room, where, despite JC's entreaties, students were almost entirely absent. Conquest delighted in poking into the corners and cupboards, anything to slow their progress. Not that he didn't give Juliette a great deal of attention too. He watched her slyly, not wanting to make her self-conscious about the way she charmed him. Their tour seemed the most immense fun. Beyond that simple thought his mind was in turmoil.

Here she is, next to me, walking around this building as naturally as if we'd know one another for years.

He wanted very much to touch her; just to brush against her would be good enough, and he managed it rather adroitly when they were passing through a doorway together. The feel of her coat was electric, as though its static charge had gone to earth through his fingers.

'I've been meaning to come back and see you again,' he said suddenly.

'You mustn't do that,' she said shyly.

He felt dizzy, with her near to him he could not find any sense of equilibrium; the plenitude of his feelings, he felt, was unbalancing his reason.

What are these feelings? Why have I never felt them before, even when I was young and free to spend my time with women? Before I met Marj, of course. And why doesn't the thought of Marj make me feel guilty about this intense...?

He did not know how to describe what he felt. He had a picture of himself that almost made him laugh:

I'm living this moment so vicariously I'll turn into a dry husk and blow away on the wind when our tour finishes. I have crested a detestable impediment. I fly, and as I fly I gaze into the abyss through a cleft in a sunlit field of clouds. It's a sublime glimpse of a gateway to nothing. How easily I've turned the tables on those wanting to trap me in a sordid assignation of their devising!

'Is it wrong to find you so attractive? I can't see that it's anything more than the way you might feel about a beautiful picture or a divine psalm.'

She seemed not to notice that he had spoken. It occurred to him that the speech had been in his head.

Why am I comparing her to a psalm?

He wondered if he should be worried that something in him was unravelling.

What is it I'm in the grip of? Am I really manufacturing it myself, or is it she?

He followed her down the corridor wondering, in his literary style, whether he was lion or lamb, base or beatific.

Juliette had come to a halt at a doorway at the end of the corridor. There was a semi-circular fanlight above the door and through it Conquest could see enough to tell him that they were outside a large, high-ceilinged room.

'What's in there?' he asked.

'It's the project room. It's sometimes used for life drawing. Shall we look in?'

'Ah, the famous life room! Of course.'

Juliette opened the door. She stood on the threshold, holding the door ajar. Conquest came up behind her and looked over her shoulder. He caught a glimpse of a thicket of easels round an empty podium and beyond a large, heavy table. And at the table, sitting on chairs, and seated on the table itself, were a number of disgruntled looking students, in poses of extreme lassitude, staring at what they seemed to consider an intrusion.

'Sorry,' said Juliette, and as she pulled the door to she stepped back onto Conquest's toes. Conquest did not fall back but deftly he encircled her waist with his right arm and put his lips into the nape of her neck. Such bliss it was! It was over in a moment: he had released her and stepped away.

That was a nuzzle, not a kiss.

She turned to face him with an expression that was startled but not hostile.

'Who were they?' he asked blankly.

'I don't know,' she said, conspiring to ignore what had just happened.

'They were oriental.'

'Yes, I think Chinese.'

'Perhaps I should make sure.' He cast about fretfully. 'Did I break the rule?'

'What rule?'

A note of tenderness had entered his voice. 'You know, the no touching rule.'

'Yes.' She laughed lightly. 'I suppose you did.'

'Well then, I should be punished.'

'You should be fined.'

'Yes, fined. With twenty eight days to pay.'

'No, not twenty eight days; it's instant.'

'Like the crime.'

'It wasn't a crime; it was flattery… of a sort.'

'Very adult of you to see it like that. I think *I* was being juvenile.'

'You were. You see, age and conduct at odds.'

'Perhaps we could agree to meet in the middle.'

'One day, perhaps. I'd have to check my bank balance first.'

'Surely I don't pay the fine to you? I never heard of a justice system like that!'

'It's the Club Beirut system: invented by plaintiffs.'

'Ah yes, I can see they would expect something for their distress.'

'Tax-free.'

'Tax-free? That's *too much*! Is it always tax-free?'

'No, but until I sell my first painting I'm tax exempt. And it has to be a perfect painting.'

'I'm sure it will be. What were those Oriental boys doing in there? Were *they* trying to paint the perfect picture?'

'I expect so; that's what we're all trying to do. Here comes Professor Promfret. Ask him, he'll tell you it's so.'

The corridor was suddenly full of bustle, the building resounding as if a hundred extras had been summoned by an impresario's hand. A stream of students leaving a seminar or lecture came toppling down the stairs. Pomfret emerged from their midst, heading in their direction. Much closer to, a squat, blonde woman Conquest didn't know had appeared at a doorway.

'Good morning, vice-chancellor, welcome to Frank Brangwyn,' the woman said with an asinine smirk.

Conquest nodded in a trance.

Damned woman! Our moment of rapport was exceptional, wasn't it? Maybe I'm fooling myself, but didn't our conversation have the perfection of a scene from a romantic comedy? I know which one too: Audrey Hepburn and Cary Grant in Charade. *I saw it on my Gran's TV years ago. The only thing is, Cary Grant didn't have a gran, only Archie Leach had a gran. The distinction is important to my self-image: am I an Archie Leach or a Cary Grant? Remember, no back story! Christ, is that woman leering at me? I suppose I'll have to notice Pomfret! Anyway, there were twenty-five years between Grant and Hepburn; that's probably about our age difference.*

'Good morning, vice-chancellor,' said Pomfret as he bustled up. 'I see JC's been showing you round.'

JC gave Conquest another idiotic grin.

'Actually, she's just joined us,' said Conquest, refusing to look her in the face.

Pomfret felt the awkwardness in the air and his sense of propriety told him that he was not about to question Juliette Burton about why she was present. 'JC's my right hand man,' he explained, gushing to hide his discomposure. 'Invaluable support in running the department. Done a sterling job in preparing for the review.'

'We have *not* finished.' Conquest snapped. '*I* was hoping *Juliette* would take me to see the studios on the next floor.'

Pomfret gave JC a quizzical look.

Her grin had frozen. 'I was detained.'

'I see.' Pomfret made a pantomime of checking his watch. 'Well, well, time *is* getting on. I'd very much like to show you our foundry.' He smiled winningly at Conquest.

It came to Conquest that if he didn't exercise self-restraint Pomfret would recognise piqued ardour. He swallowed his annoyance. 'Well, all right, of course.'

'I'm sorry I wasn't here myself for your tour, vice-chancellor, but as you know I was with the review panel.' Pomfret paused as though reflecting on his management of the review. 'Not that you'd get lost with Juliette on hand.'

Since Conquest was sure Pomfret had tried to lure him into an indiscretion, he found it disconcerting that he could not detect the least hint of irony in his blandishments. 'She's been a great help,' he said faintly.

'But perhaps we should get on; there's a great deal to see.'

'I rather gathered from Professor Czinc,' said Conquest, pulling himself together in the face of Pomfret's laughable eagerness to be obliging, 'that your meeting was due to end some time ago.'

'Ah, yes, coffee intervened,' confessed Pomfret with a contrition that Conquest found as suspect as his sincerity.

'Well, well, we'd better do as you say!' decided Conquest. Lady Caroline Lamb, he realised, would have to be left behind. The thought was a dismal one, but he hid his feelings. 'Thank you, Juliette,' he said, turning to her and trying to erase from his mind the presence of the others, 'but it seems you have been out-ranked. Another time.' He gave her a tight grimace of a smile and turned back to the others. 'Lead on and show me your foundry.'

Suddenly Conquest was so eager for action he would have taken Pomfret by the elbow had he not already gone ahead. He chased him along the corridor, gripped by an anger-induced wish to damn all academics to hell. Despite his fury a moiety of self-pity also floated in the air. It was as if for a brief moment fate had led him towards glorious, effulgent emotions but then the nature of his position and his responsibilities had reclaimed him.

Is it my destiny to be stuck with fading memories and dreams of What Might Have Been? I shit on Pomfret's head!

THIRTY-SEVEN

Juliette was left standing in the corridor. Nobody could have read a thing from the faint blush of pink to her face, but she was wondering how indignant she should be. She had come in early at no small inconvenience to herself in response to JC's plea that the studios should be populated at all times during the review. JC had stopped her in the corridor as she made her way to her studio and asked her to act as a guide for an unspecified VIP. She was beginning to suspect that she had been left in Professor Pomfret's office as bait. So this was the man who had seen her at the Club Beirut and cross-questioned her about the nude! Could it be, she wondered, that there was a plot afoot to lure him into a more serious indiscretion after the way he had picked her out for special attention at the brains trust? It seemed so.

If she was right, it followed that, in the short time since the previous evening, Terry Bragg had passed on to JC what she had told him in the students' union bar. She was saddened to think that he had betrayed her when she had believed they were sharing confidences. Her disappointment was compounded by her vexation at finding herself in the kind of machinations that the proprietors of the Club Beirut occasionally tried on wealthy tourists, although at least, she reflected, her experiences there meant she was inured to men who over-stepped the mark and practised at disentangling herself without causing offence.

'Good girl!' said JC under her breath as she passed. She slid her arm round her shoulder in a casual embrace. 'It would be nice to chat, but I must catch up.'

THIRTY-EIGHT

Conquest completed his tour of the Frank Brangwyn Building in a whirl. He expended energy furiously in his desire to appear fascinated by daubs of paint on walls, rubbish left behind doors and every inchoate artistic tableau they came upon. He was breathless by the time they reached the foundry in the basement. For his part, Pomfret – not infrequently prompted by JC – was assiduous in furnishing him with an answer to his every query. At last, the tour over, and all of them quite exhausted, Conquest had one final question for Pomfret.

'Tell me, who were those Oriental students I saw in the life room? They didn't have a model.'

Pomfret seemed perplexed by the question and, seeing his discomfort, JC stepped in. 'Models are notoriously unreliable, vice-chancellor.'

'But who exactly are they?'

'The models?'

'No, the students.'

'They must have been our "study in London" certificate students,' she said with a winning smile.

'Ah, yes,' agreed Pomfret hastily, 'our "study in London" certificate students.'

Conquest looked at them and felt, not for the first time that morning, stirrings of incredulity. He'd never heard of such a qualification, but he had not the least desire to pursue the matter now that he was at the threshold of the Frank Brangwyn Building and almost at liberty to go. Little did he think that he was about to miss his last chance to intervene in an academic injustice he would hear a great deal more of before the day was out.

'I trust their model has turned up; they seemed at a loose

200

end.' It was Conquest's final shot and it fell short; he could see from the look on their faces that his hosts had already bid him farewell. Finally free of their ministrations he stood in the middle of Tiananmen Square Green and gazed up at the Frank Brangwyn Building thinking what a fine site it would make for the digital hub.

Stop being so reasonable, so mild mannered. Don't you dare allow them to get away with their little intrigue! Swear on the withered hand of Saint Xavier that you'll tear that building down around the ears of Professor Archie Pomfret.

He straightened his tie uneasily.

By the calculations of accountants and the devices of lawyers, the Frank Brangwyn Building shall come down, whosoever Frank Brangwyn is... or was. Fuck, that sounds weak.

THIRTY-NINE

Conquest's rancour did not abate quickly. It was two o'clock and students were making their way to lectures before he could reflect that, after all, he had dealt adroitly with the tawdry embarrassment that Professor Pomfret had tried to trap him in.

What's more, it was magnificent to have at last found myself with Lady Caroline Lamb, even if she was only half there, a promise veiled, cruelly masked by that coat! Why does she wear clothes too big for her? Come to think of it, I owe nothing but thanks to Professor Pomfret and his gang. How wonderful the aroma of her hair! Now I have to plan my next step, now I have to secure another meeting with her, somewhere away from the university, somewhere glamorous. Perhaps the Caprice!

Much as he would have liked to have spent the time dreaming of Lady Caroline Lamb, he had matters to deal with. He devoted the afternoon to making the final arrangements for the following day's meeting of the university's senate. Since it was his first meeting he wanted to be certain he made a forceful impression: a leader with energy, drive and imagination. Twice he spoke to Professor "Perk" Hingley on the phone to ensure that they agreed on what would be the outcome of each item on the agenda.

Oh no, I won't allow the assorted worthies and pliant functionaries of senate to go off in some direction I don't approve of. While I'm vice-chancellor they have to understand what their role is: follow your leader!

Conquest intended to ask the meeting to approve in principle the Conquest Digital Hub, not that he thought it was quite time to attach his name to the project; that moment would come, but not until the first sod was turned. It was item three on the agenda under the innocuous sounding heading of "estate developments". He spent more than an hour drafting his arguments for an immediate start to the project.

What cloud computing is to all those Facebook nitwits, the digital hub will be to our university! Central overview of the flows of information, a storehouse of every email sent by every member of the university. By their emails shall ye know them!

By the time it was four o'clock he was feeling pleased with his preparation. Unfortunately any fantasy about a moment for tea and biscuits was given short shift by the arrival of Carole.

'The president of the Students' Union is requesting an urgent meeting. Apparently there's a sit-in in the library.'

'Sit-in?' Conquest's vision of himself sequestered in the eyrie of the master-planner, far removed from the humdrum lives of students, evaporated.

'Yes, an occupation. The head librarian's asking whether she should close.'

'Close? No, fine, tell her the library should be kept open. Tell her to ignore it and carry on as usual.'

Carole regarded him with a vaguely exasperated air. 'I think you might want to reconsider that view.'

'Oh? Why?'

'They're overseas students. She says they refuse to leave.'

'Good God! Really?' Conquest rose to his feet and paced back and forward between his desk and the sofas, his brow furrowed. 'What overseas students, exactly?'

'I expect Rob Mission has the details, don't you?'

However much Conquest might loath Mission and wish to avoid meeting him, this, he realised, was something he would have to take seriously. Experience told him that because students were normally so supine, grievances that pushed them to the extent of demonstrating were immensely difficult to resolve because the stakes had already become so high. All this was doubly so with overseas students who were generally the most assiduous and pacific members of the student body – as well as being the university's most important source of non-governmental funding.

'Overseas… occupying the library?' Conquest intoned the words as though it pained him to say them.

Carole gave him a silent look of animosity. 'He's outside, waiting to brief you. Why don't you hear what he has to say?'

'All right, wheel him in. I suppose you'd better bring us some tea.'

Even though Mission had only just begun his term as president, their relationship was already acrimonious. Relations had soured over the flying of the Palestinian flag atop the Keynes Building. Mission saw himself as the protector of the status quo of funding top-ups and other concessions that the Students' Union had wrung from the last administration and which Conquest was now threatening to dismantle. Conquest considered Mission to be one of those easy-talking pipsqueaks who get on in the public sector, but end up being a blemish on its good name. He could imagine him taking some hospital trust down the road to ruin; to endless recriminations about surgical fatalities due to his poor management of incompetent surgeons. At heart, Conquest disliked him because of the legitimacy his elected status gave him.

The only good thing about him is that he's still too new to the post to understand the extent of his powers, especially his powers to disrupt the smooth running of my university when I'm working to put the bloody thing back on its feet.

'Carole,' he said, his thoughts shooting off at a sudden tangent. 'I'd be informed if the police had any undercover officers on the campus, wouldn't I?'

She looked at him with an opaque smile. 'You'd have to ask them that. I wouldn't know. Dennis doesn't discuss things like that with me. He wouldn't, would he?'

'Yes, of course. But I'm asking about the principle. Would I be informed? Somebody should know.'

'We haven't been informed, as far as I know. But, then, why would they want us to know?'

Conquest was put out. 'Protocol, I suppose. An act of courtesy.'

She gave him a withering look. 'We might leak.'

The way she said it made Conquest feel that somewhere someone in authority had decided he was prone to leaking. He found himself scrambling to affirm his credentials as a man of probity. 'The question occurred to me the other day, for some reason,' he explained at a rush. 'I was thinking only of serious subversive behaviour, you know. The Students' Union would not be difficult to infiltrate.'

She considered what he had said with a sardonic smile on her face. 'Dennis thinks civilians are best left in the dark,' she said finally and went back into the outer office to summon Mission, leaving Conquest to reflect that she was a real ball breaker.

A few moments later she ushered Mission in: a scrawny young man with glasses, a goatee and, in Conquest's opinion, too much of a spring in his step, a certain spry energy that belied his shabby clothes and broken-down trainers.

'Hello Rob, have a seat. How are things settling down? Support staff up to the mark?' Conquest gave him the benefit of his most unctuous smile. 'I hear we have a problem.'

'*You* have a problem, chancellor.'

I see, and *are* things settling down?'

'Yes, fine, but there's a dispute brewing.'

'I heard. What's up in the library?'

'A group of Chinese students, backed by the rest of the overseas students. They say they're been cheated. Complaints blocked by the academic registrar.'

'Chinese students? That's interesting. How come?'

'They've been complaining since the beginning of the academic year and no one has lifted a finger to help them.'

Conquest regarded him with a growing sense of alarm. 'All right, let's get specific, Rob; which department are they in and what's gone wrong? You know our university and its academic provision as well as I do.'

'They're on a "study in London" course. One of them has a panga.'

'A panga?'

'That's a kind of machete.'

'I know what a panga is, Rob.'

'It's the pre-postgraduate certificate in fine art. In the prospectus there's an explicit promise that they will experience contemporary art making as it is found in London.'

'I see, Rob.' Conquest's brow darkened.

That study in London thing! The bloody Department of Fine Art. I might have known!

'I think I saw these students this morning. Is this anything to do with the fact that the Department of Fine Art is, at this very moment, under review?'

Mission looked perplexed. 'No, it's not. Why would you think that? Since they're here in London these students expected to find themselves mixing with Western – preferably British – students. Instead they're in a student group that's entirely Chinese. They say how can they learn about art in London if they never meet any actual British or Western students?'

Conquest looked at him earnestly. 'Did they come here to learn from the students, Rob? I thought students came here to be taught by members of the academic staff.'

'Well, chancellor, they see themselves as on a cultural exchange and they're not getting any.'

'Actually, it's vice-chancellor, Rob, *vice*-chancellor. Her Royal Highness is the chancellor, if you recall.'

'The point is—'

'Yes, I understand what you're saying. A cultural exchange has to be based on something tangible, and students need to engage in all manner of exchanges, including those with other students.'

'As it stands, this course is a racially-driven construct, excluding precisely – *precisely* – those exchanges. They're ghettoised contrary to the dictates of the European Court of Human Rights.'

Racially-driven construct! Begrudgingly Conquest had to admire Mission's attempt at rhetorical intimidation: the incisive "precisely", and the way he had trotted out sanctimonious objections to supposed racism and ghettoisation. As it happened, he had a fine appreciation of their strategic use from his own experience of deploying them. It all went to strengthen his instinct that Mission was a noxious twerp and the incident had the potential to cause wider ructions unless something strenuous was done.

'I doubt they're ghettoised in a way that is contrary to the dictates of the European Court of Human Rights, Rob.'

European Court of Poppicock, he thought testily.

'Look, Rob, I saw these students this morning and they did seem a little… socially excluded. I would have spoken to them had I known… You make a number of good points and I don't doubt there's something here that needs to be put right but we must avoid a rush to judgment without a complete understanding of the academic thinking behind this course. I can't proceed until I've had a chat with the academic registrar and the head of department. Heard both sides of the story, as it were.'

'I can only point out that overseas students are an important constituency of the university, chancellor, and we can't condone any recruitment of students that's racially-driven. We'll be taking action in sympathy with them, unless there's some resolution of the sit-in in the next twenty-four hours, and that's non-negotiable.'

The little ratbag! Now he's giving me deadlines! Look at you, you undersized numbskull. You can't get on unless you can look good in a suit, and you won't, ever. You'll probably always have your tie slack and your cheap M&S shirt collar askew. Better humour the bastard.

'I'm not saying you don't have due cause, Rob. It's just got to be left in my hands for a while so I can check that implementation has been fully aligned to the institutional agenda. Look, give me some time to get to the bottom of this. Come back and see me in a couple of hours – let's say half past six – and we'll have something concrete to talk about. In the meantime can we get the chap with the panga to lower the threat level?'

Mission shrugged. 'They're barricaded in so…'

'Barricaded! You mean there's an *actual* barricade?'

'Certainly: books.'

'Isn't there any way you could persuade them to reactivate the material aspects of their protest at a more… *appropriate* moment?'

Mission sniggered. 'That's not going to happen, not until the university moves on their grievances.'

He has the peevish look of the stubborn, thought Conquest. 'I'm not unwilling to act, Rob, I'm just unwilling to act without understanding what's gone wrong. If they could desist until—'

'That won't shift them; I couldn't persuade them to do anything on that basis.'

'All right, thank you, Rob.' Conquest had decided that now was not the time to parley. 'Our library users will have to put up with the disruption. Come back later and we'll sort this out. You have my word.'

When the door had closed behind him, Conquest did a little enraged war dance. He was still pacing up and down furiously when Carole came in carrying a tray with the tea he had ordered, which she placed on his desk.

'Do you need anything else?' said Carole, examining him as though through a long cardboard tube.

'I'll say I do! Get the academic registrar over here. Tell him its urgent; he's to drop what he's doing.'

She looked at him critically. 'Are you going to talk those Chinese lads out of there? You know what the Chinese are like: they're a danger to themselves.'

Conquest gave her a dark look. 'I do *not* meet with students, especially those setting up barricades and carrying weapons. They've a panga in there! I hate to think what a self-respecting health & safety officer would make of that!'

She looked him up and down with a vague and insolent air as though she were thinking that Dennis, her husband, would have gone straight in there and knocked heads together. 'I'll get Dr Cornish to drop everything, then,' she said in tones that indicated it wasn't her chosen way forward, and she made for the door in the haughty way he found particularly annoying. 'Oh,' she added as she was on the point of closing the door, 'Professor Czinc is waiting to see you. Apparently you asked him to report before he leaves.'

Conquest made a weary beckoning gesture. 'Send him in.'

Czinc entered. He carried with him a fine mist of apology and Conquest sensed he was about to say something abject.

'Vice-chancellor,' he began by way of a greeting.

'Andrew, please call me "Cliff",' Conquest reminded him as he waved him to a seat on one of his sofas. 'Have some tea? Are you aware that some fine art students are staging a sit-in in the library?'

Andrew straightened up. The question had caught him in mid-crouch as he was about to place his bottom on the sofa. 'I hope it isn't something to do with the review?'

'No, no.' He checked himself. 'Well, not directly. You saw the president of the Students' Union on the way in?'

'Rob Mission? Yes, he's one of mine. I mean, he's a sociology student.'

'Oh, is he? Really? And I thought he was an empty space between two bookends.'

Czinc pretended not to have heard. 'Very good on constitutional reform.'

'Oh yes, I'm *positive* he is. He was spouting at me about the European Court of Human Rights.' Clifford said this with considerable sarcastic force, which Czinc also chose to overlook.

'Would you like me to come back later?'

'Certainly not. A small demonstration in the library isn't going to put me off my stride... nor you off yours!'

'No, of course not,' agreed Czinc. 'I didn't mean to imply—'

'Never mind. The thing is, Mission says they're staging this demonstration because the course they are on is a "racially-driven construct". What do you think of that?'

Czinc looked flabbergasted. 'Racially-driven construct! *Racially-driven construct?*'

'Yes, I'm not surprised you're speechless. What I want to know is: what evidence have you uncovered of such a thing in the course of the review?'

'None. None whatsoever.'

'*Ah!* And what does *that* mean? It means you still haven't delved deep enough!'

'Vice-chancellor... Cliff, we've not even considered such a thing. The review's all wrapped up.'

'Wrapped *up*? What *do* you mean?'

'The feedback session finished half an hour ago.'

Momentarily Conquest was stunned. 'Half an hour ago!' he gave his wristwatch a furious glare. 'Look at that, *four thirty!* And?'

'Well,' began Andrew faintly, 'they scored threes all round.'

'*Threes*? That means they're home and free. How did that happen?'

'They have a passion to teach.'

'*Passion…!* No caveats, no reservations… *at all?*'

Czinc shook his head.

Conquest had no doubt that this was a defeat. His promise that the review process would be used to put poorly performing departments on the rack had been shown to be so much hot air. He was incensed.

This man is a huge disappointment! My assessment of him was completely bloody adrift. Where's the grit of his father?

'That's entirely unexpected, Andrew. I would have thought at least on "quality" you could have got them down to a two. They're all over the shop and wouldn't recognise best practice if it slapped them in the face.'

'Ah, well, that's where Marta Cramp came into her own.'

'*I knew it!*' Conquest clapped his hand to his head in frustration. 'So you couldn't control her? Is that what you're saying?'

Czinc was anguished. 'Let's say she's a very hard negotiator, shall we?'

'Really? Why don't we say she negotiated the other members of the panel into her corner? That's also called "intimidation"!'

Czinc looked despairing. 'Her argument is that the most meaningful measure of quality is whether the teaching is underpinned by research and in this case the level of research outcomes is indisputably high. They're all mad on research, Cliff, but I don't see that what they claim to be research is research, it's just *art*. I mean, frankly the subject's a law unto itself.'

'Oh, is it? If they're so good how come they've got students barricaded in the library?' This fact gave the lie to the whole thing as far as Conquest was concerned and he was suitably indignant.

Mercifully for Czinc, he was spared the need to answer by the arrival of Carole, holding the door open for the academic registrar, who hurried in with the air of a man who knew trouble was coming. In the flurry of his arrival Czinc tried to excuse himself.

'Don't you go sidling off,' said Conquest, pointing him back to the sofa, 'Have a seat.' He turned to greet Dr Cornish. 'You'll have some tea, won't you, Bert?' He took a quick look at his wristwatch and changed his mind. 'No, no time for tea.' He gripped Cornish by the shoulder. 'Bert, there's a small matter I want you to deal with.' He turned back to Czinc. 'Andrew – change of plan – you can go if you have nothing more to contribute, but I expect a full report before the panel's views are ratified. I cannot hide the fact that I'm rather disappointed with how the first of my reviews has turned out. I bid you good evening.'

First ordered to sit down like a schoolboy, then dismissed! The age-old ritual of princely disapproval was complete; it was almost as if Czinc had been handed a pistol and invited to go outside and use it. He rose to his feet and gave a clipped nod to both the academic registrar and his vice-chancellor.

'So much for that!' said Conquest bitterly when the door had close behind him. He looked at Cornish with a frown. 'Are we on the same page, Bert?'

'Yes, vice-chancellor,' said Cornish, holding himself unusually erect.

Conquest had a feeling that the pace of events was accelerating. It seemed he was being drawn into a trap more devilish than that of being caught in a compromising situation with Lady Caroline Lamb. He examined Cornish, still sufficiently alert to appearances to note he was wearing the trousers of a pinstripe suit paired with a blazer with some sort of flamboyant sports crest on the breast pocket. What was even clearer was that Cornish already knew why he had been called in and had decided that an air of formality was in order.

'Sit down, Bert, sit down.' Conquest waved him onto the sofa facing him. 'Don't ask me about reviews, I'm not in the mood. There are some Chinese students in the library; something to do with the course they're on.'

'Yes, I've heard.'

'I understand from Rob Mission that you've had meetings with them.'

A look of anguish crossed Cornish's face. Now that the matter was out in the open his instinctive response was to revert to informality. '*Meeting*, Cliff, I had *a meeting* with them. I referred their complaint back to the department. Seemed like a matter for them.'

'For them? *The Department of Fine Art*? Was that fair?'

'Seemed very fair,' said Cornish sheepishly.

'According to the Students' Union their course is a racially-driven construct. What do you make of that?'

'*Construct?*' Cornish looked mystified.

'Yes, *construct!* That's what Rob Mission called it. I want you to go and find out what the problem is. We don't want students claiming they've been enrolled on racially-driven constructs, do we? I don't care for that sort of language: it gets in the papers. Before we know it the whole place will be "institutionally racist"! See if you can get them to come out. Tell them you have my ear, and that I am concerned to…?' Conquest went blank. He looked to Cornish for help. 'What am I concerned to do, Bert?'

'Er, well, vice-chancellor, I should think you're concerned that their complaints should be properly dealt with and any academic deficiencies should be rectified.'

'Their complaints will be heard, Bert, *heard.*' To stress the final word he raised a prophetic finger. 'I think that's more than sufficient, don't you?'

'Yes, thank you for that clarification.'

'Fine, then perhaps you'll go now and help them to come to the decision to leave the library. Will you do that for me?'

Cornish rose to his feet, apparently fired up to please. 'Certainly, Cliff. I'll make my way over there right now.'

'Good man. And as far as they're concerned you're my point person; you're the only one they talk to. I want you to make sure they get one message, and one only. No other lines of communication. You understand? Tell the head librarian she's to close the library immediately and the porters are to make sure the students don't have any contact with the Students' Union, especially with Rob Mission. It's a health & safety precaution.' He looked hard at Cornish who seemed a little slow in grasping the full implications of the instructions he was being given. 'Do you follow?'

Cornish nodded animatedly.

'Report back; no more than an hour. I'll expect good news.'

As Conquest ushered Cornish into the outer office he signalled for Carole, who was at the photocopier, to join him. A few moments later she came through the door, notepad in hand.

'If the dean of academic affairs is in the building could you ask him to join me?'

Carole stuck her tongue in her cheek before answering, as if she were restraining some opinion unbefitting her role as his PA.

'What?' he felt moved to ask.

'Nothing. I believe he's still here.'

'Good!'

This woman is another one slow to grasp what is being asked of her.

'I need a word with him.'

Carole managed to combine reluctance and disdain in her nod. As she turned to go Conquest had the distinct impression she uttered the word "tosser" under her breath. He stared at the closed door, wondering whether he had heard aright. It seemed unlikely she had actually said "tosser" – an epithet that could have only been aimed at him – so unlikely that he found himself wondering how he could have mistaken what he had heard. "Roister" and "dosser" didn't fit the context, nor did "toaster", "lost her" or "foster". Had she said "Oh no, sir"? But that really didn't make sense, and phonetically was rather dissimilar to what he had heard. Had something rustled about her person that sounded like a muttered "tosser"? Had he seen her lips move? He was still beset by this puzzle when Professor Woolworth knocked at the door.

'Am *I* glad to see you!' said Conquest gestured at him with a copy of University London Central's prospectus. 'Are you aware we have a sit-in?'

Woolworth nodded mildly. 'Yes, Cliff. Rob Mission's been briefing me.'

Conquest bristled. 'What the hell is *he* doing briefing *you*? That's my job!'

'I suppose he thought he was being usef—'

'Never mind, Murray! The world according to Rob Mission can wait! Look at this.' He flicked through the prospectus until he found the page that he wanted and jabbed a finger at it.

Obediently Woolworth scanned the page. 'Aaaaah!' he said cautiously, once he had recognised its contents. 'One of our "study in London" pre-postgraduate certificates. Overseas recruitment.'

'No, Murray, it's a racially-driven construct. How did this course get past academic board? It's quite clear to me that you can't get on this course unless you're an overseas student. That's discriminatory, isn't it?'

'I don't think it was thought that a British student would ever need this sort of course, vice-chancellor. It's a postgraduate access opportunity for individuals who haven't been through a British undergraduate course.'

'Quite so, Murray, but the effect is exactly as the Students' Union is claiming: those Chinese students end up ghettoised.'

'I don't see how it is discriminatory, vice-chancellor. The course is open for any British citizen to apply as long as they don't mind paying overseas student fees.'

Conquest pulled an expression as though he had come upon something very disagreeable in a plate of seafood. 'What is "pre-postgraduate", anyway? If I say, "I'm pre-pregnant", that means I'm not pregnant; isn't that right? And a certificate of attendance is not a qualification worth the paper it's printed on! Murray, the Department of Fine Art seems to have created rather a mess. Don't you agree?'

Professor Woolworth did not agree entirely. He knew only too well that the "study in London" courses had been the brainwave of Conquest's disgraced predecessor. They had been thought rather a good idea at the time, but he was not about to court unpopularity by saying so. 'I think we should be circumspect about a rush to judgment, Cliff. The department's academic staff have been very distracted by their preparations for the review.'

'Ah, there we have it! Your Marta Cramp intimidated the review panel into giving them threes. Did you know that?'

'That they scored threes? Yes, I attended the feedback—'

'Yes. No! That Marta Cramp bullied the others round to her point of view. Professor Czinc has been in here to complain.'

'I find that hard to… A total score of eighteen is hardly earth-shatteringly good.'

'No, but it means they've escaped further supervision, doesn't it?'

'Yes, I suppose that's true.'

'Well, that's exactly what they wanted. And if these Chinese students reveal some scandal the review's missed I promise you I shall re-opened it... *without that woman!* Do you understand what I'm saying?'

'Yes, vice-chancellor.'

'And please don't go home until this sit-in has been dealt with. I think you need to brief me *fully* on these pre-postgraduate courses.'

FORTY

Conquest was glad to be rid of the dean of academic affairs.

Oh yes, he's got what it takes to be a pen-pushing functionary!

For three quarters of an hour he paced the length of his office, back and forth, going over the events that had unfolded since he had launched the review of the Department of Fine Art. He was prepared to admit to himself that he had initiated the review believing the department would fail it. What he was less willing to perceive was that somewhere within the moiling depths of his psyche he had been seeking a reason to interfere in the department's affairs in a way that would put him – as the darkest description of his motive would have it – orbiting ever closer to the fragrant femininity of Lady Caroline Lamb!

Karumba!

And yet the department's failure would have placed him in a position to… To do what? To take possession of Lady Caroline Lamb? To direct her education? To help her escape the Club Beruit? He was not sure. These were questions he had never really faced.

Perhaps my mind has been playing tricks on me. Has having the latitude to do whatever I want led me astray?

Events were making him think that he should abandon all attempts to reform a department that he was beginning to regard as a dangerous, subversive influence. Removing it to Potter's Bar to make way for the digital hub seemed a more attractive solution by the minute.

But then I lose Lady Caroline Lamb.

It was a quandary. He was no nearer a settled view when Carole led Dr Cornish back into his office.

'Did you see the panga?' Conquest asked with glum flippancy.

Cornish looked dispirited. 'I saw several Chinese… boys, Cliff.

One was in tears. He says his parents have spent every penny of their life savings to send him here to further his career as an artist. He is the hope of the entire village. He cannot stand the shame of going home after being treated as he has been by our university.'

'I see. That doesn't sound particularly helpful, does it?'

'I don't like the look of it, Cliff.' Cornish sat down heavily on one of Conquest's sofas. 'I thought they were going to take me hostage. There's an unhealthy air of desperation about them. They've barricaded themselves in the sociology stacks.' He gulped. 'One of them is threatening to cut off his finger.'

'Threatening to cut off a finger? I thought we had metal detectors – *or some such* – to stop students taking things like pangas into the library.'

'The one with the Stanley knife is threatening. The one with the panga is manning the barricade.'

'Really?' Conquest was pacing between the back of the sofa on which Cornish was seated and his desk. 'Well, what are their demands? Tell me that.'

'They want to be treated the same as the other students.'

'What does that mean? Which students?'

'They want to be on the undergraduate course, preferably the third year so they can go back to China with a British degree at the end of the academic year.'

'*What?* That's an absolutely preposterous demand, isn't it? They have to study for three years to get a degree. How did they dream that one up?'

Cornish looked hopelessly out of his depth, rudderless, adrift in a sea of irresolvable demands. 'I tried to explain that to them. I've been going round that point with them for the best part of an hour. Their English is not of the best. As far as I understand, they're saying that since the course is a preparation for postgraduate study then that means once they've successfully completed it they've satisfied the requirements of an undergraduate degree.'

'Really? What a surprise! What do you suggest? Surely we can get this course of theirs more to their liking; we need to get the department in on it.' Conquest ruminated. 'Such an abortion of a course – whatever the precise details – could only have been dreamt up by the Department of Fine Art. How come academic board approved a racially-driven construct?'

Cornish had no answer to that, although he knew perfectly well that several departments had been asked to recruit overseas students for pre-postgraduate certificates to boost the university's fee income; only fine art had actually succeeded in doing so.

'I was right, wasn't I, to put the department under review?' Conquest exploded furiously. 'And now they've been allowed to escape! Bert, this was the department's failure. You were quite right to send the matter back to them. Where was the orientation course, the pastoral care? We need to take a closer look at the course details, the handbook and whatever. I've a good mind to annul the outcome of the review and get Andrew to do it again. I want you to go back to the library and talk to these Chinese.'

'Vice-chancellor,' Cornish began faintly, 'they said I wasn't to go back. I am unwelcome. This Zhao boy swore he'd cut off his finger if he saw me again. That's what he said. He called me a "running dog".'

'*Running dog?* Preposterous!'

'They're only willing to speak with "the head of the university". That's what they said.'

'Playing hardball, eh?' The Americanism came from Conquest's lips with contorted weirdness. 'Expect to go right to the top. Well, we don't do that, do we, Bert?' He laughed energetically. 'Perhaps we need to take a new tack with these young gentlemen.' He went to the door and called in Carole. She came in and stood, her notebook at the ready, lines of exasperation etched into her face.

'Carole,' said Conquest, 'change of plan.' It suddenly came to him that he could no longer ignore her expression. 'Er, is everything all right?'

She nodded furiously, her lips knotted.

'Can you get Professor Pomfret here as quickly as possible, please? Thank you.' As she pivoted to leave, the impression of pent-up aggression unnerved him. The involuntary gulp of a second 'Thank you' escaped his lips as she reached the door.

FORTY-ONE

Some twenty minutes later, still radiating antagonism, Carole announced the arrival of Professor Pomfret. To Clifford's eyes Pomfret had the look of a man who was thinking he was about to be congratulated. The thought of him having come through the review unscathed made Conquest want to say something unguarded and wilful. He repressed the desire.

Bloody hell, this man actual thinks he's achieved something. No doubt he's thinking he's escaped my clutches. Well more fool him! Who was that woman he was with this morning? "My right hand man" he called her, silly fool. I'll make her head of department when his term's up. Must correct the gender balance in academic management!

What Conquest could not know, and only later was to have grounds to suspect, was that Pomfret and those members of his department involved in the review had collectively consumed one and a half cases of Chilean red since the results of the review had been announced.

When Conquest had Pomfret seated, facing him and Cornish, he mustered his diplomacy and began. 'It was good of you to spare us the time, Archie. I know you've been very busy with the review… and, of course, very well done to come out of it with a decent score, but there seems to be a problem with some of your students.'

'Really? Which students, may I ask?'

Already Conquest could feel himself losing patience.

Why is this man so bloody bland and unconcerned?

'Your Chinese students. They've barricaded themselves in the library.'

'"Barricaded"? Sounds a bit extreme.'

'Yes, *that's* what I thought. The academic registrar's been to talk to them.'

'Good. That seems sensible.'

Conquest saw Pomfret's every response as designed to irritate him. 'They seem to be dissatisfied with their lot. Perhaps they've been left too much to their own devices? A life room with no model and that sort of thing.'

Pomfret looked at him blandly. 'Quite likely… the review, you know. They are adults, after all, vice-chancellor.'

'That is *not* the point! They are in our care. I'm told they don't meet any of the other students.'

'Who, may I ask, told you that?'

'The president of the Students' Union. How can that be acceptable?'

'Well, we accepted them without making any assessment of their suitability. If we had we wouldn't have accepted them at all.'

Conquest goggled. What he had just heard was either an idiotic *non sequitur* or purblind stupidity. For a moment he was at a loss. 'I think you're twisting my words!' he said, rather lamely.

'We have five hundred applicants for the places on the undergraduate course. We spend weeks interviewing them. The Chinese students walk into the department practically without a check because they pay overseas students' fees. What am I to do? My staff don't like this anymore than you do.'

Conquest bridled at being aligned with Pomfret's academic staff. 'I am for any sensible overseas recruitment policy that produces results, and please don't think I see this with the same eyes as your academic staff. I seem to think they have failed these students, failed them utterly!'

Now it was Pomfret's turn to be indignant. 'Surely there's evidence to the contrary, vice-chancellor?'

'They say they're on a "racially-driven construct". What do you think of that?'

Pomfret gave a guffaw. 'Jargon! Some lefty's been putting words in their mouths.'

Conquest could see that Pomfret had no appreciation of the seriousness of the situation, nor that he considered it was he who needed to take responsibility for placating the students. 'Look now, bloody hell, I don't what to overreact, but I think you need to play an active part in bringing this sit-in to an end. I think we need you to be *involved*.'

'Right –' Pomfret rose to his feet, suddenly purposeful – 'I'll send in their course leader and she'll ask them to come out. I'm sure they'll see reason.'

Conquest turned in exasperation to Cornish who so far had been a silent witness to the exchange. He appealed to his good sense with raised hands. Cornish gave an involuntary shudder. It was with something like desperation that Conquest turned back to Pomfret. '"Sure they'll see reason"? These students have banned Bert – *the academic registrar!* – from the library. They threatened him… one of them has a panga! Don't you think that bodes rather ill for your proposal? *I* do!'

'Vice-chancellor, you ask me to play an active role and active role I will play,' Pomfret assured him. 'I know these students, not by name or personality but by their propensity for art. It will out, and they will out too.'

Conquest was now familiar with Pomfret's arrant assurances and this specimen did nothing to assuage his suspicion that the Department of Fine Art was in the hands of a lunatic. Before he could remonstrate with him Pomfret began again.

'I really think, vice-chancellor, that this is rather simple. I don't what to say you're over-playing the aggrieved, but I imagine this matter is easily put to rights. It's art, isn't it? We all understand where that sits in the larger scheme of things: not terribly high, in my opinion. It matters, but it doesn't matter awfully, does it? We all like it, but it mustn't be too important, must it?'

'Professor Pomfret, I suggest you sit down.' Conquest's voice had regained some of its force. 'I want Bert to tell you what he saw in the library.'

'If I'm to be involved, vice-chancellor,' said Pomfret blithely, declining to hear from the academic registrar, 'I know exactly who to delegate the task to.'

Conquest produced a flash of menace. 'You'll do it yourself, damn it! *Who* is the point person?'

'I suppose I'm the point person,' said Pomfret, at last rather put down.

'I thought I was the point person,' objected Cornish.

'No, you're not. You've been banned,' Conquest reminded him, 'Anyway, it's clear to me that Professor Pomfret should go in there and sort the students out. It's his department and I think it perfectly proper – institutionally speaking – that he should be the one to make them see sense. Professor Pomfret will report to you, Bert.' Conquest smiled a ghastly smile. Now that he had identified the appropriate senior members of staff whose responsibility it was to end the sit-in he felt an immense surge of relief.

Things will be decided by these two gentlemen, and I can let them get on with it and make a mess of it if they will, heaven forbid!

'Excellent! I'm glad we have an understanding.' Conquest rubbed his hands together breezily. 'Now I expect things to move forward. This matter must be resolved.'

Pomfret was let out, the vice-chancellor's exhortations to make the Chinese students come to terms following him as he made his way through the outer office and past Carole's desk.

Once the door had closed behind him Conquest turned to look sternly at Bert. 'We seem to have everyone on the same page at last,' he announced. 'About time Pomfret displayed some leadership skills.'

Cornish nodded dumbly as it dawned on him that although he was no longer the point person he had been manoeuvred into position at the head of the chain of command. After a few final exhortations he followed Pomfret, but once out of the Keynes Building he turned away from the George Orwell Library, and towards Kier Hardy House. He had decided that for the moment Pomfret could get on with extracting the Chinese students without his participation. The evening was turning cold and, before joining Pomfret at the library, he intended to return to registry, ensure it was put to bed for the night and collect his coat. He was hopeful the sit-in might be ended by the time he arrived.

As he crossed the campus he brooded on his own experience at the barricade. The students had been polite enough, but there was no doubt that there was a troubling undercurrent of extremism in their attitude. It seemed to him that one could not tell what they might do from one minute to the next, and as he thought of Pomfret using his leadership skills his sense of apprehension grew. An error of judgment had been made and a half-formed thought told him that he ought to turn back to the Keynes Building now – *right now* – before it was too late. For a blink of time his thoughts churned, but bold statements did not become him. Even though he counted as one of the university's senior administrators, his recent elevation meant he was far from confident it was his place to contradict his vice-chancellor. Then... *whatever*... he decided. Being almost entirely without guile, it did not occur to him that his vice-chancellor might be harbouring a wish that Pomfret would fail.

FORTY-TWO

Archie Pomfret was not in a mood to delay. If the Chinese students needed to be shifted from the library, they needed to be shifted directly, before they got settled in and the task of getting them out curtailed his plans for the evening.

'Bloody housekeeping,' he said to himself.

As he left the Keynes Building he took his mobile from his pocket and put in a call to JC McCann, with whom he had been celebrating only an hour before. 'Pick up, woman, pick up,' he cursed as he made his way towards the George Orwell Library

'HELLO.'

'Ah, JC, where are you?'

'Is that you, Archie? I'm on the train to Chingford. Where are you?'

'Oh dear! JC, something's come up with your course. I was hoping you were still here, at the university.'

'I'm nearly home.'

'I see. It's gone belly up.'

'Belly up? Course? Archie, what course? How am I supposed to know what you're talking about?'

'The study in London certificate, JC.'

'Oh, that thing. Are the Chinks on the rampage or something?'

'No levity, JC, that's precisely what's happened. Apparently they've barricaded themselves in the library.'

'Giddy godfathers! Perhaps they've taken up reading!'

Pomfret cupped his hand over the mobile and lowered his voice. It crossed his mind that JC might have drunk even more Chilean wine than he. 'Look, JC, the bosses are deeply unhappy. Some rigmarole about them being ghettoised on a racially-driven how's-your-father. We need to get them out pronto. Can you come back and sort it out?'

There was a cackle from the other end of the line. 'Racially-driven *what*?'

'Never mind. Can you come back?'

'Bloody hell! Next stop's Chingford! Can't I delegate?'

'No!'

'Archie, be reasonable!'

Pomfret was alarmed. 'Who to?'

'Well, Terry Bragg. He teaches on their course one day a fortnight. He's not been teaching them today but I can ask him to have a word, sort them out. Okay?'

'I don't know if that's a good idea, JC. I mean, is he senior enough to pull it off?'

'They seem to like him, Archie. They talk to him.'

'Do they?' Pomfrert found that encouraging; personally he found all Chinese bashful and monosyllabic. 'I suppose that's all right, then, if you think so. It's against orders, JC, so he'd better be discreet. I'd do it myself but I'm in a terrible rush.'

'I say he should have a shot. He's only a part-timer, so he'll do whatever. You know how it is.'

Pomfret was oblivious to all aspects of employment law and assumed — not that he had ever thought about it — that everyone teaching in the department enjoyed the same terms and conditions that he did, so the significance of JC's observation about the terms of Bragg's employment missed him entirely. He looked at his watch; he was running late, he was due in Dover Street. 'Keep me informed, JC. Otherwise, I'll leave it with you. Oh, and JC, tell Bragg one of them has a panga.' He snapped off his mobile and pocketed it.

FORTY-THREE

Terence Bragg had had a second busy day covering for the teaching staff caught up in the review. He had broken his own daily record by conducting nine tutorials with first year students. He felt as though he'd been exposed to every conceivable view on the purpose and meaning of art and was in no mood for anything but going home. The one person he had wanted to see – Juliette – had been missing from her studio space whenever he had looked in. He had hoped to arrange when he was going to take her to see the Morandis at the Courtauld and now he would have to wait for another week. As finally he took his leave of the Frank Brangwyn Building his mobile rang. He looked to see who was calling and saw in was JC. He was tempted to leave the call unanswered, but a spark of optimism told him he might hear something to his advantage.

'Hello, JC.'

'Terry, are you still in the department?'

'Near enough.'

'Good. There's a bit of a job for you before you go home. Boy's Own stuff you'll enjoy.'

'What's that, JC?' said Bragg, suddenly wary about where her call might be leading.

'Apparently, some of your students have got themselves holed up in the library, staging a sit-in. Prof Archie's been on to me. Can you hoik them out; they're annoying the readers.'

'My students? I don't have any—'

'The Chinese lot, Terry.'

'*Mine?* I'd hardly call… JC, I teach them one day every other week, and I certainly wasn't teaching them today!'

JC ignored his disavowal. 'Yeah, well, there was a no-show for their life class today and that might have got them a teeny bit hacked off. Look, I have to get going; the train's coming into my station. Just get over to the library and sort them out. It's fucking easy enough, for Christ's sake. Take a saunter and give them the usual chat. *Capiche*? Oh, and Terry, one of them has a panga, so disarm!'

'Yeah, JC, but what—' Bragg realised he was talking to thin air. He gave his mobile a hostile look and tried to call her back. Too late: she'd switched off and all he got was an invitation to leave a message.

The George Orwell Library was a blaze of lights, shining out into the foggy dusk. It was a big, square building in the atrium style with much promenading space and low-ceilinged quarters for the books.

Bragg found Mick the Porter on duty, sitting at a desk between the library's two sets of doors. Mick was a wiry man, middle-aged, affable, with a sharp, almost cunning look about him. It was widely accepted that in matters of a practical nature his intelligence was keener than that of most of the academic staff. He was entertaining himself with a book of reminiscences about Margaret Thatcher.

'Hello there, Terry,' he said on seeing Bragg pushing open the plate glass door. He was often on duty in the Frank Brangwyn Building and considered Terry a decent enough chap for an academic. 'What brings you here? We're closed.'

'I've been told to get over here.'

'Oh, you're here for the spot of bother, are you? It's got the high-ups running round like nobody's business.' He put his hand to the side of his mouth as if sharing a confidence. 'The academy registrar, Dr Albert bleeding Cornish, was here a while ago. He's been in and out, up and down, *and* back and forth. Never seen him so far from his office. He's a tin of tuna that needs reeling in by his secretary.'

'Why closed? Is that really necessary?'

'Oh, yes, it's ominous all right.'

While Mick was talking, Bragg had been peered through the inner glass doors, trying to make out what was going on inside. 'Are the students still here?'

'Upstairs.'

'Are the security guards here?'

Mick sucked in air sharply through pursed lips. 'Security firm won't deal with students. They've got a clause against dealing with students. I clock up a lovely lot of overtime thanks to them.' He looked mildly content.

'I'm afraid I've got to go up there,' apologised Bragg, not wanting to be thought of as willingly foreclosing his overtime claim.

Mick was dubious. 'I should retire gracefully, if I were you. They're kitted out like shoe bombers.' He raised a cautioning finger. 'I think there's a cultural misunderstanding going on.'

'You don't mean actual bombs, do you?'

'Well, no, not actual bombs. I was employing a figure of speech, but you understand what I mean? The problem is they're very bright in their own way, but in the university's eyes they're dim. It's a cultural misunderstanding, like I said.'

'Well, the fact is, I've been instructed... I have to try and persuade them to...'

'What they protesting about, Terry? Any idea?'

'I dunno. They missed a life class today 'cause the model didn't turn up.'

'They're razzed up about something.'

'Look, just let me in and I'll see what's what.'

Mick shut his book and stood up, the huge bunch of keys hanging bandolier-like from his belt jingle-jangling. 'It's not locked anyway,' he explained as they walked together to the inner glass doors. He let Bragg through.

'Will you come if I call?' said Bragg.

'Dr Cornish said I was to stay outside.'

'Come if I call.'

The inner doors led to the atrium, overlooked by the upper floors of the book stacks and study areas. The security barrier was directly ahead. It was switched off and the turnstiles were open. Bragg walked through and into the area beyond. When he reached the enquiries desk he stopped to listen and thought he could hear people talking somewhere on the upper floors. Just then Mick poked his head round the door behind him.

'They're in social sciences on the second floor.'

'Second floor,' repeated Bragg. 'Right.' He gave Mick an ironic wave and a grimace of joy as he made for the stairs. The first floor was empty and only the lights nearest the stairs were on. The studying areas with their ranks of tables shaded off into darkness. He turned back on himself to climb the stairs to the second floor. When he reached the top he heard voices again and walked towards the stacks. Beyond music and world history there was a corridor that led to an older part of the library where the social science stacks were. At the narrowest point the way was barricaded with trolleys used by the librarians when returning books to the shelves. As Bragg approached he could see that the trolleys had been crazily piled high with books. In a gap between two of the trolleys a broad, flat face topped with a fringe of straight, black hair was staring at him unblinkingly.

'Sir! Bragg!' spoke the face fiercely. 'They send you! You teach us well! We have no argue with you, nor wish make trouble for you, please.'

Bragg felt faint with fatigue. It was, he thought, all too much. Here were these students, all the way from China, reduced to some sort of demonstration. About what? He knew only too well that their course was considered a very low priority in the department and he himself had witnessed their polite disbelief at the way it was being run. 'What's happened, Zhao?' he asked hesitantly. 'Why are you doing this?'

The face suddenly contorted and was overwhelmed by a sense of the tragedy of life. 'We... We don't... We do... Sir, Bragg, is all lost?'

'Lost? No, of course not.' Zhao's intensity was giving Bragg a queasy feeling. 'But... But it's time to give this up and go home.'

The face was wracked by a spasm of pure horror. 'We never go home. We lost forever. Art is not what it seems, I think.'

'Zhao, you are taking this – *really* – far too seriously. We can get everything sorted out if you talk to us. That's all I can say, but I can assure you—'

'No, no,' Zhao interrupted, 'we hear too many assurances from this... JC.'

'Oh!' Bragg was shocked by the scorn in his voice. It revealed feelings he had not previously been aware of.

'She insults us *every* day!'

'I can't believe...' He felt the prickly heat of embarrassment, knowing what JC was capable of in an unguarded moment.

'She say we have big cheek thinking we want qualification from proper university. We see British students not gifted, no work, sail away with it. She think we don't see.'

He had to admit to himself that the remark sounded like JC at her most tetchy. 'I don't think that's what JC meant,' he said, wondered where the conversation was heading. 'Are you sure you understood her correctly?'

'So, yes, right. We understand this specific point, that, in her opinion, we not good enough before she see, even.'

Just then one of the trolleys was moved aside far enough for another face to appear, this time it was of the student that Bragg knew as "Sid". Sid beckoned for him to come closer.

'Here, squarehead,' said Sid.

'I beg your pardon!' said Bragg.

'You know we call you "squarehead"?' He laughed. 'Here we say as it is, little squarehead.'

Subversion, thought Bragg. He liked to see students showing spirit, though he didn't much care for it when it was directed at him. The Chinese were not normally inclined to such disrespectful levity, so he was impressed. 'Sid, I want you out of here.' Then he saw the panga, which was sobering. 'I was warned about *that*! How did you get it in here?'

'This is democratic protest, right? We vote to occupy this section of library. It bring attention to us, but no need to close everything. It makes big thing out of us here, so they have excuse to end it. Government technique in China too.'

'I don't think—'

'Sorry, we don't go. If we do we waste everything.'

Bragg saw the sense it that. 'All right. But are you going to stay here *all night*? How many of you are there?' He pointed. 'Can you use those toilets over there? You have food?'

Sid leant forward with a grin. 'Zhao cut his finger off if we don't get better course with proper entry to department and proper teachers.'

'I'm a proper teacher,' Terry protested.

'We see you one time every two weeks.'

'Okay, but threatening to cut off a finger isn't going to…' A thought struck him. 'You do see other members of staff when I'm not there, don't you?'

They all laughed.

'JC come in, go out.' Zhao made a little pantomime with his fingers of someone walking fast. 'Nobody else except three students from MA course. Not proper teacher. We see nothing about art here. They make us draw object on tabletop. That is traditional Western, not modern art.'

'So, *really,* what are your…er… demands?'

'We want to be with other students, real British-type students, with crazy styles… proper course. We see no white boys, or white girls. Sorry Bragg sir, you very good, but we want more. We want to be with proper British, not students only from world wide global.'

Bragg regarded him with a jaundiced eye, thinking how ill-advised and romantic was the desire that drove the many to follow the path of art. He was beginning to grasp the depths of their feelings and could see that it was not going to be possible to persuade them to leave, at least not unless they received assurances from someone with a great deal more clout than he. 'Look, I can see this is all a bit difficult. I'm going to have to consult. I'm sorry, I can't do anything right now.'

'You can help. You can take finger.' Zhao brandished a Stanley knife with a wild glint in his eyes. 'Then they know we serious.'

Bragg blenched. 'Don't do anything like that, please. I promise you'll get some action on this.'

'If you come back with empty hand, we put finger in it and send you away,' said Sid. 'You lucky we don't lock you in screening room… *as hostage!*'

Bragg leveled his finger at Zhao, as if to say they were going way too far. 'No screening room!'

'You go,' called out Sid as he disappeared behind the barricade. 'Tell them we have conviction.'

Bragg was relieved to see they had no serious intention of taking him hostage. 'I'll come back as soon as I can. In the meantime…' He pulled up in mid sentence, unable to think of anything to say about the time between now and his return.

The only response was Sid's disembodied voice. 'Tell them we're not leaving until our demands have been met. Go!'

Bragg frowned, thinking that Sid's parting shot sounded as though someone with a native command of English had put the words in his mouth. As he went back down the stairs it occurred to him that the only person immediately at hand was Mick the Porter.

Surely, Mick has not been tutoring them?

It then struck him that Mick was the only person available for *him* to consult. That hardly seemed the support he needed; the problem called for JC. He could see himself being forced to hang about all night, keeping Mick company, unless he could persuade her to assume command. He took his mobile from his pocket as he descended the last few steps into the foyer.

'They all right up there?' called Mick from the open door.

Bragg nodded, busily going through his directory. He registered the smell of chips and saw that Mick was eating. Surprisingly, JC answered her phone straight away.

'Hello JC, they won't come out.' There was the sound of human chatter from the other end and he could hardly make out what JC was saying.

'Damn it, Terry! What d'you mean, "Won't come out"? Didn't you order them out?'

Bragg laughed briefly. 'It's not like that, JC. They're taking it all rather seriously.'

'Oh, Jesus, *Terry!*'

'Can't you come and sort it out?'

'God, no! I suppose I'm going to have to speak to Prof Archie. Stay there, don't move and I'll ring you back.'

Bragg decided that the hubbub meant that JC was in a bar and that there was a disappearingly small chance of her making any contribution to bringing the students out. He wondered whether Professor Pomfret was a better bet. As far as he was concerned

Pomfret was an aloof and distant figure. JC might refer to him jocularly as "Prof Archie", he certainly never had. In fact, he'd never even spoken to him, although he had heard him briefing the staff about academic matters at a departmental board. At the time he suspected Pomfret thought him a student representative. Nevertheless, it seemed likely, he decided, that if anyone had the institutional clout to fix the Chinese's complaints he did; it seemed to be a matter of resources and he, as head of department, had, he reckoned, access to resources in abundance.

He pocketed his mobile and for some reason the smell of chips made him feel abandoned. Mick, he reflected – and this was something that had already crossed his mind without becoming a fully-formed thought – looked far too relaxed to be guarding a library under siege, occupied by an unknown number of revolting Chinese students. And *how* had he procured chips?

'They're not leaving until their demands are met, are they?' said Mick as he wiped chip grease from his fingers with some delicacy. 'Never mind, it means some bigwig from administration will have to run about a bit. Won't do them any harm; it's what they're paid for.'

Bragg reached for a chip, thinking there was something decidedly subversive about Mick's attitude. 'So, do they have a back channel up there giving them support?'

Mick smirked and shook his head. 'Nah, fire doors is alarmed.'

'How about someone who knows how to negotiate giving them advice? You're a union man, aren't you?'

Mick shook his head again and ate a chip.

Bragg helped himself too. 'It's all right for you, but I'm paid for a fixed number of hours. Look –' he offered Mick a view of his wristwatch – 'it's past six, and I'm the only member of the academic staff here!' He had hardly finished his lament when his mobile sounded and hastily he dug for it in his pocket. 'Hello, JC.'

'Stand to attention, Terry, Prof Archie is returning from Dover Street to be with you in your hour of need. If you can sort the blighters out in the next half an hour give me a ring and I'll cancel his return. Threaten them if you like. Prof Archie is not best pleased at having to come back and has no objection to the use of threats. You need –' she paused to give her words emphasis – '*you need to be seen to be effective.*' She gave a brief chortle and rang off leaving Bragg wondering whether, when Pomfret arrived, he dare ask him for extra hours' pay for having attended the sit-in.

'What do you think, Mick? Can I ask for overtime for putting up with this?'

'I should think so: my union would be after them like nobody's business if I was in your shoes... which I ain't.'

There was a loud crash from the direction of the outer doors and they turned to see the academic registrar floundering on his knees, his face flattened against the plate glass.

'Here comes his brightness,' said Mick.

Cornish rose to his feet and put himself to rights as he made a second attempt to negotiate the door. 'Good Lord, tripped! Fell straight into that glass door!' he said, as though it were a lark. He registered Bragg's presence with a puzzled look. 'Hello, who are you? I was expecting Professor Pomfret to be here.' He turned his attention to Mick without waiting for an answer. 'Anything happening up there?'

Mick looked blandly at Cornish and shook his head. 'Ask him,' he said, pointing at Bragg with his chin. 'He's been up there with them.'

Cornish turned to Bragg, indignation blossoming. 'Who authorised you?'

'Well, Professor Pomfret. I was told to come over here and sort the students out.'

'I'm surprised... and shocked! I was up there and they threatened me. I scarcely think you'd do better. In fact, if Professor Pomfret fails I think the police might be the answer.'

Mick sucked in his cheeks. 'Private property, Dr Cornish. They won't want to get involved.'

'You need –' he pointed a threatening finger at Bragg – 'to exercise caution!' He paced about a bit, steaming, and when he had calmed down he came back to question Bragg further. 'What made you think it was permissible for you to go up there?'

Bragg opened his mouth to speak, but stopped, not sure what to say. Finally: 'I teach them one day a fortnight.'

'Oh, do you?' Cornish was not mollified. 'Well, you and your colleagues seem to have made a hash of it! Where's the pastoral care? Where was the induction course? When this is over there's going to be a post mortem, I can tell you.'

'Too right!' Bragg was happy to respond in kind. He considered that as a part-time employee on a one-year contract, teaching them one day a fortnight, he was blameless. In any case he had a feeling that he was the one member of staff the Chinese would speak up for if it came to some sort of reckoning. 'I was wondering if I might claim some extra hours,' he said loftily. 'I usually finish at four thirty.'

Cornish glowered at him. 'Do you think this is the moment? One of those boys is threatening to cut his finger off!'

Bragg acknowledged the truth of what he was saying. 'That's Zhao: he tends to be a bit over the top, artistically speaking.'

Cornish suddenly looked at Bragg in a new light. 'What do you mean, "artistically speaking"? Are you saying it's a show, this finger cutting thing?'

'Well, it will be authentic finger cutting, I expect. I don't think it'll be a sham. I think they understand that much about contemporary art.'

Cornish's eyes had turned beady; his lips were compressed in a severe line.

'What I mean,' Bragg tried to explain, 'is they're not studying drama, are they? They won't be thinking about theatrical artifice, will they? They'll go for the authentic, the real, the actual finger cutting.'

Cornish raised a hand to stop him. 'I think you should keep your thoughts to yourself. You're trying to articulate two forms of finger cutting where I see no distinction – *it's a real finger!*'

Cornish's reply had a righteous simplicity about it that stopped Bragg dead. 'Fair enough,' he agreed, 'but go up there without some sort of peace offering and we'll end up with a finger and Zhao in A&E.'

Cornish looked at him blankly, not wanting to credit anything he said. 'This matter,' he declared grandly, 'is being monitored by the vice-chancellor in consultation with senior officers of the university. And where exactly is Professor Pomfret?'

'He's on his way from Dover Street. I suppose I'm the advanced guard.'

'What do you mean, "Dover Street"? He was here, on the campus half an hour ago! Professor Pomfret's the point man; that's what the vice-chancellor has decreed. "No delegation", he said.'

'Yes.'

'Stay here while I refer this back to the vice-chancellor. What's your name?'

'Bragg, Terry Bragg.'

Cornish took his mobile from his pocket and fingered it agitatedly. 'I wouldn't be surprised if he regards this as a serious breach of university policy.' He turned away and walked towards a distant corner where he could not be overheard. The call was brief and when it was over he came back with a look of relief on his face. 'We're to wait here, all of us. In the light of developments the VC's decided to come over here and see for himself.'

They did not wait long – time Cornish spent checking messages on his mobile while Mick watched him with an amused smile, anticipating exciting times ahead. The vice-chancellor's arrival was sudden and dynamic. He nodded to all three of them with apparent good humour as he entered.

'You understand,' he said without preamble, 'that it is with the greatest reluctance that I have come.'

They all nodded slavishly.

'I do not negotiate under duress.'

It was Bragg's first sight of his ultimate boss and he examined him with some cynicism. He didn't much care for what he saw. Here was a man who had subjected Juliette to a terroristic interrogation designed to embarrass and humiliate her with sexual innuendo. Had Bragg known he had unwittingly identified her so she could be "staked-out" as bait to trap the vice-chancellor he would have been mortified.

'Vice-chancellor,' began Cornish at a rush, 'I am only too aware that your presence might—'

'Never mind about that. I want this business brought to an end. Please explain to me what has happened.'

In response to Conquest's request Cornish was bold enough

to take him by the elbow and lead him away from the others. In a low voice he told him what he knew of Bragg's dealings with the students.

'Insufferable! That man Pomfret has fragrantly ignored his instructions!' muttered Conquest. He nodded in Bragg's direction. 'Is he their tutor?'

'Part-timer; says he teaches them one day a fortnight.'

Conquest gave a tut of disapproval. 'We've got to wean these departments off using hourly-paid staff: it's terribly unprofessional. What's his name?'

'Bragg.'

'First name?'

Cornish had forgotten. He shrugged.

Conquest walked over to Bragg, followed by Cornish. 'Mr Bragg, I understand you have some influence with these students.'

'I don't know… Perhaps…' said Bragg doubtfully.

'He told me the finger-cutting threat is just bluff,' said Cornish excitedly.

Conquest scratched his arm vigorously as he addressed Bragg. 'I want you to go up there and tell them the university has had enough. We cannot tolerate this disruption and they must evacuate the building immediately.'

'They've already been told that.'

'No matter, we must persevere. We cannot be held to ransom. I want you to tell them that none of their demands are negotiable until they clear the building. They are labouring under a profound misapprehension… And they must put the books back where they got them from!'

'Look,' said Mick, 'I see smoke.'

They looked up and, sure enough, a haze of smoke was rising up towards the roof of the atrium.

'*Christ!*' breathed Conquest. He gestured for Bragg to go.

'They said I shouldn't go back. If I do—'

Conquest was determined to have his way. 'Never mind about that. They're burning books; that's a quite unacceptable totalitarian trait! You must *go!*'

'Let's hope it's not the set books they're burning,' said Mick.

Conquest turned on him ferociously. 'Go and override the alarms, man! Things are tense enough without fire alarms putting everyone's nerves on edge.'

Mick considered Conquest's instruction. 'Should I call the fire brigade?'

'The fire alarms… *now!*' Conquest gestured for Mick to do as he was bid. 'Mr Bragg, you must tell them in the strongest possible terms that they're forfeiting the last shred of sympathy for their cause.'

Bragg shrugged. 'Fine.' He headed for the stairs, reckoning that since matters seemed to have come to a head and he had little option but to act, he would act with all speed.

At the top of the stairs on the second floor Sid was waiting for him. He was tending a fire in a waste paper bin. 'We get your attention with smoke signal. Soon the alarms will go, I think.'

Bragg felt another pang of despair on their behalf. 'Sid, this is not going to work. You have to tell the others.'

Together they walked back to the barricade where a third Chinese called Li was pointing a camera in his direction. It was all so casual: Zhao had the little finger of his left hand resting on the cover of the uppermost book on the trolley, which was, Bragg saw in pin-sharp focus, the *Times World Atlas*. In his other hand Zhao held the Stanley knife. Before Bragg could react, he raked the knife across the extended finger with all his might and in a moment was reeling backwards with a howl. To say that Bragg was squeamish was a vast understatement; he was sensitive to the conditions of the flesh to an acute degree. He had the sensibility of the aesthete, always ready to quail at the animal, blood-and-guts condition of the body. Cruelty to animals stirred him to anger; the kicking of a misbehaving dog or the bad-tempered shaking of a child was enough to set him quivering with rage. Now this: a bloody self-mutilation before his very eyes! As he staggered back, he was aware of two other Chinese trying to staunch the blood with paper towels. He tried to keep his balance but his head felt empty. He uttered the word, "Triage" as the emptiness took hold and consciousness ebbed away. He pitched over onto the floor.

FORTY-FOUR

When Bragg came to he found he had been moved – mostly likely dragged, he thought, since he'd lost his shoes – to the head of the stairs. He peered around, trying to get his bearings, slow-witted from the effects of his faint. It was then that he saw the finger in the nest of tissue. When the finger moved he squirmed backwards, hitting his head on the lowest shelf of a book stack. It came to him slowly that he had experienced an eidetic image of the last moment the finger had been attached to the rest of Zhao. That brought him round like a douche of cold water. He got to his feet, appalled by the token he had been gifted to deliver. He stumbled and almost fell down the stairs. When he reached the first floor the vice-chancellor and academic registrar came into view in the foyer below.

'I told you they meant it,' he wailed. Slowly he descended, holding out the nest of tissues like a relic. On reaching them he offered the nest to each in turn. He heard expressions of horror, but was much too focused on not letting the finger fall to see the looks on their faces. He felt like crying; the whole thing was just so inevitable, stupid and tragic. 'We must get this sewn back on now, or it'll be too late. Didn't I say we'd end up in A&E?'

Mick, who had just returned from overriding the fire alarms, beheld the severed finger with indignation. 'Now, look!' he scolded. 'See where cultural misunderstandings get you!'

Despite the shock, Conquest had achieved a certain serenity.

Leaders show their mettle in situations of extreme stress. When the going gets tough, lead from the front, and all that crap. Moral fibre is nothing without dash!

'If necessary,' he said calmly, 'we must storm their barricade. Mr Bragg, put that finger down somewhere safe. Bert, I want you

239

to take these two men –' he indicted Bragg and Mick – 'and get that boy with the severed... *I want him out!*'

'Zhao,' said Bragg mechanically.

'Yes, Zhao.' Beckoning the others to follow, Conquest started for the stairs.

Don't go much further. I've a nasty feeling this could go from very bad to still worse. Thank God I've already got my fall guy identified! Cornish is just what I need: a stooge to take responsibility for a student dismemberment. He's perfect: inexperienced, handled initial complaint badly. Didn't listen to the students; referred them back to the uncaring department, run by negligent professor, too old and mentally infirm. Entrusted him with putting matters right, made a hash of it. That's the sort of tale that carries the day! "Here's a tip, Bert: the bursar's post at the American University in Ankara is yours for the taking..." Yes, that's the line to take. "Bert, opportunity calls!"

'Now, this must be done with dispatch,' he told his three foot soldiers when they reached the first floor. 'Bert, you're in charge. Use whatever force you find necessary, but get that injured boy out... *immediately!* I shall go back to the entrance and await the ambulance.' He held up his mobile as though it were a talisman of good fortune. '*Go, all of you!* I'm going to make the call right now. *No negotiations!*'

The three men climbed the stairs to the second floor. Mick, who had armed himself with a fire extinguisher, laughed quietly to himself as they went.

'Desperate measures,' said Cornish as they reached the top.

'You know one of them has a panga, don't you?' said Bragg. He saw his shoes lying nearby and went to retrieve them.

'Yes, I want you to confiscate it,' said Cornish, watching him as he returned the shoes to his feet.

Mick laughed some more as he doused the remains of the fire in the wastepaper bin.

'I think a straightforward, we're-taking-no-nonsense walk-in, don't you?' Bert gabbled. 'Straight through the barricade as though it's not there.'

It seemed such an improbable approach Bragg couldn't think of anything to say. Instead he nodded gamely.

'Right, Strength in Numbers! So... close support, please.'

They made their way towards the sociology stacks, Cornish in the lead. Bragg wondered what gave Cornish the confidence to behave as though he were on military manoeuvres. Then it occurred to him that something had happened to the Chinese students. There was no movement behind the barricade. 'They've gone,' he said, overtaking Bert. 'They've done a bunk and taken Zhao with them.'

Mick shook his head, as if to register his disbelief. 'Fire escape! Turned the alarms off, didn't I? We'd have known if I hadn't.'

'*They're gone?*' Dr. Cornish looked immensely relieved. 'But that's bloody marvellous! *Marvellous! Mission accomplished!*'

Bragg was thinking ahead. 'If they've gone, what are they going to do now?' The thought filled him with apprehension. 'Don't we need to get Zhao and the finger back together?'

'Good job it isn't something important,' said Mick, deadpan, 'like his morning glory.'

FORTY-FIVE

Conquest was waiting for them at the entrance. Mick the Porter was directed to guard the entrance, while he and Cornish went outside to confer. Bragg was ignored.

'So, they've gone,' said Conquest grimly, once he was sure they could not be overheard.

'Apparently they opened an emergency exit. The alarms were switched off, so… What are we going to do about the finger?'

'I've informed the emergency services. I expect they will advise us, don't you?' Conquest paced about a bit. 'I suppose we ought to find its owner. What's his name?

'Zhao.'

'I saw those students this morning. I should have intervened then! They were in a life class with no model and I expect they stayed like that all day. I assumed Pomfret and his staff would deal with it. It's crass incompetence to leave students to their own devices, especially so soon after the beginning of the academic year.'

There was an uncomfortable hiatus. It seemed slightly ridiculous to be waiting for an ambulance with a finger, but no one thought to say so. Shortly, Professor Woolworth, dean of academic affairs, who had been summoned to join them, appeared.

'Ah, Murray!' said Conquest as soon as he was within hailing distance.

Woolworth approached with a degree of trepidation. 'Has the sit-in finished?'

'They made off through one of the emergency exits,' explained Cornish.

Conquest welcomed Woolworth's arrival as if he were his salvation. 'There's been a typical piece of student over-reaction to a situation –'

'– for which the department is *entirely* culpable,' jumped in Cornish.

'Bert, if you will allow me, *please!*' Conquest was finding Cornish increasingly annoying; he suspected he was revelling in the situation. 'One of them – a Mr Zhao – severed his finger… off.'

He said the last word so softly that Woolworth was unsure he had heard aright. 'Off…?' he goggled. 'Accidentally…?'

'Apparently not, although the motive is not entirely clear.'

'I see,' said Woolworth as though in a trance. 'Students do the strangest things.'

'What is *that* to do with anything?' snapped Conquest, but before he could fully express his exasperation a gabardine mac caught his eye, flapping lazily in their direction. It was Professor Pomfret who had just arrived back from Dover Street.

Pomfret hailed them. 'What *ho!*'

'Your department,' Conquest informed him coldly, 'is responsible for a major disruption of University London Central's teaching and learning environment.'

'I say… *what?*' responded Pomfret, like a genial nitwit.

'If it weren't for the complexities of employment laws and their restraining hand on higher management, I would be venturing to say that *someone should consider their future!*'

Pomfret was beginning to sense he was at the centre of a maelstrom. 'Has it all gone tits up?'

'Bert,' commanded Conquest, 'go and fetch that finger!'

Pomfret looked about him in an airy sort of way. 'Not the fickle finger of fate, I hope?'

'The finger of one of your students who elected to cut it off to show his displeasure at the way you and your department have been treating him! There! Do you follow?'

'I…'

'Yes, you might well be lost for words! Bert, the finger, please!'

'I…'

'Vice-chancellor,' said Woolworth, 'I'm not sure we should be bandying—'

'Bandying what? Words with a chump?'

'No, I meant the fing—'

'Surely this is all rather excessive,' said Pomfret unhappily.

'Bert, if you won't fetch the finger, I will. I intend to show Professor Pomfret what he has wrought.'

'Vice-chancellor,' said Woolworth, attempting to intervene again, 'I don't believe it would help matters to bring the finger into this.'

'Oh, really?'

'Yes. I think to would be much better if Professor Pomfret were sent off to find these Chinese students. Could it be that they've gone back to the Frank Brangwyn Building? If not, perhaps they're making their way to their hall of residence. Professor Pomfret should perhaps start to repair some of the damage done by this unfortunate affair.'

'You really think so, do you Murray? You think he's the man for the job?'

Woolworth quailed before Conquest's penetrating gaze. 'Yes, I think, "fair enough".'

Conquest uttered a highly-charged snort of amusement. 'I believe,' he said, 'that Professor Pomfret was given every opportunity to put an end to this business over an hour ago. What did he do? He bunked off! What do you think of that?'

Woolworth was already regretting having been so firm in his opinion. He was far from sure that Pomfret was capable of dealing with a band of Chinese desperados. Pomfret had, he felt, no institutional gumption, and this business called for gumption *and* guile. He could not know that Cornish had experienced similar thoughts, but his disquiet intensified when he noticed the lopsided smirk on his face.

'Nevertheless...' Woolworth muttered lamely. He had staked his judgment and now it was too late for him to change his mind. Already he had a prickle of foreboding that something was bound to go wrong with what he had proposed, added to which was his growing realisation that Pomfret's performance thus far probably indicated he was not entirely sober.

'Fair enough!' said Conquest. 'That's good enough for me! Professor Pomfret, go and do your worst. We will be in my office

awaiting your return!'

Contrary to Woolworth's suspicions, Pomfret had been considerably sobered by his reception and the realisation that the severed finger was real. 'Vice-chancellor, I will do my best. As for my earlier remarks, I assure you they were in jest. I had not appreciated the gravity of the situation. If the Chinese students can be found, I will find them.'

'That's right, leaving with arrant nonsense still ringing in our ears! Good for you.'

At that moment they heard the sound of sirens in the distance.

'I expect that's the ambulance,' said Conquest.

'Or a fire engine,' added Cornish as a large red truck with a multitude of flashing blue lights came into sight on the service road.

'Fire engine? Who called the fire brigade?' demanded Conquest.

Bragg was standing apart from the rest. Mick the Porter drifted up too him. 'What a lot of chieftains on the run!' he commented. 'They've got the blood of a martyr on their hands. There'll be a price to pay.'

They watched as the mighty machine drew up and its crew began to climb out in a business-like way. Conquest stood his ground defiantly.

'Evening, gentlemen,' said the fire officer. 'Who's in charge here?'

'I am,' said Conquest bitterly. 'And there is no fire. I called an ambulance!'

The officer looked at his watch. 'We had a fire called in seventeen minutes ago.'

Cornish intervened. 'There was a small fire – deliberately lit – in a wastepaper basket. It's been put out.'

The officer was not to be deflected from his professional duty. 'We'll have a look, if you don't mind, sir.' With that he turned towards the George Orwell Library. 'In there, is it?'

'Yes,' intervened Woolworth. 'I'll show you.'

'Some of your students, I expect. Always up to tricks.'

'Yes. Ha, ha!'

'Funny there's no alarms going.'

'They were turned off for health & safety reasons,' said Conquest reluctantly.

The officer gave a bemused laugh. 'You'll have to run that past me again.'

Gamely, Woolworth attempted to shield his vice-chancellor. 'To facilitate an orderly end to the sit-in,' he said.

The appearance of another fire engine on the service road, blue lights flashing, distracted the fire officer's attention. 'Look, here's Freddie's lot,' he said. 'Oh, hello, there's an ambulance right behind it.' He turned back to Conquest. 'There you are, sir, your ambulance has arrived.'

'Thank you, officer,' said Conquest through gritted teeth. 'Bert, perhaps *now* you would fetch the finger!'

FORTY-SIX

As Archie Pomfret hastened towards the Frank Brangwyn Building he received a call on his mobile. It was JC.

'Archie, how's the chinks' tea party?'

'JC, it's not. And less of the blasphemies, *please!*'

'What's going on?'

'Chaos. One of them's cut his finger off and now they've given us the slip.'

JC seemed unable to grasp the concept of finger cutting and it wasn't until he had told her the story three or four different ways that she was satisfied she understood. 'Archie, there's going to be hell to pay over this so remember my advice: keep your head down and you might not find yourself in the firing line.'

'Thank you, JC. Since it's your course I thought you might be the one in the firing line.'

'Archie, that's a low blow! How can I be in two places at once? You said, "Set them projects" so I could do the dogsbody work for the review. And don't forget: Marta single-handedly turned the panel.'

'Don't worry, I'll back you up with the Chinese when the reckoning comes. They speak so highly of you, too.'

'Being cutting does not become you, Archie. I take it we agree the powers-that-be will be looking for a sacrificial lamb, eh?' JC was already thinking ahead. 'Well, obviously if you're a part-timer you need to be smart, although in Terry Bragg's case I'm not completely sure that's true.'

'Yes, Bragg was hanging about when I reached the library. He seems to have *much* too much of an interest in the Chinese sit-in. Is he teaching in the department tomorrow?'

'No, he's done his two days this week.'

'Well, get him in anyway. As he was the departmental representative at the time of this... this finger cutting business, we should have words; I've a suspicion he was egging those Chinese students on.'

'Steady on! We asked him to go there! Don't you remember?'

'Your suggestion, JC. I'll have to do something about the Chinese. Maybe I should take them out to lunch. Really, I don't understand why this happened; in my day it was enough to be given the opportunity to make art.'

'Archie, that was then! Listen, I'll give Terry a call. You'll have to offer him extra hours, you know.'

Archie gestured irritably. 'Whatever, JC; it always comes down to money! Just get him to come in! Meanwhile put out feelers. I need to find the Chinese students and reel them in.'

FORTY-SEVEN

Once the emergency services had been sent on their way there was nothing for Conquest to do but to retreat to the Keynes Building in the company of the academic registrar and the dean for academic affairs. Ballantyne was summoned to join their conference. Once they had settled themselves with glasses of Conquest's whisky it became rapidly clear that the disappearance of the maimed Mr Zhao and his colleagues was an opportunity for both scandalised speculation and a sort of horrified breathlessness. Conquest felt obliged to make a call to the police to inform them of what had happened. A police officer, Turnbull by name, large, bluff, with a military moustache, arrived. He brought his own special form of suspicion to the gathering by wondering aloud whether some immigration infringement might not lie behind the Chinese making themselves scarce once they realised they'd overstepped the mark and the authorities were about to descend on them. While he thought of the owner of the severed finger as a renegade, the severed finger – put into cold storage by the ambulance crew – was regarded by him, and the wider gathering, as an object of concern, concern of the reverent sort. In a sense, it had become a little corpse. After much discussion of the evening's events, the police officer's opinion was that no crime had been committed during the sit-in, certainly none that Conquest felt the university could press charges over. Both the disruption and the setting fire to waste paper in a bin were dismissed by Turnbull as no more than typical components of "A Domestic". However, Turnbull took a dim view of the train of events as a whole. It struck him that it spoke volumes about the anarchic, lefty nature of universities.

'They can only keep that finger in good condition for so long,' he kept pointing out to the gathering. 'After that...' He shrugged.

His audience tried to look impassive, as if to say the matter was out of their hands. For the third time, Conquest gestured to him with the bottle of whisky, and for the third time he declined the offer with a shake of his head.

'I am on duty, sir, though I thank you for the thought.'

Ballantyne gladly held up his glass for a refill since the circumstances, being ex-financial, inclined him to the belief that he was off-duty. Cornish also seemed in need of frequent top-ups. Conquest may have looked tranquil and in control as he acted the part of host, but his mind was a ferment.

The bloody posers hanging about here. What do they want? Me to fall. That's it. Me brought down. And how has this happened? Students and plots. It's quite clear what's happened. The bloody staff want me emasculated and this is their way of doing it. Catch me out with Lady Caroline Lamb; saddle me with a mutilated student protest scandal! They want a power vacuum so they can return to their fancy former ways. They want to spend money they haven't earned, assume privileges they don't deserve. I damn them all in the name of an ethics that will not stand for a culture of sanctimonious twaddle. I cannot bear – No! – I cannot bear this living hell of being civil!

After half an hour Professor Pomfret came in breathlessly. His reception was icy. He reported that neither the Frank Brangwyn Building nor Clifton House, their hall of residence, had provided the least clue as to the whereabouts of the Chinese students. It seemed they had fled the campus and where they might have gone he was at a loss to know. While delivering his news he somehow procured both glass and whisky although, thinking about it later, Conquest couldn't recall giving his consent to either.

Strange to report, but Pomfret's news was a relief to the gathering. Without discussion, a consensus took hold that some third party – the police, the NHS – were now responsible for the severed finger.

As the silence that followed Pomfret's admission of failure lengthened, Carole sidled into the room and beckoned to Conquest. She had about her the superior look of one who had known from the first that he would cock up the student sit-in. Since it was now firmly impressed on Conquest's mind that she was a critic of the way he handled things, he was reluctant to go over to her. Nevertheless he went, thinking he must look like a beaten dog.

'The president of the Students' Union is outside. He says you asked him to come back.'

'He's late… and anyway there's no longer any need for me to see him. The sit-in's over.'

'Believe me, you want to hear what he's got to say.'

He looked at her with exasperation. 'Do I? What is it?'

She pulled a face of longsuffering. 'He's waiting outside and I'm going home – unless you need me. Or shall I send him in?'

'*In?* No, definitely *not!* I'll be there in a second.' He ushered her out and turned to the others. 'I'm just going to confer with the president of the union. I'll be right back.'

As he was leaving he heard someone laugh and say, 'What union?' He wondered who it was but didn't want to acknowledge he'd heard, by looking back.

What bloody berk is taking things lightly after everything that's happened? Could it be the policeman? Or was it one of us? Whoever it was it's traitorous to laugh like that. I bet it was that Pomfret man. What does he think this is, a moonwalk competition?

'Chancellor, we meet again.'

Christ, now this one's being flippant! What has got into everyone? They all think they can cheek me because they think I can't snap back at them. I'll sort out the whole lot of them when this is done.

'Good evening, Rob. It seems that the occupation of the library has come to an end.'

'Chancellor, I—'

'Vice-chancellor.'

Rob Mission rolled his eyes in a way that said they were dealing in pedantic niceties. 'Vice-chancellor, you should know that a video is about to appear on YouTube. I think you can guess what it shows.'

'I have no idea…'

'The finger. Being severed.'

Conquest went pale. He saw that the situation, which he

thought had been stablised, was again slipping out of control. A touch of hysteria entered his voice. 'Look, we have that Chinese boy's finger. It's not too late. Where is he?'

'He's not with me.'

'Yes, but you know where they've taken him, don't you? Don't you understand? *We have the finger!*'

'Vice-chancellor, you may think you can put this back together again as though nothing's happened, but it's too late.'

'Are you *trying* to cause a scandal? Is that what you're about?'

As he finished speaking, Officer Turnbull emerged from the inner office and rolled towards them, knocking papers to the floor as he passed the secretaries' desks.

'I think I'll be going,' he said, clearly weary of the whole business. 'Let me know if I can help further.' He took a firm grip of Conquest's hand and shook it.

'Thank you, officer.'

'I expect it'll blow over –' he looked ludicrously doubtful – 'all things being equal.'

Conquest nodded. 'I'll always be glad of your advice.'

Turnbull looked Mission up and down as though making an appraisal of his character. 'Don't bother, I'll let myself out,' he said and made for the door.

'Thank you.' Conquest muttered, already turning his attention back to Mission. 'Well, thank you for bringing me your news, Rob,' he mumbled as he tried to regain his equilibrium, 'but what, *exactly*, is it you want?'

'I'm not here to gloat, if that's what you think. My constituents – those students – need to go back to China at the end of this academic year with a proper qualification. That's what they were promised when they signed up with the recruiting agent.'

'But Rob, that's asking the university to beggar its qualifications! It can't be done!'

'Yes, it can, and worse has been done, vice-chancellor. If they can do it in the English department for sexual favours I'm sure you can do it in fine art to save your skin.'

'Rob, you ask too much. There are principles involved here; important institutional principles! You must give me time to think;

I recognise the countervailing principle of restitution for these students. Of course I do!' Conquest put his hand to his brow. 'I don't suppose this posting on YouTube...?'

Mission shook his head.

'Very well, Rob, you must let me think what we can offer them that doesn't compromise... I suggest we meet again tomorrow, in the morning. Can we do that?'

'Oh, yes, we can do that. That would be splendid. You sleep on it; much the best thing. And I'll see you tomorrow. What time?'

'Nine?'

'Suits me.'

'Fine, Rob, nine o'clock it is.'

FORTY-EIGHT

The unquiet night had passed and the participants in the previous evening's events found themselves hurrying back to the university as though to revisit the site of a disaster that had haunted their dreams. Professor Pomfret was aghast that it was his students who had staged the library sit-in just when he was hoping that he, and his department, could slip back into the shadows having successfully negotiated the review. He left his mews house in Kensington before seven, his mind full of how he would handle the Chinese students, once he had run them to ground. Over a cup of strong tea bought in a café near South Kensington tube station he was the first member of the university to see the *Sun* headline on page 5. It read "SNOGGING UNI BOSS IN SELF-HARM SCANDAL". For a long moment he could not compute what he was reading. It was all weirdly familiar, but he couldn't bring himself to believe that it was his university, his vice-chancellor and his students that the article was talking about. All night he had been obsessing about what he thought of as "The Chinese Insurrection", now here was the incident exposed to the full glare of national publicity! He studied the three photographs alongside the headline, his head swimming. They weren't very sharp but what they purported to show was the vice-chancellor in the act of nuzzling the nape of a young woman whose face, half-turned towards the camera, had been pixilated. He turned his attention to the story. The first sentence in bold read: "Yesterday University London Central was in turmoil as foreign students went on the rampage over poor teaching." He winced. The rest of the story went downhill from there: "A group of Chinese art students staged a sit-in in the university's library. In a gruesome attempt to draw attention to their complaints one of them, Zhao Tai, mutilated his own hand, saying, 'I accuse

254

University London Central of neglecting our studies and using our fees to subsidise other courses'. The video of the finger cutting has already become an internet sensation. While the Chinese students were staging their severed finger protest, randy, cheating uni boss, Clifford Conquest, was caught on camera groping a female art student. He was secretly filmed stealing a kiss outside the very room where the student protest started. Students' Union kingpin Rob Mission pointed *his* finger at his new uni boss saying he was too intent on "predatory sexual conduct" to take an interest in the Chinese students' protest. Students set fire to the library as the dispute escalated and four fire engines attended the blaze. The police were called in to restore order. University London Central is expected to issue a statement later today."

'Good god!' Pomfret breathed. He switched his attention back to the photographs. There was no doubt about it: he recognised the doorway and the architectural surround. It was definitely the entrance to one of the studios in the Frank Brangwyn Building. He marvelled at what visual images – even photographs as lacking in focus as these – could suggest when put to the right storyline. It shocked him that someone should have been so unsporting as to snap the vice-chancellor in such a compromising pose.

'It looks,' he said to himself, *'as if he's trying to mount her from the rear!'*

It was then that it dawned on him that the photograph must have been taken very close to the moment he had arrived to take the vice-chancellor on his tour of the building. He recalled the scene, and who was present. And that meant that the subject of the vice-chancellor's attentions was... *Juliette Burton!* He let the newspaper slip to the table.

Good god, that's it! Juliette Burton! I've been waiting for someone to be smitten by her since she joined the department. I knew she was a pocket femme fatale if ever I saw one... but the vice-chancellor!

He was stunned and it took a little time longer before he began to wonder whether JC might have had something to do with the taking of the photograph. He seemed to recall that she was hanging about in the corridor when he caught up with the vice-chancellor.

It had occurred to him at the time that there was something forced about her manner and now he was beginning to suspect he knew the reason why. What he was struggling with was a motive for her doing such a thing. Was it a plot to discredit the vice-chancellor? Perhaps JC had taken it upon herself to organise the incident to protect the department. Had she set it up with Juliette Burton's connivance? And what about the Chinese students? They were on JC's course, so had they too played a part in the plot? His mind reeled.

No, no, too much of a stretch. Nobody playing a part in a plot like that cuts off a finger. I'm over-exercising the imagination: too many moving parts.

But still he had to admit the whole thing had something of JC's creative cunning about it. 'My goodness,' he groaned, 'it certainly reads *very* badly! JC's right: somebody's going to have to take the blame for this!'

FORTY-NINE

At the same moment that Pomfret was hailing a taxi and speculating on the amatory powers of Juliette Burton, Conquest had the *Daily Mirror* open at page three where the headline proclaimed "STUDENTS IN SEVERED FINGER PROTEST". Accompanying it were the same photographs that Pomfret had already seen in the *Sun*. Conquest was scrutinising them closely.

So, it was a trap after all, and they were spying on me, waiting to take compromising photographs if they could. Let's see, the photographs were taken from behind, but at a slight angle as though… Where was I? I was standing in the corridor in the Frank Brangwyn Building and Lady Caroline Lamb was looking through an open door. Where was the door, at the end of the corridor, or to one side? Yes, at the end and it was the room where the Chinese students were. She stepped back into me. My arm slipped round her. Yes, I remember that. And then… So where were the photographs taken from?

He studied the photographs afresh.

Behind, but somewhat to one side. I was absorbed in what I was doing. Lady Caroline Lamb was just there, close to. We were talking, and she was being so charming! Pomfret approached down the corridor, coming from the direction of the stairwell. Yes, we were at the end of the corridor and Pomfret was coming from behind and he must have had some kind of camera. He slipped it in his pocket when I turned… no, before I turned. He's definitely not the giddy fool he pretends to be, the bastard!

Conquest was not particularly visually-minded and lacked the acuity of eye to see that the angle was wrong for Pomfret to have taken the photographs. Even so, his analysis would have been a little more forensic had he not been mortified at having allowed himself to fall for such a blatant trap.

One thing is sure: Lady Caroline Lamb is innocent. She would not have been part of such a sordid plot. These people besmirch her very existence.

With an inward sob, he turned his attention back to the accompanying story and, having scanned it briefly, he dropped the newspaper to the floor and stepped on it.

Ballantyne eyed Conquest warily, uncertain of his state of mind. 'What are you going to do?'

'I don't know, Tommy. You tell me,' he said wearily. 'What are my options?'

'Brazen it out…' Ballantyne's pause hung heavily in the room. 'Or go, I suppose.'

Conquest brushed off the latter with a wry smile. 'Well, we were ever brazen, weren't we, Tommy? Although I'm not sure I'm not losing my nerve. That Carole has been giving me the willies these past few days. She acts like she's got my number all the time. Makes me feel very uncomfortable.'

'Sack her, Cliff. Give her the boot. We laugh at industrial tribunals, don't we?'

'She's long-serving; at least five vice-chancellors.'

'Amalgamate your office with the office of the dean of academic affairs. A new administrative entity; call it *the Vice-Chancellor's Strategic Secretariat"*. That silly sod Woolworth can be your quality assurance supremo. A new administrative structure means you can make both Carole and Woolworth's secretary redundant.'

'Create a new post?'

'Yeah… one or two.'

'Strategic secretariat! I like the sound of that, Tommy. *That* I like the sound of! We'll call the new posts, *"administrative officer, strategic secretariat"* and, *"deputy administrative officer, strategic secretariat"*. We'll encourage them both to apply for them if they want to: equal opps.'

'And if they meet the job spec we'll appoint them!'

'PhD in Astrophysics.'

They both laughed. Not for the first time Conquest found himself reflecting on how it was always Tommy who lightened the load on his shoulders when it reached oppressive proportions. But when he looked up he saw Carole was standing in the doorway. For a moment he thought he'd been found out, but, no, she was quite wrapped up in her own importance. She held a printout in her hand with a prim look of disapproval on her face.

'This is from the *Independent's* website. Shall I read it out?'

When Carole had arrived, as usual, dead on eight o'clock, Conquest had asked her to look for news updates on the web and it was clear from her manner that she had found one she thought brought shame on his head. Read it out? That he was *not* having. He strode across the room and held out his hand. 'I'll read my own press stories, thank you.'

'Suit yourself,' she said with a smirk.

'Carole, we are in conference and we need coffee. Rob Mission should be here at nine. Can you let me know when he arrives?'

When she was gone, Ballantyne gave Conquest a meaningfully smirk in imitation of Carole's. 'Strategic secretariat,' he said in a mincing voice.

Conquest held up a hand and began to read out loud. '"7.23am: It seems it takes severed fingers to get someone's attention at University London Central. Now what everyone wants to know is: who was the student warding off the attentions of university boss Clifford Conquest when he was snapped subjecting her to unwanted amorous attentions on campus? The photographs are making headlines because a student protest – one that ended in a self-mutilation sensation on YouTube – was at that moment developing right under the vice-chancellor's nose. Now it is reported that the *Daily Mail* is offering fifteen thousand pounds for the reluctant *inamorata's* story. Will she come forward? That is the question everyone is asking."' Conquest gave a scornful snort.

'"Early on the case this morning was Sandra Torpington, press officer of the university, who issued a statement by fax saying: 'Professor Conquest is not available for comment at this time but denies all accusations of inappropriate behaviour'. 'Not credible,' says student leader Rob Mission who has been lambasting, 'impropriety, evasions and cover-ups'. He comments: 'The vice-chancellor needs a thorough re-education in interpersonal relations. He should meet with the students involved in both incidents and offer restitution for the traumatic experiences they've suffered. A situation of this gravity calls for immediate mediation by the university's trauma councillor at the Students' Advice Centre.' Meanwhile, following the intervention of the Chinese Embassy, the student who severed his finger in the protest has been admitted to a clinic for a surgical procedure. The Chinese ambassador has made no statement but is believed that feelings at the embassy are running high. No senior officials of the university have as yet made themselves available for comment."'

Conquest gave Ballantyne a drooping look of exasperation. 'I'll strangle that Mission boy when he gets here. And what about this Sandra Torpington? I suppose I've met her, have I? How come she's issuing statements on the fly?' He passed him the printout.

'You know her: she's the bint in the public relations office.' Ballantyne scanned Sandra Torpington's statement and gave a hollow laugh. 'Once you've got a press officer the press expects press statements.'

'That's a point; we should make sure we don't have one.'

'Too right, another redundancy.' He handed him back the piece of paper like someone getting rid of something distasteful. 'Well, we don't want any more hostages to fortune like that, do we? Let's not do anything silly, eh? Keep things nice and steady.'

'Ah, Tommy! I have been shown considerable disrespect by certain members of this university.'

'I appreciate that, Cliff, but if revenge must follow, take it by stealth, eh?'

'As you say, Tommy, by stealth. I'm not finished here, I've only just started!'

As Conquest paced the room making a silent vow to crush his opponents, Professor "Perk" Hingley, chair of senate, came creeping into the room, unannounced. When Conquest realised he was there he exclaimed: '*Good God, Perk!* How did you get in? I thought Carole had the door sealed.'

'I came as soon as I heard. Fortunately, I have a journalist contact at the BBC.'

Conquest could tell he was supposed to read "compassionate

concern" on Perk's face. He watched in silence as Perk fetched a bundle of folded newspapers out of his briefcase.

'You've seen this morning's red tops?'

Conquest indicated the *Daily Mirror* lying on the floor. He made no comment, curious to see what line Perk would take.

'This is a rum turn-up.' Perk tugged at his collar and, having wandered about a bit, he sat down on one of the sofas. He pulled a handkerchief from his pocket and made a business of blowing his nose.

'You certainly look agitated,' said Conquest finally.

Perk looked at Ballantyne. 'I think I need five minutes alone, if you wouldn't mind?'

Ballantyne nodded, rose to his feet with a grunt, and headed for the door.

Conquest felt like telling him to stay, but he decided to let the matter go. 'Tommy,' he called after him, 'I'll give you a call when we're done.'

Once the door had closed behind Ballantyne, Conquest sat down opposite Perk with a bland, expectant smile on his face.

Perk held his breath for a moment before proceeding. 'You realise there's a meeting of senate this morning, don't you?'

'Of course.'

'If you attend I'll have no alternative but to move for your suspension while these allegations are investigated.'

'Oh, will you? You know this is all a lot of tommyrot, don't you? I've been framed!'

'Were you in the library last night when this boy *cut* his finger off?'

'Yes, I—'

'You *ordered* the fire alarms switched off.'

'Yes, but—'

'There was *a fire*!'

'Only in a waste paper basket.'

Perk didn't look mollified. 'The fire brigade *turned out*! And this *student* you've been photographed with?'

Conquest took a deep breath, stood up and walked over to the far side of the room where he could see out of the window. 'Actually, she's the only real thing in this whole story.' He turned to fix Perk with a stare. 'The body exquisite: it's a gift from on high, is it not?'

'*Excuse me?*' Slowly it dawned on Perk what he was saying. 'I see,' he said with a sighing exhalation of air. 'And have you any idea how long it will take the press to get to her and ask her about these photographs?'

'What does it matter?'

'I don't know, Cliff, you tell me. I don't know *who* she is or *what* she'll have to say. I suppose she has a name?'

'It's all prurient nonsense. I haven't touched her. Well –' he gestured to the crumpled *Daily Mirror* – 'the evidence is barely conclusive, is it?'

'Does she know this has blown up?'

'I doubt it.'

'Sorry to ask, but I must be clear with you: this is serious! What about stalking? Molestation? Other indiscretions?' Perk looked grave. 'I really feel… I'm sorry to say… I *cannot* have you going to senate with stuff like this coming out. They'll crucify you.'

Oh feeble little Perk, stop yapping like a dog! I really can't see how you could ever make a judgment that would make sense! You're feeble, so feeble! What do you understand of anything! Whine, whine, whine away, then I'll tell you what's really going to happen.

'Look, Perk, it's not in my best interests to be shut out of senate,' he insisted.

Perk was exasperated; over a period of fifteen minutes they argued his point at least three different ways. Conquest remained adamant but Perk was determined he was right. After all, he knew the likely temper of the members of senate, Conquest did not. '*I'm* the one thinking of your best interests.'

'Really? Well, clearly we disagree. I understand what you're saying, but I have to address senate. If they give me a hearing I believe I can convince them of my side of the story.'

'I repeat, I am not trying to shut you out of senate. I think allowing senate to convene is a bad idea. We don't want someone doing something in haste. It's safer to postpone and allow this business to play out.'

Oh please, stop being so feeble.

'I can stop at least some of them from coming. I'll call the members myself.' Perk stood firm, having had what he hoped was the definitive last word.

There was a bang from the outer office followed by the sound of voices. A second later the impassioned figure of Sir Norman appeared in the doorway. 'What the bloody hell is going on?' He strode into the room. 'I have never before seen...!' He threw a wad of folded newspapers down on the coffee table in front of Perk. 'Morning, Perk.'

Oh my god, don't tell me: now I'm going to have to suffer Sir Norman's views being rammed down my throat!

'This tittle-tattle has to be answered, Clifford. Get out there and speak, man! If you take this sort of stuff lying down you're a goner. You know that, don't you?'

'Sir Norman,' said Perk determinedly, 'I am advising Cliff we should postpone today's meeting of senate.'

'Why? Senate should be rooting for him. Give us the message and we'll take it out there! She's not under-age, is she?'

Conquest dismissed the notion with a flick of his wrist. 'Of course not.' He saw in Sir Norman's attitude a change of fortune.

'Has she made a complaint?'

Conquest and Perk shook their heads.

Sir Norman looked baffled. 'What's the problem, then?' He stalked about a bit, as though looking for a fly to swat. 'Anyway,' he pointed accusingly at Perk, 'you can't get rid of a second vice-chancellor.'

'That would be awkward,' agreed Perk, wringing his hands.

'Too bloody right!' responded Sir Norman. 'No, it's not on.'

'I have been maligned and defamed,' interjected Conquest.

'Of course you have!' agreed Sir Norman.

'There's been unpleasantness with the Students' Union,' said Perk for Sir Norman's benefit. 'We must suspect it's behind these Chinese students.'

'You mean this Mission fellow who's been speaking to the rags?' Sir Norman seethed. 'An absolute, disloyal, asinine *swine*!'

'He's been put up to it, you mark my words,' said Conquest smoothly.

'And who's put him up to it?'

Conquest shrugged. 'Some of the senior academics. They don't like being put straight. They preferred the old regime. The lax behaviour my predecessor allowed suited them. We need to show them we won't stand for it.'

'We won't! Got any names?'

'Pomfret,' said Conquest. 'Pomfret's one of them: head of fine art. The review of his department should have shown him up for the incompetent he is but the old guard connived to let him escape.'

'Head of department? Small fry! You can get the swine on the mat later.' Sir Norman took himself over to the sofa. 'Tell me, Perk, does the vice-chancellor have the power to dispose of Students' Union officers.'

'No, of course not! Out of the question.'

Sir Norman was disappointed. 'In that case, Clifford, since you haven't the power to sack this Mission swine, you'd better make peace with him. We need to get him on side over these Chinese students. Is there anything else to come out?'

'No.'

Sir Norman looked at him closely. 'Are you sure? What about the digital hub? Is there anything there I don't know about?'

'No, no, there's nothing else. And don't worry about the bloody senate; I'll deal with them. What we need is a council of war.'

'Right enough,' agreed Sir Norman who always relished a fight. 'Mind you, I wouldn't want to be waging a war with that lot watching my back.'

'The senate keeps this university safe!' Perk reminded them, piqued by their comments.

'Really?' said Sir Norman dryly.

'I wouldn't be surprised,' worried Perk, 'if the Chinese embassy doesn't take up this finger business: diplomatic incident!'

Sir Norman was dismissive. 'I doubt that!'

'As a matter of national pride,' persisted Perk, 'and we know how much national pride means to the Chinese.'

'If they wanted national pride they shouldn't have opened Chinese takeaways all over the place, should they?' said Sir Norman.

'That's ridiculous...' Perk dropped his chin, adding, *'and xenophobic,'* in a cross undertone.

'Let's not exaggerate unnecessarily,' said Conquest, bolstered by Sir Norman's bullish attitude. 'There are Chinese students being mistreated by institutions of higher education all over the country.'

'Exactly,' agreed Sir Norman. 'What's a finger in the grand scheme of things?'

'Quite a lot I should think,' Perk bleated. 'I dread to think what our colleagues are thinking.'

'Oh, why's that?' said Clifford. 'They're probably thinking about having breakfast or taking the dog for a walk.'

'I mean, your reputation. Damage control and all that. Nobody wants you to look a fool.'

'Well, that's patently false; half the senior staff of this university want me to look a fool.'

'Quite!' agreed Sir Norman.

Perk was cornered. 'Fine, have it your own way!'

Conquest saw that Perk was beginning to sense a lack of respect for his opinions and thought it prudent to backtrack. 'Of course, I have to take responsibility for what's happened. *And I do!* Mind you, the acting academic registrar made a mess of the Chinese student thing right from the start. I'm not sure he's up to the job.'

'I'm not surprised!' said Sir Norman. 'Who is he? That fellow you bumped up?'

'Never mind about that!' said Perk, showing a spark of annoyance. 'Now is not the time for that kind of talk. I just hope you're ready to make your peace with Rob Mission. I understand he's waiting outside.'

'Oh, he is, is he?' said Sir Norman in a voice that suggested he was about to go out there and give him a good thumping.

'And remember, you can't intimidate him.' Perk gave a moment's consideration to what he had just said. 'Well, you can try, but not by threatening him.'

'Yes, yes, I'm going to intimidate him with mellifluous turns of bloody phrase,' said Conquest, making to usher Sir Norman and Perk out of his office. He turned to Perk. 'And if I come out dragging him by the roots of his hair you'll know I've failed.'

'You don't imagine we're going to let you see him by yourself, do you?' said Sir Norman, throwing himself down on the sofa. 'Stay, Hingley! We're going to make sure you've witnesses, Cliff. No more misrepresentations!'

Carole was called in and Conquest asked her to fetch Mission. She regarded the gathering of suited men with serene condescension. 'Made in Hong Kong,' she said under her breath, *apropos* nothing.

'Now then, Rob,' began Conquest, when Mission arrived, 'these gentlemen represent senate, the body responsible for the governance of this university. They are going to stay and ensure fair play.'

Mission eyed them contemptuously. 'In that case I want a witness.'

'Fine, have all the witnesses you want,' said Conquest as though the whole thing were beneath him.

Mission made an inspired leap into the unknown. 'I only want one: Juliette Burton.'

'Really?' Conquest's smile had gone rigid.

Seated on the sofa, Sir Norman looked unconcerned until Perk leant towards him and whispered, 'That must be the girl.' The effect of his words was galvanic: Sir Norman propelled himself to his feet, bristling. 'Now look here,' he growled, 'that's just mischief-making!'

Every inch a crane confronted by a monstrous bullfrog, Mission stood his ground, although he couldn't prevent a squeak of anxiety entering his voice. 'She's just as much a part of this as you.' He jabbed a finger in Perk's direction. '*Or him.*'

'The audacity!' stormed Sir Norman. 'You've exceeded your remit at every turn since this business began.'

'You're making a great mistake, Rob,' said Conquest calmly. 'It's a bit like putting the Palestinian flag back up five times after you've been told to take it down: *over-reaching*! You think she'll make some sort of complaint against me, don't you? Well she won't.' He turned to Sir Norman. 'Let him have his way. It's all right.'

Sir Norman raised a warning finger to Conquest. 'This is student extremism of the worst kind, and if you allow it you'd better be prepared for the consequences.'

Mission was exultant. 'It's justice if she sees you lot grovelling.'

'Fine, Rob, fine,' said Conquest. 'Bring her in.'

Mission took half a step back as he contemplated the practicalities of pulling off his coup. 'She's not here; I have to fetch her. And if you want this Chinese business to end I want the academic business we were talking about last night fixed.'

'I'll do what I can.'

'And we're going to fly the Palestinian flag for Eid.'

'Fine, fly the flag. And I'll want your cooperation over the digital hub. Students' Union backing for joint facilities.'

Mission nodded, a gleam of triumph on his face.

Bloody scrawny swine!

Conquest consulted his watch, relieved that Lady Caroline Lamb was not waiting in the wings. 'Right Rob, senate's meeting at eleven. You've got until then. I think you misjudge me, Rob, and perhaps Juliette Burton will help you to see that. You think me a predator; she will say otherwise. I have no objection if you want to bring a delegation of the Chinese students too.'

Mission tried not to show it but Conquest's ready acceptance to his terms was cooling his sense of triumph; he feared he had been manoeuvred into offering terms that the vice-chancellor found all too acceptable. It also troubled him that demanding Juliette Burton be a party to their negotiations might be a mistake. It would be glorious to see their discomfiture, but he knew only too well that he was dependant on his officer without portfolio (activities) to make it happen. If his officer without portfolio (activities) could only get her to come to his office, he reckoned he had an excellent chance of persuading her to follow his lead. After all, she was a victim! She had been grievously put upon! Nevertheless, his thoughts were turning to the need to cover himself if things went badly.

'It's important to understand,' he announced in emollient

tones, 'that I represent the Students' Union, and I reflect what my members tell me. If they've got it wrong, I've got it wrong. Whatever else, they have a right to have the things that are wrong put right, not more bad stuff heaped on the existing bad stuff. I hope you follow my meaning.'

In other circumstances Conquest would have laughed out loud but instead he managed to nod his head in such a way as to withhold both his agreement and his approval. He guided Mission to the door, said, 'Before eleven!' and ushered him out.

There was silence. Sir Norman took himself back to the sofa and sat down besides Perk.

'There is actually something rather cleansing about this process,' said Conquest, his eyes half closed as though touched by some form of ecstasy. 'I don't know what it is, but...' He had gone to his desk and his hand hovered over the telephone.

Perk huffed and pulled a face. 'I thank my sainted aunt he's not one of the student representatives on senate.'

'I wished he worked on one of my building sites,' reflected Sir Norman. 'I'd have a brick dropped on him.'

Conquest was not listening. He had the receiver of the phone to his ear. He was calling Professor Andrew Czinc.

'Andrew, good morning.'

Much surprised, vaguely alarmed, Andrew stuttered a greeting: 'Vice-chancellor! Good m-m-morning.'

'You'll recall this, won't you? There was a woman holding Professor Pomfret's hand during the review; the cretin called her his "right hand man". You know: the blonde, dumpy woman?'

'Jennifer McCann.'

'Yes. You must have made an estimation of her capabilities. Leadership material?'

Czinc replied cautiously: 'I suppose so. Seemed sound enough.'

'Any chance you could get hold of her? Must do something about the gender balance –' Conquest's voice had taken on dreamy suavity – 'and I think she's the makings of a chair, university committee. Important to nurture talent... Long-term investment. Could you arrange something?'

'I'll ring Professor Pomfret.'

'No, no, don't do that.' Conquest gave a yelp of amusement. 'Better if you contact her personally. Don't want any ruffled feathers, do we? Give me a call when you know something.' He cut off Czinc before he could respond and replaced the receiver. Sir Norman was still rumbling away like a summer storm.

'…insubordination from stroppy employees was always put down.'

'Doubtless,' said Perk disagreeably.

'Sorry, Must keep the administration going,' said Conquest. 'I seem to have lost the thread, Sir Norman.'

'Eh? I presumed you were planning a counter-attack, otherwise, if I were you, I should concentrate on the matter at hand.'

'Quite so. Shall I arrange for coffee?'

'I still don't think –' began Perk, but Sir Norman raised an admonishing hand and he was silent.

FIFTY

For most students the workings of their university at the highest level, at the level at which its responses to the diktats of the state are crafted, at the level at which the politics of academic administration are deliberated upon – in short, at the level of the vice-chancellor's office – are as mysterious as the customs of the lost Amazonian civilization of the Paititi. The students' world is bound – as is the world of most of the academics that teach them – by subject concerns: the nature of the unconscious, the behaviour of genetic material, the historical precedents for monetary union... So it was that the machinations that lay behind the affair of the severed finger and the stolen kiss in the Frank Brangwyn Building were at nine o'clock that morning only known to a small handful of the more politically-motivated members of the student population, principally those who had temporarily set aside their studies for paid employment as officers of the Students' Union. Amongst them was the part-time officer without portfolio (activities), who was in his cubbyhole of an office unusually early that day. The officer without portfolio (activities) had something of a roving commission, occupying, upon election, a post that had originally been created to bolster the club sports that had fallen out of fashion amongst the students and become embarrassingly absent from the activities that, so it was thought, a students' union should be seen to foster. The Students' Union's ultra-conservatism when it came to its own affairs meant that the post had continued even though club sports had long since swung back into fashion amongst the hearty types. In the absence of abolition, a curious tradition had established itself whereby the post was monopolised by students from the Department of Fine Art, even though the department had a reputation for lounging rather than straining the sinews on pitch or field. Low turnout undoubtedly contributed to this electoral success. Be that as it may, it never occurred to the returning officer to query the yearly result. The latest student beneficiary of the arrangement was Oswald, owner of the renegade dog, Mr Fantastic. Oswald had arrived at the Students' Union late the previous afternoon while excitement over the Chinese students' sit-in was at its peak. Rob Mission had just returned after seeing the vice-chancellor. News of his refusal to cooperate with the vice-chancellor over the removal of the Chinese students from the library had earned him a tumultuous reception. Various union officers were still milling about in his office talking excitedly of heroic exploits in the face of oppression when one of them, who was checking the union's emails, opened one entitled "VC With Pants Down", and three photographs popped up.

'Jeeee-sus, it's the vice-chancellor!' exclaimed Mission.

That much was clear, but who was the woman with him? Only one union officer recognised her. That profile was unmistakable. His sense of protectiveness told him to keep what he knew to himself.

FIFTY-ONE

Oswald had had no success in contacting Juliette until the following morning, the reason being that she had performed at the Club Beirut until 4am and had only heard his message at about the time the morning's newspapers arrived in the all-night cafés of Shoreditch. Now she was sitting in Oswald's office, looking – so he thought – surprisingly small and vulnerable as she studied the *Sun*. Oswald felt a rising sense of indignation on her behalf.

'If this Chinese student hadn't cut off his finger nobody would be interested in this,' said Juliette, holding the newspaper out with a faint air of disgust. 'The photographs aren't very sharp, are they? Anyway, I'm fuzzied out and completely unrecognizable.'

'Believe me, photographs with no fuzzing exist. I've seen them and I knew it was you right away. In one your profile is unmistakable,' said Oswald. 'Did you know he was going to kiss you?' he wondered.

Juliette had not been to bed and her normally cheerful disposition was eclipsed. She felt exasperation at the furore she had been dragged into, and at having had to come straight to the university from work. 'No, but I suppose he thought we were flirting.' She said this with a sort of weariness. 'He was trying to be charming. It's pretty obvious there was a misunderstanding, isn't it?'

'I suppose so.' Oswald was slightly affronted by the idea that she condoned in any way the vice-chancellor's advances.

'So, what happens now? What am I supposed to do? I shouldn't be here.'

'Rob Mission has some idea about getting you an apology. Restitution.'

'An apology!' Juliette's tone made it clear she regarded the idea with grave suspicion. *'From the vice-chancellor?'*

'Yes.'

She gave a small snort of laughter as though he had said something truly ridiculous. 'You think I'm one of those office ice queens getting offended because some man opens a door for me? I told you, it was a misunderstanding.'

Oswald had a sudden glimpse of things from her point of view and saw how little of a threat the vice-chancellor had been; in her eyes he was an irrelevant inconvenience that had crossed her path. He had noticed it about her before, but now he saw very clearly how self-contained, how wrapped in a protective coat of her own making she was, and it intrigued him: she was someone intent on her own story and – as far as he knew – not really concerned with anyone else's. She was regarding him with a quizzical smile, challenging him to make something more of the vice-chancellor's peccadillo.

'He was a silly man, with low self-esteem. That's all,' she concluded, daring him to ascribe some deeper meaning to his – or her – behaviour. 'All I want to know is how I can stop myself being dragged any further into the limelight by a scandal that seems to have burst into life out of nothing! Look, it was just this *silly* man...' she repeated with great emphasis... '*being silly*. He got carried away, that's all.'

'Only Rob knows about this. You should wait to hear what he has to say. There's a great deal of money on offer if you'll give the press your story. He's got the details.'

She sat forward, bubbling with amused vitality. 'No way!'

At that moment Rob Mission walked in. He made a swift appraisal of the scene and made a ducking movement almost as if he were bowing to Juliette. 'Hi, I'm Rob Mission.' As he shook her hand he examined her carefully as if trying to assess what kind of person he was dealing with. 'I'm sorry you've been dragged into this.'

'Me too!'

The asperity with which she spoke was a chill to his hopes for a confrontation with the university authorities. What was evident was her self-possessed ease in circumstances where he had been hoping for a victim, ready to bemoan the abuse she had received at the vice-chancellor's hands. He couldn't help but notice how startlingly good looking she was, and how unusually mobile her features were.

'Terrible… and entirely uncalled-for.'

She pushed a strand of hair behind her ear. 'It's all very petty.'

Mission could see she was amused that he and Oswald were taking things so seriously.

'It was inadmissible that he should have behaved like that.'

'It was,' she replied.

'Look, all you've got to do is tell your side of the story and there's fifteen thousand pounds waiting for you. Fifteen thousand!'

She shook her head with a grin.

Oswald looked disbelieving. 'Aren't you tempted?'

'Of course not, and I don't want you telling them who I am. It was a mistake.' She saw he was looking at her sceptically and shrugged.

'Look,' began Mission, running his hand through his hair, 'I've just come from his office. He's there with the chair of senate. They know they're on the ropes. If you don't want the money you can at least get an apology; you can get whatever you want!'

'I told you: it was a mistake.'

'I'd do it whatever, if I was you,' said Oswald, horrified that she might throw away an easy payday.

She warded off his words with a raised hand. 'They'll never forget if it comes out who I am. What would happen? Nobody would take my paintings seriously. I'd be the "Necked by the vice-chancellor girl". I have painting, and that's what I want to do, seriously.'

Her words were spoken with passion and Oswald found himself thinking, not for the first time, how lovely she was. He saw Mission's resolve was slipping before her intransigence and he wondered again whether she was aware of the effect she had on others. It wasn't as though she was particularly effusive or demonstrative, but there were moments like this when she seemed utterly self-assured and aware of nothing but her sense of mission, even if – it seemed treachery to admit this – he could not take it entirely seriously.

On the other side of the negotiation, Mission was finding it hard to credit such purblind idealism and was staring at her in grudging admiration. 'Look,' he said plaintively, 'a high-falutin' university honcho tries to take advantage of you and deserves to be punished.' He tried to tear his eyes away as he realised he was losing momentum in the contemplation of her.

'Not at my expense; not with my cooperation. I'm sorry, but you'll have to trap him some other way.'

'So you won't help to expose his rottenness, even for the sake of the Chinese students?'

'Certainly not! They can fight their own corner: there's lots of them and one of me. Why do you think I'll sacrifice myself for somebody else's cause?' Even though she was sitting she stamped her foot. '*I won't do it!*'

It was no good; Mission had come to the end of his arguments and realised he was beaten. He sank into thoughtfulness. He had played his hand to the best of his ability, he had come close to the comprehensive humiliation of his adversary, but ultimately had failed. Now he would have to negotiate like any other politician. The thought was rather depressing. He much preferred to think of himself as a heroic revolutionary, but apparently that was not to be... not this time.

'Perhaps we should be flying the Tibetan flag too,' he mused.

Juliette quit the Students' Union with a feeling she was far from being in the clear. She needed to be careful about being seen, but since she was on the campus she was determined to make use of her time by crossing to the Frank Brangwyn Building to take a look at her latest painting. As she reached Tiananmen Square Green she saw Terry Bragg heading in the same direction. She called out and ran to catch up with him.

'Terry, did you let on about what I told you happened at that stupid brains trust on Monday?'

Bragg had had a storm-tossed night. He had got up several times and paced his meagre living room trying to work out how culpable he was for the evening's events. Could he have prevented Zhao cutting off his finger? There was something about cutting off one's own finger that would not let him rest and set him brooding about fanatical martyrs and suicide bombers. Such an aspect of the human spirit was alien to his nature. He saw martyrdom as contrary to the principles of staying the course and out-lasting one's opponent. He was, he recognised, of the latter persuasion: the conscientious objector type who chained himself to some morally repugnant manifestation of state power. He had tossed and turned in his bed, plagued by thoughts of the footloose, alienated subject in modernity; the disaffected loser ready to perpetrate some monstrous act on the toss of a coin. Had it been ever thus, he reflected gloomily, or was it only the modern subject who was adrift in a mirror maze of self-absorption? Before crawling back beneath his duvet he had found his bank statements and run through his monthly expenditure to check how dependent he was on his salary from the university. *This,* he had brooded as he pushed the statements back into their manila envelope, *is what becomes of compromising one's principles by teaching.*

Finally a wintry dawn had broken and it had been time to drag himself from his bed and set out for the university in response to JC's curt command to, "Get there by nine, Terry; no ifs or buts, you're the day's star turn."

He bought a copy of the *Sun* from the newsagent at the entrance to the Holloway Road tube station. Soon enough he reached page five. He read dispassionately the story beneath the "SNOGGING UNI BOSS IN SELF-HARM SCANDAL" headline, until he realised what it was he was reading. Then it required no great deduction to identify Juliette as the girl in the photographs. Had he not told JC about the brains trust? What had JC said? "Lovely sprat to catch a mackerel." He stiffened at the thought of Juliette trapped in a tawdry incident that could only have been designed to discredit the vice-chancellor. The whole production smacked of JC's kind of mischief, although what justified going to such lengths, and at Juliette's expense, he could not imagine. Horrified, he lowered the newspaper to his lap and gazed out into the blackness of the rushing-by tunnel wall.

'Do you know what I mean, Terry?'

Now, as he stood there facing her, he was ready and willing to commit whatever act of atonement Juliette demanded. It was the only way to redeem himself for his betrayal, and for the way he had treated all the Matthews of his teaching career. He looked into Juliette's face and could tell that she already knew the answer to her question, and was about to rebuke him. He put his hand to his head as though he was in pain. 'Jesus, Juliette, I didn't mean to get you into this. I did tell JC. It never occurred to me...'

She was straight and dignified in her indignation. 'This is my life being messed with. I don't want reporters snooping around looking for me, Terry. It's appalling!' She knew only too well that it would give a further twist to the scandal if it were to be discovered that she was a pole dancer. She was beginning to wonder whether she might have to disappear for a week or two. 'I'm here to study art, you know.'

He held up his hands in an act of supplication. 'Look, I promise you, I'm going to put a cap on this business. I won't let them hound you. Leave it to me.'

'Yes, Terry, please. I'd be really grateful.'

He lowered his arms slowly, regretfully, as if she were a ghostly apparition he could only reach out to in vain. Then a figure caught his eye emerging from the door of the Frank Brangwyn Building. It seemed JC had been waiting for them.

'Come on in, lovebirds.' She beckoned to them. 'Terry, your head of department needs comfort and glad tidings, so I hope you're feeling generous of spirit.'

Bragg glared at her. 'Did you take the photographs, JC?'

JC embraced them with an innocent smile. 'Lovely, lovely tryst, but no, *nothing* to do with me.'

FIFTY-TWO

Archie Pomfret's dander was up. What with the review, and now this, his week had been traumatic, and it was still only Wednesday! 'Now look here, Terry, I know you went up in the library and saw those Chinese students before they disappeared. You must have some idea where they went. JC says you talked to them. The department's reputation is at a nadir... Tatters, zero!'

Bragg opened his mouth but before he could speak his mind, Pomfret picked up speed.

'You may not have seen them but the newspapers are full of photographs of the vice-chancellor with one of our students: Juliette Burton. Yes, I know it's her; I saw her with him yesterday when he was touring the building. I'm sure we didn't encourage it, but you know how bad that sort of thing looks. Outrage has been piled on outrage! I've told JC we can't have the blame for this coming back to the department. We have to limit the damage and recoup lost ground by getting the Chinese students back on board.'

'It was me in the photograph. They've got it all wrong.'

'*You?*' The confession was so novel and unexpected, Pomfret could only stare at him, open-mouthed. 'It didn't look like you. It looked like the vice-chancellor.' He gazed at him as though he were a scientific curiosity while he floundered for something further to say. 'Although you were *in* yesterday, I suppose,' he said finally, wondering whether there was a joke somewhere he didn't get.

'Yes, it was me. They're poor, aren't they: the photographs? And I'm taken from behind. Juliette will confirm it was me though. I suppose you'd say I was caught committing an indiscretion with a student.'

'Well, yes... and no.' Pomfret stared into a corner of the room without speaking while he gathered his thoughts. 'I mean, did she consent?'

'She didn't mind terribly, but I made a mistake. I've apologised.'

'Good. Well, if there won't be trouble… We're all adults after all –' Pomfret wished he still had his copy of the *Sun* so he could refresh his memory of the photographs – 'though I'm not sure I can keep this as a departmental matter, you know.'

'Do whatever. I've decided to give up teaching. It's too competitive for me.'

'Really? Not over Ms Burton, then?'

'No, not exactly.'

'I can't say I blame you; artists tend to be thin skinned. If I had the money I'd give it up like a shot.'

Bragg swallowed, unable to confess to this mild-mannered, assured, utterly alien and unreachable man that he *couldn't* afford to give it up. 'I suppose I'll need to find something else.'

Pomfret put his hand to his brow as though deep in contemplation. 'Whatever you decide to do, it's important to keep your energy for the studio. One mustn't divide one's energies. Roly Gilbert's opinion was no less than five hours, come rain, come shine. He worked in a tithe barn in Suffolk. Big as a house it was and *still* he claimed he couldn't get back far enough.'

'If it's all right, I'll go and get on.'

'Oh, yes. So… you have no idea where the Chinese…? No, I suppose not, but you'll keep your ear to the ground?'

Bragg indicated he would.

'Yes, get on. Don't do anything sudden. I suppose you want me to inform the vice-chancellor; tell him we've found the real culprit? I'm sure he'll be very relieved…' Pomfret felt tempted to be forthright and tell Bragg that the longer he dwelt on the idea the greater his difficulty in believing it was him in the photographs, but to do so would be to doubt his word and that would be… well, *unsporting*, so he cast about uncertainly. 'You are sure you're right about this, aren't you?'

Bragg nodded, gave Pomfret a brave smile and left the room with an enormous sense of relief. At last he'd done the honorable thing and absolved himself of any harm he might otherwise have caused Juliette. He could – as he thought of it – "go forth!" He would begin again, rededicating himself to what he liked to think of as his "concrete conceptual musings", even if it meant a menial night job.

Left behind in his room, Pomfret was wondering whether he needed to discuss what he had just heard with Juliette Burton.

'No, after all,' he decided, 'this is not a nunnery.'

He looked out unhappily on Tiananmen Square Green, thinking his time was passing away, and what had just occurred was proof that the old ways of doing things no longer worked. No longer could one take a fellow by the shoulder and have a heart-to-heart: too condescending – the "old school" way, he supposed – and yet it upset him to see how a lack of empathy allowed what he now saw as a questionable confession to coalesce into a convenient truth, not that he could fathom who benefited from Bragg's sacrifice except the vice-chancellor. Still, it would confuse things, even if it did not entirely defuse what had now become a very public scandal over the Chinese students. He thought of a finger, a heraldic dismemberment. The image of St John the Baptist in the painting by Leonardo da Vinci came to him; St John pointing skywards with curious insistence, guiding the viewer towards thoughts of salvation through baptism.

Sentimental.

Ponderously he rose to his feet. Now the dispensable part-timer had confessed and done the decent thing, it was time, he decided, to run JC to ground and make sure she found the Chinese students.

FIFTY-THREE

It was raining, not dramatically, but steadily with the dogged persistence that rain has in November. There were semi-furled umbrellas drip-drying in the corridor outside the room where senate was gathering. Beyond the varnished oak doors there was a muffled hubbub. As Conquest entered with Perk the chatter subsided. Senate had twenty-eight members: he had counted the names on the distribution list attached to the agenda, but the room seemed to teem. The air was charged with anticipation and he ducked involuntarily as though brickbats were already flying. At the far end of the room the representatives of the university's academic staff were gossiping in one corner – most certainly about him, he reflected – and in the other stood the two student representatives, looking suitably awed. Between these two, around the coffee urn, were gathered a larger group of external members of senate, their backs to the door. One of them had just finished recounting something to amuse and the others had succumbed dutifully to guffaws of laughter.

A few nods were directed in Conquest's direction and a jolly little man with a bow tie came over and greeted him profusely. Conquest guessed that the man was friendless in this particular gathering and had not yet been given the wink over the press story. His name was Carlton Vestibule, or that's how his introduction lodged in Conquest's brain. While Conquest scoped the room, the man reminded him that he was the director of a charity concerned with homelessness. Conquest found himself gazing at the effeminate officer of the Arts Council with the stork-like neck who was extraordinarily absorbed in buttering up the local MP. Perk, he noticed, had become breezily affable and plunged straight into what appeared to be a half-finished conversation with a man

Conquest knew to be the chair of a notorious quango that had long deliberated on arcane matters to do with public sector services, the efficient delivery of which was impinged upon by the division of powers between local and central government. Conquest tore his eyes away from the officer of the Arts Council; he felt impelled to move on but once he had escaped the company of the charity director he regretted having done so. It was not so much that he was afraid of being given the cold shoulder by members of senate. No, what troubled him was the thought of being assailed suddenly by Rob Mission. There had been no sign of him since he had gone off to find Lady Caroline Lamb. Conquest's relief had gradually turned to anxiety as the time for senate had approached. Now he was feverish with nerves, fearing he was not safe from a scene caused by Rob Mission bursting in, dragging Lady Caroline Lamb after him, until senate was in session. He looked at his watch, saw that it was on the brink of eleven, and held out the dial in a silent appeal for Perk to start proceedings.

'Yes, must begin promptly,' said Perk, tearing himself away from the chair of the quango.

Nancy Spurling, the newspaper columnist, surprised Conquest by winking at him as he took his seat.

Damn me! At least somebody thinks this business has made me a bit of a celebrity.

As he checked that he had his agenda, shrill laughter reached him from Nancy Spurling's direction. Before he had a chance to confirm it was her, there was a commotion at his right shoulder and Sir Norman loomed over him.

Sir Norman had his hand over his mouth as though he were afraid someone might read his lips. 'Show them the edge of your steel!' he said. There was the glint of battle in his eye, and Conquest could have sworn Nancy Spurling and Sir Norman exchanged winks as he made his way to his seat.

Perk was on his feet. 'Welcome everyone to the first meeting of senate this academic year. Glad to see we have a full house for this extremely important meeting.' He gave a twitchy smile as he gazed into some other-worldly space above the heads of the assembled company. 'Now I know there are certain conventions we respect in the conduct of our meetings and I know you've received an agenda... but events overnight mean that it's imperative we amend our order of business to allow the vice-chancellor to make a statement.' He looked around uneasily as though expecting an ambush from he knew not where. 'He will tell you there has been a calumny... an-an-an-and he calls on you all to support him. I have absolute – *ABSOLUTE* – confidence that he is a man of his word and we can trust in his good name. Events may have put him in temporary difficulties but he is a man of honour on who we can all rely.'

'Here, here,' rumbled Sir Norman, an intervention that Conquest noticed was in marked contrast to the silence from the rest of the gathering.

Perk gulped. 'It is most unfortunate that this should have occurred now, at our first meeting with Professor Conquest. I had hoped you would spend today hearing his plans, but we have been overtaken by events...'

It was clear to Conquest that the support Perk was offering him was only half-hearted and, worse, he was now beginning to flounder. He decided it was time to stand up and put an end to his plight. He pushed back his chair with a loud scraping noise.

'Thank you, chair, for those kind words of support. Members of senate –' he engaged the room with an expression of droll frankness – 'I think we all know that events have a way of happening.'

There was a moment's silence and then somebody laughed.

'Yes, they've been happening to me, and I want to make sure they don't happen to *us*!'

There was a second laugh and a faint wash of tittering.

This is easy. They're already taking morsels from my hand. What on earth was Perk thinking to try and prevent me...?

He picked up his theme with studied care. 'If today we don't have time to discuss all the issues I was hoping to seek advice from you about it would be unfortunate. Yes, a great pity, but at least the events that have overtaken us – apologies, I mean *me* – provide a context in which to make some remarks about the task I have been labouring at since my appointment.' Conquest paused to give his audience a significant look. 'We all have moments – I want to share this with you – when we find ourselves at the centre of mighty forces, caught in a web we haven't woven and cannot cast aside. These are occasions when we might fly but for such hindrances. I have found myself battling for the soul of this university. Yes, for *the students* of this university... and all the other stakeholders *too!* It has not taken me long to realise that the mountainside up which I'm pushing the rock of other people's inertia is steep... and potholed. This university has suffered from a lack of...' Conquest stopped, as though considering how exactly he should phrase what he was about to say.

'How shall I put this? For some time the university has been in need of a thorough recalibrating... I mean upwards, of course. Such things cannot always be accomplished without breaking eggs. Of course, omelettes can be very tasty, and that is where we are: in the middle of making an omelette. I defy anybody not to find it delicious when it is made, but for now it looks a mess.'

He paused, expecting another round of laughter but the room was silent but for some uneasy creaking of chairs.

'Yes, this is University London Central: a work-in-progress! The young folk who throng the corridors and lecture theatres expect the best, and why not? I am here to deliver it for them; that is my mission, my passion and my duty. Who in his – or her – right mind would stand in the way of that? I would never tell you I suffered for my job. It is my vocation, after all, and many students of this university will tell you what a marvellous thing a vocation is! It is true that the humdrum cares and concerns of running a great institution like this sometimes make trying to untangle the mysteries of the character of Bobby Kennedy a daunting task. So be it! I ask for no remission of those cares and concerns. Biography is a great calling, but for me the greater calling is this university.

'Now, members of senate, it is my duty to report to you where we are – where *I* am – in this process of putting right the harm done to this university by the last administration. Let's be clear, this was not structural. There was a lack of humility; there was abuse of privilege, dishonesty, and yes, *corruption*! But even more, there was ineptitude in the management of this institution that set

284

faction against faction, academe against administration. That's an ugly thing, and I have been at pains to heal those rifts by placing the demands of a greater loyalty upon all concerned. By so doing I may have stirred up some enmity against my person, but *so be it!* Right and conscience and loyalty to the collective endeavour cannot be wished away. Has my character been impugned? Yes, it has! I have been doubly accused in the muckraking rags of Fleet Street... or Wapping... and other sites in Docklands, as now are. It has been claimed –' and at this point Conquest took up a wad of folded newspapers – 'that I am a rake!' He gave a snort of derision at the absurdity of such a claim. 'I am no more a rake than a garden implement, if you will indulge a play on words; no more than I sowed the seeds of the regrettable diplomatic incident that was played out in our library yesterday evening. There is an entity within this university you will be hearing a great deal more of before I've finished this morning: the Students' Union! It bears considerable responsibility for what has happened. There was a breach of security instigated by officers of that union. They enflamed a dispute between the university and a group of Chinese students whom we bear no grudge against for protesting if things are not quite right. Naturally, *I uphold that right!* On this we all agree, I think. Yes, I can see it is so from your expressions. But who here is about to condone arson and violence and self-harm as instruments of politics? Not one right-thinking person! The fact is that the president of the Students' Union lent clandestine support to a student action that was a gross contravention of health & safety rules *and* breached the university's security protocols. To discomfort me his administration has broadcast far and wide the story that I was too busy chasing female students to hear their protest. Not true! I was simply not informed by their head of department, even though he was there, at that time, having satisfied – *apparently* – an academic review panel that his department knew what it was doing – which was plainly false, and terribly misguided of the review panel, meaning *lacking in judgment* – which I suspect had been infiltrated – the panel, I mean – by a supporter of the head of department's completely aberrant behaviour and academic ideas... *apparently*. The fact is that no one feels for the students

– appreciates their needs, their aspirations, their enthusiasm for learning, their thirst for knowledge – more than I do. I am with them at the barricades, so to speak, the barricades of scholarship and creative thought, of the interdisciplinary quest, if I might so describe it. Not the barricades of arson and confrontation where books are abused!

Conquest came to a momentary halt. The room was spinning, so it seemed. The torrent of words that had poured from his mouth had left him breathless and disorientated. He spread out his arms to embrace the meeting in what seemed to be, depending on the members of his audience's susceptibility to what he had just said, either an appeal for solidarity or a benediction. He was seized by the need to hurry on, to complete his vindication and crush his enemies utterly.

'Now I want to be perfectly candid with you: there is a cabal of staff – some quite senior – who regret the passing of the old regime. It suited them that there was slackness and a general lack of direction from the university's leadership. It meant they could get away with things they know I will not tolerate. They will do anything to prevent themselves from becoming the subject of scrutiny. I have instituted departmental reviews! Efficiencies of the sort I am introducing are anathema to them. And it is they who have stooped so low as to collude with the Student Union's most irresponsible faction.'

Around the room people were beginning to catch one another's eye with frozen expressions. *Was this seemly?* This was the question seeping into senate's collective consciousness. Here an eyebrow twitched and, in response, a fleeting grimace touched the corner of a pair of lips.

'I cannot tell you how many minor provocations have been directed at me. The Palestinian flag has been a persistent bone of contention with the Students' Union. There has been collusion from some keyholder to give representatives of the Students' Union access to this building to run up that flag. On this issue, in an act of good faith, I have conceded to the Student Union's wishes. I'm happy to announce the flag will fly for Eid. Reasonableness is the mark of good governance! I negotiate! I defy anybody in this room to describe me as unreasonable. My work as a senior administrator has always been tempered by my scholarship. My work in American studies – latterly my life of the Kennedy brothers – has always kept my feet on the ground. When you are researching a subject like that you develop a respect for the radical thought, the sudden perception that begins something new. I understand the impatience of the bright student when the academic framework is unresponsive, passionless!'

'Oh gawd,' said Perk to himself under his breath.

Conquest looked up and caught sight of Sir Norman in profile. The look on his face was one of a man who had seen his dog run down by a car. Clifford felt his insides quiver and turn to jelly. The thought of Sir Norman's disapproval was too much for him.

This is not going as well as I thought. I must exculpate myself. Perhaps some of them here don't understand: those of coarse fibre who will greet my admission of having sensitivities with derision. Something of that kind is always possible with tenderness, and expressions of feelings of tenderness, and when what provokes tenderness is confessed to. There we have it: Oh brutish world!

'Now, if you'll permit me a little more time, I have a way of conveying these ideas,' Conquest announced, pulling himself together with a supreme effort. He wiped his moist eyes with a tissue he produced from his jacket pocket. 'Sorry about that. If I may, I wish to cite a perception from my own research.' He smacked the back of his own head as though chastening himself. 'You may not know this, but there's only one photograph of President Kennedy with Marilyn Monroe. It was taken at a party after Monroe had performed her famous rendition of *Happy Birthday, Mr President* at JFK's forty-fifth birthday celebration at Madison Square Gardens.

'What do you need to know about this photograph to understand the point I'm trying to make? Well, Monroe is in profile smiling at JFK, but he's turning away, showing his back to the camera. On their left, in the foreground, is Bobby and it's as if the photographer has sneaked up behind him, in his shadow almost, in an attempt to catch JFK and Monroe unawares. Why was JFK turning away even though it was the official White

House photographer taking the photograph? Because JFK has already decided: no photographs with Monroe! It is only by a stroke of luck that this one has survived. But what on earth is Bobby up to? All along, Bobby was JFK's fixer, his Attorney General, yet he seems to be engaged in ensuring that precisely what his brother doesn't want happens. Was it because he knew the powers of suggestion of such a photograph would override all other considerations?'

Conquest came to a sudden halt, startled by the idea of sibling betrayal he had developed. When he recommenced it was in the voice that had taken on a deeper, more mellow timbre. 'Because this picture, like a lot of pictures – dare I say, like the photograph some of you have seen in this morning's papers? – is capable of different interpretations, depending on what you imagine is going on. JFK was a man of vision; JFK had an instinct for these kind of things, and could see quite plainly that any photograph *at all* of him with Marilyn Monroe was likely to look compromising. A clumsy action caught at the right moment can look far from innocent. This is the trap of representation.'

Conquest looked around the room and suddenly realised that facing him at the further end of the table, with something that looked uncomfortably like a smirk on his face, was Dr Albert Cornish, his academic registrar, the only person in the room who knew that Juliette Burton was more than a misunderstood image. Was that a copy of the *Sun* poking out from beneath his committee papers? Conquest could recall vividly that evening in registry when they had shared a bottle of rum. Hadn't Cornish compared him to Dickens, who was known to have harboured a prurient fascination for fallen women? He remembered that he had promised himself he'd get rid of Cornish, yet here he was, a gloating presence across the table, the one person who knew that he had searched through the university's records to find his Lady Caroline Lamb amongst the thousands of other students.

'No, I shall not be deflected from my aim by this miserable misrepresentation. I remain steadfast in my determination that this university shall thrive. I see a vision we must share: I see the green pastures of academia spread out before us as we go forward to a new, bright place; and this place of learning is full of excitement and innovation. *We must be there!*'

At that moment there was a strange gagging noise from the right-hand side of the table and glancing in that direction he saw that Sir Norman had half-risen to his feet. His face had a strange vacancy and the gagging noise was issuing from his mouth. He canted to one side and slumped backwards. His chair made a shrieking noise as his collapse impelled it backwards. Slowly he subsided into the gap that opened up between it and the table, the expression on his face making a ghastly impression on the meeting.

'I do believe...' Conquest heard Perk mutter as he rose from his chair.

With a clatter, everyone was on their feet, apart from Sir Norman's neighbours who were already down on their knees beside him.

'*Call an ambulance!*' cried one of them, looking up briefly. '*He can't breath!*'

'I do believe...' said Perk again in his fretful voice.

That's great! All my effort in vain. Now Perk'll call for a suspension of the meeting and I'll have to start all over again. What the hell's happened to Sir Norman anyway? His ticker playing up? Maybe he's fainted and he'll be all right in a minute or two.

Conquest found that Nancy Spurling had moved round the table and was standing next to him.

'Poor thing! That's definitely a stroke,' she murmured close to his ear with great certitude. 'If ever I saw a stroke, that's one!'

'It is what it is,' said Conquest in a kind of trance.

'I think you should take charge,' she said.

'Yes,' agreed Conquest, 'I will.' When he didn't move she prodded him sharply with her foot.

'You know the ropes. Get someone to call the medical centre... *now!*'

Goaded into sudden animation, Conquest headed for the door where he found himself being jostled by Professor Woolworth, who was about the same mission.

'I'll call an ambulance,' said Conquest brusquely. 'Leave it to me.' He rushed across the corridor to his office. 'Carole,' he yelled as he crashed through the door, 'call an ambulance. And call the medical centre and see if Doctor Magwar is there. We've got an emergency in senate: Sir Norman's collapsed. I wouldn't be surprised if it was a stroke.'

Carole lived for such moments of emergency and instantly became a whirl of activity. For his part, Conquest was overcome by a feeling of finitude, as though he had completed his task. He wasn't strictly needed for anything in particular. In fact, he felt rather like a lie down.

A sense of lassitude! I was, after all, in full rhetorical flight. It's always the same when one gets cut off in mid-flow.

He drifted into his office, out of the back door and along the corridor, past the temporary kitchen where his office staff made tea and kept their snacks in the refrigerator. Beyond was a door and beyond that the crooked stairs that led up to the terrace beneath the cupola.

FIFTY-FOUR

Sometimes, Conquest reflected, he experienced time passing slowly; sometimes it ripped along. He knew it was a defeat of logic, but today was a case in point: time seemed to slow down and then speed up in entirely unpredictable ways. One moment he was holding forth and time was positively rushing by, the next he was on the roof of the Keynes Building and everything seemed to have stopped. *It is what it is,* was what he thought about it. *It is what it is.* He was watching for Lady Caroline Lamb crossing the campus but the walkways between the buildings were nearly empty.

'Where are the students? Gone every one,' he said to himself. It sounded so melancholic he said it again. 'Gone, gone, every one.'

He waited patiently, and eventually he was rewarded by the sight of the academic registrar and the dean of academic affairs making their way towards the George Orwell Library.

They're out of senate! That means the meeting's over. Did they endorse my digital hub? Did they vote for me or against me? No, wait a minute, the meeting was abandoned because Sir Norman had a seizure! No, no, that's irrelevant. I settled everything with my speech. Perk only had to wrap up and get the hell out of there.

Coming in the other direction was Professor Andrew Czinc. Conquest watched intently as Cornish and Woolworth stopped to talk to him.

Ah, they're discussing me, and my speech. Think you've got the rest of the morning off, don't you? No! Wrong! Stop gossiping and get working on something else!

Conquest was feeling quite cut up about Sir Norman. He had become something of a talisman, keeping him from harm, unwavering in his support for the digital hub, vanquisher of his foes, and now he was laid low by some catastrophe of the arterial system. It didn't seem fair, just when he needed him resolute beside him. What had Ballantyne said first thing in the morning?

"Brazen it out… or go." No doubt what Sir Norman's opinion was! I know they're lurking in the corners of the senior common room where sunlight never falls, waiting to get me. Well, you little rats, you won't, because you're feeble, and I see you there in the shadows, too frightened use your hat pins unless I'm already wrapped in clingfilm!

He wasn't sure how long he was up there, waiting for time to start.

A long time in no time.

Eventually he came down from the roof and entered his office as he'd left, using the back way, avoiding Carole and the rest of his staff. There were wine glasses everywhere and his office reeked of sauvignon blanc. Plates of half-eaten food had been abandoned in the strangest places. It was as though everyone had left in a rush. In the midst of this festive wreckage stood a wheelchair with its back to him. It was occupied by a figure, inanimate, slumped to one side. Clifford circled round warily to see whether he recognised the occupant and was startled to see it was Sir Norman. For a moment he had the fancy that his corpse had been left there in the aftermath of a riotous bacchanalia, but for once there was a healthy flush to Sir Norman's face. What's more, he could see the rise and fall of his chest as he breathed.

In a moment he's going to start snoring.

Conquest found a half empty bottle of wine and poured himself a glass. He contemplated Sir Norman in the wheelchair as just one more still life object amongst the glasses and abandoned food.

'How do, Sir Norman,' he said loudly when he'd had his fill of looking at him.

Sir Norman opened his eyes with a start. He attempted to get up and then remembered where he was.

'Ah, sorry, Cliff. I needed that! Little nap. Damn-well choked on the cap of my pen, but that handsome PA of yours saw me to rights.'

Conquest looked at him blankly. 'Carole?'

'Heimlich manoeuvre: did the job! Strong woman! Hellish

powerful!' He patted the arms of the wheelchair. 'Strenuous morning! She insisted I take a rest. Used to work with dementia patients. Did you know that?'

'Really? No!'

'Ah, Cliff, damn fine show. Bravura performance. Not a dry eye in the house. I thought you carried off the injured innocence marvellously.'

'I thought you disapproved; hated it!'

'*Hated?* Not a bit of it! Confused the buggers!'

'You were looking daggers.'

'No, no, I was giving that damn fool Perk the evil eye. I hate it if the chair doesn't keep still when someone has the floor. He's a milksop! Where've you been, anyway? He told me you were driving around in your car to calm down.'

'I don't have a car; not here.'

'Typical: just the sort of milksop thing a milksop would say. Masterly presentation by your finance bod. They fully endorsed the digital hub. Couldn't have done it myself, not sneaky enough. I hear some idiot is claiming he's the man in the snaps, not you. Who paid him?' He gave a guffaw. 'What with no damsel in distress and the Chinese students apologising I'd say you're home and dry.'

'*Chinese apologising?*' Conquest was having difficulty keeping up.

'Yes, abjectly. Mind you, it's being said that somebody has fiddled them enough modular credits to warrant putting them straight into the third year of the undergraduate course.'

'How can that be?'

'Prior professional practice, or some such tommyrot. Your academic registrar was rather keen to slip me the word.' Sir Norman gave a shrug that indicated he was but a babe in arms before the dark arts of academic administration. 'He strikes me as a bit of a spiv.'

'I was thinking of giving him the sack.'

'Good idea, but later. Anyway, they've apologised for their behaviour. Strict instructions from the embassy, I understand.'

Conquest was struggling to come to terms with the turn of events. 'How can this be?'

Sir Norman took on the look of one about to impart something in strict confidence. 'Friends in high places. *Connections!* I think you've met Lord N'Garbi, haven't you? He's been working his magic on your behalf. Can't compromise the digital hub, can we? N'Garbi's big with the Chinese; they value his advice greatly. Say not a word, but cruise ships are the coming thing. *Imagine: factories of pleasure in western seas!* No disrespect to Perk, but N'Garbi's the sort of chap we ought to have chairing senate. Time to build, Cliff, time to build! Take a good look at this building: it's all fancy staircase and had its day. Leave the façade and bung in the hub behind it. It'll only cost a million more... best of both worlds! You're not the sort of chap who needs grand accommodation like this. *Budge up!*' He slapped the arms of the wheelchair. 'Apparently they took the last vice-chancellor out in this. We're made of sterner stuff though, aren't we? Senate all gone home in jolly spirits. Lovely lunch. Must push off myself. Perhaps you would get Carole to wheel me to a cab? I wouldn't mind a few more of her ministrations! Hey-ho, strange days!'

In the profound silence that followed Sir Norman's departure, Conquest tried to comprehend the enormity of what had happened. Sir Norman's news would not compute. He preferred the feeling of being beleaguered. It satisfied him more; it was what it meant to be God's mercenary.

Somebody else embracing Lady Caroline Lamb? Chinese students in abject apology? Conquest digital hub sanctioned by senate? Presumably, reputation restored!

It was not acceptable; the aesthetics of resolution revolted him. 'Better buy a new suit,' he said to himself, for such was the armour of the public-sector samurai.

FIFTY-FIVE

JC McCann had finished for the day. She came down the steps of the Frank Brangwyn Building fully occupied by her attempt to put up an umbrella against the rain. That's why she didn't see him until the last moment. The sight sent her scurrying back up the steps and straight into Professor Pomfret's office.

'Archie, he's standing on the green. The vice-chancellor: he's standing on the green.'

'In the rain?'

'Yes, he's standing there, waiting... in the rain. Waiting like a statue. I think he's stuck.'

Pomfret, who had been busy manoeuvring coloured geometrical cut-outs around a sheet of graph paper, responded to the alarm in her voice with surprising alacrity, almost as if she were bringing news he had been expecting. He switched off the overhead lights and went to the window with her. They kept a little way back but still had a perfect view of Tiananmen Square Green. There he stood, unbending in the slanting rain of the storm, imperfectly illuminated by the several sodium vapour lamps that edged the green.

JC went forward and pressed her nose to the glass. 'I think you should go and talk to him. It's awfully wet out there.'

Pomfret had seen enough of the vice-chancellor's resolutely immobile figure to share her opinion. 'You're right, I should... It does no good, this sort of thing.' He hooked his coat off the back of the door.

Together they stood at the front door of the Frank Brangwyn Building while Pomfret plucked up his courage, then he threw his coat over his head and went down the steps. As he approached Conquest he noticed – silhouetted against the lights of the building across the green – that rain was dripping off the end of his nose – or he was crying. He had no idea which.

'Excuse me, vice-chancellor…'

Conquest started as though caught unawares. 'Ah, there you are. Call me "Cliff", *do*. "Breezy": that's the note I want to strike!'

'You should come in out of the rain.'

'Not very clement, is it?'

'No, it's rather grim.' Pomfret regarded him warily.

'Tell me, Pomfret, are you a cunning devil or a complete bloody fool?'

Pomfret laughed self-depreciatingly. 'That's rather a good question. I don't know that it's for me to say. Are you waiting for someone?'

'Yes, Lady Caroline Lamb.' There was an almost ethereal otherness in the way he spoke the name.

'I see, Lady Caroline Lamb.' Pomfret rubbed his chin in puzzlement. The name was vaguely familiar, but in what way it was of significance to his vice-chancellor he had no idea. He was rather more concerned that while speaking, Conquest had not shifted his eyes for a moment from a spot midway up the Frank Brangwyn Building that he had been fixedly staring at since they had first noticed him.

'Is she expected?'

'I suppose so, unless you've kidnapped her.' Conquest laughed curtly at the idea.

Pomfret decided he might rouse him if he administered a bit of a shock. 'I don't think she's coming. Not tonight.'

'I suppose you expect me to find that upsetting.'

'Not a bit of it. I was hoping you'd be relieved.'

Conquest abandoned the fixity of his gaze as though his thoughts had begun to wander. 'Yes, I suppose you would. There's a total eclipse of the moon tonight, you know.'

They both glanced up into the teeth of the downpour.

'Did this… ahhh… Lady Caroline arrange to meet you here? I mean, in this exact spot? Surely you could shelter over there.' Pomfret pointed to the entrance of the Frank Brangwyn Building.

'Ah, no, I'm not allowed. It's quite forbidden.'

'I was about to go home. Don't you think it's time you went too?'

'I've always found the start of a new academic year quite electrifying. The sense of anticipation, the new beginnings.'

'Yes, I suppose it's good to empathise with the students' experience. Even so, it's time we were going.'

'The headhunters want me to speak to Ofwat, you know.'

'Tomorrow.'

'Yes. So, no Lady Caroline Lamb?'

Pomfret shook his head.

'I see, so no point in waiting. Busy day tomorrow? Diary full?' Conquest didn't seem inclined to move.

'I expect you have; always busy.'

Conquest found that amusing. 'No, I meant you: Mr Busy Bee. My diary is actually rather empty. I know this terribly good club. Bags of atmosphere; sort of thing you might find visually arresting. How about a glass of something white?' His enthusiasm was clearly waxing. 'Give me a moment, I'll call a cab' He began to delve in his pocket for his mobile.

Pomfret waited while he put through the call, throwing the occasional glance back towards the Frank Brangwyn Building to see if JC were in sight, hoping for support, or even rescue. He wanted to return to his office, but his conscience pricked him: clearly the vice-chancellor was in no condition to be allowed to wander off alone. He wasn't quite sure what was troubling him but what crossed his mind was the story of several academics from the Department of Political Science who had gone missing with a troupe of ladyboys while at a conference in the Far East. The explanation for their behaviour: "I was on medication at the time". He wondered if the vice-chancellor might have slipped up on his pill-taking regime; taken a double dose of something. As the idea became settled he knew he would have to humour him by accepting his invitation – anything to get out of the rain even though, from what he knew of Conquest, he imagined their destination would be some glum place in St James's with wooden paneling and MCC ties.

'After all,' Conquest assured him, 'if she's not here, she's probably there.'

'Quite so,' agreed Pomfret, good-naturedly reconciled to the asymmetry of their companionship.

'Consider yourself sworn to secrecy.'

'I do.'

And so off into the night they paddled on a journey that was to culminate in an awakening of sorts; not an awakening to trouble Conquest, for he had already chosen his path, chosen it knowing that in his line of work there were no backbenches for miscreants. No, it was an awakening for Pomfret. He was humbled by a renewal of his acquaintanceship with the beauty of the nude, recalling the tender and fierce passions of his youth. Passions which since then, he was horrified to realise, had dimmed to an academic vestige. *Ah, how the promiscuity of the eyes arouses the other senses!* Had he been canvassed to give himself a character reference – he found himself musing on this later as he took a taxi westwards to Kensington – he would have sworn he was a sensualist, a connoisseur of female beauty. In fact, he would have declared himself so *fervently*. Was he not the inheritor of a visual tradition that had canonised the female form? Was he not of a line of artists that had striven to capture its beauty, stretching back through Renoir, Rodin, Boucher, Rubens, Titian...? Was he not the living embodiment of this heritage? *Clearly not!* He had succumbed to the cold science of geometry that iconoclasts adored while they shrouded the beauty of their women in black! He experienced a moment of divine discontent. His belief in the nature of his own character was crushed. He had to acknowledge that a fire had been extinguished he had not even noticed paling through the years.

'Ahhh...!' he exclaimed in wonder as the crossbeams of light revealed the pole dancer with their luscious embrace. With new comprehension he looked at Conquest and saw the rapt expression on his face. 'I see! So *that's* Lady Caroline Lamb!'

GJ BABB'S
ART WORLD TRILOGY

Lara Bliss Loves Rose Madder Genuine
is available now at your local bookshop or on-line.

Of Art And Eros
the third novel in GJ Babb's Art World Trilogy
will be published in 2021.

Lara Bliss Loves Rose Madder Genuine

Another novel in GJ Babb's Art World Trilogy

The Emsbury locals call them "grockles", summertime visitors that flock to the beautiful estuary of the river Em. The most famous grockle is Meade Daguerre, controversial artist with an international reputation to uphold. Lara Bliss, local artist and president of the Emsbury League of Artists, sees Daguerre as one of her own and takes him under her wing when she hears that journalist Jack Palanga, "the Celebrities' Confidant", is in town after a story.

Palanga is playing his cards close to his chest, but gradually it transpires that he suspects the crew of Daguerre's racing yacht, which is berthed in Emsbury marina, is using it to smuggle something – possibly illegal immigrants – ashore.

Daguerre is beset by another distraction: nighthawks searching for a horde of gold with metal detectors have plundered an archeological site on his estate. The archaeologists guarding the site are attacked at night in an apparent attempt to drive them off. Matters become more serious when Daguerre discovers a bloody chaos in the cabin of his racing yacht. It appears a murder has been committed there, and the five members of the crew have disappeared.

As July unfolds, the police, amateur sleuths – led by Lara Bliss – and journalists seek to solve the twin crimes. As Bliss navigates her own way to an understanding of who are behind them she begins to see that the clash of two communities – and two cultures – means that things are never quite what they seem…

LARA BLISS
LOVES
ROSE MADDER
GENUINE

A NOVEL

GJ BABB